A SHADOW
IN THE FLAMES
BOOK ONE OF THE
NEW AENEID CYCLE

MICHAEL G. MUNZ

Red Muse Press
Seattle, WA 2016

Cover Design by Amalia Chitulescu

Previously published as *A Shadow in the Flames*, Virtual Bookworm, 2007; and self-published (revised edition), 2013

This is a work of fiction. Names, characters, places, brands, media, and incidents are either the product of the author's imagination or are used fictitiously. Any resemblance to similarly named places or to persons living or deceased is unintentional.

PRINT ISBN 978-0-9977622-1-1

Library of Congress Control Number: 2014918415

ACKNOWLEDGMENTS

Special thanks to my parents and sister for all their support, and to beta-readers Brian, Linda, Sarah, and "Calypso" from way back before the first edition was released. Thanks as well to Scott, Sean, Kevin, Mark, Matt, and Kristi: You know who you are, and you know why you're here.

Additionally, thank you to Terry Brooks and the eleven of my fellow authors in his PNWA workshop who gave input on the first draft and provided the kick in the bum that I needed to do some major rewrites.

Oh, and thanks to caffeine, without which my writing would not be possible. Also chocolate.

For Marina, in memory.

I

MICHAEL FLYNN FELT NAKED. The sidewalk outside of a transit station on the edge of The Dirge was far from the safest place to stand alone at night. Even so, waiting there to rendezvous with his roommate was less risky than walking home into The Dirge alone.

He glanced up and down the street from his vantage point atop the steps that led back down to the transit bay. The other passengers who had left the bus with him dispersed into the night along isolated paths. A homeless woman sat hunched beneath a small overhang, silently begging as they passed without taking notice. Michael supposed he could be in a worse situation than having to stand a few extra minutes waiting for his roommate to meet him. The woman had been in the same spot when he had left that morning. Did she have a place to sleep?

Sleep. He'd welcome it after such a fruitless day. Maybe, if he could just get home and relax, his problems might go away for a bit. They might even look better in the morning.

A soft rain began to fall. It spattered on a fallen poster that proclaimed the arrival of the new 2051 model year Uhatsu sedans. The woman's bare feet pressed on the pavement as she tried to better position herself in the dry spot beneath the overhang. Michael watched her and doubted anyone in the neighborhood was in the market for a new luxury car. Then he noticed something more.

She'd worn shoes that morning.

He cursed under his breath that someone would have stolen them from her, and his wallet was open before he'd really even thought about it. What insignificant cash he had clung to the inside and made the empty space there all the more prominent. He stared at it for a few moments and then put it away again. Soon he would need to worry about how to feed himself.

Yet there was still no sign of his roommate. After casting a few more glances along the street, he found himself meeting the woman's chance gaze. The resignation in her eyes struck him; they were devoid of hope and heavy with loss. Michael's heart sank in the brief moment before she turned away, and, once the contact was broken, he looked down at his own shoes, barely six months old. He'd bought them just before coming to Northgate. Though the city had marred them a bit, they were still in solid shape.

He reached for his wallet again and walked the short distance to the homeless woman with the regret that he wasn't better equipped to help. At the very least, he wished he could have caught whoever had taken her shoes.

Her hands were chapped, weathered, and dusted with the grime of street life. She took the few bills he offered, and her dirty fingers briefly brushed Michael's own before withdrawing, almost apologetically, from the contact. After a moment, he took out another five and passed that to her as well. Tired eyes looked up at him and a melancholy smile passed over her worn face before her gaze quickly dropped again.

"Thank you," she whispered.

He opened his mouth to offer some form of comfort, but any words he could think of only sounded hollow. He cast his eyes about in a search for what to say, yet all he managed to find was the sight of his roommate's arrival. His roommate kept his distance down the sidewalk, waiting in the evening drizzle. Michael left the woman with a weak smile to cover his loss for words, and then hurried to join him.

His roommate turned and began to walk as Michael reached him. "You've found a job, then?"

"Well . . . " Michael shrugged. His search that day had been a bust. "Not really, no."

"You shouldn't be throwing away money on strangers," the other said. "Thought you said your savings are running out."

"Yeah, I know." It was true: he was twenty-two with almost nothing to show for it, and giving her a portion of what little money he had left probably wasn't the smartest thing he could have done. "But . . . she probably had less."

"It won't help her. You might need it." He quickened his pace toward the bridge ahead. "Come on."

Michael looked ahead of them, across the water. The clouds broke along the horizon, and the Moon was just beginning to rise over the degenerating slums where he lived. Most just called it The Dirge, a violent, forgotten section of the city where police seldom went and those elsewhere tried to ignore. Roving gangs had long ago torn down the security cameras that were otherwise common on public streets and in the corporate-run sectors of the city. Even so, his pace quickened to get there. Meager though their apartment might be, it was a place to call home, and sometimes just the fact that he had a roof over his head was a comfort. At least it was in one of the more subdued quarters of The Dirge. Still dangerous, yes, but there were worse places, and it certainly wasn't expensive.

Yet he still had to eat, and if he didn't find a source of income soon, well, he wasn't exactly sure what he would do. The small sum he'd given the woman might buy her a meal or two. Even so, his roommate was right. If he wasn't careful, he'd be in the same position.

Still, there were so many like her.

"Uncle Frank always used to give to charity. Even as the farm was going under," Michael said suddenly.

"He was a good man. Hard worker. I liked him. But in the end he couldn't afford to pay the hands. Things changed."

Michael nodded, forced to agree. "I am trying to find a job, you know," he said. "It's just—no one wants to hire a bodyguard without experience. They all want real freelancers. I figured that Aegis course would be enough—they certainly said so when I enrolled—but even they won't hire me."

"They only hire from their elite courses," the older man said. "Give everyone else the rest."

Michael grimaced. "Yeah, well, they forgot to tell us that."

Most of his money had gone into Aegis Security's training program when he'd first arrived in the city. They'd seemed the best place to start. They were the largest security corp in the world. They handled most of the downtown corporate district's policing. Everyone respected them.

"I don't know," Michael said. "I just figured security would be the way to go. Protect myself, protect other people."

"So you've said."

Michael blushed at his venting. "Well, it's what you do, right? I'm starting to think everyone else had the same idea. I don't know. I guess maybe I'm just not looking in the right places."

He caught his reflection as they passed a darkened window, and beside his roommate's silhouette, he saw the short brown hair and youthful green eyes of the man for whom no one seemed to have a purpose. At least he had the build for security work. Years of laboring on his uncle's farm had helped to develop him, and while he was not quite as tall or muscular as his six-foot-three roommate, Michael hoped to one day be just as imposing.

His roommate grabbed his arm and stopped them both. Michael turned from his thoughts to find him looking into the distance of the sparsely lit street ahead. "Trouble," he said. "Better cross over."

With that, he let go of Michael's arm and started across to the other side of the street. Michael followed, peering in the direction his companion had indicated. "What is it, Diomedes? Gangers?"

One of the streetlights ahead was dark. He wasn't able to make out much in the gloom, yet Michael trusted that his companion had seen something. While Michael's eyes were the same ones he was born with, Diomedes had replaced his with cybernetic implants. Not only were they marginally better than the norm, they also had a few enhancements installed that Diomedes would rarely speak of.

"Maybe."

They reached the opposite sidewalk and continued walking. Michael kept looking for some sign of the group ahead and was soon able to make out a small pack of figures. While he still couldn't tell if they were gangers or not, Diomedes had seven more years' worth of experience than he and knew what he was doing. Michael might not have seen them on his own until it was too late.

Diomedes, on the other hand, was a freelancer: a modern-day knight errant, part of a new caste of society that supplied security and protection for those who needed it. The very word excited Michael's imagination. Michael wasn't sure if Diomedes was in service to any particular company. Only some freelancers were affiliated. In a time when a corporation might control more land than some countries, a few freelancers even signed lifetime fealty contracts. Most, however, had more freedom to find their own causes. Diomedes's attitude made it clear that his own affiliation was not to be discussed. To Michael, that only added to the mystery and adventure that surrounded this man, through whom all of his dreams had come.

"How much was it?" Diomedes asked suddenly.

"How much?"

"How much did you give her?"

"Oh," Michael said. "About ten."

"Here." Diomedes pressed a twenty into Michael's hand. "Don't give it away."

He was right. Michael pocketed it. "Thanks."

His roommate only grunted.

Across the street, the group of people Diomedes had spotted ran past them. Cackling, laughing and screaming in a way that Michael had once only attributed to the mentally disturbed, they took no notice of the two men on the other side of the dim street. He tried to steal a glimpse of them as they passed by, avoiding direct eye contact in an effort not to attract any attention.

"I hate when they do that," Michael muttered.

"Just noise."

"Yeah, but it seems like every single ganger in the city has to do it."

"I told you you'd get used to it. So get used to it."

"Yeah, but . . . Yeah." Not wanting Diomedes to think less of him, Michael left it at that. At least the fact that it didn't bother his roommate was still some comfort. Geez, how he could hope to be as strong as Diomedes when he couldn't even deal with a little screaming? "I'll get used to it," he added, almost to himself. *Eventually.*

A brief while after the howling group had continued onward, Michael looked up from his thoughts to see that they were nearly to the run-down apartment building where they currently lived. "It's dingy, it's ugly, it probably should have been condemned years ago," he mused, "and it's still good to see it."

"Don't complain."

"I'm not, really," Michael insisted, genuinely glad for a safe place to sleep. "You rigged up some great security."

"Never trust a lock that's not yours."

Michael nodded and took a few more steps before deciding to ask something. "Why do you still live here? If you can afford the gear you've got in there—"

"Shut up about that out here," his roommate whispered.

Michael winced. "I only meant—"

Their building exploded without warning. Debris ruptured out of the front entrance, framed by fire that billowed out and up into the night. Though Diomedes seemed to duck on instinct, the force of the blast and sheer surprise caught Michael off guard and knocked him down. The explosion reverberated off the other buildings around him as he lay stunned on the concrete. He blinked to clear his eyes and raised his head up.

God, did that really just happen?

They'd been only half a block from the building when it erupted. While technically still standing, the old tenement was now a gigantic bonfire. Flames jetted from windows and the hole in the front, lighting the rubble that had been thrown into the street by the initial blast. Michael, still struggling to his feet and hindered more from shock than the explosion itself, saw Diomedes running at full speed toward the fire. Others rushed about the chaos.

What the hell happened?

Diomedes made straight for the section of the building where their unit had been. He bolted past the few shocked residents staggering out, and Michael realized that Diomedes was going to attempt to salvage whatever he could of their belongings from the flames. Michael stared, his head still swimming. Their building had just exploded! Feeling as if he would vomit, he ran to help.

Michael's world became a blur. The initial shock of the explosion gave way to frantic, desperate despair as he rushed into the blaze after Diomedes. He was barely able to force himself in against the blast of heat and acrid black plumes of smoke that filled the hallway. Chaos and heat engulfed him before the sight of a wall painted in flames greeted him with the terrible realization that his bedroom lay on the opposite side. The door to their unit was wide open. Michael hoped that meant Diomedes was somewhere ahead of him inside.

Half blind, and with the front of his shirt up over his mouth and nose, Michael pushed on. He got only as far as the middle of the room immediately inside, which had served as their kitchen and common space. Fire was nearly everywhere. What wasn't aflame was wrapped in smoke that stung his eyes and fouled his sense of direction.

He nearly panicked then; he couldn't be sure where anything was. The next thing he knew, Diomedes came rushing past him, and Michael's confusion was such that he was nearly sent toppling into the flames. His roommate paused with a backward glance as Michael caught himself, and then disappeared again towards his own room.

Cursing himself for standing in the way like an idiot, Michael moved in a half-blind, rapid crouch. The heat intensified with each step. It scorched and slapped him as he passed into his room, and what little hope he had of saving anything almost completely evaporated then and there. Just a few feet away lay nearly everything he owned, swallowed in the fire. He barely spotted his tablet just ahead atop a burning dresser, but the flames seared his hands and forced him back from retrieving even that.

There was nothing he could do. His heart was pounding. He could barely breathe, could barely see in the choking heat. There was no longer any doubt: if he didn't get out immediately, the next thing he'd lose would be his life.

Two hours later, the whole affair was a haze of flame, smoke, and loss. Michael vaguely recalled Diomedes yelling at him to get out while Michael had fought through a storm of panic. It had filled his senses even as they had finally abandoned their home and, shortly after, taken refuge in a midtown bar. Now, sharing a booth there with Diomedes, that storm had narrowed into a single stain on the table at which Michael stared.

Dried and red, it was entrenched within the cracks of the table surface. Age had turned it almost as faded as the gray color of the table itself. Michael didn't think it was possible for gray to fade, yet apparently it had. He stared at the stain, clenching his fists and struggling to keep from thinking about the mess that his world had become. He didn't want to think about it. He would not think about it! He had to be strong.

Life had been difficult since his uncle had died, and now that he looked back on everything that had happened since, at all of the failures and catastrophes that resulted in him being nearly broke and unemployed, it seemed . . . well, he didn't exactly know how it seemed. All he knew was that no matter what he did, he didn't do it right. No, some things he did right, but then it never seemed to matter. Having a stable and semi-decent place to live was the one thing he'd had going for him.

Now he didn't even have that anymore.

Now he had nothing.

It wrenched his stomach like a punch to his gut. He saw himself lying in the rain where the homeless woman had been, abandoned and forgotten, his resources gone. He could almost feel it: soaked to the bone, shivering, hungry. He was lost in the world without a lifeline or anchor. Michael began to well up and squeezed his eyes shut against the tears, forcing them back angrily and cursing himself.

Pull it together! Michael gathered up his grief, swallowed it down, and silently traced his fingers along the stain to distract himself.

He hadn't cried since his uncle's heart attack. Uncle Frank had been his only family since he was a little boy, and his farm had been all Michael had known. He'd stood alone on the porch of his uncle's house after the funeral, head in his hands, grief pouring out of him. He'd felt ashamed of it then, and no one had seen him. He would not let Diomedes see him so weak now.

Yet what was he going to do? How could he possibly pick up the pieces? Before, he'd been able to sell what was left of the failing farm and follow his dreams into the city. What options were left to him this time?

He looked up and across the table to where Diomedes sat silent with rage, as he had been since they left the scene of the fire. Michael had asked, multiple times, what they were going to do, but dark, angry looks had been his only reply. After a while, he gave up asking. He should have known by now that Diomedes would want to be left alone. Michael was just glad that he'd been allowed to follow when the older man had stormed off from the ruin of their home.

In fact, Diomedes hadn't even moved since sitting down except to slowly turn his glass with his eyes focused through it, through the table, at some point beyond the ground. Though thankful not to be alone, Michael wished to God that Diomedes would offer him some reassurance, but the longer he sat, the more Michael could sense only fury. Diomedes was thinking within his anger, but of exactly what, there was no telling.

"What're we going to do?" Michael asked again before he could stop himself. *Dammit.*

Diomedes didn't move.

Michael reached out for a paper napkin and grasped it tightly, just to have something in his hands.

At least I still have him.

Diomedes had worked on the farm when he was younger, and Michael counted himself lucky to have found him again a few months ago. Though the older man had shaved the dark head of hair he'd once had, Michael still recognized him immediately by his stern face and the determined look in his eyes. He'd helped Michael more than a few times since, either teaching him about city life or protecting him from its more dangerous elements. A weight had lifted the day Michael persuaded the freelancer to let him move in.

Michael managed a smile despite himself. In truth, he'd more or less idolized the man soon after he'd come to the farm. It didn't seem so long ago. Michael had been twelve and Diomedes around nineteen, though he hadn't taken the name Diomedes yet. Diomedes would not respond to his real name anymore, save for the occasional burst of anger at its use. Michael had decided it best to think of him in terms of his new alias as well.

It was, after all, what freelancers did.

At least I still have him, Michael repeated, struggling to find comfort in his friend's presence. He rubbed his eyes to try to force out the sting of the smoke.

Nearly everything else he had was lost in the fire, probably destroyed before he'd even made it inside. The printed pictures he'd kept from his days on the farm had surely burned as soon as the heat had neared them. His memory alone would have to serve him now. Even the digital copies he'd had were lost. The tablet computer that held them, only recently purchased, was among the small bit of expensive equipment he had. All of it was gone. Michael squeezed his eyes shut again. *Dammit.*

Diomedes coughed as if about to speak. Michael looked up in hope of guidance, but all that followed was a renewed scowling. The older man must still be dealing with the smoke as well.

All in all, Diomedes had lost even more than he had. All of his expensive equipment—a collection of weapons, armor, and miscellaneous gadgets—was hidden away in a small, concealed room with an electric lock on it to keep it safe from random break-ins. Michael cursed himself again for getting in his roommate's way. One small path through a roomful of fire and he'd stood like a cow in the middle of it.

"I'm getting a beer," he said finally. He doubted that he'd be able to put the money to better use anyway, and he didn't want to think about the fire anymore. Diomedes had no response for him. Michael slid from the booth to make his way to the bar.

Though The Flaming Pyre—the bar's name had taken on a sickeningly fitting quality—was a favored hangout for Diomedes and other freelancers, Michael had only been inside with him a handful of times. Reddish light and low metal music bathed the place, the latter disguising most of the noise of the patrons. Rarely in Michael's brief experience did the voices become loud, and when they did, it usually meant trouble.

Michael's gaze traveled around the other patrons rather than over them as he approached the bar. Diomedes had taught him to look that way, to avoid the possibility of provoking someone who might mistake a casual glance for a challenge. *Don't let your eyes rest on anyone. Use your peripheral vision.* And that was only for when you actually had to look for something. All other times, you just looked straight ahead and minded your own business in places like this. Though the habit seemed a little paranoid to Michael, he gave Diomedes's experience the benefit of the doubt. He'd be like him one day, with the ability and confidence to command respect. He hoped. Attaining such glory from his current situation seemed impossible now, even with Diomedes to guide him.

Use your peripheral vision.

A man was staring directly at him.

Michael looked away after the initial flick of eye contact, trying to act as if he hadn't seen his observer. He was sitting across the room, just barely in view behind a table where three Aegis-affiliated freelancers sat. Michael did what he could to avoid the stranger's gaze and focused instead on ordering his beer and watching the bartender fill the glass. Still, the stranger remained in the corner of his eye, a cool presence in a posh overcoat, watching him.

Michael didn't know how long he'd been watching. He didn't even remember seeing the stranger come in. From the brief moment of eye contact, he didn't seem to be threatening, merely observing. Maybe he'd caught the stranger's eye too long the first time and the man was merely watching him for any further challenge. When his beer was ready, Michael did his best to inconspicuously return to his roommate's booth. He sat down again with Diomedes's silence and stared into the beer without drinking.

"It was no accident," Diomedes said.

Michael turned his attention back to his friend. Diomedes was still staring through his glass, but the words he'd spoken were loud enough to make Michael think he might be speaking to him. Despite Diomedes's sudden breach of silence, Michael briefly wondered if he should say anything. He decided to chance it.

"Are you sure?" It was an old building, after all. An accidental fire could have hit a gas line and caused the explosion. Michael wasn't an expert on such things, but it seemed feasible enough to consider.

Diomedes fixed him with a stare. "It was no accident."

Michael glanced down at the table. "How do you know?"

The freelancer regarded Michael and seemed to consider his reply "Don't ask me that question."

Michael waited a few moments for a more satisfying response before he once again regarded his drink with an inward sigh.

A new voice entered the conversation. "Your friend is right."

Michael jumped at the voice, feeling foolish for it even as he did so. Diomedes didn't flinch. The voice belonged to the man who had been across the room watching him only moments before.

I I

THE STRANGER MUST have approached while Michael was concentrating on Diomedes. Now that he was closer, Michael was able to get a better look. He pegged the stranger at about six feet—roughly Michael's own height—and of average build, though the overcoat made it hard to be sure. A suit and tie were just visible through the bit that hung open. A black ponytail seemed the only prominent feature of his otherwise unremarkable features. Hands held in his pockets, he looked between the two men. Michael looked back to Diomedes for guidance.

The man with the ponytail paused, also waiting for a reaction from Diomedes. Getting none, he continued. "He is right," he said to Michael, "but beyond that, I doubt he knows any more than you do."

Diomedes grabbed the front of the man's coat at the neck and pulled him down in a motion almost too quick to see. Only after the man was caught, his head pulled level to his captor's, did Diomedes turn to look at him. His voice was frigid. "Do you have a point?"

The stranger smiled and, comfortably, clasped his hands behind his back as if bending down of his own accord. "Oh, I have more than a point. I have a proposition." Michael was impressed by the stranger's composure. "Although," he continued, "I'd much prefer to deliver it sitting down."

Diomedes regarded the man for a moment. He then grunted quietly in reply, slid farther down the seat, and pushed the man absently onto the other half of the booth. "Talk."

The man settled into his new seat and turned first to Michael. "I can see your friend is, understandably, not in the best of moods. I'll attempt to be brief. As I said, the destruction of your building was no accident." Here the stranger glanced at Diomedes's tightening grip on his glass and added, "Nor was it an attempt on your life, if that's what you're thinking. As a matter of fact, I can't give you much of an idea of the reason behind it, other than to say it was arson. I don't know how much attention you pay to the news. The few other little fires started around the city recently?"

"It was just a random arson," Michael whispered despite himself. A random crime, not a random accident. Somehow the idea made him feel even more helpless. Diomedes glanced at him, his stern expression unchanged.

"Yes. Perpetrated by the same man who set the others."

"You're sure of that?" Diomedes asked.

The stranger paused and turned to look at the freelancer. "My employer is. He is also sure of his identity, at least—"

Diomedes spun in the booth. His hand shot to the man's throat, this time pinning him against the back of the seat.

"Tell me," he whispered. "Now!"

Though it faded quickly before being replaced by his previous confident manner, Michael could tell the man was caught off guard. Even aware that Diomedes had enhancements to speed his movements, Michael couldn't help feeling surprised along with the stranger. Diomedes's rage had worn through his patience the way Michael's own helplessness had worn through his hope, and the stranger had caught the result. The stranger smiled, a trace of nervousness on his face, and glanced down at the hand at his neck.

"Ah, perhaps now would be a good time to tell you of my proposition."

Diomedes's hand tightened. "Wrong. Now would be the time for you to tell me who the bastard is."

"You want to kill him?" the man managed to gasp.

"I'm going to kill *somebody*."

"That's—the proposition." The man managed a smug grin. Diomedes watched him silently for a moment, not seeming to have heard. The stranger looked back with a clear expectation of freedom after his last pitch. His smile faded as the grip about his neck continued to hold. He glanced at Michael, who watched, unsure of what to do. He didn't think that his friend would kill the man, but he realized with more than a little nervousness that he didn't absolutely know that he wouldn't, either. Probably he was just trying to frighten the stranger. Diomedes had once told him the importance of maintaining a powerful image in this sort of situation, but the man didn't seem frightened so much as — like Michael — unsure.

And then, as if by some unseen signal, Diomedes released the man and turned back to the table. "So tell."

Aside from rubbing the growing welt on his neck as he settled back into his seat again, the man continued as if nothing terribly unusual had happened. He laid his left arm on the table and rolled up his sleeve to expose the underside of his forearm. His hand clenched briefly and, a moment later, a rectangular panel of skin about five inches long folded upward to reveal a data pad touch screen. It blinked to life.

The quality of the artificial arm was impressive. Michael knew enough about cybernetics and synthetic skin to know that the seamless concealment of the computer was quite expensive. Whoever this man's "employer" was, they obviously paid him quite well.

The stranger touched a few keys. Michael and Diomedes both watched closely as the image of what looked to be a warehouse appeared.

"Where's this?" Michael asked.

"One of the other arson sites. Watch."

A figure appeared on the screen, running along the warehouse's roof. There was no sound with the image, but if there had been, it seemed that they might have heard the breaking of glass as, after going a short distance, the figure swung down over the side and disappeared, feet first, through the window.

"This was taken a few days ago by a rather resourceful person who then sold it to my employer. Considering what little can be made out so far, it doesn't seem to have been such a wonderful bargain. Though if you'll watch a little longer . . ."

They obliged. About ten seconds later, the figure was visible again, jumping out of the same window to the ground and then running away from the building in the general direction of the camera. A second later, the building erupted in a way familiar enough to feel like a punch to Michael's gut. He glanced at Diomedes, who returned the gaze before looking back at the screen. The stranger tapped a key, and the image paused.

The flames cast a bit of light on the figure. Michael could make out a little of some type of full body suit, although its flat black coloring made it difficult to see entirely. An occasional glint of metal could also be seen in places, but the camera was too far away to discern a face.

"A little bit better," the ponytailed man remarked. "If we enlarge here and enhance the image . . . " He pressed a few more keys. Soon they were looking at a close-up of the figure's face, half illuminated by the light of the fire. The other half was just a shadow in the flames. Michael studied the face without recognition.

Diomedes matched Michael's scrutiny. "That's him." It was more a statement than a question.

"Do you recognize him?" the man asked.

Diomedes stared at the picture again. "No. Who is he?"

The man closed up his arm and pulled his sleeve back down. "We don't know."

Diomedes glared. "You said—"

"Had you allowed me to finish my sentence earlier," the stranger advised, "you would have heard me say that we know who did it, not exactly who he is."

"Not exactly?" Michael asked.

"We do know one additional thing about him." The man paused, as if searching for a way to say something. "He seems to match the general description of someone who's rumored to be calling himself 'Wraith.' Apparently he fancies himself a vigilante, fighting 'evil-doers.'" The man gave a mocking chuckle. "Gangers and the like. Though as you can attest to, he sometimes misses the mark a bit."

"And you want him killed," Diomedes said. The man nodded.

"Why?" Michael asked.

Diomedes flashed him a stern look.

The stranger shrugged. "I'm just a facilitator. I don't ask, they don't tell me."

Michael almost asked who 'they' were, but thought better of it. It didn't seem like the man cared to share that with them, and, as Diomedes hadn't touched on the subject, he figured it wasn't something you asked. He made a mental note to talk to Diomedes about it later.

Diomedes turned to face the man, for the first time making eye contact without assaulting him. "How much?"

"Ten thousand. Two up front. Plus, of course, the information I've already given you."

"Information we need for the job anyway."

"Granted, but one could argue that was given out of trust that the job would be accepted." The man smiled.

"You gave it because your neck was squeezed. That was your choice. You pay for it."

The ponytailed man scowled. "I hardly think that—"

Diomedes cut him off. "Fifteen. We have to find him, first."

The stranger looked at Michael, who had been listening silently. "Your friend here is bold. Given his previous behavior, he planned to do what the job requires even before it came along." He looked back to Diomedes, a trace of smugness in his expression. "Now he seeks to throw away the chance of compensation."

Diomedes's pale eyes narrowed. "I said I was going to kill somebody. You're still an option."

Though he appeared unfazed by the threat, the man nevertheless responded after a few moments. "I can do as much as twelve. I'd suggest you take it before I decide to leave."

Diomedes turned back to the table. "Twelve. With three up front."

"Done," the stranger replied, not seeming to care. He placed the money and a card on the table and stood up. "Call when it's done," he said, indicating a number written on the card. "He shouldn't be too hard to find. Maybe," he added, "if he hears you're looking for him, he'll help you out and come to kill you. Gentlemen."

With a farewell nod and a smirk, the ponytailed man turned and left the 'Pyre. Diomedes watched him go. It was plain from his expression that whatever he was thinking about the man wasn't good. Michael had never known Diomedes to be a fan of smugness.

For his own part, Michael's spirits were rising. The fire that took almost everything away from him was giving him some of the things he never had—a chance to do something adventurous, something to help people. Catching a vigilante-turned-arsonist could prevent more useless destruction. The fact that the man in question called himself "Wraith" only made things more mysterious, if a touch absurd.

Although, Michael considered, were they really going to kill the man? On the one hand, he had little faith in the justice system. The ideas behind it were noble enough, but he had heard too many stories of corruption and inefficiency, and seen too much crime going on unchecked, to have much practical faith in it. Sometimes the individual needed to act on his own. Corporations and others who could afford it did so every day, hiring freelancers and private investigators. On the other hand, the actual thought of killing made him wary. Yet Diomedes was a part of this, and if he thought it necessary, then it was necessary. If the man was an arsonist, lives would be saved.

"Diomedes," he said, "how can we be sure about what that guy said?"

The large freelancer looked up from his own brief thoughts to Michael. "Trust the money, kid," he replied distantly. "It's a constant."

Michael nodded at the advice. They were going to have to find the man anyway, and that process would likely help to answer his questions. It suddenly occurred to him that he had no idea how they would go about tracking him down, and he mentioned this to Diomedes.

"I'm thinking about that." Diomedes looked absently at the wall. "May need to hire some help with this one."

"What?" Someone else? Was he going to be left out? "Aren't I—"

The freelancer frowned. "To find the mark, dumbass. You don't know where he is any more than me, do you?"

Michael nodded, relieved to still be included, despite the way Diomedes had said it. He hadn't meant it as an insult, of course. That was just the way Diomedes was. And he was right. If he said they needed help, they needed help.

"There's someone I know . . . " Diomedes scowled.

"But?"

"He's a jackass. Also the best guy for the job."

Michael remembered a man who had once come to the apartment for Diomedes to consult about something that the freelancer hadn't let him hear. The guy had seemed nice enough in the brief time Michael had spent with him. He'd seemed to have a rather constant sense of humor, which might have been part of why Diomedes found him irritating. One thing Michael had noticed on the farm was that Diomedes lacked a real appreciation for humor; following their reunion, he appeared to have little tolerance for it at all.

Or it may have been something else entirely. Michael didn't really experience enough of the visitor to tell. He couldn't even remember his name. He asked Diomedes if this was the man he meant.

Diomedes nodded, still scowling. "Hiatt." Putting his hand over the payment he had put in a coat pocket, he paused for a moment before appearing to come to a decision. He pulled out his phone. "If anyone can find the mark, it's him."

Michael permitted himself a quick smile at his friend's attempt at self-persuasion and waited while Diomedes was on the phone. Just possibly, things might turn out alright. Maybe that was just how his life worked: hope from tragedy. When he was four, his mother died of cancer after his father had run off, yet his uncle had raised him well. His uncle's death had meant the loss of his only family. Yet if his uncle were still alive, Michael might still be on the farm, helping him "for just one more year" to keep it going, the way Michael had done each year since he had originally planned to leave at eighteen. Though it had been Michael's own choice, he had secretly begun to think of the farm as an invisible chain that kept him from experiencing more of the outside world. He smiled sadly. Maybe soon he'd be able to have the gain without the tragedy.

Diomedes finished up on the phone and rolled his eyes. Michael watched him for an explanation with an expectant look that took Diomedes a few moments to notice.

"He'll meet us here soon." Diomedes sounded less than pleased. "Looks like you're a real freelancer now, kid," he said before taking a drink.

Michael smiled at the thought and tried to focus beyond the night's losses. A new stage of his life was finally beginning. Diomedes was no longer just a role model; he was about to become his mentor. The thought was enough to make him forget the day's earlier disaster for a moment.

Diomedes set the glass down. Stern, artificial eyes fell on Michael. "Don't screw up."

I I I

A FACE FLOATED like a ghost above the lunar landscape. The face was Parker's own, reflected in the clear polymer windshield of the dual-passenger rover that kept them safe from the choking, cold near-vacuum outside. The Earth hung in the sky beyond, the only spot of color in a view of white, black, and gray. It was always there. Parker hadn't realized until he had arrived on the Moon that the same facts of orbit and rotation that kept one face of the Moon perpetually facing the Earth also kept the Earth in the sky above that face constantly. It was a sight that he found comforting in its constancy. Parker had wished more than once that everything were so straightforward.

His hands remained at the controls of the rover, guiding it along the smoothest course along the Aristarchus crater and following the tracks of the mining transports that had made the journey in the past few days. The rover's only other occupant, the woman from ESA, stood patiently beside him, occasionally shifting her weight as they navigated the route from the operations center.

In 2035, the European Space Agency had completed Alpha Station, humanity's first major lunar base. Since then, ESA had claimed the right to stewardship of the territory surrounding it. As its resources were primarily those of exploration, it became more feasible to dispense mining contracts to independent companies instead of going into the mining business itself. ESA would bear the responsibility of transport to and from Earth in return for a percentage of the profit. The Saratoga Mining Company, Parker's employer, was one of many firms to take up ESA's offer, with multiple plots available to mine at its discretion.

Parker steered them across one of those plots until the mouth of a tunnel opened in the surface ahead of them, and then he eased the rover inside. "Here we are again," he announced. "Have you had a close look at it, yet? Gotten out and actually looked close at the surface?"

"I have," she answered after a beat. "Shortly after arriving. As you reported, Mr. Andora, very . . . remarkable."

"I've sure never seen a thing like it."

His crew had found it barely six days ago. At the time, Parker had been in his office working on the paperwork for his crew's hasty transfer from their previous site. The company had pulled them out before they had reached the standard ESA mining limits, which made for an administrative nightmare. Parker had figured that the Aristarchus site must be richer and that Saratoga wished to mine it first, but from the initial survey data he'd had, the place wasn't any better than the old site. In some ways, it was worse. Yet if his crew didn't mine enough out of the new site, someone in administration wouldn't like it, and he'd catch the blame.

He had been agonizing over the survey estimates and wishing for a distraction when he'd gotten his wish in a signal from the crew's outfitting bay. He'd turned, opened the frequency, and responded, perhaps too eagerly, with, "Is there a problem?"

"Heh. That's a good question, sir," came the response from the speaker. Rayburn's gruff voice had echoed from the bare walls of the airlock in which he stood. *"You wanna come out here and take a look at this yourself?"*

Parker had looked out his window and down at the equipment below. "Take a look at what?"

"Hell, if I could tell you I wouldn't be callin' you out here."

Though the tone in Rayburn's voice had hinted otherwise, Parker had headed down to the airlock with the thought in his mind that whatever he was being called to look at might help in some way with increasing the production estimates. He put on his pressure suit and followed Rayburn over the dusty landscape, the hope still with him despite the other's silent refusal to elaborate until they'd reached the site. The appearance of something else soon overshadowed that hope and brought its own unique dilemmas.

Rayburn had led him down toward the center of the Aristarchus crater, to where a depression in the exposed rock cradled an area where the miners had begun clearing it. A short distance from there, Rayburn stopped and pointed. At first he seemed to be pointing at nothing beyond the immediate lunar geology, but after stepping closer, Parker noticed a difference. After a moment of uncertainty, he had approached further and reached out to touch it, almost gingerly. Of the jumble of thoughts in his mind at the time—a mix of confusion, worry, and amazement—the one thing he could clearly remember was his own voice asking with a slight air of annoyance, "Now what the hell is the protocol for *this*?"

Whatever the exposed object was, it appeared to extend farther back and down into the rock than what little had been revealed. It was composed of some type of metal, although the specific type was impossible to determine with a mere visual examination. The metal had a strange ethereal quality to it, at once both uniformly gray and somehow transparent, as if he could see a few millimeters into the surface. It felt rather like gazing through a fog at clouds beyond it— yet it was genuinely solid nonetheless, sending the light from his suit dancing in a faint lattice of crystalline reflection. After the initial shock and wonder had worn off, Parker had promptly decided that this was not a situation for him to be handling, and it wasn't long before he contacted his own superiors. He had been relieved to be told that all he was required to do was to wait for further instructions.

Considering the nature of the situation, the instructions had come quicker than expected. On the other hand, they were generally simple to carry out. Deciding what should be done in this case wasn't the kind of responsibility he'd signed on for, and he was more than happy to just be a cog in the wheel. He was to maintain authority over his crew, of course. That was the job he was qualified for, and what he had been told to have them accomplish was easily within the confines of their ability. Soon the crew had begun to dig again, following the object back into the rock.

In the time between then and now, they had created a tunnel that sloped gently into the Moon's surface. On one side was the strange metal object, clearly much larger than Parker had been able to discern during his initial look. It had been slow going. They'd had to widen the tunnel, now almost one hundred yards long, to give the people and machinery enough space to work. Supports had been put in to keep the tunnel safe, and that had taken time as well. But with the entire crew's effort concentrated on the one task, they were going as quickly as possible.

Parker refocused on the present as the rover neared the end of the tunnel where his crew was working and eased the vehicle down to a slow creep. The piercing light from the cutting that carved the lunar rock reflected in the rover's windshield. As the rock was delicately sliced from its foundation, miners moved about, strapped into the large, robotic skeletons that hydraulically modified their own movements and allowed them to carry away carvings that would otherwise break a man's back, even in the Moon's lower gravity. Larger vehicles took the heavier pieces that such exo-chassis couldn't handle, and both loaded the rock onto belts that conveyed the rocks along the tunnel to the surface, where they would then be hauled to the material processors.

Normally, once the rocks reached the processors, crews would begin the procedure of extracting any usable material. Only now the processors did not operate. The rock was beginning to pile up. Parker had ordered the initially surprised crew to concentrate solely on digging.

"Your crew works quickly," the woman commended him.

"They're the best," he said, easing the rover to a stop.

For a time, he and the woman watched the crew in silence. She had arrived at the dig site a little more than two days ago, introducing herself as Field Chief Marette Clarion, an ESA overseer. French by her accent, so far she had been true to the title, content to only watch while Parker directed the crew. Even so, he was glad of her presence, for the most part.

From the onset of the excavation, Parker had supervised almost constantly. ESA had told him what they wanted him to look for, and although he had instructions to not inform the crew of specifics, he was fairly certain they had an idea of their objective as well. Whether any of them would know it or not, if they saw it, was another question. That was one thing that made him uneasy, as Parker didn't even know exactly how to recognize it himself.

When they began, he had opted not to worry about it until there was a change in the featureless metal surface that they were uncovering. When Clarion had arrived, he'd taken some comfort in the assumption that she would help him to make the distinction, yet she hadn't been willing to shed any more light on the subject. Primarily, she watched, tight-lipped, and answered most questions with the assertion that it was best to avoid premature speculation. He assumed—or hoped— that she would speak up when the time came.

On the other hand, despite the fact that Parker was allowed to continue supervising the project (he had more than half expected ESA to completely take control), Clarion's presence made him uneasy. She had assured him she was only there to see the results of the dig, but as her relative silence continued, Parker couldn't shake the feeling that he was being evaluated as well. The idea was ridiculous, he'd told himself; the woman was from ESA, not Saratoga. It was just his nerves reacting to the circumstances. The fact that it was a non-routine project was enough to cause him stress, even without the incredible details. But somehow realizing this didn't seem to help the feeling that Clarion was studying him.

A change in the usual rhythm of the digging caught Parker's attention. As he looked over toward the edge of the excavated wall, the crew's comm-channel broke the silence inside the vehicle.

"You told us to say when we uncovered anything different, Parker," came the female crewmember's voice. *"Looks like we just did."*

Parker glanced over at Clarion, who was peering out at the operation. "Can you give me a bit more details, there?" he replied.

"Looks like an indentation in the metal. Doesn't seem to be much larger than ten feet square, though we're still uncovering it."

"An indentation?" Parker asked while trying for a better view. "Like a dent?"

"Mm, wouldn't call it a dent. Definite corners."

"All right." He took a deep breath. "I'll be out there in a minute to have a look."

Parker guided the vehicle in closer to the spot in question. As the crew continued to cut away the rock around the indentation, he slipped into the rear airlock and closed it off from the cockpit where Clarion remained. Designed for only one person at a time, the airlock was cramped, and it took a few extra moments of awkward bending to get the suit on. He then opened the outer door, walked over to the wall, and ordered the crew to stop their work. As they backed off, he was able to get a better look. Just as described, the indentation was around ten feet high, although it extended horizontally at least a little farther. The left edge remained concealed by uncut rock, but the right was uncovered, all with a uniform depth of about six inches. Again Parker gave in to the impulse to touch it, gliding a hand along one side. His thumb traced an edge that formed a perfect right angle.

Parker stared for a time to let his gaze roam the indentation's full width, scanning corners, peering into the mysterious metal, and wrestling with the decision before him. What business did he have even making this distinction? If he screwed this one up, they'd surely hang it on him, but they could only expect so much of him, couldn't they?

Well, Parker? Yes, or no?

"I think," he started. "I think this might possibly be what we're looking for."

*   *   *

In the rover, Marette Clarion watched the uncertain foreman study the find. Marette herself was not entirely positive about her own assessment of the indentation—she doubted there was anyone who would be—but she was responsible for making a decision, so she made it. She would sign off on the foreman's report to ESA when he submitted it, but first, there were others to be notified. She reached for her watch and pressed the signal button just above the etching of the Palladium, never for a moment taking her eyes off the uncovered space that, for all intents and purposes, appeared to be a door.

I V

FELIX HIATT was haunting the offices of Marquand Cybernetics when the humorless freelancer called. Felix didn't work there, or at least he didn't work there for Marquand. He was "working" there for himself, and as far as Marquand was concerned he probably shouldn't have even been in the building. Non-employees weren't normally allowed in the majority of the facilities. He would have been no exception, were it not for an acquaintance who managed to hook him up with a minimum-access employee card. It didn't give him free run of the building, but very few people had that privilege anyway, so it wasn't a major concern. It was enough, for the moment.

Despite the minor inconvenience of procuring the pass card, Felix had no specific purpose in the building other than trolling for information. Sitting alone in the cafeteria, he attempted to overhear any interesting conversations. He'd managed to discover a few days earlier that a certain hotshot cybernetic engineer had been hired, and if the woman would be helping out with any particularly interesting hardware, he wanted to know. The annual cybernetics convention was due to happen in just over a month and new things were bound to be in development. As to what Felix might do with the information when and if he got it, he didn't quite know himself. He might find someone interested in paying for the information, or he might not. Perhaps another use of the knowledge might present itself. Even so, he still enjoyed the search—almost as much as he enjoyed the knowledge itself.

Besides, he had a reputation to consider.

It was this same reputation that had caused Diomedes to call him, Felix figured. What little the freelancer had told him hinted at a solid job, which was more definite than his current objective, and just the fact that he had called him at all spoke of a challenge. Diomedes liked Felix about as much as a kick in the teeth, and anything that would get him past that attitude certainly involved something big. Knowing Diomedes, it involved a big sum of money. Felix had to smile when he thought of the mental struggle the freelancer must have fought between the want of the money and his dislike of Felix's company.

No doubt about it, Felix thought, this was going to be fun.

A short time after getting the call, Felix arrived in The Flaming Pyre. He checked the handgun he kept under his coat at the door, and then stopped just inside, where his eyes scanned the room from behind the mirrored sunglasses he'd recently taken to wearing on a whim. Most of the light inside came from the central bar, ringed by orange neon and a few overhead fluorescents. The orange mixed with smaller, reddish lights along the walls and the ceiling, overpowering the white to bathe most of the establishment in a rusty ambiance.

Felix spotted Diomedes in a booth near the back. If the freelancer had seen him, he gave no indication, though Felix guessed that he most likely had. One thing about Diomedes, he was observant, even if he wasn't always discerning enough to properly classify the things he observed. Felix recognized the younger man with him as his roommate . . . Michael, he realized after a moment's concentration. They had met once, briefly, and although Felix didn't think he'd spent enough time with him to form an accurate impression, he'd seemed like a decent enough kid.

Felix smiled to himself, feeling old because of his mental reference to a man in what looked to be his early twenties as a kid. At thirty-one, he realized he sometimes felt he was a kid himself, even though Felix could still clearly remember being Michael's age and feeling completely matured. He hoped the kid knew what he was doing, hanging around with someone like Diomedes.

Felix resumed moving, heading not for the booth but instead for the central bar. Not looking anywhere near the direction of the freelancer and his roommate, he took a stool and ordered a drink. The bartender smiled in recognition of his customer and then shook his head disapprovingly as he accepted Felix's order of, "Water, on the rocks."

Felix smiled back at him. He knew this man, too.

A few moments later, Felix sipped slowly at his ice water and wondered how long it might take for Diomedes to come over and haul him off the seat. He probably shouldn't be doing this. He was extremely curious about what Diomedes had called him for, and playing with the freelancer's patience probably wasn't the wisest thing to do in any case, but Felix still couldn't quite resist. Should he turn around and wave? Felix chuckled. That would probably be going a little too far. This way at least he could claim to not have seen him if it came to making an excuse, albeit a flippant one.

Felix took another sip of water and motioned again for the bartender, a rough-looking man in his mid-forties.

"Yeah, Felix? Somethin' wrong with your water?" the bartender joked.

"Oh, not at all." Felix held the glass up to the light and made a show of admiring it. "I'm very impressed with it. Nice bouquet. It's, what, a 'thirty-three?"

The bartender smiled again—a barely perceptible upturn at the corner of his mouth. "Good year for water. So, what is it?"

"Oh, just wondering if there's been anything interesting going on here."

The bartender shrugged. "Eh, it's been dull as dust lately. Some new guy named Patterson got a little wasted and smashed up a table last night. S'probably the most exciting thing that's happened."

"What about Diomedes?" Felix asked. He cocked his head back in the freelancer's direction.

"Ah, he's been here with that other guy for the past hour, I guess. Seemed pretty pissed about somethin' or other." The bartender smirked. "Though with him it's hard to tell. Some suit talked to him for a bit. Had an armor-laced overcoat, but I saw the suit under. Diomedes had him by the throat a few times. After that he left." He shrugged.

Felix nodded. "Thanks, Lars," he said, slipping him a twenty. "This should cover the water. And keep your eyes open for me, eh?"

"Can do," said Lars. He took the cash and moved off.

A hand tapped Felix's shoulder a few moments later. Felix was sure even before he turned that it was someone other than Diomedes. If it was Dio, he'd gotten a lot more polite.

"Felix?" Michael asked.

"Yep," Felix nodded and glanced over the kid's shoulder to where Diomedes sat. "Michael, right?"

"It's Romulus now, actually. Diomedes sent me over here to ask if you'd join us."

"Yeah, I'm sure that's exactly how he would've put it, too," Felix said with a grin.

Romulus hesitated, opening his mouth slightly and seeming unsure as to how to respond to the sarcasm. Felix grabbed his water off the bar, deciding to end the kid's awkwardness. He started towards the booth. "I see you've decided to take a freelance name."

"Sure have."

Felix shook his head. "Got to say, I think that's a shame. Always thought that whole street alias business was a little foolish. Your choice, I suppose." Felix also noted with some dismay that his chosen name was—like Diomedes's—from classical mythology. Felix liked mythology, but the choice indicated that the grim freelancer definitely had some influence over his younger roommate. Felix suddenly smiled, remembering something: Diomedes was a Greek hero during the Trojan War, but Romulus was supposedly the founder of Rome, a people descended in theory by fugitives of Troy who were led out of their falling city by Aeneas. Felix wondered if either roommate was aware of the irony. He guessed not.

He never had found out just why Diomedes had chosen his alias. Whatever the reason, it was something interesting; the man had refused to answer and then nearly clocked him when he pried. It remained on a mental list Felix kept of things he wanted to someday discover. Diomedes held onto the secret like his life depended on it, so he figured it would stay on that list awhile. Then again, the list wasn't for the easy stuff.

Felix slid into the booth next to Romulus and greeted Diomedes's blank glare with a smile. "Diomedes," Felix said. "Grinning ear to ear as always, I see."

"Took you long enough to get here," the freelancer growled.

Felix shrugged. "They have good water here. Although, now that I think about it—who wants an orange whip? Orange whip? Orange whip?" he asked brightly, looking and pointing to Romulus and Diomedes in turn. "Three orange whips!" The drink order was directed at a passing patron who continued walking without response. Felix grinned back at them before he had to sigh and shake his head. "No one gets that joke anymore." He leaned in to Romulus. "Not that they ever really did in my lifetime anyway. Maybe I should stop making references to things from a different century, huh?"

The kid gave him a confused look. "I guess so," he answered, looking over to Diomedes, who was rolling his eyes.

"Are you finished?"

"Oh, that's right!" Felix chirped. He had wondered how long Diomedes would let him banter on. He turned back to face him and leaned over the table. "You wanted to talk to me about something, didn't you?"

"We need to find someone."

"A particular someone, or just someone in general?"

"Shut the hell up and let me finish." Felix opted to oblige. "Someone's hired me to find some whacked-out vigilante bastard. For some screwed-up reason he calls himself 'Wraith.' You're helping us find him."

"'Wraith,' huh? Well, it could be worse. Could be something like . . . 'Batguy.' Or 'Irving the Terrible.' Though maybe you should check the comic book stores anyway?" Felix grinned. "It still sounds like he might have read a few too many."

"Dumbass suggestions aren't the kind of help I had in mind."

"I know, I know. I swear, Diomedes, the day you manage a laugh will be the day hell freezes over," said Felix.

"It wasn't funny."

Felix smiled again. "Well, I suppose you have me there, but it was the best I could do at the time." He paused again to sip his water. "Okay, seriously: I've heard of this guy, mainly rumors. I take it you have enough cause to take them at face value?" Felix had reasons of his own to believe the rumors, but he wanted to see what Diomedes would say. His only response was a nod. "Next question. Whoever it was that hired you, why do they want you to find him?"

Romulus seemed about to say something when Diomedes cut him off: "Why should you care? We're hiring you, all you worry about is finding him."

Felix shook his head. "Information has to flow both ways on this, Dio."

"Don't call me Dio."

Felix ignored the demand. "Knowing why you want him is almost sure to help me determine where we should start looking. Unless there really isn't a Wraith and you just enjoy my company," he added with his best wolfish smile.

"The sonofabitch torched our apartment," Diomedes said a moment later.

Felix nodded. "That would explain your subtle lack of affection for him. But why would someone else hire you to find him for that?"

Romulus spoke for the first time since the start of the conversation. "They think he also set all those warehouse fires recently."

"See, now that makes more sense," said Felix, turning to Romulus. "Question is, why would someone who's only toasted warehouses suddenly decide to burn down an apartment?"

"That's your job, Hiatt," Diomedes said. "Figure it out."

"So I'll be doing that while you sit here and soak up the atmosphere?" Felix was reasonably certain it wasn't true as he said it. Diomedes was also a control freak.

The control freak shook his head. "We'll be with you to keep you on track. I just don't want you following us around getting paid for nothing."

Felix chuckled. "Now that actually brings up another question: how much *are* you paying me?"

The two took a few moments to haggle over Felix's fee. They wound up with a small sum, to be paid upon finding the vigilante. Although he was reasonably happy with the agreed upon amount, Felix still made a show of being disappointed. In truth, he admitted to himself, he probably could have gotten at least a little more. He hadn't taken the time to truly bargain seriously. As with the search at Marquand, the hunt was enough to satisfy him—especially when it involved looking for the truth behind a rumor magnet like this Wraith person. Any money he got in the bargain purely kept him fed and reasonably comfortable, and even if the money he got from Diomedes hadn't been enough for that, he knew of a few other groups who would pay for the information. More than one gang was offering cash for the vigilante's identity, presumably to avenge comrades whose death he'd allegedly caused. Though he hadn't made mention of it, Felix assumed that was ultimately what Diomedes planned to do as well. There was rarely any other reason to involve a freelancer in something like this, and the fact that he allegedly burned down Diomedes's home pretty much sealed the deal.

If he was to be working with Diomedes, though, he would have to watch his back; there was no doubt about that. It wasn't specifically that he didn't trust Diomedes. He didn't, of course, but that wasn't the issue. Felix was certain that the freelancer didn't trust him, and that was the problem. Diomedes's common view of people often bordered on the paranoid, and this made for an unpredictable and undesirable element. He didn't trust anyone completely, so far as Felix could tell. Diomedes obviously placed some measure of trust in his roommate, but Felix hadn't spent enough of his time with the pair to sense how much.

As for Romulus, or whatever Michael preferred to be called, Felix wasn't worried at all. Felix still believed him to be a better man than Diomedes, although how much hanging around with Diomedes would change him was yet to be seen. What he could tell from Romulus's body language spoke of respect for his roommate, if not plain admiration. Felix realized that if his impression of that kid were accurate, it would be a shame if Diomedes influenced him too much.

He'd have to keep an eye on that.

*   *   *

Romulus sat back in the booth as Diomedes and Felix argued quietly over compensation. The discussion of the money held less interest for Romulus than the actual matter of stopping the vigilante-turned-arsonist from doing more harm. How much help would Felix be to them? Regardless, he seemed like an interesting person to have along, at the very least.

He didn't truly know quite what to make of the man's sense of humor, though. This little interaction had already confirmed that Diomedes found it deeply irritating, but Romulus had found himself smiling inwardly from at least most of the quips. So far he didn't think he understood everything that Felix had joked about—he didn't know at all what to make of the "orange whip" comment—but he could still sense the comedic intention behind it.

Was that . . . appropriate? Was "appropriate" even the right word? Diomedes had always taken everything seriously for as long as he had known him. Romulus looked around at the other freelancers who filled the bar. Some looked as tough, or tougher, than Diomedes: large hulking brutes bristling with muscular enhancements, cybernetic limbs, and designer street armor. Others were smaller, yet no less imposing: a quiet, strong presence of deadly confidence. And the ones who commanded the most respect? Rarely, if ever, did he catch them laughing. Theirs—especially Diomedes's if he was to truly be his mentor—was the example to follow.

Yet it did feel good to smile, however little, from Felix's antics. Maybe keeping it hidden was the important thing. Further thought on the subject was cut short as Romulus sensed a conclusion in the money matters.

"Now that that's been settled," Felix announced, "let's see if we can't find your little friend." Romulus nodded, excited to be going, and began to slide his way out of the booth. Felix glanced at him. "You have somewhere to be just now?"

Romulus looked back at him, confused. "But, aren't we—" Hadn't he said they were leaving? "I thought you said . . . " He inched back into the booth.

"We need to do a little thinking before we can start acting, Romulus," Felix said. He looked to Diomedes. "Didn't you teach him that yet?"

Diomedes didn't respond.

Romulus wanted to try to explain himself, but after a second or two of searching for the words he decided to just stay quiet and try not to look any more stupid in front of the other two. It wasn't that big of a deal anyway, he told himself. Felix's tone had been simple, not scolding. *Just chalk it up to a learning experience. Let it go.* Easier said than done. He wished Diomedes hadn't seen it. He felt like a child.

Felix took off his mirror shades, clasped his hands in front of his face and leaned on them, thinking. "Incidentally," he began with a glance at Diomedes, "who exactly was it that hired you?"

"I didn't find it necessary to ask," he replied.

Felix chuckled lightly. "I guess that means his money was good. It might've helped us if you'd found that out."

"I didn't find it necessary to ask."

"Yes, so you said."

Romulus found himself wanting to question the procedure again. Was it usual to ask, or was it something best left unsaid? How might it help them?

He kept quiet. This probably wasn't the best time to start asking questions like that, especially after nearly vaulting out of the booth a moment before. Besides, if he listened well enough, he might find the answers he was looking for anyway.

"Do you at least remember what the man you talked to looked like?" Felix probed. "Maybe I'd know him from somewhere?"

Diomedes gave a brief description of the man with the ponytail as Felix listened. Romulus tried to form his own description, hoping to redeem himself a little by adding any details Diomedes left out. As it happened, he could.

"He also had a touch screen data pad that folded out from his left arm," he offered after Diomedes had finished.

Felix nodded. "Was the arm metal or skinned?"

"Skinned," Diomedes replied. There was a hint of annoyance in his voice that did not go unnoticed by Romulus, who returned his blank stare with a mildly perplexed one of his own.

"Yeah," said Romulus, looking back to Felix. "Looked pretty expensive to me."

"Know a lot about organic synthetics, kid?"

"Er, well, as much as most people, I think. Why?"

Felix shrugged. "Just curious. You remember a brand name on that data pad?" Romulus shook his head. Felix looked to Diomedes. "Dio?"

"No," the freelancer insisted. He turned to stare at the wall.

"Just checking," Felix said, seeming to ignore Diomedes's impatience. He then closed his eyes. For a moment, it seemed to Romulus that Felix was lost in thought before his eyes opened again and he shook his head with a frown. "I don't know him."

"You sure?" Romulus asked.

Felix smiled. "Kid, my memory is one of the few things in this life that I very rarely question." He sighed. "But seeing as I don't know this guy, it's probably a moot point anyway."

"The man we are actually looking for," Diomedes sniped. "What do you know about *him*?"

"Like I said, there's a lot of rumors out there I've heard. Sorting them from the truth is always the tricky part." He smiled. "I wouldn't be surprised if he turns into Northgate's own Sasquatch soon. People'll start seeing things and call them 'Wraith,' if it hasn't happened already.

Gets to be fashionable, even if it's a bit ludicrous. Sort of like some other things I could mention, eh, Romulus?

"As a matter of fact," he continued before Romulus could ponder his last comment, "I'm reasonably certain the man we're looking for isn't even called 'Wraith.'"

Diomedes furrowed his brow. "Explain."

"I put that badly. I should've said he doesn't call himself that. I've heard that 'Wraith' was what some drunk on the street called him after he saved him from some gangers. The name stuck for a lack of something to take its place."

"You're sure?" Diomedes asked.

"Like I said, it's hard to sort the rumors from the truth. I put more stock in this mainly because it seems to make a tad more sense for a name like that to come from a wino, if you'll pardon the term."

"That's assuming things make sense in this city," Romulus broke in.

Felix smiled gently. "Things always make sense, kid. It's just that most of the time you don't know the whole picture. Machinery behind the scenes, systems that command them. I'd give you an example, but I think I've tried your roommate's patience a little much already. He's waiting for me to explain how what I've just mentioned about the name will help us, and if I wait too long he may cease to be his usual smiling self."

Diomedes's expression confirmed the smaller man's assertion. "How does it help us?"

Felix shrugged. "Don't know. But you asked for information. It might help us, it might not—but there it is. That's not all I know, of course. One thing that's nearly definite is his method. His main focus seems to be gangers, though there's rumored to be a few times others have been killed, too."

"What kind of others?" Romulus asked. He didn't exactly like the sound of that.

Felix shrugged again. "The only others I've heard about have been creeps who didn't seem connected to gangs but were involved in some sort of violent criminal activity."

"The guy who talked to us said his vigilante work missed the mark a bit. Have you heard anything about that?"

"Nothing specific," Felix replied. "Now that you mention it, most of his actions that I've heard of could be argued to be good. Not many people would feel too sorry for most of those gangers. But then, history's written by those who survive it."

"This bastard cost me a lot," Diomedes grumbled. "I don't see any damn good thing about that."

"Didn't say there was. It's just that before now, I hadn't heard of this sort of thing. I'll be the first to admit that we shouldn't rule out the possibility that it's happened before."

But it had happened before, Romulus thought. "What about the warehouse arsons?"

"That's what I'm talking about. Until now I hadn't known anything about our boy being connected with them." Felix paused to take another sip of water. "But we can go over that in a few minutes. First let me finish my original thought. Most gang deaths fall into two categories. Those caused by guns of whatever kind—which is about, I'd say, fifty to sixty percent—and those caused by other means: knives, bare hands, combat cybernetics—both standard and black market—and your good old-fashioned blunt object."

"Anything that isn't a gun," Diomedes summarized dryly.

"Exactly. But from what I've heard, our vigilante friend exclusively prefers the second category. Most of his alleged victims have been either cut up or beaten to a pulp."

Romulus swallowed. "Cut up?"

Felix gave what seemed to be a weak, comforting smile, obviously having detected a hint of fear that Romulus wished he had disguised better. "I said cut up, not shredded. As I understand it, the attacker's intent was to kill, not to torture. Not much more comforting, though, I suppose."

Romulus nodded, finding it to be at least a little more comforting.

"Cut apart with what?" Diomedes asked. The subject did not seem to bother him. "Knife? Sword? Slashers?"

"You have to remember that we're still dealing primarily with rumor yet, but most talk I've heard indicates the cuts were made by some type of slasher, yeah."

Romulus grimaced. Slashers were any of the number of various types of blades implanted in a hand. Some ran along the palm and inside of the fingers, others on the backside, and still others could extend from the base of the knuckle. All types were concealable to at least some degree, and nearly all were illegal. From what Romulus knew, they usually required a cybernetic hand into which they could be hidden and anchored, but he had heard of small versions being expensively installed into actual flesh. Someone with slashers had once attacked Diomedes. He hadn't shared the details, but Romulus had seen the scar: a particularly nasty looking gouge. The marks made it seem as if some hideous animal had clawed him.

"What's more," Felix continued, "is that the accompanying beatings were done by either an exceptionally strong person, or by someone who definitely had cybernetics. Given the existence of the slashers, I'd go with the latter option."

"Kicks or punches?" Diomedes asked. It took Romulus a moment to realize the relevance of the question. He was trying to determine which limbs were artificial.

Felix chuckled and shook his head. "You'll have to introduce me to some of these people you know that do autopsies on every street punk they find dead. You're asking for information that's pushing the limit of what you get from mere rumor. We could probably find out with a little checking, but for now I can't say for certain." Felix paused again, considering. "Though if I had to make a guess," he added, "I'd be inclined to say both. It might explain a bit about his behavior."

"Stop being vague, Hiatt."

Felix looked at Diomedes with a flicker of mock surprise that Romulus barely caught. "Why, Dio, one would think that you of all people would know what I mean."

Diomedes slammed his fist down on the table. Romulus thought he saw it crack and that Felix would see the same fury that his roommate had shown to their current employer. "Don't call me Dio," he whispered through clenched teeth.

Felix had not moved. For a moment there was something in his eyes that could have been anger before his previous demeanor washed it away. The smaller man only waited. Romulus looked down at the table as Diomedes brought his arm back up slowly. He had indeed cracked the tabletop.

"Fine," Felix said finally. His tone was calm. A moment later he turned to Romulus. "Ever heard of cyberpsychosis, kid?" he asked, cheerless. "That's what I was getting at."

Romulus nodded and wished Felix would stop calling him "kid." He chose not to mention that while he had heard of cyberpsychosis, he didn't know nearly as much as he wanted to. It was some type of mental instability, a psychological abnormality that seemed to result in some way from artificial augmentations or replacements to the body. Romulus tried to dredge up all he had on it in an effort to give a better response to the question than merely a simple yes, but little was forthcoming. He could recall that most cases were different in some way, and he thought he'd heard that more conspicuous implants had a greater influence, but he wasn't sure about the last part. He had no idea what caused it. The question had once been a curiosity that had since been overshadowed by more pressing concerns, but the current discussion opened up the topic anew. Would asking about it only make him seem like more of a kid? It was too late anyway. Felix had already accepted his nod and moved on.

"If it turns out that that's the case—that your friend is suffering from some form of cyberpsychosis—then it's a fair bet CPMC has a file on him." Felix's smile returned. "But I'd also bet that the name on the file is not 'Mr. Wraith.' Call me crazy."

Romulus recognized the name of the cybernetics watchdog agency, but couldn't remember what the 'CPMC' stood for. Maybe there was time still to ask about it all.

"Even if they do, they're not just going to show it to us." Diomedes had spoken first. "You said you'd say something more about the arsons. What is it?"

"I was going to say that we should try to discover more about them. How they were started, what was burned, and so forth."

"Something makes you think that would help?"

"Maybe he did them for a specific purpose. Knowing that purpose might help us know where to look."

"What's he need a purpose for? He's a freak," Diomedes shot. Romulus couldn't help but agree with him. Didn't it stand to reason that whatever caused him to do the killing had simply flowed into the arena of arson?

"I won't argue the possibility, but you shouldn't discount what I'm saying, either. It's worth checking out. Besides, even if he doesn't have a specific purpose, does it make sense to you that after three warehouses he'd suddenly go for an apartment?"

"A Dirge apartment is easier to get into than a warehouse." The thought sprung from Romulus's mouth even as it was formed. "Maybe he didn't want to keep risking so much?"

"Not a bad point, kid," Felix said. Romulus couldn't help but feel a twinge of pride. "But my gut's still telling me there's another reason." Felix watched him a moment more, still thinking, before he broke into a grin. "Then again, maybe apartments are just lighter in calories. At any rate, I think there might be someone I could talk with to find out. Later, of course." Felix took the last sip of his water.

"So what do we do now?" Romulus asked. Both he and his roommate awaited Felix's answer.

The small man put his empty glass down. "Now," he began, "we take a quick break while I get more water." He slipped out of the booth, taking his glass with him. "Always drink eight glasses a day, kid. Kidney stones are a bitch." With a wink, he left for the bar.

"My uncle had a kidney stone once—"

"Never volunteer information like that," Diomedes whispered harshly. Romulus looked up, truly not knowing what he meant. "The screen, the synthetic skin, he didn't need to know that. This joker makes a living off selling information. We don't give him anything for free that he doesn't need to know. No one's going to hand anything to us."

As the all-too-familiar feeling of naiveté settled upon him once again, Romulus nodded. He sat back to await Felix's return and resolved to keep quiet for the rest of the discussion.

*   *   *

Felix walked the short distance back to the bar, glass in hand. As the droning sounds of industrial rock continued to blanket the establishment, he overheard Diomedes whisper to his younger roommate, "Never volunteer information like that." Felix shook his head. Diomedes didn't change. He didn't give Romulus enough credit. The kid was smart, although he didn't seem to fully realize it himself.

Felix approached the bar and motioned for Lars, deciding he should probably stop using the term "kid." But he was already resolved not to perpetuate "Romulus."

Lars slid down his way. "More o' the same?" Felix nodded and handed him the glass, which the bartender quickly filled with ice water and returned. "Diomedes's gettin' a little excited over there. Wanna do me a favor and tell him to ease up on that table? We're runnin' low as it is."

Felix chuckled. "Tell him yourself. Just, ah, don't call him Dio."

The bartender snickered. Felix headed back to the booth, passing a younger, slightly uncomfortable-looking red-haired man who took his place at the bar. Sipping again on his water, he pondered their options. A moment later he was back with the others.

"Something's just occurred to me," he began. "There's a cybernetics convention here in just over a month. Aegis Security's rumored to be working on something that they plan to unveil then. I've been mildly interested to find out what they've got cooking, but I haven't turned up much that you can't find through regular channels."

"Get to the point, Hiatt," Diomedes said.

"I am. Be patient. What I do know is that it's something to do with keeping the peace in more violent sections of a city. 'Urban Control' is what they're calling the project. Aegis doesn't do much technological design on their own, but it's been known to happen. It's more probable that the project is in conjunction with someone else. The point is that *maybe* the guy we're looking for *is* that project."

"You think the killing and the arsons are part of some damned field test?" Diomedes appeared to consider the idea.

"Like I said before, there's not many people who'll miss a few gangers. Maybe they're taking advantage of that. Additionally, it is compatible with Aegis's usual approach to their products, based off individuals and trained manpower. It might explain this Wraith person."

"Doesn't explain my building."

"Maybe whatever they've created doesn't know its own strength?" Felix shrugged. "It's just an idea. Might be completely wrong. Maybe we'll have an answer when we find out more on the arsons. It gives us a direction to go in at any rate." Felix glanced over at Romulus, who returned his gaze without comment. He hadn't said a word yet—a fact that Felix quickly attributed to Diomedes's scolding of him a few minutes ago. Perhaps it was better that he just listened; it was a skill often overlooked and misunderstood, in Felix's opinion.

"Nosferatu," Diomedes said suddenly. Felix recognized the name and guessed what the freelancer was getting at. It was an interesting idea, but if Diomedes meant what he thought he did, Felix didn't put much faith in it.

"I take it you think this might have something to do with them?" Felix asked.

"You said he used slashers. Any evidence that some of the cuts were from fangs instead?"

"I can neither confirm nor deny that statement," Felix replied with a grin. "Sorry, I like saying that for some reason. But it's true. They might've been, but it's impossible for me to tell you for sure from what I know."

"So it could be them."

"I don't know." Felix shook his head. "I'm not sure it's quite their style."

Diomedes looked at him, incredulous. "Slashers, fangs," he listed. "If that's not their style then I'd sure as hell like to know what is!"

Felix was about to answer when he noticed the confusion in Romulus's eyes. "Know who we're talking about—?" He caught himself as he almost said 'kid,' leaving the question to hang awkwardly in the air.

"Nosferatu?" Romulus asked. "Um, well, I know I've heard the word, I think, but I don't know who it refers to." Felix considered for a moment the possibility that he was feigning ignorance based on Diomedes's last words to him, but dismissed the idea swiftly. He truly didn't know.

"Nosferatu comes from an Old Slavonic term for, well, vampires. I assume you've heard of those. Big teeth, got a thing for blood, dangerously prone to sunburn, etc."

Romulus nodded. "Stakes through the heart."

"Yeah. But just make sure it's a wooden stake—tossing a T-bone at 'em only makes 'em mad—if you believe that sort of thing."

"Which you shouldn't," Diomedes added.

"I don't."

"Well, there's some that do—or they at least think they do, and here in our fair city there's sort of a cult—I'd personally hesitate to call them a gang—who are pretty into that sort of thing. Fascinated by vampires to the point of acting like them. And I mean *really* acting like them, twenty-four seven. Some even think they are vampires, or at least they put on a good show of it." Felix leaned back in the booth. "I'll admit to being personally intrigued by vampire legends and lore, but these people are on an entirely different level."

"Fanatical maniacs is what they are," Diomedes spat.

"On the other hand, they *are* snappy dressers," joked Felix. Romulus grinned slightly. "One thing they are not, however, is homicidal maniacs, ironically."

"That you know of," Diomedes said. To Felix it sounded like he had already made up his mind on the subject.

"It's my job to know these things. It *is* what you're paying me for, isn't it?" He considered pointing out that he didn't tell the freelancer how to kill people—but he wasn't sure of the reaction he'd get, and he didn't want to go down that road. "I know they're suspected in their share of assaults, and, yes, the occasional death, but nothing along the lines we're talking about. Usually with the Nosferatu, you leave them alone and they'll do likewise. The Wraith attacks are all around the city. And those warehouses that burned aren't even near where the Nosferatu usually are found."

Diomedes continued to press the idea. "Full moon last week. They're usually more active then, yes?"

Felix sighed. "Yes," he begrudgingly admitted, "but you're not listening. We're talking vandalism and minor property destruction, not mass hunting of other gangs."

"Arson?"

"It's been known to happen," he was forced to admit. "But I have to warn you: I really think this is a dead lead, no pun intended. It's just not them. Call it a gut feeling. There are other options. We still haven't talked about seeing what we can find out from CPMC."

"We're through discussing it," Diomedes declared. "We won't know who's right by sitting here. We're finding some Nosferatu." He slid out of the booth and stood up.

Knowing it was pointless to try to change the stubborn freelancer's mind once he had made it, Felix moved out of the booth as well. "These aren't just some kids out having a role-play," he warned as he stood.

"They've got a nasty territorial streak. Don't expect them to be good hosts if you drop in unannounced."

Diomedes ignored the comment and looked down at Romulus, who quickly got out of the booth behind Felix. "Let's go," he said, and turned towards the door. Romulus followed, and Felix fell in beside the younger man.

"What's your last name," he asked of Romulus, "if you don't mind my asking?"

The kid hesitated for a moment before replying. "Flynn."

"Flynn," Felix repeated, listening to the sound of the name. "Flynn," he said again. "I like it." He gave the kid a pat on the back. "Let's go learn a few things, Flynn."

*   *   *

From his seat at the bar, the redheaded man Felix had passed earlier watched the three men leave.

Two days ago, Brian Savagewood had balked at his assignment to find the truth behind the Wraith rumors. It was goose-chasing fluff, a junk assignment designed to keep him busy until his boss could find a good enough reason to fire him from the junior investigative reporter position his father had gotten him at the network. He'd have gotten the position on his own merit, of course, if he'd been given the chance. His name might have gotten him noticed, but he'd deserved the job for his credentials alone. He was sure that no one else at the network thought so, however. He could feel it in the way they looked at him. The assignment was just another sign of that.

Yet he wasn't going to let it stop him from doing the best damn job on it as possible. Find out about the Wraith? Hell, he'd do more than that. He'd get a damned interview with the man. But just the effort wasn't going to be enough, he'd realized. He'd have to dig up something or risk making a credulous ass of himself, like some guy who believes that the word "gullible" isn't in the dictionary.

Two days of scant progress had led him to the 'Pyre. He had sensed more than a few haughty stares in his direction as he, a mere scrawny nobody by their standards, walked in the door of the dangerous establishment. The decision to come there had not been altogether easy, but he couldn't let something as childish as fear stop him.

Brian almost couldn't believe his luck when he'd overheard the group speaking about the Wraith so soon after entering. The aural enhancements he'd let his dad buy him had paid off, and, pleased at his skill and good fortune, he'd focused in on their conversation. It was as if fate had brought him here, as if some omnipotent force had guided him to this spot. He knew that it was, in truth, his own decision — his own *deduction* — that someone with the apparent cybernetics and violent behavior exhibited by the Wraith stood a good chance of being a freelancer — or at least somehow connected to one. But "fate" sounded a lot more dramatic.

He slipped off his stool, hurried to the door, and followed the men.

V

THE WANING GIBBOUS MOON existed in the clear, black sky above the city, sharing the dark expanse with the few stars bright enough to be seen through the city's own unrelenting light. While the ever-present amber and neon glow of streetlights and billboards lit the busier districts, the Moon itself was indiscriminate, bathing even the darkest parts of the urban landscape.

Felix watched it through the window of the floater with his usual appreciation. He had never actually been to the Moon, though he hoped to change that one day. For as long as he could remember—a span of time longer than he had a right to—he had always been amazed by its simple beauty. He wondered if that would change if he actually went there. Would it cease to be a white orb of placidity if he ever tread upon it the same way as he did upon this sometimes depressing and misdirected planet? He remembered the descriptions the first humans to walk on the Moon gave of the Earth, floating beautifully amongst the stars. It occurred to Felix that perhaps it was not his vision of the Moon that might change.

Flynn, Diomedes and he were soaring towards the stadium at an altitude of about five hundred feet. Earlier, they had walked from the bar to a public storage facility a short distance away. Diomedes had stored some additional equipment there and intended to get it before going any further. It didn't surprise Felix that the freelancer would have such a cache; it was a practice that made sense, even without being as paranoid as Diomedes. There was paranoid, and then there was prepared. What *had* surprised him was the size of the cache, its main component being a van-sized floater. Floaters were the common term for any number of typically boxy craft that hovered and maneuvered on a combination of vectored thrust engines and stabilizing electromagnetic repulsion lifts. Felix didn't bother to ask where he'd acquired it. Floaters were usually parts of a corporate fleet and used for limousines, for shipping, or by hospitals and the better-funded police departments. Private floaters were far from unheard of, but not so widespread that it would seem usual for Diomedes to have access to one. Regardless of how he'd come by it, Felix was certain the freelancer wouldn't offer any details.

"Like I said," Felix continued, still watching out the window, "*Nosferatu* is derived from an Old Slavonic word." Since shortly after their take-off, he had been sharing random bits of vampire lore with the other two. Diomedes, of course, hadn't cared to even appear interested, but Flynn seemed attentive enough. "The actual word it came from was *nosufer-atu*, more or less borrowed from the Greek *nosophoros*, meaning 'plague carrier.' Back then, vampires were thought to be connected with the spread of tuberculosis and other wholesome treats. They didn't know the entire truth then, of course, so, as is human nature, they filled in the gaps in the truth, and that all led to the idea of spreading vampirism with a bite. I've read that although the word has been in use for quite a few centuries in Romania, it's not actually in any dictionaries, although that seems odd." Felix knew he was rambling. Rambling was fun! "Can't believe everything you read, I suppose. When Bram Stoker wrote *Dracula*, a character based off a rather morbid gentleman named Vlad Tepes, he incorrectly gave the word the meaning of 'undead.' But as to how—"

"You don't shut up, do you?" Diomedes grumbled from the pilot's seat.

"Dio, if I don't keep talking, poor Flynn here's liable to fall asleep from your deafening silence." Felix turned to Flynn with a smile. "It's getting to where I can't get a word in edgewise with this guy."

The sudden ring of Felix's phone broke into the minor argument. He pulled it out. "This is Felix—coming to you from thousands of miles below the Earth's crust!" He covered the mouthpiece for a moment and leaned forward to Diomedes. "I didn't figure you'd want me giving away our position."

"Good," Diomedes said. Felix honestly wasn't sure if he picked up on the joke or not. Without commenting further, he leaned back and listened to the voice on the other end.

"*Below the earth's crust, eh?*" the voice said. "*Right, how is it down there?*"

"Dark," Felix said. "But no Morlocks."

The voice belonged to a contact of his at the fire department involved in investigating unknown burns. A while ago Felix had helped him with a bit of free information that had led to the capture of an arsonist responsible for seven separate fires. Felix had traded favors with the man ever since. Felix would go to him if he needed to find out some sensitive information, and in turn he'd keep his own ears to the ground for anything that might help with any new investigations. He had called the man shortly after they had arrived at the storage facility. He hoped he was calling back with good news. "What've you got for me, Albert?"

"*A little info I think you'll thank me for. From a quick check, I've found out a bit for you on what the arsonist used to start the warehouse blazes.*"

"So it's verified as arson."

"*You bet. The fire was intentional. An explosive was used—preliminaries are that it wasn't fancy—probably something homemade.*"

Felix nodded his understanding. "That's certainly interesting. What about the apartment building on the edge of The Dirge?"

"*The seventh just got that one out a short while ago. Too soon to know anything, Dirge or not. You said you needed what I got ASAP, so you're hearing what I could dig out of the files in a few minutes.*"

"I know, I know," Felix said. "Just thought I'd check."

"*Uh huh. So why such a hurry, anyway?*"

Felix looked out the window again and down at the moonlit ground below. "I'm going somewhere foolish and I wanted to find out what I could before I got there. So is that it for now, then?"

"*Not quite. I took the liberty of looking up who owned those warehouses. Figured I'd save you the trouble of asking.*"

"Let's hear it." Felix only knew that the first one was owned by a clothing manufacturer.

Albert confirmed the clothing warehouse and then continued. "*The second was Oranni Shipping. That one was a hoot, let me tell you. The biggest of the three. They were just barely able to contain it before it spread to the place next door.*"

"Uh huh, uh huh," Felix said, trying to hurry the other along. They were nearing the stadium and Diomedes was starting to take them in for a landing.

"The third was a warehouse used by Raven Defense Technologies. Wasn't quite as big as the second, but that one had the added danger of the ammunition stored there exploding. Wasn't as bad as it might've been, though. That's all I've got for you just now."

"RavenTech? Thanks, Albert, I appreciate it. If you get a chance, let me know anything else you can manage. I'd better get going here myself."

"No problem. Does this bring us back to even, or do you owe me now?"

Felix smiled. "I think it makes us even, but who's counting? Give me a call if you need anything yourself."

After a few more friendly words of parting, Felix hung up the phone and put it back in his coat. He quickly relayed what Albert had told him to the others.

"The interesting thing," he continued, "is the explosive used. What do you think that tells us, Flynn?"

"Whoever did it didn't have access to anything fancier," Flynn answered. "Or," he added after a moment of thought, "he did, but he didn't see a need to use it—or didn't want to?"

Felix nodded slightly. "That's true, although I might add that the important thing for us to remember is that 'or.' But I was actually getting at something else." Felix watched him, wondering if he knew enough about this sort of thing to know. Felix could tell that he was pondering the question; he seemed to care about his answer. That was a good sign.

Diomedes banked the floater around the stadium, searching for a landing area. Felix held onto his seat while Flynn braced himself against the dash.

Flynn snapped his fingers. "It was premeditated. He planned it."

"Another good point, which begs the question: did he, or she, or they, plan to burn that particular building, or just to do one in general? Usually arsonists who burn for the sheer thrill of it will use whatever's available. They'll see an opportunity for fire and take it. Pyromaniacs might carry around lighters, but not bombs. I'd bet money that these buildings were hit for a reason. We need to find out that reason."

"You'd bet, but you're not completely sure, are you?" Flynn asked with a glance to Diomedes. The floater leveled out and hovered, then descended slowly, engines whining.

Felix looked Flynn straight in the eye to be sure the kid knew he was serious. "I try very hard not to let myself get completely sure about anything. Closes the mind to possibilities." After a moment of letting the statement sink in, he suddenly produced a wide-eyed, maniacal grin and shouted gleefully, "And possibilities are our friends!"

Flynn burst out with a chortle that Felix could tell he tried to suppress. Before either of them could say anything, the floater bumped the ground in landing. Without a word, Diomedes shut down the engine completely and got out of the pilot's seat. He moved in a crouch under the floater's low ceiling toward the back of the vehicle.

Extending six feet to the rear wall from the back seat where Felix sat was an open space where this particular style of floater could be outfitted with various option modules, depending on its intended use. He had once seen firsthand the bio-medical module that was used in most floater ambulances, but he knew there were others. That there was none in this one meant it was either previously used for cargo transport, or one had simply not been attached when Diomedes had acquired it. What it did have were storage compartments rising up from the floor and built into the back wall. Diomedes went to one on the floor and opened it.

As the freelancer rummaged through the compartment, Felix glanced out the window. They were on one side of a wide alley. Ahead of them and to the north, framed by dirty brick walls, the stadium rose out of the concrete parking lot just across the street. The buildings on either side were tall, allowing only a reflected glow from the unseen streetlights to penetrate a few feet into the alley. Even the Moon, now blocked from view by the building tops, barely managed to illuminate only the upper portion of the alley, leaving the lower parts covered in an eerie half-darkness where bits of trash, scattered by the descending floater's engines, lay strewn about the ground and on top of a set of dumpsters. All in all, Felix thought to himself, your basic dark alley.

"They're in the sewers," Diomedes said behind him. It was more of a statement than a question.

Felix nodded anyway. "Right." He assumed Diomedes was referring to the Nosferatu. They were most active around the stadium. Rumor had it that they lived in the sewer and electrical tunnels beneath it.

Diomedes was busy strapping a gas mask to his face. "Romulus and me will go in." His baroque voice echoed through the mask in what Felix found to be an amusingly familiar way. "You wait here."

They had already gone over this when they were leaving the storage facility. Felix guessed the freelancer felt the need to reassert his plan. "Yeah, I know. Just watch that you don't go nuts down there. It's always convenient when the person you bring back for questioning still has the ability to answer."

"Leave that to me," Diomedes assured him through the mask.

Felix almost laughed out loud. He couldn't resist. "Diomedes, are you up on classic films from the twentieth century?"

"What?" Diomedes's tone indicated that not only did he not know what Felix was talking about, but that he also had absolutely no desire to deal with it.

Felix couldn't help but grin. "It's just that, well, with that mask, and your voice, you . . . " He trailed off, still smiling as Diomedes glared at him impatiently. Felix shook his head with a grin. "Forget it. I doubt you'd appreciate it anyway. You see any lava floes down there, though, you come right back, huh?"

The freelancer only rolled his eyes and moved for the side door. Flynn followed, adjusting his own mask that Diomedes had lent him. They opened the door and stepped outside. Flynn gave him a quick glance.

"Hey, Flynn," Felix said. "Watch yourself down there."

Flynn nodded. They closed the door. Felix watched them go. Wearing gas masks and body armor, carrying auto-pistols and gas grenades, they opened up a manhole, pitched a grenade down, and, when the hiss of the gas had stopped, lowered themselves down after it.

*   *   *

Brian stepped from the taxi and checked his watch: ten after nine. He was probably a little behind the three men in the floater, but ground traffic had been reasonably light, and he had made fair time. He glanced around the area in front of the stadium; there was no sign of them. On the other hand, it was a large area with any number of alleys and side streets to land in. He'd overheard them talking about both the stadium and the Nosferatu. They had to be headed here.

Brian began to stroll the perimeter of the stadium parking lot, alert for both the floater and any sign of trouble. It was only a matter of time before he found them.

Unless they had known he was listening and intentionally let him hear the wrong information? No, that was impossible. Or, at least, highly improbable. They were talking about the Nosferatu when they were still in the bar, and what kind of idiot didn't know that those gothic freaks hung out in this area?

He had trailed them after they had left, unseen and unnoticed. While he wasn't able to hear the men as easily, it didn't appear that they were saying much while in the open anyway. Brian surmised that they were wary of being heard by anyone on the street. If they only knew, he thought. He'd been ready for a trick, some kind of test the men might try to see if they were being followed. He had even come up with a few strategies if they simply decided to run. As it turned out, they were either oblivious, over-confident, or both. Except for one backward glance by the smallest of the men, they did nothing. For a moment, Brian feared he had been seen, but the short man with the mirror shades said nothing to his companions and made no attempt to try to shake any pursuit.

When they arrived at the public storage facility, Brian hid himself behind an adjacent building while they opened the door to their garage locker and busied themselves within. Disappointingly, most of their movement was blocked from his vision by the building itself or the unmarked floater that was inside—Brian himself was a little surprised at seeing *that*. From what he could tell, they were loading some amount of equipment onto the floater, an idea later supported by the fact that the space was completely empty after they left, save for a few rectangular outlines of dust on the floor.

They had spoken briefly, however, and the bit that Brian overheard further supported the stadium as their first destination. There was also something about arson then, and he didn't know what to make of that. His information said absolutely nothing about the Wraith being involved in any arson. Either they knew something he didn't, or they were planning something of that nature themselves.

It made Brian wonder just what he'd stumbled into. He thought of all of the movies he'd seen where a reporter ends up getting caught in some sinister corporate plot or criminal scheme. If only he were so lucky. This didn't sound too corporate, but he might still have something.

It had hit him then that perhaps his imagination was getting a little too active. He resolved to concentrate on the task at hand before getting carried away. After the men had taken off, he hailed the taxi that had taken him here.

A stretch of the East Side Viaduct ran over the parking area on the west side of the stadium. Brian walked beneath it, deciding to follow it until it curved off towards the rest of the city. From there he would check the street to the south of the stadium and stay only at the edge of the parking areas until he'd completed a full walk around the streets that framed them. If he hadn't found anything by that point, he would explore the lots closer to the stadium itself. There were fewer places there that one could conceal a floater, and the stadium's floater lots were secured from unauthorized use. Brian thought it more likely they would simply choose an alley.

He continued on through the lot under the viaduct, keeping to the better-lit areas when he could and staying alert for anything or anyone in the shadows. Not all of the lights were working. A few flickered erratically; others did not shine at all. He was doing his best to be as silent as possible, but when his feet weren't crunching on the graveled areas, his hard-soled footfalls echoed off the supports of the viaduct. Other sounds drifted to him as well: the partially muted car engines passing on the viaduct overhead, a trace of music from a nearby bar, the occasional rustling of movement nearby . . . Brian looked toward the mysterious noises whenever he heard them, half expecting to find any number of things looking back at him. He saw nothing. Most likely rats, he hoped.

He could see the headline now: "Reporter killed by lunatic street gang on assignment." No, he thought: passive, and possibly ambiguous. "Lunatic street gang kills reporter on assignment." Better. They'd find his body the next day in a pool of blood under the viaduct. Or maybe his body wouldn't be found at all, dragged underground for God-knows-what purpose by the Nosferatu or whatever else was out there. He doubted the story would make the front page, of course. Probably they'd put it somewhere in the back near the personals. At least his boss wouldn't have to put up with him anymore. Brian smiled despite the thought.

Besides, he reminded himself, he was wary. He was careful. He'd be able to hear anything dangerous coming, and he wasn't completely without protection. He'd be fine.

A bright light to the right caught his peripheral vision. He spun. A ground car had turned down an alley across the street, heading for the road that ran beside the stadium. He zoomed his vision to check the occupants in case it was one or more of them trying to double back, but it was only a taxi. Brian continued on.

Exactly what kind of men were those he was following? Brian pondered the question as he neared where the viaduct passed over the cross street ahead of him. He'd only caught one of their names: the quiet one had told the smaller man his name was Flynn. Flynn wasn't as large as the one with the shaved head, but he still looked to have some bulk to him. He was pretty sure the larger man was a freelancer, so it made sense for Flynn to be one as well. Brian wasn't certain, though. The man hadn't said much. Probably he was either the strong, silent type, or just the stupid type. Given his near total lack of participation in the bar discussion, it was clear that the larger man, whom Brian had considered the leader, was not including him in the decision-making process. This Flynn was probably just a hired thug. Whether he really was stupid or not was still up in the air, but there was definitely something out of place about the man. Perhaps that was it.

Brian was less sure about the other two. Though the large man was likely the leader, Brian had less of an idea of the purpose of the smaller man with the mirror shades. From what Brian had been able to filter out of the intentionally masking ambiance of the bar, "Shades" seemed to have a lot of information—at least about the Nosferatu. Was he some kind of consultant? Brian doubted the possibility. He had heard enough to know the man was against the idea of visiting the Nosferatu, yet the leader had ignored him. If he were a consultant, wouldn't the leader have listened to him more? So what was his part in all of this? If he wasn't a consultant, then he must have his own agenda. Perhaps the two had been partnered in some way by someone else.

Brian looked up at the Moon as he walked and remembered again about the subject of arson that Shades had mentioned. He considered again the two possibilities: either they knew of some connection between the Wraith and the arsons, or they were more directly involved with the fires themselves. Yet if they had started the fires, what did that have to do with the vigilante?

Unless, he thought suddenly, they planned—or at least Shades did—to somehow try to pin the fires that they were responsible for on the vigilante! Brian scowled. Then why are they trying to find him? Was there more than one purpose that the men both kept, or did each have a separate objective? That would certainly explain their arguing. It was obvious the two men didn't get along.

The answer, Brian realized, must lie with the leader.

"So what the hell are you going to do," Brian muttered to himself, "just walk up and ask him?" Trying to answer his own question, he continued in silence along the south edge of the parking lot, keeping watch in the alleys across the street for the floater. The shadows were less abundant now that he was out from under the viaduct, yet dark places still lurked beneath the landscaped trees. Places, Brian cautioned himself, that could still conceal unwanted surprises.

Brian supposed his course of action upon finding the men would depend on which of them, if any, were with the floater. If they really were going to look for the Nosferatu, it stood to reason that if anyone stayed with the vehicle, it would be Shades. Brian scowled. Of the three, he considered Shades the least approachable—or at least the one he'd feel least comfortable approaching. The others he knew more about. With Shades he'd be going in with a lot more questions than answers, and he couldn't predict how the man would react to whatever approach he used. Brian doubted he would be terribly open to sharing any information, assuming he was even still in the vehicle. Maybe Brian would get lucky, and it'd be the leader who had stayed behind alone.

Something was behind him.

Brian sensed it more than heard it: a small twinge of awareness in the back of his mind. He turned, cautiously, and saw absolutely nothing.

Brian stood for a moment in silence, watching and listening for anything. There was no sign of movement, no trace of a follower. Only a deadly quiet.

He didn't hear anything, he told himself. He didn't see anything. He just . . . sensed it. Brian laughed inwardly at his imagination. Sensed it? What the hell does that mean?

"It means you're some kind of paranoid . . . " Brian heard his own voice trail off into the night air before he could come up with an appropriate noun. He shook his head and continued on.

Brian tried to pick up where he'd left off. If simple was what he was looking for, he'd be hoping for Flynn to be there. Unfortunately, Flynn probably wouldn't be able to tell him too much about what was going on. The other two surely wouldn't tell a hired gun any more than was necessary. On the other hand, Flynn's being a mercenary did open up the possibility of buying some information out of him. But why would the leader hire someone and then leave him behind in the floater? Brian decided to forget it.

He glanced behind himself once more. Nothing still followed him, and Brian decided the dark feeling he sensed was just his nervousness about what he would do when he caught up to the men. It only made sense. He might hear someone, possibly see something to indicate a pursuer, but he put no faith in the "feeling of being watched." It was all just his own unease. Content in that fact, he walked on.

Brian still felt something back there.

He continued on and instead focused on brainstorming ideas on how to approach whichever man was still in the floater. He had only walked a few yards when suddenly it was there. In a wide alley, almost crouching in the shadows of two taller buildings, was the hunched lump that could easily be the floater he was looking for.

He had been walking towards it since he had left the viaduct, but concentrating as he was on searching the alleys and buildings across the street to his right, he hadn't seen it until now. Brian needed to zoom in a bit to be certain he wasn't merely seeing a large dumpster, but after a moment of study, he was certain he had found it.

The alley fed out onto the street that framed the east side of the stadium area. Even with his vision zoomed, it was dark enough so that he could only barely make out the glint of the front windshield. Though unable to tell if anyone was inside from this distance, moving closer risked their recognizing him, and Brian preferred to surprise them if at all possible. He turned and crossed the street to his right with the intent to circle around and approach the floater from the rear, where the vehicle had no windows.

As he walked past the better-lit buildings on this side of the street, Brian noticed suddenly that the dark feeling was gone. So it had been all in his mind. Now that he'd actually found the floater and crossed over to the busier street to circle around, he was easily more confident.

Despite the confirmation that it was merely a conjuring of his own psyche, he was still relieved by its absence. He disliked skulking about in dark alleys enough as it was, and being haunted with such a feeling hadn't helped.

Brian walked on, a spring in his step. After passing by various closed storefronts, a bar or two and a few dilapidated office buildings, he neared the street that framed the east side of the stadium into which the alley holding the floater fed. Taking a deep breath, he turned off down a different alley to his right. He would head out just a little and then double back through the alleyways to a point directly behind the vehicle. What happened at that point would depend upon whom he found.

This first alley he entered was dirty, but the lighting from a neon hotel sign above provided a strong red glow that illuminated things more than they would be otherwise. The alley itself was deserted, which didn't surprise him. There were few enough people on the main street. The stadium stood near the edge of the city, and little else of note was out here. Still, Brian had been prepared to see at least someone, even if it were only a harmless wino rather than a wandering member of the Nosferatu. He hadn't checked inside the two dumpsters to his right, of course. He didn't plan to, either.

A brisk walk took him towards the end of the alley, where he belatedly glanced at the hotel fire escape above him. Thankfully no one was looking back. If anyone had been up there, Brian realized, they could have easily surprised him. *Careful.*

Brian continued through the alleyway, keeping as far as possible from any places that might hide anything at all. He was beginning to feel as he had before. The dread itself was still absent, but his alertness was starting to border on fear. It was the fear that surprised him. In previous situations he had been aware of the possibility of danger, but he had never gone anywhere that made him feel like he was in over his head. This time should have been no different.

He rounded a corner and checked the fire escape above again. Empty. It suddenly occurred to him—and why he'd let it slip by him before he didn't know—that he hadn't even considered the possibility that two of the men might remain. Or perhaps they all were there, waiting on some mysterious rendezvous. One he could talk with, but all of them? How could he have overlooked that?

It was behind him again. The dread had returned, this time unmistakably stronger. The night air seemed to go colder, and even with his enhanced hearing, a deathly silence seemed to descend. He froze and looked back again, and again saw nothing. But this was more than a feeling. He was being followed—watched from a place he couldn't see.

Brian turned forward again and fought the urge to break into a run. It would only make him easier to catch. The macabre feeling wasn't just in his mind. This was real. He couldn't understand how, but he was sure of it, and that certainty itself was frightening.

Heart racing, he moved as silently as he could, keeping to the wall of the alley, trying to use the darkness to his advantage. A pile of discarded crates loomed up in his way. He dashed around them and glanced behind him. Someone was back there in the distant darkness; the glow of its eyes confirmed the figure's presence. Brian continued to flee, feeling his blood pound through his veins.

Why was he running? It made no sense. He had a taser. It was just one man! Brian could confront him. Yet all his instincts told him to flee. It was getting closer, and the feeling of unnatural death grew with it.

Get out of there!

Brian turned another corner and tripped over something. He couldn't tell in the dark what it was, and he didn't have time to look as he spilled forward, head glancing off the side of another dumpster. There he remained still in the darkness in an attempt to regain his bearings, feeling almost chilled to the bone. Fear rushed over him. He was cornered. If he ran it would only catch him.

His only hope was to surprise it.

Quickly, he felt his way around to the other side of the dumpster, sure even then that the pursuing specter was already upon him. He turned and crouched against the wall, concealed by the trash bin, and faced the way he had come. Brian gripped his taser in a sweaty hand. He couldn't stop shaking! All thought fled from his mind, save for the burning feeling that hunted him through the alley. He sat. He waited. He listened to the tick of his watch and tried to shake off the irrational terror that threatened to consume him.

. . . tick. . .

His knees trembled as he crouched.

. . . tick. . .

Something drew closer. Again he felt it.

. . . tick. . .

Brian waited in agony.

. . . tick. . .

He double-checked that the taser was charged. A hand touched his shoulder. The fear would not let him move.

. . . tick . . .

VI

THEIR FIRST GAS GRENADE turned out to be unnecessary. The only things that awaited Diomedes and Romulus upon their entrance were two unconscious rats. Romulus felt sorry for the apparent waste of a grenade, but more than understood the need for caution. Diomedes seemed to agree; he reacted with only silence, and then nudged the creatures into the murky water beside the walkway while Romulus replaced the manhole cover.

"What now?" Romulus whispered.

Diomedes shushed him with only a glare and a finger pressed to his own lips before staring down the tunnel in either direction. Grimy bulbs lit the sections of the walkways stretched between the shadows and illuminated both lengths of pipe along the ceiling and gutters of muck below. Apparently satisfied, he moved off in the direction of the stadium and motioned for Romulus to follow.

The two crept their way through the dreary stone tunnels. The minutes drifted away. Not a sound reached Romulus's ears, save for their footfalls and an omnipresent yet untraceable dripping that echoed from somewhere in the distance. Romulus had always considered himself able to move quietly when he tried. To amuse himself when he was younger, he would creep around the grounds of his uncle's farm, but even the faintest sound he made here seemed to have its own thundering echo. He couldn't be sure if the echo was due to the tunnels or merely a trick of his own ears. He could barely hear Diomedes in front of him; the man moved silently, experienced.

Deep down, he realized, he was nervous. Who would they find? How would he react? He forced his self-consciousness away, drawing on Diomedes's silent presence and his own training to keep it in check.

His worries faded, soon after replaced by the pride he took in their banishment. He could do this, he told himself. He *was* doing this! He'd taken the first few steps on a path to the type of man he wanted to become. He was alert, doing his best to be silent, and, for the most part, felt ready for whatever might lay ahead. They might even find exactly what they were looking for down here.

His foot kicked a pebble by accident. Romulus winced and kept moving, focusing on the ground ahead and following his mentor who still had not, Romulus scolded himself, kicked any pebbles.

After traveling to a point Romulus estimated to be somewhere beneath the stadium's inner parking lot, they passed a metal door set into the wall. Diomedes continued past it without more than a glance, so Romulus ignored it as well, despite the feeling that something better might be found behind it. He had just passed by the door himself when Diomedes stopped and, after a moment of regarding the distance of tunnel ahead, turned back towards it.

On first inspection, it appeared to be locked. A large deadbolt sat squarely above the knob, and the door itself looked secure and solid, its metal weight obvious as it sat on thick hinges. After motioning for Romulus to stand to the other side, Diomedes opened it with barely a pull. Instantly his auto-pistol was inside, trained on whatever was in the space beyond. Unable to see where the gun pointed, Romulus waited for his mentor to either open fire or indicate that it was clear.

After a long few moments, he received the all-clear. Diomedes stepped back and pointed to the edge of the door as Romulus came around from behind it. From there it was clear that the lock had already been broken: Where the thick deadbolt should have been was simply a hole. Someone had apparently removed the lock, broken it, and then replaced it to make it appear to be still in working order. Romulus gave a questioning look to his mentor, who pointed in response to the wear and tear on the outside of the door. Did he mean to say the Nosferatu had broken the lock? It was certainly possible, but it could just as easily have been caused by someone else.

Diomedes had apparently already decided and moved cautiously inside. Romulus followed, unsure if they were on the right track. Yet when he closed the door behind him, it occurred to him that the lock, unlike the old door that was scratched and dirty with age, was new.

The original knob assembly had been replaced before and broken again, possibly more than once. Romulus smiled. That must have been what had made Diomedes so confident. Whoever had broken the lock must have done so repeatedly, and that would fit with cultists living somewhere in these tunnels.

They were on the right track.

The thrill of it flared in Romulus's heart and reminded him of the stories Diomedes used to tell back on the farm—stories of an older brother who'd lived in the city. They were noble, glorious tales of thrilling acts, such as stepping unseen into a dangerous place to rescue an abductee that the police couldn't help. Those stories were more exciting than any movie he had ever seen, and Romulus had once memorized them by heart. Though most of the details had faded now, their excitement and adventure had stayed with him all those years and spurred him to seek it in his own life.

Now he was living them out.

Unfortunately, after what seemed like at least five minutes, there was still no sign of the Nosferatu. The tunnel they were in was smaller than the sewer tunnels, with more pipes along the ceiling and various turns and crossing corridors. Romulus wasn't worried about getting lost; at each corner there was a map for any utility crews that may have used the tunnels. Yet it was apparent that their search might be more difficult and painstaking than he had anticipated.

Realizing that Diomedes had probably seen the clues on the door instinctively as he walked by it the first time, Romulus realized he should stop navel-gazing and concentrate on his own observations. Most of the tunnel was bare save for the grime and decades-old paint that coated the walls and ceiling. The only things of note were the lights, the maps, and the ceiling pipes. Romulus instead searched for breaks in the pattern, checking the walls for any telltale clean spots or other markings. Diomedes would surely pick up on anything important, but it was still good practice. Maybe he might even be able to impress his roommate by noticing something without having to have Diomedes point it out.

They went on down the tunnel, with Romulus now less worried about making noise than missing anything important. Though nothing seemed to be out of the ordinary, suddenly he knew he had missed something. Diomedes had stopped in front of him, holding back a hand for him to halt. Romulus peered into the tunnel ahead. It continued on into the damp gloom, but twenty feet or so ahead, another passage opened to the left. Had there been a sound beyond the corner Romulus hadn't heard? At once he regretted only having concentrated on visual clues. A sound he might have missed.

Diomedes pointed to the base of the tunnel wall to their left. Romulus examined the area, but it seemed to be unremarkable. Feeling somewhat inept, he tried to silently communicate his confusion to Diomedes by looking back at him and shaking his head. His mentor regarded him blankly for an instant, and Romulus felt his chance to impress him slipping away. Diomedes shook his head a moment later. After touching two fingers to his own eyes, he pointed in a hooked motion around the corner. Romulus nodded suddenly, relieved that he understood. As his roommate pulled a second gas grenade from his belt, Romulus checked the seal of the mask on his face.

He hadn't seen what Diomedes was pointing at because there was no way he could have. He wasn't pointing *at* the wall but, rather, through it. Something or someone was behind that wall in another room, the door to which was likely around the corner. Diomedes must have spotted the heat source with his implants. What exactly he had seen was an obvious question that Romulus wished he had the luxury of asking. Regardless, it was clear that his roommate intended to subdue whoever it was with his second grenade.

Diomedes had checked his own mask and then disappeared silently around the corner. Romulus followed.

* * *

"You know," said the voice from behind Brian, "I think you're the first person I've seen in a long while with red hair that's natural."

With the voice came the sudden ability to move again. Brian jerked the speaker's hand from his shoulder and spun around in his crouched position. It put his back to the dumpster that a moment ago seemed the only thing between him and his phantom pursuer. His still-shaking hands held the taser protectively in front of him. Words didn't come.

The man stood before him, but stepped back slightly. "Is it?" the voice added. "Natural, I mean?"

Brian watched his assailant carefully. What was he saying? Something about his hair? Brian's hand stopped shaking finally and he renewed his grip on the taser, ready to zap the man the instant he made a move towards him.

"If you don't mind my asking, of course. It's just that everyone seems to be dyeing or replacing their hair nowadays. I expect you must get some envious looks."

What the hell was this guy talking about? He had chased him through the alley to ask—? No, Brian thought, he'd come from the wrong direction. He glanced over his shoulder and saw nothing.

When Brian turned back around, he realized that the man who seemed to be fascinated with his hair color was Shades. The elusive floater sat no more than fifteen feet beyond him in the dim alleyway. He must have run farther than he knew in his flight. "Do you always quiz people about their hair color in dark alleys?" Brian blurted.

"As things to do to people in dark alleys go, asking about their hair color isn't too bad, I'd say."

"You may have a point there," Brian stood up. He was feeling more at ease now, though he still had to figure out how to deal with Shades. He glanced over his shoulder again. Still nothing.

"Yeah, I suppose I might have a point." Shades seemed to consider the statement and then grinned. "Then again, I might not. I'm a little funny that way."

Brian nodded, unsure of what to say and wondering just how sane Shades was. Was he just playing with him, or was he waiting for the right time to jump him?

"If I may say so, though," Shades continued, "standing around chatting in dark alleys in general isn't something I'm terribly fond of. Care to join me inside, Brian? And then you can share why you've been following my happy little group."

This was going easier than expected. Though the expression on Shades's waiting face was unreadable for the most part, his eyes appeared welcoming enough. And despite the absence of the foolish terror he had felt before, standing around in the back of the alley was still not something Brian cared to do. The floater would be safer, and being inside it would most likely give him a look at whatever cargo they had—information that might tell him of their connection with the Wraith. At the very least it would give him a better handle on asking about it.

On the other hand, Shades had known he was following them. He must have recognized him from the bar. Perhaps this was a trap. The other two could be waiting in the vehicle . . .

In a flash Brian realized he'd missed something.

"How'd you know my name?"

Shades smiled. "I'm good with names. Brian Savagewood, junior investigative reporter for our local Media Star Network if memory serves."

Brian nodded, feeling both unease and pride that someone had noticed him. But Brian himself hadn't had any real exposure, and he definitely did not recognize Shades from the station. Who is this guy?

"Don't be spooked," Shades said. "I'm just someone who keeps his eyes and ears open. And, as I said, I'm good with names." He put his hand forward and Brian almost brought up the taser before he realized he was offering a handshake. "Felix Hiatt."

Brian switched the taser to his left hand, shook the strange man's hand silently, and then realized that he must look rather dumbfounded. "I'd give you my name," he found himself saying in a sudden effort to seem intelligent, "but . . . "

"You could always make up a new name if it makes you feel any better," Felix suggested. Brian assumed he was kidding.

"No thanks." Brian released the handshake. "My own works for now."

"Refreshing. C'mon."

With a wave of his hand he turned towards the vehicle. Brian followed and switched the taser back to his right hand to hold it inside his coat pocket, just in case.

"By the way," Felix said as he neared the door, "you won't need that taser. But at the risk of being a cliché, next time you do need it I'd suggest taking the safety off." Brian felt for the switch inside his pocket. He swore under his breath and followed the odd man inside.

As it turned out, Felix's two larger associates did not jump him when he entered the vehicle. They weren't even there—a fact that both comforted and, curiously, disappointed him. While it was much less complex this way, he had briefly amused himself with thoughts of getting out of such an ambush. The two could probably easily overpower him, but he would have enjoyed the chance to slyly talk his way out of the situation. No matter. Perhaps Shades would be more likely to let something slip, alone as he was.

"So what exactly was back there, if you don't mind my asking?"

"What?" Brian said, distracted. Felix had taken a seat in the front and was turned around to face him.

"No offense, but you seemed a little spooked. At least that's how I've felt on a couple occasions that've found me crouched behind a dumpster myself."

"Oh, yeah. I was just, I don't know, a little—I thought I heard something and decided I'd better stop and see what it was. Must have been paying more attention to what was behind me than what was in front. I stumbled a bit before I settled in to wait for whoever it was." Brian glanced out the window. "I guess it was nothing, but there's some weirdoes around here. I was being careful."

As he talked, Brian took in the floater's interior. It was surprisingly bare, though what he had expected to find he didn't know. Perhaps there was something more interesting in the few storage compartments.

"I suppose I should be flattered, then," Felix responded. He didn't look like a Felix, though. It probably wasn't his real name. Not that Brian blamed him much for the deception.

"And why is that?"

"Well," the strange man continued in what Brian thought was a slightly patronizing tone, "you must consider whatever reason you're following us important enough to slink around in the alleys with the 'weirdoes.' You also gave us enough credit to go to the trouble of circling around behind us after you found where we were. You could have surprised me if I hadn't seen you first."

"Recognized me from the bar, did you?" Brian asked, deciding to go along with his patronizing line of questioning.

Felix nodded. "From the bar, yes. And from behind us on the street, and at the storage building. I didn't recall who you were until after you started following, though. I was a bit curious why you were back there, but it seemed you'd show up and tell me when you were ready."

"And I suppose your two associates are, what, off looking for me right now?" Brian added. He was more than a little serious about the question, but he also hoped it would lead Felix to reveal a bit more of their purpose out here. Then again, they could be out looking for him and this Felix character might only be stalling him until their return.

"Anything's possible, I suppose, but to my knowledge they never noticed you coming. If they had, don't you think they would have found you by now anyway?"

Brian realized he had a point. He also realized his weak leading question had gone nowhere. Perhaps being slightly more direct would help. "So why didn't you go help them with whatever it is that they're doing?" he tried.

"Because I was waiting for you, of course," the odd man replied with a smile. "And now you're here, to ask me whatever it is that got you to follow us all this way out of that ever-so-pleasant establishment where you didn't even seem like you belonged in the first place." Felix held up an apologetic hand. "Not that I always judge a book by its cover, of course. But so far it's the only part I've been given to read."

In other words, *tell me what the hell you are doing here before I toss you back out,* Brian translated. "I'm here because of some things I overheard from the three of you."

"My, what big ears you have. So what caught your interest?"

"A number of things." His host watched him, still waiting for more. "The name 'Wraith,' for one."

Felix raised an eyebrow. "And why would you be so interested in that?"

"I might ask you the same thing." This could be tricky. He had to find out their relation to the Wraith and at the same time try not to come off as obnoxious, on the off chance he might want to try to tag along.

Felix chuckled, sighing afterward. "Look, Brian, I'll be honest. I want a favor from you."

"A favor? Anything in particular?"

"Don't know yet. I'll know later when I need it. But in my line of work it's convenient to have an extra set of ears in a position like yours from time to time. I'd like us to be able to help each other out."

"And just what exactly is your line of work?"

"I guess you could say I'm in the business of knowing things. And people. I'd like to know you, Mr. Savagewood."

"Like you know the Wraith?"

"No," he replied, "I think I already know you better than that. You I've actually met. Him I haven't."

"I thought your job was to know things. And people."

"Ever known something you didn't have to find out first? The point is I might be able to help you here. Now. Maybe we could help each other. Then, later, when one of us needs to know something, we'll have established a precedent. But I can't help you now unless you tell me what you need."

Brian's mind was still racing. This was too easy. Either things were finally starting to go his way or this was part of a trick, and Brian was a firm believer of Murphy's Law. Was Felix trying to get him to tell him all he knew, so he could then kick him out? Or worse? What did he think Brian knew, anyway? He didn't know anything at all about the Wraith. Brian had no reason to trust him. Come to think of it, why would Felix trust *him* that much? What kind of idiot trusts someone he's only known for a few minutes?

His host sighed. "Brian, you can either sit there and stew or you can work with me. Neither of us has anything to gain without the first step."

Brian realized Felix wasn't going to tell him anything otherwise. It was either this or leave empty-handed and continue tailing them. Through the whole city. All night. With his quarry in a floater. Reminding himself of the importance of risk, Brian spoke up. "It's mine," he said.

Felix looked confused for the first time in their entire history. "Come again?"

"My hair," Brian said. Felix wasn't the only one who can make a joke, he thought to himself. "It's natural. Now what else should I tell you?"

Felix grinned.

*   *   *

Despite his training, Romulus still found his heart pounding as he rushed into the room behind Diomedes. He held his auto-pistol in front of him, ready to train it onto anyone still standing after the flood of the gas grenade. No one remained. Not until his mentor broke the silence with a curse did it occur to him that something could be wrong.

He looked over to the location that Diomedes had previously indicated as the heat source and saw what triggered the curse. Behind a small stack of piping, among a pile of rubbish, were at least a dozen unconscious rats. Romulus lowered his weapon and groaned silently. He spun about to examine the room and tried to still the adrenaline still running through him.

The room wasn't much larger than a section of the hallway. Spare pipes and boxes of what looked to be supplies sat about the storage area in a slipshod fashion. A collection of discarded food wrappers and other rubbish lay near the rats' nest. Romulus checked behind a stack of boxes that he thought might conceal a door, but found nothing.

A wet cracking sound that turned his stomach came on the heels of another curse from Diomedes. Romulus turned to see his roommate wipe his foot across the ground, trying to remove the blood of the rat he had no doubt crushed in frustration. Romulus understood. They had wasted two grenades and still found absolutely nothing. He pointed to the one in his own pocket and mouthed, "I still have one."

A shake of the head and a dismissing wave was the only response. He watched as Diomedes scanned the room and then locked onto something behind him. Romulus turned to spot a small grating near the ceiling and watched while Diomedes began to test the dirty edges of the metal. It did look like the hole would be big enough to crawl through, but—

Almost immediately after Diomedes touched it, the grating fell down from the concrete ridge that appeared to be the only thing supporting it. Diomedes caught it and set it against the wall without a sound. Romulus continued to watch, glancing warily between the doorway and the wall as Diomedes jumped, grabbed on to the ledge of the hole, and pulled himself up halfway.

After peering into the hole for short seconds, he dropped back down silently and motioned to Romulus, ready to boost him into the hole. He was going first? A wave of unease swallowed him. Diomedes must have seen it; he scowled and motioned more rapidly a moment later. Romulus moved closer. "Me?" he mouthed.

Diomedes grabbed his arm and pulled him in to whisper, "You can't get up without help and I can't turn around to pull you. Move."

Romulus swallowed and nodded to his mentor, steeling himself. Diomedes was right, of course. After a step up, boosted by his roommate's hands, he was in the hole. It was dark, but he moved forward nonetheless, feeling his way along the cement. This had to be the right way, he was sure of it, and the thought pushed him ahead into darkness. He continued straight, cautiously probing the area ahead with his hands in case of any turns or holes.

Behind him, Diomedes clambered up into the darkness and followed. Though he could not see him, he could still sense his dominating presence close behind him in the tunnel. Too close, in fact. Romulus realized he was holding the other up. He quickened his pace through the darkness to accommodate his roommate's pace.

His hand jammed into solid cement that bent his middle finger back with a crack. A muffled groan escaped his throat before he could stop it, and he only just managed to stop short of knocking his head on the same wall. Romulus paused to put his weapon down and rub the pain from his jammed finger.

Diomedes waited behind him. Romulus could hear him shifting. He recovered himself, picked up his gun, and had begun to feel for the way the passage might have turned when he heard a tiny snap behind him. Twisting to look back as best he could in the confined space, he noticed a soft green glow in the darkness. Diomedes slid the plastic tube of a chemical flare up the crawl space to him.

Not wanting to break the already cracked silence with an expression of gratitude, he took the flare in his hand and noticed two things. The first was the continuation of the cramped tunnel to his right. The second was the jagged black "N" painted on the wall that his hand had discovered so abruptly. At least, the eerie green light made it look black. It could have been red. It occurred to Romulus just before he continued that it could have been dried blood. Would blood turn to black if dried on cement? Romulus thought so, but had never seen any to know.

He moved on, thankful at least for the fact that he wasn't claustrophobic. After a step or two of crawling with the flare in his hand, he thought better of it and lifted his gas mask to hold the plastic casing in his teeth.

Crawling another twenty feet or so brought them to a crossing tunnel. Romulus paused, took a breath, and peered around the corner. Darkness alone stared back at him from both directions, and a moment later he realized the folly of trying to remain unseen. Even before he looked down the cross passage, anyone who might have been there would have been aware of him from the flare's glow.

Unfortunately, bringing the flare around the corner did very little besides give him away and illuminate the area a few feet in front of him. Beyond that, the blackness swallowed it up and made the three possible paths identically unknown. With his eyes useless, he tried using his ears, but the only thing he could hear was the breath of his waiting mentor right behind him.

"What do you think?" Romulus whispered, hoping Diomedes noticed something that he'd missed.

"They're close," came the answer. It wasn't the answer he was looking for, but at least if they were close he would know to turn back soon if they went the wrong way and found nothing. He chose not to make a turn and continued on straight through the tunnel.

Another ten feet, a turn, five feet, another turn, and then there was a change. Romulus stopped just around the corner when he saw it. A light came from an opening ahead; though dim by usual standards, in the darkness it glowed like a beacon. The tunnel seemed to open out into a larger space—a room, possibly their destination. He pulled back around the corner and whispered of it to Diomedes.

His roommate pointed to the flare and shook his head. Romulus nodded and sat it down along the tunnel wall. Guessing this was probably the time to use their last grenade, he took a chance and pulled it from his belt. Diomedes's only response was to check his mask. Pleased with himself for thinking as his mentor would, he turned back around the corner, pulled his own mask back down, and began crawling toward the dim opening. He moved slowly, watching and feeling his way along. What if whoever was in the next room heard him before he had the chance to gas the area? Suddenly it occurred to him that he didn't know for sure if anyone *was* in the room. What if he used their last grenade on an empty room?

He stopped in the tunnel and strained to hear any sound ahead. Diomedes stopped behind him. Did he understand what Romulus was doing? Or, having already sensed a presence in the room ahead, was he growing impatient at Romulus's hesitation? He waited and prayed for a sound in front of him, afraid to hold Diomedes up and afraid to let anyone ahead hear him first. If he heard nothing, he'd keep going, but—

From ahead came a tiny shift of something on stone! They were there, maybe heading for him already! He flipped the timer and thrust the grenade down the tunnel. It reached the edge and seemed to teeter there for entirely too long before falling over. The crack of its impact with the cement floor was followed almost immediately by the hiss of the gas, and for a moment Romulus hesitated again, unsure how long to wait, until Diomedes's impatient nudge at his heels sent him scrambling forward. He was rushing down the hill now, moving to the end of the tunnel like a bullet out the barrel of a gun. His own gun was ahead of him. He had to reach the room while its occupants were still confused.

He reached the edge of the tunnel, going too fast. Momentum carried him forward and sent him sprawling through mid-air. His vain flailing for a handhold amid the gas ended with him slamming into the ground a second later in a disorganized jumble of arms and legs. Somehow he managed to keep his head from smacking onto the floor too hard; his mask stayed on.

Yet the fall had knocked the wind out of him. If he just lay there he'd be vulnerable to anyone in the room not affected by his clumsy hurl of the grenade. Tightening his grip on the gun to reassure himself that it was still in his hand, he tried to pull himself up from his pain. Fifteen feet away, on the floor near the far wall, a prostrate figure lay in a heap of black robes. Romulus scrambled toward the figure and struggled to draw breath, unwilling to remain long enough to take in any of his other surroundings. He reached the figure in a flash and had managed to get to his feet when he heard Diomedes land in the room behind him—on his feet by the sound of it.

Romulus had almost verified that the robed figure was unconscious when there came a loud hiss behind him and a grunt of impact from his roommate. Romulus spun to see his mentor at the other side of the small chamber. Another figure in black was on his back. The figure clutched a knife that Diomedes struggled to keep from his neck.

Romulus fought to pull breath into his lungs. It was as if he could see himself standing there, useless, as his roommate struggled. *Do something!* Romulus brought up his near-forgotten auto-pistol, wondering even as he did so if he would ever have a clear shot.

Before he had time to judge, the robed figure from the floor behind him sprang up and pinned Romulus's arms down at his sides. The gas hadn't affected him! Romulus fought to free himself, hoping his mask would stay over his face. His mentor struggled with his own opponent miles away across the room. Romulus tried to hurl himself back against the wall to knock the robed man off, but he was off-balance and still weakened from the shock of his fall. He tried to pull his gun arm free, but the figure held it fast. All around him was chaos, and he only half saw Diomedes connect with a backward elbow jab and fling his stunned assailant to the floor with disproportionate strength. Romulus himself could manage no such feat and cried out as a sharp pain stabbed into his wrist. He looked down in time to see his gun fall from his hand, bloodied from where pointed black fingernails had pierced his skin deeply. Another hiss filled his ears, this time from his own attacker, and he turned to see the glint of fangs poised to sink into his neck. He was trying to pull away when a sharp retort filled the room. Warmth splashed the side of his face in the same instant that his attacker slumped away.

A split second after looking down the barrel of the gun that had saved him, Romulus spun belatedly away from his fallen attacker. He intended a glance down at the body to assure himself that the man wasn't still coming for him, but that glance turned longer until Romulus was staring at the sight of the cultist lying wrecked and lifeless on the floor.

"He won't get up," Diomedes said finally.

Romulus nodded and pried his eyes from the body. His own heart continued to pound in his chest. "Thanks," he managed.

If Diomedes heard the expression of gratitude, he made no show of it. "There's no more up there." He motioned with his gun to an alcove, located above the tunnel from which he and Diomedes had come. The second cultist must have been hiding there. The gas hadn't worked on either of them. Had he thrown the grenade wrong somehow? The thought echoed in his mind; everything else was strangely absent.

"I screwed up." His gaze fell again to the body before he had to look away.

His mentor only grunted and bent down to the body of the man he had thrown from his back. That one had been in the alcove when the grenade burst. It made sense that the gas hadn't affected him, at least at first. But the other had been right in the middle of the cloud. Why hadn't it worked? It had to be his fault. If things had worked correctly, the cultist would have been out completely when they entered. He wouldn't have attacked him.

He wouldn't have gotten shot.

"This one's alive," Diomedes said. "We'll take him and go. Before more come." In one quick motion the large man had the body up over his shoulder and was waiting for Romulus to climb back into the tunnel. Things were moving swiftly. Romulus knew he was falling behind. He pressed the thoughts quietly filling his mind back into a dark corner and started for the tunnel.

"Hey," Diomedes began, looking at him. The tone of his voice suggested he had noticed something. Romulus turned.

"Wipe that blood off your face," his mentor said. "We'll look suspicious enough carrying this around."

Romulus blinked for a moment and then touched his fingers to his cheek. The warm sensation he now recalled feeling earlier returned as his fingertips pulled away red. "Oh, damn," he whispered. He stared at the crimson gel. Why in God's name hadn't the grenade worked?

"Use the dead one's robe. Just get it off and get in the tunnel." Feeling queasy, Romulus nodded and followed his mentor's orders.

VII

THE REPORTER SAT SILENTLY in the floater, his eyes wandering occasionally as Felix acquainted him with the circumstances surrounding their own search for Wraith. He still seemed to be taking everything with a grain of salt. His body language told Felix that he had begun to trust him a little more—his arms had uncrossed, at least—but he still appeared to hang on to the possibility of a trick. Felix supposed he couldn't blame him too much, but hoped he wouldn't hang on to it much longer. It remained for Felix to see if it was the immediate situation that made Brian so cautious, or if he was just another victim of paranoia.

Felix hoped it was the former. It was already going to be difficult enough to get Diomedes to allow the reporter to join them. Maybe things would work a little smoother if he prepped Brian for that beforehand.

"So you're sure he's tied in with the warehouse arsons?" Brian asked. "There's nothing in my files to even suggest that." He'd been skeptical of that idea the moment Felix had told him of it.

"No," said Felix. "But my associate seems to have evidence to that effect."

"Diomedes, you mean."

"Yeah, and I wouldn't press him on the matter too much until he's had a chance to accept your presence in this little venture."

"Uh huh. And that would be when?"

Felix chuckled. "About five or six years should do it."

"Great. Sounds like a friendly guy."

"Well, I'm not completely certain how, ah, comfortable he'll be with letting you join us. As I said, he's the one that hired me, and he wouldn't even've done that if he didn't think it absolutely necessary. He'll be worried about you getting in his way or stabbing him in the back somehow—or maybe writing about him. He'll certainly be worried you'll try to get yourself a cut of his pay. If I know him as well as I think I do, that is."

"I'm just after an interview. I couldn't care less about money or anything else."

"All the same, might be better if I do the talking when they get back," Felix said. "Unless I'm wrong—which I realize is a foolish colloquialism—"

"What is?"

"'Unless I'm wrong.' We're all correct about everything unless we're wrong. There's no point in saying it."

"So why say it?"

"As I said before, I don't always have a point," Felix reminded him with a smile. "Just a habit of mine. But as I was trying to say, Diomedes might have a problem with the interview, too."

"And why is *that*?"

"Call it a hunch. It's that whole 'unless I'm wrong' thing."

"So you did have a point," Brian said.

"I suppose I did. Isn't life amusing?"

What Felix suspected was that Diomedes, if he was truly planning to kill the man in question, would certainly see the interview as an obstacle to that—or at least to doing it cleanly. As for telling Brian his reasons, Felix decided to hold off. No sense in telling him of things that he only suspected just yet. Besides, he didn't know how well Brian would be able to conceal that suspicion from Diomedes, and getting the man to let the reporter in would be hard enough without any other leaks in discretion.

It occurred to Felix that he was hiding things from the reporter: the very man he was asking to trust him. Felix thought he reasonably understood the workings of the freelancer's mind enough to help the situation work out for the best, but even so, he was dealing with the freelancer's suspicion and lack of trust with a lack of trust of his own.

It made him a hypocrite. Yet was Felix strong enough to do it any other way?

"So what about the other one?" the reporter probed. "You called him Flynn?"

"You mean should you worry about him?"

"Well, that, among other things. What can you tell me about him?"

"I don't know him quite as well, but he's nowhere near the . . . ," Felix paused to search for a word, "individual Diomedes is." *Not if I can help it, anyway.* "He's definitely looking forward to being so, but I'm not sure if he's got the—"

"Brains?" Brian asked. He seemed to regret it as Felix cocked his head.

"I was going to say 'heart.' Or the lack of it, rather."

Brian shrugged. "It's just that he didn't seem to be saying much, just blindly following you two."

"Mr. Savagewood," Felix observed, "you seem to hear a lot, but I'm not sure how much of it you listen to."

After a moment of confusion, Brian nodded and tapped his ears. "Oh, yeah. They're implants. I can tune into one conversation and tune the others out to a pretty reasonable degree."

Felix blinked at him. The man had both completely missed and proven his point at the same time. He decided not to belabor the point for the time being. "I thought so, considering what you overheard in the bar. And seeing how you spotted our floater from a distance in the dark, I'm guessing your ears aren't the only artificial senses you've got. I'd say it's a good bet your head is one big sensor?"

"Damn right. The best money can buy," Brian said. "The eyes are Opticell 2600s, with a few special features."

Felix gave an appreciative chuckle. "Sounds expensive. They must pay you well."

"Well, yeah, they're expensive." Brian glanced away with a shrug and shifted in his seat. "But that's pretty much all I'm getting. I'm not about to go hacking limbs off for metal."

"Not ever?" Felix asked. He sensed an interesting conversation.

"Well, okay, I've thought about it. But who hasn't, right?"

"There is an odd lure to it for a lot of people." Though cybernetic limbs were initially resisted upon their introduction, they had eventually made their way into fashion like an expensive technological tattoo.

"And jumping off cliffs has an odd lure to lemmings, but does that mean they should?"

"Lemmings aren't suicidal, they're just hungry and stupid. In their rush to find food they occasionally stumble off a cliff, and the ones following are too dumb to pay attention until it's too late."

"Hungry and stupid, hmm? Still sort of fits then, doesn't it?"

Felix shrugged. "Just making a correction. Another habit of mine."

"My point is that it's a little too risky, even if you've got the money to do it right."

"Psychologically speaking, you mean," Felix stated. "Incidences of mental collapse from one limb replacement are pretty uncommon, from what I understand."

"Maybe, but the risk is still there, isn't it? And it's not exactly something they can predict."

"In some cases they can," Felix said, "if the patient has had a previous history of mental instability."

"But they're not the only cases. I've heard of all sorts of cases of perfectly normal people whacking out in all sorts of ways."

"Oh, no, they're not the only cases; I was just pointing out the current knowledge." *All sorts of ways.* The reporter was right. Sometimes it manifested itself in a sudden flare of uncontainable violence. People just snapped. But sometimes it was less obvious, surfacing in varieties of paranoid delusions or schizophrenia.

"And even if they can predict it in some cases," Brian went on, "they're still not sure why it happens."

"There are some theories. Though most of the concepts that support them are barely theories themselves."

"The only thing I've heard was something about the EM radiation messing with the brain, but that's not very well accepted, is it?"

"Not exactly," said Felix. "There are so many other similar devices — cybernetic and non-cybernetic — that if there was an effect it shouldn't just be in those who have them attached to their bodies. Though I believe there's a small group of people who think the close proximity and constant attachment to the body may give enough additional exposure to push things beyond some critical point."

"And what do you think?"

"I think they might have the right cause — constant proximity and attachment, that is — but not the reason for the effect."

"What do you mean?" Brian asked. At least he seemed more relaxed.

"There are some schools of thought, whose origins I believe lie in Eastern philosophy, that say the mind doesn't reside completely in the brain—that it's also resident in the rest of the body."

Brian smirked. "What, so if you cut off your arm you lose a bit of your mind?"

"You're thinking too physically. You've heard of amputees waking up and scratching limbs that weren't there? Same thing. The energy, chi, soul, spirit, whatever you want to call it is still there."

"So the new replacement messes that up somehow."

Felix shrugged. "The idea's got some merit. I'm sure whatever it is, it's a mix of influences. You have to admit, it does give one a certain unnatural feeling to be able to hear the way we do with nothing more than a thought."

"Well, I don't know what the hell causes it. I just don't want to mess around with it. I wouldn't be surprised to find out you're right, though."

"I wouldn't be surprised to find out I was wrong, either. People thought the earth was flat once, too." Felix grinned.

"Whatever. It's not something to screw around with is my point."

"And yet you still have yours."

"That's different! With what I've got—well, the risk, it's not nearly as big."

"It's still a risk," Felix countered.

Brian crossed his arms, seeming slightly agitated. "There's a difference between crossing the street and physically hurling yourself in front of a truck, wouldn't you say?"

Felix held up his hands. "Sorry, I didn't mean to seem like I was judging you. Unless I miss my guess, I've certainly taken at least a little more of those risks than you, myself. My point is that you obviously felt it was justified based on the benefits. By that same token, others obviously did as well. I'm not saying whether it's right or wrong. Just one of the pitfalls of the modern world, same as it's always been."

"I still say you have to be crazy to mess around with that stuff to the point some do."

"Well, if they're already crazy then it's not exactly a risk now, is it?" Felix shot the man a grin. To his slight relief, the reporter chuckled. Felix decided to take the moment to nudge the subject to one side. He glanced out the window for any sign of Diomedes and Flynn, and asked, "So would you be a fan of CPMC, then?"

The reporter made his own search out the window, mirroring Felix. "You mean Big Brother?" he asked with a glance up at the alley wall.

"That'd be a no, then."

"Well, it's sort of a deal with the devil, isn't it? I mean they serve their purpose when someone goes berserk, but at what cost?" Brian's tone took on that of someone reciting a prepared speech. "Constantly monitoring anyone who even gets a minor implant, tracking their behavior, following their movements. They scrutinize every deviant activity no matter how minor—"

Felix cut him off. "Taking a little license with exaggeration aren't you? Cybernetic Psychoses Monitoring and Control. It's in the name but they haven't got the resources to—" He stopped mid-sentence as he heard a sound outside the floater.

Beyond the tinted windows, Flynn pulled himself up out of the manhole.

"They're back," Felix said. It sounded more like a warning than he had intended. "Remember, let me do the talking," he warned again. (Why break a trend?) "And try not to piss him off."

Brian settled a bit in his seat. Felix inched forward, waiting for the fun to begin. A few moments later the floater door opened. Diomedes's eyes locked onto the red-haired newcomer from the start. Neither said a word, but Brian quickly folded under the freelancer's dead stare and looked to Felix. Diomedes's eyes followed an instant later.

"Who's this?" The curiosity came from Flynn, who stood in the door just behind Diomedes.

Felix looked at the younger man. "This is Brian Savagewood. And to answer your next question," Felix turned to Diomedes, unable keep from flashing a grin, "yes, that is his natural hair."

*   *   *

They appeared quickly, though their speed surprised only some. In reality, they had been given instructions to be prepared to go at a moment's notice. As the one who had given those instructions upon arriving with them at Alpha Station days ago, Marette Clarion's reaction to their rapid response was one only of satisfaction.

She met the team at the operations center of the mining camp just under one hour after she called for them, which was shortly after the mining foreman, a rather worrisome man by Clarion's estimates, had reported the "door." She hadn't needed the foreman's opinion, but ESA didn't want her to move without it. For the moment, what ESA said was what she would do.

Foreman Andora was, for the most part, cooperative and even welcoming of Marette's authority and presence as the ESA overseer. Marette had even noticed more than a little apprehension when she had left the foreman alone with his crew in order to report back to ESA and call in the team. It wasn't until she had given the man instructions to widen the chamber near the door that the apprehension seemed to fade. The tunnel did not really need to be widened—not yet, anyway—but it kept them all occupied. It was not until Marette returned with the team and their equipment and told the mining crew to evacuate the tunnel that Parker Andora began to get curious and demanded an explanation.

Truly, it had been more of a request than a demand, which made it easier for Marette to deflect him with a reminder of just whose authority allowed Saratoga to be here.

"If you have any issues with that," she had stated, "talk to your superiors, have them talk to ESA, and then ESA will talk to me. In the meanwhile, just let me handle things as I am required to, and you will be fine."

Andora had sheepishly replied that he thought it was understandable to be curious about exactly what was going on, but he left things at that and took his crew back to the surface without another word.

Marette waited until they had moved out of sight and gave the order for her team to unpack the container that they had brought with them into the tunnel from the shuttle. The boulder-sized cargo container split into three parts, the first two of which were light enough to be carried by her team unassisted. The final was the largest of the three and massive enough to need to be unloaded from the transport belt by team members in exo-chassis borrowed from the mining crew.

Marette watched as they carried the components of the portable airlock over to the door, where it would be assembled. The two smaller cargo containers were moved near the door as well, their contents set to rest until the airlock was ready.

As all eight members of the team began to assemble the airlock, Marette watched without supervising. The team knew their jobs as well or better than she did. She only needed to wait . . . and wonder.

VIII

"**LEAVE.**"

Felix watched the single word hang in the air in front of the reporter.

"What?" Brian stalled with a glare at Felix.

"Leave." Diomedes stepped to one side of the doorway. "Now."

"Diomedes," Felix tried to make his scold cheerful to disrupt the tension, "where are your manners? No 'Hello?' No 'How are you?' No 'May I offer you some custard pie?' If you're going to keep treating my friends so rudely, then I may have to stop bringing them to visit." Felix glanced at Flynn for a supporting grin, but the young man was focused on Brian and Diomedes.

"We have business." Diomedes stood motionless, glaring expectantly. Felix realized the journey into the sewers must have gone well, or he wouldn't have been in such a pleasant mood.

"Obviously. Why do you think I asked him here?" Felix replied. "Well okay, I guess I really didn't *ask* him here," he continued without giving Diomedes an opening. "We just ran into each other in the alley. We hadn't seen each other in a bit so we've been here catching up. Met in college—not when I was in college, of course, I'm not that young. He was taking classes and I was just sort of there." Felix was rambling and he knew it. "But at any rate it's a good thing he happened into the alley back there because he'll be a big help. So what'd you find down there, Flynn?" He asked the last question in cadence with his rambling, not missing a beat and looking straight at Michael.

The young man blinked as if caught off guard by the question. He stood formulating an answer, and Felix thought he caught a trace of regret in his expression.

Diomedes spoke first. "What we found is something I tell you when he's gone."

"So you did find something, then," Felix stated. The freelancer didn't respond beyond a long glance back at the manhole. Diomedes was being stubborn, but that was to be expected. They had obviously found something, but Felix would still bet it wasn't the answer they were looking for. "That would seem to be a yes." He shot to his feet. "It seems you don't need me anymore, then. Come on, Brian. I'll buy you a beer."

Diomedes moved to block the door. Felix only smiled at him. "We're not through yet," said Diomedes.

Felix sat back down. "I stay, he stays. It's a package. You paid for my help. Don't make your money worthless by taking away my contacts." Felix hoped that would get Diomedes's attention, but the freelancer's face was characteristically hard to read. Flynn was staying out of the discussion, hanging back in the alley, looking about. "Now why don't you just bring up whatever it is you two found down there and let's get this thing going again."

At this the freelancer turned back towards Brian, presumably sizing him up. Brian met his gaze impatiently.

"Diomedes," Felix went on, letting a little exasperation of his own show in his tone, "what's he going to do?"

"Exactly. What is he going to do?"

"Brian happens to have certain connections in a rather omniscient news agency. There are things he can find out—and resources he can access—that I can't get as . . . discreetly."

"And I'm not going to make a stink about anyone who roughs up the occasional Nosferatu, either," Brian chimed in.

Felix winced internally as Diomedes stepped toward him, anger in his eyes. "You told him?"

"You just crawled out of the sewer in an alley behind the stadium," Felix tried. "Anyone who knows half as much about this city as I do could guess you're either looking for Nosferatu or sneaking in for the next Ultimate match. Brian's no idiot. He notices things. Things I might miss. Another reason to have him here."

Diomedes remained silent and fixed Brian with a dead, unrelenting stare. Felix could tell he was thinking. If there was one thing he knew about the freelancer, it was that he was proud. He wouldn't simply relent and release control of the situation, not for nothing at least.

"It's your choice," Felix pressed. "He stays or he doesn't. If my redheaded friend screws up, if he doesn't help us finish your job, then you keep my fee." Felix ignored the suspicious look Brian himself gave him at this. "Which is it?"

Diomedes sized him up for a moment more, then abruptly turned from the door and walked back to the manhole. As soon as he was away, Brian whispered, "You're the one saying I can help! I'm not paying you if—"

Felix hushed him, watching as Diomedes crawled down into the hole. "The fee's hardly anything," he lied. "I don't need it."

A moment later the freelancer lifted a body from the hole, brought it to the floater, and dumped the leather-clad figure on the floor. "You stay," he spoke, pointing at Brian. "Tie him to the seat."

Felix watched as Brian took some rope from the back and bound the darkly dressed cultist in one of the near seats. Diomedes kept his auto-pistol trained on the Nosferatu the entire time. Felix assumed his primary purpose was to guard against the cultist regaining consciousness too early, but Felix guessed that he was watching their new companion just as carefully. Felix shook his head behind the freelancer's back and glanced through the doorway at Flynn. The young man had moved in again after his roommate had accepted Brian. He was also watching the Nosferatu carefully, though something in his eyes betrayed an inward distraction.

Diomedes checked the knots after Brian had stepped back. "I'm no expert, but I think those oughta hold," Brian whispered.

The freelancer ignored the comment but seemed satisfied. He motioned for Flynn to come inside. "Close the door." Flynn nodded and did as he said. He then took a seat in the front passenger chair and turned it to face the rear.

"So how far'd you have to go to find this lucky gentleman?" Felix asked as he regarded the cultist. He was covered from neck to ankle in muted black—almost like a jumpsuit but tighter and made from dull, heavy leather. His hair was short, a contrasting white, yet only slightly paler than the cultist's own skin—at least the bit that was visible. Of this, half of it was covered in a crimson tattoo of a spider's web running from eye to ear on the left side of his face. A delicate silver chain hung about his neck. Felix found the combination of color to be actually quite striking, and also found himself wondering if the cultist might have once been an art student.

"Heating room—beneath the stadium," Diomedes answered.

Felix saw no sign of physical harm to the cultist, though given his outfit, he supposed he couldn't be sure. "Gassed him, did you?" he asked of Flynn.

The young man hesitated a moment. "It wasn't . . . "

"No," Diomedes interjected with a look at Flynn. "He jumped me. Knocked him out the hard way."

"Ah."

Brian spoke from where he crouched behind the Nosferatu. "Was it just him? I thought I heard they go in packs."

The freelancer frowned at him. "Does he look like he's in a pack?" His tone was sufficient for Brian to turn his gaze back to the unconscious figure. Moments slipped away as they watched their captive breathe.

"So what do you plan to do when he wakes up?" Felix asked finally.

"You're going to ask him some questions. If I don't like his answers, I'll ask some of my own."

"And just what would you have me ask? It was your idea to take him."

"You said don't tell you how to do your job. You know what we're looking for."

"Do I?"

"He's awake," Flynn said.

Everyone looked at the Nosferatu as he sat calmly in the seat. His unnaturally green eyes—most likely simple contacts—were fixed squarely on Diomedes, staring with quiet menace as the cultist breathed faster.

"Where," he demanded, taking a short, quick breath as the word was spoken, "is Ranth?"

"Who's Ranth?" Felix asked.

"My blood mate," the cultist replied with another quick, almost lizard-like breath. His eyes did not wander from Diomedes. They only traveled up and down his body. "The other with me, when he defiled our lair." The cultist's neck shifted like a hovering snake as he regarded Diomedes. "Where is he?"

Felix waited to see if Diomedes would respond.

"He's dead."

It was Flynn who had spoken. The Nosferatu shot him a look of fury before he smiled an instant later to show prosthetic fangs. "Not for long," he whispered. His neck twisted back to Diomedes. "Be forewarned. My kindred shall find me. They shall find you."

Diomedes continued his silence.

"I don't suppose you'd care to answer a few questions for us while we wait?" Felix asked.

"Why should I answer the questions of a mortal?"

Felix stepped forward slightly and slipped his hands in his pockets as Brian glanced out the window into the alley. "Because my large friend here has told me that if you don't answer mine, you *will* answer his—something I'd imagine to be a little more uncomfortable."

Felix caught a flash of apprehension in the cultist's eyes. Though he might say otherwise, and even perhaps make himself believe otherwise, he must still have known deep down that he was possessed of the same mortality as anyone else. "He lacks the power to truly harm me, though I will speak with you as it suits me until my brethren descend upon you." The delusional shield was up again. Felix found himself pondering slightly what would happen if the others did come.

"Do you know why we brought you here?" he began.

The cultist grinned. "Should I?"

"There's someone," Felix began, pausing for dramatic effect and hoping to appeal to the man's own delusions, "or some*thing* that has been attacking, killing, perhaps feeding on other gangs and people in the shroud of night." He paused again to compose further melodrama. "Stalking them. Perhaps . . . tearing them apart with claws and fangs, leaving the blood to stain the streets of the city. My friend here thinks it's you or your brethren."

At this, the cultist hissed and turned to Diomedes. "So like a mortal, so driven by fear! By ignorance! For centuries your ilk has blamed and persecuted our—"

Felix cut off the rant, raising his voice. "I disagree with him, but I do think you may know something if it." Felix would have been surprised if the cultist did know anything new, but there was always a chance.

"And if I do?"

"Oh, I doubt it's a question of 'if.' I'm sure there's quite a lot you and your brethren have seen from the shadows." Again, Felix doubted his own words. The Nosferatu traditionally kept too isolated to have any information of value outside of their own immediate grounds.

"You are correct, human." His eyes narrowed.

"Where did you see him?" Brian asked from the corner.

"I have not. Nor do I expect to. But I know of him."

"How do you know of him, then?"

"I have been told."

"How much have you been told?" Felix pressed. It smelled like little more than common knowledge of the rumor, but something that the cultist had said did intrigue him.

"Of his existence," the cultist said. "More did not concern me."

"Because you didn't expect to see him," Felix stated.

"My reasons are clouded beyond your vision." Felix chose to take that as a yes.

"And just why exactly don't you expect to see him?"

"We do not concern him. And he knows our power."

"Oh yeah?" It was Brian again. "And just how do you know that? Can you read his mind?"

The cultist peered at Brian with contempt. "*I* cannot read minds. I was told."

"Who tells you these things?" Felix added.

At this, the Nosferatu's eyes glowed with an almost sinister delight. "The One Who Sees," he whispered.

"Ah!" said Brian, rolling his eyes. "So *he* can read minds!"

The cultist continued to stare at Felix in a way that he couldn't help but feel was slightly unnerving. "He sees. His power is . . . to be feared."

"Who is he?" Felix asked. He was intrigued. This was a title he had not heard before.

"He is The One Who Sees."

"That much I understand."

The cultist shook his head. "You do not understand."

Felix shrugged. "Okay, then help me understand. What's his name?"

"I will not speak his name," he said quickly. "There *are* things I fear."

Brian snorted. "You're afraid of his name?"

"I do not fear it, weakling," he hissed. "But I fear his wrath, should I speak of it to you."

Felix glanced at Diomedes. He remained motionless, apparently content for the moment to listen and watch. "So, he's your leader?" Felix tested. To his knowledge the Nosferatu had no leader, though they did seem to pride themselves on remaining hidden and mysterious, even from the rest of the "mainstream" goth crowd.

"He is not. One with such power does not seek to lead. Only to . . . inspire."

"If he's so powerful then why haven't we heard of him?" Brian asked. "Why hasn't he used this power to make everyone fear him?"

"He shall, but for The One Who Is."

Felix couldn't tell if the Nosferatu believed what he was saying or was just trying to be enigmatic, but Felix was becoming at least mildly fascinated by the riddle he presented. "And who is this One Who Is?" he asked. "Does your One Who Sees fear him?"

"Most mortals know The One Who Is. And yes, he shall fear him, until the coming of The One Who Will Be."

"Oh, Lord," Brian mumbled, giving Felix a look that clearly said this was getting them nowhere. Felix motioned for him to wait. Brian was probably right, but this was too interesting to not hear the rest of it. Okay, so maybe he was a sucker for this sort of thing. It was fun.

"And this One Who Will Be, he'll replace The One Who Is?"

"So says The One Who Sees."

"I take it that I would consider this a bad thing?"

"For you and your kind. Upon the coming of The One Who Will Be, men will seek death, but will not find it. They will long to die, but death will elude them."

Felix turned around to Flynn. He was looking out the window at the covered manhole. "Bummer," Felix said before turning back. "Interesting prophecy. The One Who Will Be isn't coming before next Tuesday, is he? I've got a friend coming in from out of town that day that I'd rather not miss."

"You do not believe," the Nosferatu stated, eyes narrowing.

"Oh, no, I believe. It's just that I'd rather not be longing to die just yet, and I have a tendency to cope using humor. Your One Who Sees is certain of all this, is he?"

The Nosferatu flashed Felix another unnerving grin. "They shall come to pass unless The One Who Might Be can stand against The One Who Will Be." Felix raised an eyebrow. Brian choked down a laugh. Okay, so this was becoming ludicrously convoluted.

Diomedes smacked the Nosferatu across the face, startling him and the others alike. "Enough!" The side of the cultist's face flushed from the impact. "Now I ask."

Felix moved forward to speak with the freelancer, trying to nudge him back so he could do so privately. Diomedes neither looked at him nor budged. "He doesn't know anything," Felix whispered. "Not what you want. Don't punish him for it. This is a dead end here."

"He hasn't told you everything." The freelancer didn't bother to lower his voice. His gaze remained anchored to his prisoner.

"That's because he doesn't know it. We don't have time for this."

Diomedes looked down at him. "No, we don't. Get out of my way."

"You're not going to kill him," Felix told him.

"He'll tell me what he knows."

"They will come for you!" the Nosferatu hissed from behind them.

In two swift motions, Diomedes knocked the cultist into unconsciousness and pointed at Flynn. "Go outside, across the alley. Stand watch." He turned back to Felix. "Go with him."

"I'm not leaving you alone with him," Felix said.

Diomedes turned to Brian after a moment. "You. Stay here." The freelancer lowered an expectant gaze on Felix as Flynn moved for the door. Felix turned, considering, as Flynn checked his gun. He waited as the younger man stepped from the vehicle, and then he looked back to Diomedes. Perhaps one more thing . . .

"Just remember," he whispered, "leaving a trail of bodies around doesn't make it any harder for Wallace to send the wrong kind of attention your way."

In the split second after the freelancer's hand wrapped around his throat and pressed him against the window, Felix cursed artificially boosted reflexes. He looked back at Diomedes and forced himself to appear calm. "That wasn't a threat. It was a bit of advice."

The freelancer relaxed his grip slightly but still held him. "How'd you hear?"

"I keep my ears open. And I'm not the only one who does. Ken Wallace is slime, but I'm sure there are others who wouldn't care. Just be careful is all I'm saying. I don't need anything happening to one of my steadier clients."

The freelancer dropped his grip. "I'm always careful," he said with a nod.

Felix stepped for the door. "You're always paranoid, Diomedes. There's a difference." He moved to close the door, adding, "Just make it quick so I can get on with helping you find who you're really looking for."

With a last glance at Brian, he slid the door shut.

I X

WHEN THE INTEGRITY of the airlock's seal against the excavated structure was confirmed at one hundred percent, Marette ordered the team to prepare for the first entry attempt. As the team moved towards the remaining smaller crates to unpack the weapons and sensing equipment, she opened a channel.

"Alberto," she said, "join me inside, please." For a moment she considered giving a specific reason for the order, but Alberto knew the reason well enough, and fabricating one for the others' benefit would only call more attention to the command. She gave an order, and it would be followed; for them that would be enough.

After Alberto was inside and the outer door was sealed, Marette joined him in the junction to the rover's airlock as he removed his helmet. She handed him the small device she had been fingering in her pocket. "Connect this to the transmitter on your sensor junction." Alberto nodded and opened a compartment in the leg of his pressure suit to install the device. "I want you to double check that it is active before you go in. We must ensure we get our own source copy."

"What's our comm-channel?" he asked, resealing the compartment.

"Keep the channel the team is using. I will be speaking to you all on that. Anything specifically for you will come through on thirty-two. Keep them both open for receiving but remember you will have to manually switch to thirty-two if you need to send a private transmission to me. I do not want you fumbling around with comm-channels while you are in there, so switch only if you absolutely have to. Otherwise stay focused on your surroundings. Understood?"

"Of course. Anything else?"

"Just this: keep to the rear. If things grow out of hand in there, I need you to be able to get out quickly. Do not forget where your loyalties are."

"Let's just hope it doesn't come to that," Alberto told her. He took a deep breath and pulled on his helmet.

Oui, let us hope. "Plan for the worst to prepare for the best," she quoted.

A few minutes later, Alberto had rejoined the rest of the team outside the vehicle. Marette watched him attach a sensor boom to his helmet. This was a simple device that every member of the team wore, consisting mainly of a video and thermal imaging system with a few miscellaneous functions. As one of the three primary sensor technicians, he also took one of the bulky Class II scanners. The other five team members, unencumbered by such a scanner themselves, slung recoilless ARG-rifles specially designed by ESA for extraterrestrial use. What they would be used on here, if anything, was something at which Marette did not attempt to guess.

Yet first they would need to deal with the indentation that they still considered to be a door into the mysterious structure. She continued to watch from inside the vehicle as two of the sensor techs brought in the tools that would help them either open or cut through it. The plan was that the armed members of the team would cover the two while they breached, with Alberto keeping a wide scan for anything behind the door. Once the door was open, the two would take up their scanners again and mix with the rest upon entry.

The entire team was now in the airlock with the outer door sealed against the vacuum of the excavated tunnel behind them. They would keep the vacuum within the lock itself in place until more was known. The airlock's inner door, its seal flush against the door of the structure, remained open to allow them access to the strange, ethereal metal.

"*I can't read past it,*" reported one of the sensor techs—another man, named Freitz. "*But I think it's at least sixteen centimeters thick.*"

"You think?" Marette asked.

"*Harder to tell when I don't know what it is I'm reading through. It's some sort of alloy by the initial scans, but determining anything beyond that would take more time.*"

"Hold off on the composition for now until it becomes necessary. Check for breaks in uniformity."

Within a few minutes, the tech reported bands of denser material within the metal. The bands extended the length of the door along both the top and bottom. Other than that, nothing was detectable, not even in the space framing the door.

"Try to make a hole between the bands," she ordered, watching the view from Alberto's camera on her screen. The third tech, a woman with the last name of Littlefield, brought a laser cutter to the mysterious surface. "Lowest setting," Marette ordered, probably unnecessarily. A blue light flared and reflected off the visors of the team.

It burned, for a while.

"*Doesn't seem to be doing much,*" the other tech reported. "*Switching to a higher level.*" Marette's only response this time was a nod, letting the tech do her job. Another blue light flared, pulsed for a short time, and again winked out. "*Looks as though we might've made a little progress,*" came the report. "*It's starting to glow a bit where we cut. Permission to switch to the highest setting? I think we may be able to punch through with that.*"

Marette scowled. "It will take longer at that intensity," she remarked. "Proceed." There wasn't much point in complaining about it. A third time the brilliant blue light flared. Marette waited.

"*It's glowing again. Quicker this time. And a little brighter. We'll know in a minute if it's going to work.*" On the camera, the laser drill continued to bore against the surface, which glowed whiter by the second. "*God, that's bright!*" Littlefield exclaimed. "*Freitz, do you think—*"

She screamed.

Marette's screen burst with light. It continued to glow as she switched to other cameras and the voices of the team came through the speaker.

"*Is he okay?*"

"*He's hit—! His helmet's cracked!*"

"*Freitz, report!*"

"*His suit's decompressing!*"

"*Freitz!*"

Marette watched as the light faded and the camera cleared. Littlefield and another were holding onto Freitz while he thrashed on the airlock floor. "Siri!" she called to the head of the team, "What has happened?"

"*Pressurize the lock! Now!*" It was Siri's voice, but he wasn't speaking to her.

Freitz's helmet had been compromised. How? The hiss of air filling the lock followed shortly, and Marette waited for a report as things calmed down. Freitz, still on the floor, stopped thrashing.

"Siri! Report," she ordered after a moment.

"Freitz's helmet was cracked. His suit was depressurizing. He's breathing now."

"I'm all aces," came Freitz's voice. *"Just a little shaken."*

Marette watched Littlefield help him to his feet. "What hit you?"

"Don't know. All I saw was the flash."

"I think it was the drill, ma'am," Littlefield said. *"Like it just reflected off the surface. It happened so suddenly I—"*

A sudden, dull humming came from within the structure.

"God," Alberto whispered. *"It's opening."*

Marette switched to his camera as the team turned in unison towards the slab of grey metal that was now quietly sliding back into the side of the previously lifeless structure. Marette said nothing as the darkness unveiled itself beyond what was now assuredly a door. For what seemed like an eternity, the door rolled open. Nothing moved beyond it; nothing broke the blackness that seemed anything but empty. There was no rush of air, no escaping hiss. Marette realized the pressure must be equal on both sides, but beyond acknowledging this in the back of her mind, no other thoughts would come. No words passed her lips.

And then it stopped, and all was quiet.

"Looks like we don't need to drill . . . "

The comment from one of the team went unanswered while they regarded the opening. From what Marette could see on the screen, the blackness continued beyond their vision. How far the light would penetrate—

She stopped short. "The air!" she exclaimed. "Check the air! Get Freitz to the rear of the lock!" The pressure might be the same but that was no guarantee against poisonous gases. Freitz obeyed quickly while Littlefield and Alberto analyzed the structure's atmosphere. Marette considered their options if it was poisonous: They could close the lock on the structure's side, but with no helmet there would be nowhere for Freitz to go, and the air would already have mixed to some extent. The small vehicle she waited in would not fit to the exterior side of the lock. The only way to get him out—

"*This is incredible,*" came Littlefield's voice. "*Seventy-eight-point-one percent nitrogen, twenty-point-nine percent oxygen, point-nine percent argon. Trace amounts of carbon dioxide, methane, noble gases. The thing has nearly the same atmosphere as Earth.*"

"Alberto?"

"*Stand by. Scanning for lethal trace gases,*" he replied. "*I'm reading identical here. Nothing hazardous.*"

"*That can't be right, and I'm the one that has to breathe the stuff. Hang on.*" Freitz ran a scan of his own, with the same results. "*Thank God for coincidence.*"

"Coincidence or no, I am not letting you move in without that helmet," Marette said.

"*Begging your pardon, ma'am but how would you suggest I get a new one? The lock wasn't designed for that rover you're in—or anything else we're going to fit in this tunnel.*"

"*There is another way,*" Siri said.

"*I don't relish the thought of EVA without a helmet, sir.*"

"*No. You could wait inside the structure while we vent the lock and bring in a new helmet.*"

"We do not know what's in there yet," warned Marette. "Can you make out the confines of the room, Siri?"

"*I can't, no.*"

"*That may just be because the walls are so dark,*" Alberto suggested. "*According to the scanner, it's not much larger than four hundred square meters—long and thin into the structure.*"

Marette clasped her hands and tapped her chin in thought. She didn't like it. "Siri," she said finally, "lead them in and secure the room. Freitz—"

"*If it's all the same to you, ma'am, I'll go with them, helmet or not. I'm not much use hiding in here.*"

"Granted. Take your position."

They entered.

Marette watched through Alberto's camera, viewing from his position in the rear. The walls were intensely black: completely void of light and utterly strange. The light from the team seemed to simultaneously reflect off of and yet become absorbed within the midnight surface. The walls, floor, and ceiling seemed to be made of the same substance. It almost reminded her of liquid tar, though it was obviously solid.

The footsteps of her team echoed through the chamber. She watched them explore.

"Can you get a reading on the material of the walls?"

"*It's not something the scanners recognize. I'm reading carbon, silicon . . . in varying amounts. Possibly some organic material.*"

"Possibly?"

"*Sorry; it is organic. Parts of it, anyway.*"

"Do you mean to say it is alive?" For a moment the image of the team walking into an enormous stomach flashed in her mind.

"*No. No more than a log cabin would be called alive, I think. But . . .*"

"It smells like a forest," Freitz observed in audible fascination. "*Like the forest just after the rain. The air feels humid.*"

"*Chief, I'm not seeing any other exits from this room,*" Siri reported. "*That would make it easier to secure, but it would seem our door may have led us nowhere.*"

"Or it could be we do not know where to look," she answered. "Sensor techs, can you determine the thickness of that substance?"

"*Not from the passive scans,*" reported Littlefield, "*but give us a moment.*" The scanners were already collecting and analyzing low-level data about the chamber, but for some things a more intensive scan was needed.

"Freitz," Littlefield said, "let's do a coordinated gamma burst on the right wall."

Marette watched through Alberto's view as the other two techs turned their scanners. A moment later there was a change.

"*Look at that,*" Freitz whispered.

Like the still surface of a pond broken by a child's stone throw, the previously solid wall began to react, rippling out from where the scanners were concentrated. The ripples grew in size in less than a second, and the black substance withdrew with them.

"Littlefield, Freitz: terminate the burst."

Both techs acknowledged Marette's order, but still the inky tar withdrew soundlessly. Behind it was a material visually identical to the outer hull. The black over-coating retreated to reveal almost half a meter of the grey metal, and then, before Marette could tell it had stopped, it began to reseal the bare area.

"*Looks to be just under four centimeters thick, ma'am,*" Littlefield said. "*Though that wasn't how I expected to find out. Given what we just saw, I'd say you're right about hidden doorways.*"

"Sweep the walls," she said. "Find them."

The techs traced the gamma bursts along the walls, parting the strange black substance in their wake. Marette wondered at the purpose of the inky quasi-solid and how difficult it would be to collect a sample. Once Freitz's helmet was replaced, that would be their first task.

"*Ma'am, I think I've got something. It might be another door.*"

Before Marette could switch to Freitz's camera, another voice broke through. "*It's moving! At the end of the chamber!*' Marette looked. At the far end of the chamber the black covering was indeed rolling back—but differently than before.

"Sensor techs, is anyone scanning that area?" The reports came back negative as she observed the opening. It moved faster than the others, but even more unique was that it was retreating in rectangular form. By the time she heard Siri order the weapon techs to form up, it had opened two meters wide and was on its way to reaching the ceiling.

"Is that opening to a door?" By the time she finished the question, it had been answered. The black had withdrawn up to the ceiling and the grey metal behind it was swiftly sliding away.

"Stay back, Alberto," she said on the private channel. As she finished the words, the door had opened completely. For a moment the chamber beyond was just as black.

And then it came out.

Marette watched the metallic object float out to the team. It looked like nothing so much as an upturned porcupine; thick protrusions and bristles covered the rounded bottom while the top was smoother and flatter, though slightly concave. It made its way into the chamber and then stopped five meters from the team, where the top began to glow a dull red.

"*Somebody want to tell me what that is?*" Siri ordered.

"*Working on it, sir.*"

Light flared from a lance of lightning-like energy suddenly connecting the object and the floor. Less than a second later, it swung up towards the team. The video feed was lost instantly. It wasn't until a few seconds later that the screaming stopped.

X

ROMULUS NUDGED a broken bottle with his foot as he and Felix waited and watched in the alley.

"Stubborn, isn't he?" Felix said after they had stood awhile.

"The cultist?" Romulus shrugged. "I don't know. He seemed willing to talk after a bit, I guess. Though it wasn't what we needed." He looked up at where the Moon hung over the alley. "He's more evasive than stubborn," he added absently.

Felix made what might have been a chuckle. "I was talking about Diomedes, actually."

"He does what he has to do, I guess." *And he does it right.* He was still thinking about whether he was somehow to blame for the gas not working. So far as he could tell, he'd done it correctly. Had he thrown it wrong? Had he somehow given an accidental warning? His attacker should have been unconscious. As it was, Romulus had nearly gotten killed, and would have been if Diomedes hadn't . . .

He left the thought unfinished and brushed his fingertips across his cheek, checking them for blood.

"Flynn?" he heard Felix say.

"Hmm?"

"I asked how long you've known him," said Felix.

Romulus drew a blank. "Known who?"

"Diomedes."

"Oh." Romulus glanced about for any sign of trouble and then, after a quick calculation, responded with, "Ten years, off and on."

Had it really been that long? Diomedes had left the farm for his own adventures when Romulus was nearly sixteen and had been out of contact for most of the time after. From the little information Romulus had managed to get from him after their reunion, he had first spent time in the military, although Diomedes wouldn't say which branch or for how long. Wherever it was, the experience had trained him well.

"Something bothering you, Flynn?"

Romulus turned to the smaller man at the question. Felix was looking up at the Moon as well, but turned to meet his gaze.

Romulus opened his mouth to say something, at least to vent— to a man he had only recently met, and someone whom Diomedes had warned him about talking to. "Ah," he said, shaking his head. "It's nothing."

"You just seemed a little distant there."

Romulus looked towards the darker end of the alley. "Just thinking."

"Well, thinking is good. What about?"

Again Romulus glanced at Felix. The man met his gaze quietly, an expectant look in his eye. What good would it do to tell him? Felix wasn't there. He wouldn't be able to tell him what he'd done wrong. Romulus looked away to the floater, to where Diomedes interrogated the cultist behind tinted windows.

He needed to talk through it with *somebody.*

"I was just trying to make sense of those things that cultist told us," he lied. "What it means. Or if he just made it up."

"Did sound a bit ridiculous, didn't it?" Felix said. "He seemed to know a bit of scripture, though. Do you know the Bible well?"

"Just the basics. What did he say?"

"That 'upon the coming of The One Who Will Be, men will seek death, but will not find it. They will long to die, but death will elude them.' That's a great deal like Revelations 9:6."

"Sounds like you read it a lot," Romulus said.

"Not as often as you'd think. Though I do like what it has to say on the nature of love. But mainly I just have a spectacularly good memory."

"All right, so he quotes the Bible, that doesn't make him a prophet."

"No," Felix said. He stretched. "But not everyone makes the best choices when deciding who to follow. Sometimes . . . sometimes the words that have rung true in the past can influence someone's judgment in a time of weakness."

What exactly was Felix trying to say? "So he added that part in to, what, try to influence us?"

"Maybe. Or maybe he was just repeating what his 'One Who Sees' told him. Not much is really known about the Nosferatu. Mostly people just let them be, since no one really cares to try to find out much. From what I've heard it's safer not to. This is the first I've heard of the One Who Sees."

"So do you believe it?"

"The prophecy or just that he exists?"

Romulus shrugged and watched a rat scamper across the alley. "Both."

"I don't think I have enough information. I wouldn't rule it out. But I'd be more inclined to believe in the existence of the One Who Sees than the total truth of him, or that prophecy." Felix looked at him. "For the moment, anyway," he added with a grin.

"Well it's not a help to us," Romulus decided aloud. "We might as well forget it."

"I didn't say it wasn't interesting," Felix said. "I'd be glad to find out more. Maybe after we get the job done I'll venture down into those tunnels myself," he said cheerfully.

The wave of guilt covered Romulus again at the mention of the tunnels. It couldn't have been entirely his fault, right? There were too many other factors, but he still had a lot to learn and no real clue what they might be. Geez, maybe he should mention it to Felix.

"Doesn't look like you much liked it down there," he heard Felix say.

"No," Romulus admitted. "Er, well, no. I mean, it felt good—exciting—the searching I mean. Like we were making some progress."

"But?"

"But . . . " Possible words flashed in his mind. "But it was a little cramped. And, the smell wasn't the best." A tiny lump formed in his throat. Maybe he shouldn't bring up his trouble. Diomedes had told him not to say too much, after all. Change the subject. "Who's Wallace?" he asked.

Felix seemed to pause just a moment. "Diomedes hasn't told you?"

"I don't know everything about him."

"Indeed," was the reply, more a statement than a question. "I can tell you who he is, but as for specific details of what happened, those are facts that escape me, too."

"What happened with what?"

"Wallace—Ken Wallace is his full name—is a V.P. for Raven Defense Technologies, and not the sort of person you'd call completely legit.

From what I can tell, he's handled a few of the company's more shadowy dealings. Industrial espionage, a little Wall Street-style extortion. Did you hear about those black market tac-impers who were murdered a few months ago?"

Romulus nodded. Dealers in cybernetic tactical weapons implants. He remembered hearing something about three men, whom CPMC had reported as black marketeers in the trade, all being found dead within a week. From what he remembered, it was thought to be from their own treachery.

"I've heard some indication that it was RavenTech who hired the freelancers who were behind it, taking out their competition and retaliating for the theft of their property. And that possibly Wallace had a hand in it."

"Head of the dirty tricks division, it sounds like."

"Not the head—I don't think—but from what I hear he's demonstrated quite the knack. If he were the head, I doubt Diomedes would be nearly as calm. Dio got mixed up in something with Wallace. I don't know the intimate details. Wallace screwed over your roommate and nearly got him killed. Or he tried to kill him. One of the two. Probably the latter given some things I know, and the fact that my source says Dio swore revenge—something Wallace surely isn't too happy with."

Romulus wondered if that might be the reason his mentor was so bristled. He remembered Diomedes disappearing a few weeks ago for a short period, and being in a silent rage when he resurfaced. "When did this happen?"

"A little under a month ago. Though I only got wind of it a week ago myself."

Romulus nodded but realized that aside from the immediate rage, his mentor's demeanor hadn't changed remarkably from before his disappearance. "Who told you about it?" He lived with Diomedes and he hadn't heard of him swearing revenge on Wallace, or even mentioning the name until now. Curiosity tugged at him.

"How about a trade? I'll tell you that if you answer something for me."

Romulus once again heard his mentor's warning in his head. "Answer what?"

"What happened to Ranth?"

The warnings turned to alarms. "What, so you can sell us out to the rest of them?" Romulus belatedly thought of grabbing the man by the neck, but it seemed too late for that. Diomedes would have had Felix against the wall before saying a word.

Felix regarded him calmly. Was that disappointment? "Because something's been bothering you since you came back out of that hole. I just . . . want to know. That's all. I give you my word it won't go beyond me, and I hold my word sacred."

Their eyes locked for a moment as Romulus wrestled with the decision. Felix spoke before he could. "C'mon, if I'm lying you can beat me to a bloody pulp. Or tie me up and force me to listen to country music," he finished with a wink.

"You don't like country?"

"Absolutely abhor the stuff." The man's smile faded into a somber look of listening.

"Diomedes shot him." The words left his mouth before he'd known he would say them. "He had to," he added, looking at where the floater rocked slightly. "He saved my life."

Romulus watched the ground, waiting for Felix to make a comment, but the man was silent. After a moment Romulus continued. "We—I— gassed the room before we entered, and I was the first in. It looked like he was down but either he was only stunned or he was faking because as soon as Diomedes followed and I turned, he was on me. Then the one we captured," Romulus realized for the first time that they never asked his name, "jumped Diomedes, but he was able to pull him off quick enough. I couldn't do the same to mine—to Ranth." The words were spilling from him now. "He was about to slash my throat when Diomedes saved me. He—he died instantly. I think."

Romulus's mind suddenly became blank but for a single question, the question that had burned in his mind for the past half hour, the question that now somehow seemed terribly foolish as he prepared to speak it aloud. While he hesitated, Felix beat him to it.

"You're wondering if you threw the grenade wrong."

Romulus nodded. "Stupid, huh?"

"Was there gas?"

"Yes?"

"Either a grenade goes off or it doesn't. Yours went off."

"I still could have done it wrong. The wrong placement, the wrong timing. Or something else I don't know."

"Did the gas fill the room?"

"It looked like it but he wasn't affected, filled or not."

"Well then that's hardly your fault, I'd say," Felix said.

"But what if I—"

Felix cut him off. "Flynn, you seem to be determined to find fault with yourself. Questioning your own thoughts and actions is healthy, up to a point. But take it to the point where you're banging your head against the wall, and you're going to drive yourself nuts. And let me tell you, I'm plenty bonkers for the both of us." Felix smiled. "You said it stunk down there right?"

The abrupt question caught Romulus off guard. "Yeah, it's a sewer," he said in a tone that was more annoyed than he had intended.

"Imagine living down there like they do. Don't you suppose you'd want to find a way to avoid smelling that?"

"Um," Romulus replied before he saw what the man might be getting at. "Are you talking about nasal filters?" He hadn't considered it before, but it did make sense. Nasal implants helped to filter out the pollution of the city and certain noxious gases. They certainly could have been at least partially effective against the gas, and they were cheap and self-installable.

"It's certainly a possibility," said Felix. "And as I said before, possibilities are our friends!"

Romulus nodded, realizing his mind was put to rest, slightly. Though . . . "I still wish he hadn't died."

For a moment Felix said nothing and glanced up at the Moon. "Good."

Another moment of silence passed. Somewhere beyond the alley a chorus of drunken voices rose suddenly and then faded away.

"It's your turn to answer my question," said Romulus.

Felix chuckled but before he could respond further, the floater's engines started with a whine and the door slid open. The reporter whose name Romulus had been too preoccupied to remember stepped out with the body of the Nosferatu a moment later.

"Your friend says we're leaving," the reporter told them. He laid the body against the alley wall. Romulus looked at the silent figure as he and Felix moved to the door. "He's still alive."

With a relief that surprised him, Romulus nodded and closed the door, once again taking the front seat near his mentor.

XI

IT WAS HALF past ten beneath the light of the evening moon, and people moved with quiet purpose throughout the streets of the corporate district. Some were leaving their offices for home, or maybe a night on the town. Others were simply stepping out of the skyscrapers that lined the streets for a quick bite of food before continuing to work into the night. Regardless of their purpose, the companies in control of the district would keep them safe from the assorted populace usually found on the streets: muggers, winos, gangs, and the general homeless who were too lazy and weak to better their lives. These were problems that plagued the rest of the city; there was no place for them here. Corporate security kept a close watch on those who entered the semi-privately owned district, and cameras stood in a comforting vigil above.

From his apartment on the other side of the city, Marc Triton "borrowed" access to one of the cameras and slowly panned it across the multitude of faces on the sidewalk below. A great many of them, he knew, were good, kind-hearted people, no more responsible for the corporations' cold, compassionless ideology than pebbles were responsible for an avalanche. They had families to feed, rent to pay, and they could hardly be blamed for wanting to be safe. But the upper echelon, those in the towers who molded the corporate polices and secret mission statements—Marc had long ago decided that they played a large part in causing the very conditions they kept out by force. A number of corporations commanded more resources than some governments; their influence on the world and its inhabitants could be argued by only the most foolish of people. Even without their bribes and connections to government regulators, they could hardly be considered to be taking responsibility for the consequences of their actions beyond the standard public relations smokescreens designed to keep the average person from speaking out.

Marc frowned and tried to concentrate on his search. A group of people stood patiently at a crosswalk, waiting for the light to change. Though their corporate ID badges made them less likely to be the man he was seeking, he checked each face. None were a match. He zoomed out and moved on.

When he had satisfied himself as much as possible that the object of his search was not within sight, Marc allowed the camera to return to its automated sequence and sent after it a minor worm designed to erase any records of his presence. Waiting for it to accomplish its task, Marc chafed at his inability to use more than one camera at a time. While it was easy enough, if meticulous, to access a single camera without being detected, security countermeasures made using two or three too complex and too risky, let alone trying to use them all at once. His fellows at the AoA were working with him on finding a way to do so, but at the moment, a solution was a ways off.

Marc leaned back in his chair, drained the last of the root beer in his glass and looked over at the remnants of the pizza in the box on his coffee table. If he had another piece, he'd regret it before he could finish it. Instead, he popped a Lifesaver into his mouth and stood up, rubbing his temples. This was not how he had wanted to spend his evening.

He believed in his purpose, of course. If the man from ESA was truly planning to betray his own organization and sell the secrets of the Space Agency's discovery, Marc's group needed to know. Intelligence, information—those were the keys. The AoA needed to know what the ESA mole was up to before they could decide how best to act. If it turned out to be a false alarm, calling attention to him could lead to the AoA's own exposure, but if the man truly meant to compromise the security of future secrets, it would need to be determined just how much damage he might cause. The AoA was considering putting the project on hold if security could not be guaranteed. It was a threat they needed to contain.

Unfortunately, the tail that had followed the mole into Northgate had lost him at the airport due to a stupid mistake. Had that not occurred, Marc would have had a fix on the mole hours ago and could now be tracking his movements. As it was, Marc needed to spend his time instead in the effort to find him again, and locating one man in the entire city wasn't much better than trying to find the proverbial needle in the haystack. What was it Felix had said once? "The likelihood of anyone ever actually dropping a needle in a haystack, much less wanting to find one, is incredibly small." Good for a chuckle, but not all that helpful. There were so many faces to check, and no real way to check them all. He could record the footage and view it all back later, but by then it wouldn't matter. Marc made a mental note to work more on the minor artificial intelligence he was constructing. He could have used an A.I.'s help here.

Cramped from sitting at his desk so long, Marc lay down on the couch and linked the computer into the data visor that he habitually wore over his eyes. The interface was a bit awkward, but he needed to stretch out. He pushed a pillow under his head and settled down into the cushion. Much better.

He returned to the search, unable to resist glancing at the time once more. Even if he did find the man, it would probably be too late. The AoA suspected there would be a middleman. Such a meeting had most likely already taken place, which meant it was no longer possible to trace the middleman to the person or persons that were to finally be contacted. As the minutes passed, it became less and less likely that he would have a hint of the man's purpose tonight.

They were not without recourse, however. Eventually, it would be known whom he'd contacted, middleman or not. There were too many ears listening. Just as they'd discovered the mole's intention to approach an outsider, so too would they discover the identity of the person he approached. Marc was sure steps were already being taken. *Plan for the worst to prepare for the best.*

Marc accessed a camera over a section of downtown where crowds moved among the popular bars and clubs. At this point he was just hoping to get lucky, and the more faces he could scan, the better his odds. From what he understood, his target was not the most social of men. He was more likely to be holed up wherever he was staying than out on the town, but perhaps the lure of the active urban nightlife would draw him out. At this point it was Marc's only hope. The local hotel registers couldn't be checked—or rather they could, but it would be a time-consuming process with even less hope of a lead. The man had used a false name for his airline tickets and would be certain to use another for hotel reservations—if indeed he was even staying in a hotel. The man was already cautious, and it was imperative he not know he was being followed, to say nothing of who was following him.

An unmarked floater crossed in front of the camera, obviously privately owned and most likely not his target. And yet, for a reason whose origins he couldn't pinpoint, Marc couldn't help but feel he should follow it. The hunch was more than he'd had for most of the evening. As quickly as he could, Marc disengaged the current camera, covered his tracks, and then accessed the next one along the floater's course. It continued on and turned. Again Marc switched cameras, feeling a growing concern that he would lose it, despite not having any cognizable reason to be following it in the first place. He got the next camera in time to see the floater disappear from view. There was no time to make the switch to the next. Gambling it would continue on the same course, he skipped ahead to a camera farther down. A moment later the vehicle passed by, turned a corner and began descending.

Marc switched to what he suspected would be the last camera for the moment. It gave him a view of the front of the Northgate Municipal Justice Tower. He panned the camera and then spotted the floater coming to rest in a spot across the street from the building, nearly directly beneath his viewpoint. As it sat there silent, its doors still sealed, Marc briefly let himself believe that he had found his man. It was unlikely, of course. His inexplicable feeling that something important was inside was most likely just a product of his need for some relief from the frustration born of a night spent in a fruitless search.

The door opened. He readied himself for disappointment.

The man's hair was red, and therefore not the man he wanted, but he was not alone. He stood by the open doorway speaking to someone inside. Marc scowled and found another camera. The streets around the justice building boasted more than most areas. Now watching from one on the building itself, lower to the ground, he zoomed in to see if he could discern any of the occupants.

Two figures sat in the front. Before he could get a clear look at their faces, another man stepped out from the back. Something was familiar about him, but he turned to the pilot before he could see his face. Still, it looked like it might be . . .

Marc chuckled. It was.

Felix Hiatt.

Marc could make him out clearly now as Felix looked across at the tower. Well, speak of the devil. For a brief moment he entertained the thought of calling Felix just for kicks, but he dismissed the idea. Not before he could learn more about the two still-unknown figures with him. Unlikely as it was, Felix might very well be the middleman for all he knew, and letting the others know they were being watched could be catastrophic.

Marc tried to zoom in a bit further. Getting as close a shot of the two figures as he could, he captured the image and then enhanced the frame to extrapolate whatever facial details he could from the low resolution. In a few seconds he had a clear enough picture to find that both men struck a familiar chord with him, though Marc couldn't recall anything specific. Neither was connected to the ESA mole, however, that much he did know. What were they doing with Felix? Marc decided to check on it later, if he had time.

The sight of Felix had Marc considering asking him to keep his eyes open. He toyed with the idea briefly, but then set it aside. Felix Hiatt wasn't AoA anymore, and while he could be trusted to keep their existence secret, Marc doubted that using him as a resource would be looked upon favorably. Perhaps later.

With a quick glance up at the Moon hanging promisingly in the sky, Marc resumed his search.

XII

THE MUNICIPAL JUSTICE TOWER rose out of the street to dwarf the buildings surrounding it. The actual tower was a dark slab of glass and metal some thirty stories tall, built upon an older stone building spread out along the base. The latter's Romanesque features merged with the tower in an eclectic combination of twenty-first century architectural style. Contained within were courts, the central precinct of the Northgate Police Department, crime labs, a high-security holding facility, a host of legal offices, and sitting near the very top, the local and regional headquarters of Cybernetic Psychoses Monitoring and Control.

Brian chuckled to himself at the audacity of blatantly jaywalking in front of the building that was the center of the city's police activity. Perhaps audacity was too strong a word. He very much doubted that officers would descend upon him and Felix. Then again they might, just as a matter of principle. With the growing crime rate and a public police force so underfunded that it only concentrated on crimes against actual verified taxpayers, the income from easy jaywalking citations might sound welcome. He increased his pace, just to be sure.

"So what did Diomedes say to you in there?" Felix asked as he stepped quickly up onto the sidewalk from behind.

"Rather blunt, aren't you?" Brian answered. Was it that apparent that he'd been spooked?

"Just asking. I figure he must've said something to you, or I don't know him as well as I think I do."

They were approaching the entry to the building. Brian didn't want to go into detail at the moment. "He just asked a bit about me — who I was and such — while he waited for the Nosferatu to wake up." Brian remembered the look in the freelancer's eyes saying much more than his words. "I'm pretty sure he knows about the interview. Or at least suspects. I wish you'd told him about it already so he doesn't think we're tricking him."

"What did he say?"

Brian found his eyes rolling. He didn't want to try to explain. Gut feelings, in his experience, were usually non-transferable. "He didn't *say* anything specifically beyond telling me that I had better stay out of his way, you know? Haven't you ever had a gut feeling?"

"Sometimes," Felix said. They passed through the front doors. "But that's a standard greeting for Diomedes. I wouldn't read too much into it."

Brian scowled as they stopped at the security checkpoint inside the entrance. It had to be obvious to the freelancer that Brian had his own reasons for helping. Diomedes must be suspicious of what was in it for Brian. Brian certainly would be, were the situation reversed.

But there was little point in trying to explain that now as he stood waiting, his body being scanned for dangerous cybernetics, with every bit of information no doubt being recorded by CPMC above. He checked his taser, signed in, and then moved past the checkpoint to wait for Felix.

"So you'll wait for me back here?" Brian asked him when he came through.

Felix nodded. "Yeah, or in the floater. It shouldn't take you more than twenty or thirty minutes to get your request processed."

"I have done this before, you know."

In an effort to put to good use some of the info Brian had on possible cybernetics used in the alleged attacks, they had decided to request a list of installs for the past year. The information was public domain, but because of CPMC regulations it had to be retrieved through face-to-face request. Brian had his doubts about how useful the list would be to them. It was primarily assembled from legal, legitimate installs, and the wacko they were looking for was likely to have at least some black market tech in him. The only time black-tech was on the list was if the buyer was already busted or if the installer was caught, and very few of them kept records. It was still worth checking out, of course, and it was more comfortable than sitting in a dark alley.

"So what're you doing while I'm getting the list?" Brian asked, eyeing the elevators across the sparsely populated lobby.

Felix removed his shades and looked around, giving the appearance of thought. "I'm not sure yet. Maybe look for some donuts. I haven't eaten much today." The man grinned.

"Ah. Not going to tell me."

Felix chuckled. "I'd tell you if I knew myself! I'm going to poke around a bit, see what turns up. Get going. I'll meet you back here when you're done and let you know what I've got."

Brian shrugged, realizing he didn't have much to say to that. He wished Felix luck and turned for the elevators.

*   *   *

Tall buildings had always impressed Romulus. He stared from inside the floater up at the blinking lights atop the Justice Tower and wondered why that might be. For most of his life, he had only seen them in pictures, and on the few occasions he'd been to a large city and seen them up close, they had filled him with such awe. They were so much bigger than what he was used to; surely that was part of it. Maybe it was just the inconceivability of how such a thing could be built and what it must take to construct and fill such a behemoth.

More often than not, though, it wasn't the base or the sides of the building that he'd stare at, but the top. Who or what was up there? Why? How had they earned the marvel of engineering beneath them? Romulus tried to imagine what it would be like to earn such a high place himself. Was that desire born of his fascination, or vice-versa?

Suddenly feeling juvenile for staring up at a building, he leaned back in his seat to watch Felix and his reporter friend climb the steps to the tower. He didn't quite know what to think of Brian yet. So far, he wasn't sure he liked him.

"Diomedes, what do you think of Brian?"

"He's nothing," was the delayed reply. "He won't get in the way if he knows what's good for him."

Romulus was surprised to find his mentor sounding less suspicious than he was himself. "How do you know?"

Diomedes watched Felix and Brian disappear into the tower and then turned to look at him. "You can tell a lot about someone by how they respond to threats."

Before Romulus could ask what Diomedes had said to the reporter, his mentor sat back and spoke again. "We're not waiting long for them. Too many cops here."

Unsure of how to respond, Romulus sat back himself.

Would Brian be able to help them? Their first lead had so far turned up very little. Diomedes and Brian had gotten nothing more from the Nosferatu. Though Romulus was sure that some measure of force was used in the questioning, Diomedes wasn't terribly descriptive about what they had asked, and Brian seemed unwilling to say much either. It was a fact for which he was sorry but a fact that he also supposed couldn't be helped. If Diomedes had taught him one thing it was that verbal persuasion could only take you so far. Beyond that, you had to back it up with force or it was all a bluff.

Diomedes hadn't killed the Nosferatu, Romulus reminded himself. It was foolish for Felix to think he would have, really. The cultist didn't look terribly well when Brian had brought him out, but then he didn't look terribly well to start with either. Who knows how bad of a condition he was in before he jumped Diomedes?

So about all they had discovered was that, in all likelihood, the man they were looking for wasn't a Nosferatu. Unless he was a Nosferatu gone rogue, though somehow that didn't seem to make much sense. They did have the few leads about the arsons though, and maybe that would get them somewhere. They knew the fires were probably intentional. Maybe Felix's contact at the fire department would know more about that—especially the arsonist's reason for picking their apartment in particular. He decided he'd have to tell Felix to check with that contact again when he returned, though it was getting late.

"Diomedes, where are we going to sleep?" he asked.

"In here. Easy to defend."

Romulus nodded to his mentor, though he didn't particularly relish the idea. Their apartment was far from perfect, but at least it was a building. What reason could there be for burning it? It was old and worthless. It probably would have fallen apart by itself anyway.

Insurance? He scowled. Why would a psycho vigilante care about insurance? Had someone been inside? Though that still didn't explain the warehouses. It occurred to him that he was trying to second-guess the thoughts of a probable madman. All Romulus knew was that he wanted to stop him before he did more damage, before he destroyed anyone else's home. But how the hell were they supposed to find him?

Questions weighed upon his thoughts, yet all he could do now was sit and wait.

* * *

Felix had never been satisfied with his level of penetration into the city's police force. While there were a handful of beat cops with whom he was on a first-name basis—and only some of those amicably so—he had yet to establish a positive relationship with anyone in a substantial position of knowledge. He knew the names of a few detectives who had nothing against bribery, of course, but he preferred to keep his costs to a minimum. Besides, those detectives weren't likely to put out any extra effort to discover anything for him that they didn't already know, even in the event that they had the necessary resources. Any effort at developing something more had, so far, always been doomed to fail.

Felix blamed this on some manner of witch's curse. He didn't believe it for a moment, but it made him chuckle, so there was, at least, that.

If he did have a good friend on the force, he wondered just how much attention they would have given to someone with the vigilante's M.O. As far as popular rumor went, he'd kept his victims to gangers and the like. No upstanding, "tax-paying" citizens. Public opinion of the Northgate Police Department was low enough without them standing up for those most people considered to be street scum.

On the other hand, if the police did know anything, Felix thought he might still know someone who would possibly be of a mind to help him.

If she was in a good mood.

And if the stars were aligned just right.

Northgate Police Department's Captain Abigail Brittan was heavily rooted in forensics, but that was only part of the reason for Felix going to see her. He also knew the secret of the group for whom she really worked, and they, in turn, knew him.

He sat and waited where he was asked, deciding that the middle of the Municipal Justice Building wasn't the prime place to try anything more amusing. He considered himself lucky both that she was working this late and that she hadn't sent word for him to be escorted out when she was notified of his request to see her. How long she would make him wait was another matter.

As it turned out, it was only fifteen minutes. Abigail Brittan was a tall woman with a face that was normally stern and somber, and it was beginning to show the stress of her career despite her relative youth. Her hair, cropped and mostly brown, showed a hint of gray at the roots. She did not greet him with a smile.

"Mr. Hiatt," she said in a tone that was forcibly formal. "I'm told you wish to see me. Keep it short." Brittan motioned to a chair.

"Thanks for seeing me, Abigail." Felix began to close the door.

"Captain Brittan, please," she corrected. "And leave the door open." Felix felt that curse reaching for him again. "What sort of information do you need this time?"

He chuckled. "Am I that predictable?"

"Quite frankly, yes. You have been asking for privileged information on the few occasions we've met."

"Unprivileged information's so dull. And it is a favor I am perfectly willing to return, you know."

"I doubt you could tell me anything I couldn't find out through my own sources. I've never consented to give you anything, Mr. Hiatt. One wonders why you keep asking."

Felix shrugged. "Call me a squeaky wheel. One wonders why you keep agreeing to see me."

The captain paused for just long enough to glance behind Felix at the open office door. "Because I know you're a friend of the AoA," she replied, mentioning the name of her true allegiance, "and I think, one rare day, you may have something to say that's worth listening to. But I'm sure you know that. Now, you've already taken a minute of my time. Why don't you tell me what you need so I can tell you no and we can get this visit over quickly."

Brittan had never been terribly friendly to him, but tonight she seemed even shorter than usual. He opted for the direct approach.

"I'm looking for the vigilante who's rumored to be out there. Some have dubbed him 'Wraith.'"

She nodded. "The alleged gang-slayer. I've heard of him."

"At the risk of being blunt, can you tell me what you know?"

"No."

"So there's no formal investigation?"

"You seem to be under the impression that we've got the resources to track down every single inter-ganger crime. Things are spread thin enough just trying to protect the law-abiding, to say nothing of trying to keep the gangs from clashing."

"So there's no investigation. The police haven't discovered anything."

"I didn't say that," Brittan said. "They may or may not have, but it's not a matter to be discussed with the public at this time."

"Not with anyone?"

"That's the current policy, yes."

"And is it a matter to be discussed with," Felix paused to consider how to best hint at her secret loyalties, "other non-police groups?"

"I don't see what that has to do with it."

Felix lowered his voice. "I just don't see how you can be willing to violate policy in one way and not another."

Captain Brittan leaned forward over her desk. Felix noticed her hand moving to cover the Palladium symbol on her watch as she did so and wondered if it was intentional. Her eyes locked onto his. "That's hardly the same thing."

"It used to be," he said. *Come on, I was one of you, once.*

"Yes. And just why *did* you leave the AoA, Felix Hiatt?"

"I had my reasons."

"It seems we both are withholding information, then."

"Yes, but I *want* the information I asked for. I doubt you care one way or the other about what you asked."

"No argument there. Now perhaps you'd care to leave?"

"You're not going to tell me a thing."

"I'm sorry." It was more polite than sincere.

"Not even to help stop an arsonist who's blown up a tenement?"

She cocked her head, eyebrows raised. "Where did you hear this?"

"I have my sources."

"Are they accurate?"

Felix sighed. In the long run it did not pay to lie to this woman. "Jury's still out on that. If it's true and you give me information that helps, you have my word that I'll tell you what I turn up." Felix watched her glance at the open door again. It was an uncomfortable silence. "Please, Captain. We both know policy isn't a thing you take completely seriously." Felix winced internally, knowing even as he said the words that she wouldn't take them well.

The captain bristled. Any trace of listening in her expression vanished. "On the contrary, Mr. Hiatt, I take it *very* seriously. Your time is up. I have nothing more to say."

Felix stood and wondered if he could maintain his balance with a foot in his mouth. "I'm sorry," he said and left it at that, opting for a quick retreat from the office.

* * *

Romulus stood by a public Web link across the street from the Justice Tower, feeling conspicuous. After Diomedes had left, he'd spent the first five minutes on the link searching idly through the news sites for anything of interest about the arsons or the man they were looking for. When his time ran out he had found next to nothing useful. He had decided not to waste any more of his money and so had spent the time since standing around, alert and waiting. It must have been about fifteen minutes until he caught sight of Felix and Brian heading down the steps of the building, the former carrying a small paper bag. He waved until they saw him.

"What happened to the floater?" the reporter asked when the two men reached him.

"Dio abandon you here, Flynn?" Felix asked.

Romulus shook his head. "No, he just had to leave for a bit. He told me to stay here and wait for you to come back."

Brian rolled his eyes. "Nice of him to tell us that before we went in."

"He didn't want to wait around here is all. He'll be back soon to check for us."

Felix nodded and looked skyward. "He doesn't like being around police."

"Eh? Why, what's he done?" Brian asked.

Felix glanced at Romulus a moment before smiling to the reporter. "I'll let you ask him that yourself." Brian only grunted.

"Anyway," Romulus continued, "he said he'd come back and check for you every twenty minutes, and that was just about twenty minutes ago, I think." A moment of silence passed. "So did you find anything?"

"I got the local install list, though I'm not thrilled about sifting through it," Brian told them.

"I did some poking around to try to see if the police knew anything. Didn't have much time, though, and people were rather tight-lipped. About the only thing I found out is that they aren't commenting on it to the public at all, which doesn't allow us to draw too many conclusions, I'm afraid. I do have slight reason to think that they hadn't connected our vigilante with the arsons yet." He glanced at Brian. "But that's only a . . . gut feeling."

"Who'd you talk to?" Romulus asked. If the man did know as much as Diomedes had implied, Romulus couldn't help but wonder at how he found it all out, or how he found the people to talk to.

"No one in particular. Oh!" Felix opened the paper bag. "Want a donut?"

The sound of a floater approaching above distracted Romulus from his answer. The group moved back as the weighty hulk set down beside them. Romulus quickly opened the door and entered the vehicle. He moved to the passenger seat beside his mentor while Felix and Brian repeated to Diomedes what they had told him. Romulus did note that the complaining reporter mentioned nothing about Diomedes's temporary absence. Felix may have simply beaten him to it, however.

"Had to take off for a bit, did you?" he asked, taking his seat.

Diomedes re-powered the engines. "Being careful,"

"Ah, yes, you're always careful. I nearly forgot. Incidentally, where *did* you get this floater?"

"We'll land a few blocks over," the freelancer said. "Then we decide what's next."

Romulus watched out the window as they rose. Three police cars ejected from the building up the block with sirens flashing and raced up the road away from them. He did wonder where the floater came from.

"So I'm to understand," said Felix, "that no one, *at all*, wants a donut?"

XIII

"**HAVE YOU GOT** the money?"

The fat man was sweating, though less from nervousness than the heat of his own bulk, given his otherwise calm exterior. He waited, one eyebrow arched, for an answer to his question.

Before giving one, Raven Defense Technologies Vice-President Ken Wallace took a drink and glanced around the bar. A few customers in suits and dresses engaged in private conversation in the plush leather seats and polished wood tables scattered about the place. Light jazz piano floated in the air with the soft haze of cigarette smoke that filtered the lights of the city hundreds of feet below. He set the drink down. "Is it verified?" he asked the fat man.

"Is what verified?"

"That it is what they suspect it is," the other said. "Has it been verified?"

"Have you got the money?" the fat man repeated.

Wallace smiled. "You can tell your contact that the money is being acquired. I have more than half already. Getting the rest is a paltry matter of, shall we say, finesse. He'll have it, when it's time, provided there is something there worth paying for. So again I ask, has it been verified?"

"Not yet, from what he tells me. But he wants you to know they're close. I'm supposed to contact you with a yes or no to that tomorrow. But he needs to know tonight if you're in, and if you have the money. Otherwise it's not worth him sticking his arse in the fire." The fat man snorted.

"You can assure him I'm in, if the find is what they suspect," Wallace told him. "If I find out tomorrow that it isn't, the whole thing is off."

"Of course," the fat man said. "He also wanted me to remind you of the consequences of backing out once whatever this is has begun. Or of not having the money."

Wallace smiled and lifted his glass once more. "Ah, yes," he chuckled before sipping. "The required veiled threat. It's good to hear. Assures me he's on the level."

The fat man grinned. "You have an interesting way of thinking, laddie."

"I'm sure he's given you the same threat?"

The fat man snickered. "You realize I have no solid idea of what the hell the two of you are dealing about. He only tells me what to ask of you and what he thinks I need to know."

"Language, sir," Wallace scolded. "This is a class establishment."

"All I know is it's a damn big secret. He doesn't use details when he talks to me, and he chose me because I don't ask questions."

Wallace said nothing for a moment, sure that this corpulent middleman must have figured out a few details on his own, or had made at least a few guesses. Whether or not the fat man knew his contact was from ESA would certainly indicate how much he might have guessed. Wallace had not expected to deal with a go-between. The ESA contact must be more worried about being traced than dealing with the loose ends the fat man would create. Wallace had, after all, never actually met him. Loose ends could always be tied up, one way or another. "So you'll contact me tomorrow?"

The fat man nodded.

Wallace downed the last of his scotch and stood. "Then it appears we're finished. I look forward to a confirmation."

The fat man pulled out a cigarette and lit it in one complete, practiced motion. "And I'll relay your commitment to my employer."

Wallace looked down at the other from his full height as he pulled on his overcoat. "Good evening. And enjoy your cigarette here awhile longer." With that, he turned his back on the man and moved for the elevator. Moments later, the elevator doors slid closed and he was on his way to the parking level far below.

The fat man, with his poorly-tailored suit and UK accent, was a loose end. This was truer for his contact than for himself, but still a worry. Yet now that he was fully committed, Wallace had more pressing concerns.

His plan for getting the money had nearly come to fruition. Nearly. It was even more vital now that things resolve themselves as planned, unless the entire deal was based on a false assumption. He thought to himself that he might be more surprised if the verification *did* come, though he hoped for such a surprise. Besides the obvious financial and career benefits to him if it did, he had already set risky events in motion to acquire the capital—events that he would prefer to be worth the danger.

The elevator opened. Wallace walked the short distance to a waiting limousine whose door opened for him automatically.

"Good evening again, sir," said his driver in greeting as the door closed behind him. "Where may I take you?"

Wallace was tired. Sleep would be welcome, but he had a few loose ends of his own to check on. "Head for the docks," he ordered after a moment.

The limousine headed into the city.

XIV

THE SOUND of a floater passed overhead. Romulus woke with a start, thrown into confusion by both the fading chaos of a forgotten dream and the waking realization that this was not his own bed, or even any bed. It sent him slipping off the seat where he lay, and in the blink before he hit the floor, he recalled that he was in the back of the floater. The fact was emphasized by the hard surface that smashed his hand when he tried to catch himself—a pain followed by another as the bite wound on his wrist opened again.

He lay there a moment, regaining his bearings, resting and remembering. He and Diomedes were spending the night here, both sleeping and watching for any sign of the vigilante. Felix had told them that this area near the Brooks Transit Station, one of those closest to The Dirge, was the location of at least two rumored sightings. The actual station itself was closed past two in the morning and primarily located below ground, but according to Felix the sightings had occurred just outside of it, around the part of the rectangular structure that rose above the ground, and beyond the scope of any existing cameras.

They had decided to call it a night shortly after leaving the Justice Tower. The idea was initially Felix's, who had suggested that it was too late to really investigate any more leads beyond just staking out an area for the night. Diomedes had actually agreed quickly, probably, Romulus guessed, having had enough of the man for one evening.

Romulus himself recalled being suspicious when Felix made the suggestion, though it took him a moment now to remember why. As Romulus had planned, he had reminded Felix to call his fire department contact, but when the man had pulled out his phone, Romulus caught a flash of worry across his face. It was then that he made the suggestion and explained that it was probably too late to call the man, but that hardly seemed to justify the anxiety in his eyes.

Romulus had meant to mention it to Diomedes but got distracted by the discussion of their respective tasks before meeting up again tomorrow: Brian, a man whom Romulus felt himself resenting for reasons he couldn't pinpoint, was to sift through the CMPC data. Felix would look into the arsons and talk more to his contact, and Romulus and Diomedes would stake out the transit station. They had, after all, nowhere else to go.

"Diomedes?" Romulus tried, moving to a sitting position on the floor.

His mentor was still in the pilot's seat, presumably awake and watching out the tinted windshield. "What?" he answered.

"Did you notice anything . . . weird about how quickly Felix left?"

"Everything about the man is weird."

"Well, yeah." Romulus stood and moved to the passenger's seat, fingering his bandage gingerly. It probably needed changing. "But he seemed to decide it was time to go suddenly there at the end."

"I don't trust him, either. But we haven't paid him yet." His mentor turned to glance at Romulus's bloodied wrist. "You're bleeding again," he said with a hint of concern. "You're dripping everywhere. Christ, don't you know how to tie a bandage?"

Romulus said nothing for a moment. "I couldn't do it quite right with just one hand, I guess."

Diomedes got up from his seat, moved to the back, and opened one of the compartments. He returned a moment later with a fresh bandage. "If you're going to do it, do it right," he muttered, taking Romulus's wrist and unwrapping it.

Romulus listened as Diomedes dressed the wound and instructed him on how to do so better himself. Not for the first time in the months since he came to the city, he was glad he had found Diomedes again. The man had a history of coming to his aid.

"Do you remember back on the farm when the barn loft collapsed under me?" It was one of the first times he'd helped Romulus. He had fallen, fracturing his wrist and breaking two ribs when he had hit the ground. Diomedes had found him first and carried him, unconscious, into the house.

"It was Max's fault. Your uncle told him to replace the rotten wood," his roommate stated.

Romulus grinned. "I remember. You and Uncle Frank nearly tore him a new one for that."

"It doesn't matter anymore. Max is gone. Your uncle's gone. They're all gone, except for you."

His roommate's tone made his own smile retreat a bit. Still, he had always admired Diomedes for helping him back then, and for going after Max for the danger he'd put him in. Romulus had never been too angry with Max himself, despite his injuries, but it had been nice to know that Diomedes was looking out for him.

But, for the moment, his mentor was silent once more.

Howling yells followed by a gunshot broke the silence. Diomedes leaned forward to get a better view. "What was that?" Romulus asked. Another group of howls sounded, their source not visible, yet not distant.

"Don't know." Diomedes got up while still watching out the window. He checked his gun and moved for the door. "I'll check. Stay here."

"Stay here?" Romulus asked, not wanting to be left out.

"Stay here." His mentor was nearly out the door.

"What if you need help?"

"It could be a trick." Without further explanation, he closed the door and dashed across the street. Romulus watched his mentor duck into the shadows and hug the building until he slipped out of sight around the corner of the station.

Romulus watched the entrance for any sign of who might have fired the gun, or any sign of his mentor. Motionless shadows were his only reward, and once again, he was waiting.

How much of his life had he spent waiting? Waiting to grow up, waiting to leave the farm, and just waiting for things to happen for him. The one thing he had actually done was to come to the city, and that had only led to more waiting. He sighed and tried to remind himself of the reality of his situation, that he had accomplished things. Yet all he had left of his life now was his goal of becoming a freelancer, and what was he doing? Hiding in a floater while the one person who could teach him had left without him. Was Diomedes mad at him? Didn't he have faith in him? He said a silent prayer against the thought. Diomedes was all he had left.

A burst of gunfire echoed in the night, followed by more yelling from a source he couldn't pinpoint. Romulus ducked down for protection on instinct.

Why the hell are you ducking? You're supposed to be watching!

He moved back up in the seat in time to see movement atop the station. Someone was running across the roof. It was the arsonist. It had to be! And there was no sign of Diomedes. Seeing his chance, Romulus clambered for the door and bolted out of the vehicle.

The figure was gone. Romulus ran across the street regardless. The figure couldn't have gotten far. Should he yell for Diomedes? No, that would only give him away. Romulus darted around to where the figure had been running and rounded the corner as the gangers' howling increased. God damn it, he hated that sound.

A pair of dumpsters sat beneath a high window to the station. Wincing at the pain in his wrist, Romulus climbed one dumpster and pulled himself up to the ledge in the hope of catching sight of their mark from higher ground. A brief look down yielded nothing but vertigo.

Another round of shots rang out. A scream of pain. It was on the other side of the station. Romulus looked up. The roof was just above him. He might make it with a jump, but if he missed . . .

Another shot broke out and made the decision for him. His fingertips barely caught the edge, and he strained to pull himself up the remaining distance.

A moment later he was at the top, cradling his wrist and running, dodging around a skylight that shone down the four-story drop to the transit tunnel below, and thanking his luck that he had seen it in the shadows. A yell of anger that had to be from Diomedes met his ears a moment before Romulus stopped short at the edge and looked over.

Diomedes was there beside a kiosk. Three gangers that Romulus couldn't identify surrounded him. One was on the ground, but the other two—both quite large—had Diomedes held and were trying with all their might to maintain their grip. His mentor strained against them, but his eyes were fixed on neither. Romulus followed his mentor's glare to a whirl of howling movement below and to Romulus's left. Five more gangers surrounded the same figure in black he had seen on the roof—the same figure he was now sure was Wraith.

Romulus watched, transfixed, as the gangers attacked the vigilante en masse. He kicked one backward instantly into a cement pillar. A second howled in pain just after Romulus saw the flash of blades at the man's neck. He fell quickly. The others pressed inward.

Diomedes's bellow simultaneously turned his attention back to his mentor's struggle and made him conscious of his own inaction. Though unable to do much else, Diomedes's captors looked to have him well enough held so that he was unable to fight back.

Romulus reached for his weapon and cursed. It was gone; he'd left it in the floater! A crack of bone came from Wraith's melee and he froze, unsure how to help.

Do something!

With a shout, he jumped the distance to the ground, forced into a controlled roll by his own momentum. He shot to his feet and rushed the ganger on Diomedes's left, crashing into him. Surprised and off balance, the ganger's grip on Diomedes broke as Romulus slammed him against the kiosk. Romulus held the man back a moment before the ganger head-butted him. He fell back, catching himself on his wounded wrist and wincing in pain as his mentor swung the other ganger around to smash him into the kiosk, where he remained.

In the same motion Diomedes turned and ran for the other struggle taking place across the station entrance. Romulus braced himself for the other ganger's counter-attack, but when he looked a moment later, the man was scrambling for the safety of the shadows across the street.

Romulus sprang up and turned toward a sound to his right. An old man lay on the ground beside the outer wall of the station, cloaked in dirt and weathered clothing and clutching his stomach in pain. He looked at Romulus a moment in fear before his features softened in confusion.

"Was it you?" the vagrant asked.

The yell of his mentor's frustration jerked Romulus's attention away from the old man. Diomedes now dueled with Wraith among the fallen gangers. His mentor fought valiantly, attempting to grab the vigilante while at the same time trying to block the slashers that Romulus could clearly see even in the dim light. The vigilante connected, slashing into Diomedes's arm with an unusual clashing of metal. Wincing in sympathy, Romulus ran to help him a second later.

The vagrant's voice trailed behind him. "No . . . "

Romulus ran to Diomedes without thinking. The vigilante's eyes fixed on him a moment before a blaze of light flared from the palm of his hand.

Thrown off balance and blinded, Romulus stumbled. His hand struck a pillar but he managed to catch himself and regain his balance fast enough to keep his momentum and continue blindly toward Diomedes. Before he could think to stop, he struck hard against a stone surface that he realized was another pillar a second before he lost consciousness.

"I don't know, I told ya!" The voice was ragged with anger and fear. "Don't know who he is! Don't know who you are! Don't know bleedin' anything!" The voice broke on a sob. "Leave me alone . . . "

As the voice trailed off and footsteps approached him, Romulus became aware again of his own consciousness. He was sitting propped against a pillar. A throbbing pain grew on the side of his forehead, and he groaned as he opened his eyes. A dark floater flew overhead behind the shape of Diomedes standing over him.

"He escaped," Diomedes said.

"Is that him? Eh?" Romulus heard the other voice ask. He looked over to see the vagrant he had spotted previously. "Oh. No." The man shook his head.

Romulus looked to his right, still dazed. Near the kiosk were the fallen gangers he and Diomedes had fought. To the left were—Romulus winced at the sight—more gangers, bloodier than the others. One's throat hung open, torn by the vigilante's blades. Blood ran down his chest. His mouth gaped. His eyes turned back in a ghoulish expression of— Romulus forced himself to look away.

"What happened?" he asked.

Diomedes stood, brooding. It was a moment or two before he spoke. "Things got fucked. The noise was them attacking him," Diomedes explained, indicating the gangers and vagrant. "Then the mark appeared and attacked them."

"Told ya I don't know him," the vagrant mumbled.

"Shut up!" Diomedes thundered. "I couldn't get to him," he continued. "Then you showed up." Romulus's brief smile in anticipation of praise for his help melted quickly as his mentor's already existing scowl deepened. "I told you to stay with the floater."

"I—I was following him! I saw him on the roof and I was trying to help!" Romulus bit his tongue before he could say more.

"He saw you coming and hit us both with a stun flash. Bastard ran when my guard was down. Slashed my arm."

Romulus glanced at his mentor's arm. The clothing was torn above a nasty pair of scratches on the metal beneath. If the arm weren't cybernetic, Diomedes would have been in a lot of pain. "How long was I out?"

"Not long."

Romulus stood and looked toward where the vagrant crouched in a corner at the station entrance. "Shouldn't we do something for him?"

"We need to leave before cops come by. He'll live." The freelancer walked to the kiosk, retrieved his auto-pistol, and then checked and searched the bodies of the fallen gangers there. "So will they," he said.

Romulus found himself returning to the bloodier collection of gangers where the vigilante had been. "They won't."

"It's what they deserved. Don't touch the bodies. Let's go."

Diomedes handed Romulus some of the money from the unconscious gangers and turned to go back to the floater. Michael waited, regarded the cash a moment, and then passed it to the wounded vagrant before following after his mentor.

Later that night, as he sat in the rear of the floater unable to sleep because of the throbbing of his head, he watched Diomedes sleeping in the pilot's chair. Earlier that evening, Romulus had trouble finding sleep because of where he was forced to take it. Now, mere hours later, it struck him how comfortable he was with the idea. Perhaps after seeing the old man by the transit station, he was just comforted to have shelter at all—something to protect him from the kind of cruelty he had seen tonight in men who would prey on an old man for their own sick enjoyment.

It troubled Romulus slightly that the person responsible for visiting the same cruelty on him, destroying his only meager home, was the same person who had tried to save the vagrant. At least that's how it seemed, to hear Diomedes tell it. He recalled what his mentor had told him, reviewing what he knew once more, just in case. There wasn't much to interpret, though. The gangers were beating the vagrant, and then the vigilante appeared to attack them.

Had Diomedes stood and watched until Wraith arrived, even as the man was being beaten? There was a definite lapse of time between when his mentor left and when he first spotted the vigilante. No, that was ludicrous. Diomedes had been trying to move quietly. That meant caution; it would have taken him some time to get there. And Diomedes was a man of few words. Just because he had left out an unnecessary detail certainly didn't mean that he'd done nothing. It was a foolish thought.

Of course, he could always just ask . . . Romulus glanced at his mentor again and decided against the insult that such an implication would make. How would Diomedes react to that?

"He'd probably tell you to quit talking and go to sleep," Romulus said to himself. And he'd have a point. Romulus nodded and listened to his mentor.

In the early morning, Romulus thought he had awoken to find Diomedes checking and redressing his wounds. It was only for a moment before he had quickly fallen back to sleep, and later, he couldn't be sure if he hadn't dreamed it.

XV

FELIX HAD MADE a discovery. He loved doing that, even the small ones, and the one that he now held in his mind like a child with a new toy was a little more than small. It wasn't huge, it wasn't the final piece of the puzzle by any means, but it was enough to make him soon forget—here Felix chuckled at his own thoughts—to *overshadow*, he corrected—the previous night's unpleasantness.

The problem that had caused him to leave the freelancer's company so quickly had turned out to be modest. Only a few minor adjustments were required. He had been relieved to find that out, but he was sure that at least a bit of his panic at not being able to remember Albert's name had shown to his companions. With something as important to him as his memory, he had a tendency to assume the worst.

Still, Felix had never regretted his original decision to participate in the experiment. When they had first approached him three years ago, the initial idea was more than intriguing enough. When they'd discovered the added side effect of a near-photographic memory, he couldn't believe his luck. He was glad they had the time to implement the changes to help him more fully utilize that aspect before the project lost its funding. The occasional side effects were, so far, something he could live with, but it was sometimes difficult not to worry.

The discovery he'd made was simple: there was a connection to the arsons—or three of the four of them, anyway. After speaking to Albert and doing some poking around of his own, he had found it.

"RavenTech," he told Albert. It was only fair. The man had helped him, after all. And it wasn't such a big secret that someone else wouldn't have figured it out soon anyway. "Each warehouse had a connection to Raven Military Technologies."

"What sort of connection?"

"The third one's obvious. It's a RavenTech warehouse," Felix told him. "Remember what you said about the second one at Oranni Shipping? You said they were just barely able to contain it before it spread to the place next door. RavenTech *owns* the place next door."

"And the first?"

"Had its security provided by RavenTech."

Albert chuckled. *"There's a fact Aegis Security's probably already planning to exploit."*

"I hadn't thought of that," said Felix. RavenTech and Aegis were competitors. While RavenTech was stronger in combat hardware, Aegis's forte was more centered on security manpower and training. Even so, each was trying to carve a niche in the other's specialty. Perhaps there was more merit to a Wraith/Aegis connection than he first thought.

"So what do you think's the connection to the apartment fire?"

"Don't know," said Felix. "But since you've already confirmed it was started the same way, I'll bet there is one. For now, I just wanted to mention that to you."

"I appreciate it. So why're you looking into this, anyway?"

"Can't tell you that, I'm afraid," Felix replied, and hoped Albert would leave it at that.

There was a pause. *"Mm. Well, let me know if you find anything else."*

Felix nodded, useless as the gesture was over the phone. "Will do." A few moments later, Felix climbed aboard a bus bound for The Dirge.

It was nearly four in the afternoon. He had spent most of the morning sleeping after maintenance on his memory problems kept him up until near dawn. He had used the time after that to check in with Albert and search for information that led to his RavenTech discovery. He had an hour before he was to meet up with Diomedes and Flynn again. The tight-lipped freelancer had relayed the fact that they had seen the object of their search last night, and Felix looked forward to picking their minds for details. For now, however, the focus was on their former home.

The late afternoon sun was shining through clouds of rain and smog when he arrived. It bathed in a dirty, golden light the charred pile of what some people used to call home. A stray dog dug through the rubble not far from where a man worked at shaping some of the debris into a shelter. A gunshot echoed from far in the distance, covered a moment later by a boy yelling at his friend as they explored the ashes of the ruined building.

The investigative crews were long gone, most likely having wrapped up as quickly as possible the previous night. Most people didn't linger in The Dirge if they didn't have to, even if it was just on the edge. Most of the caution ribbon had already been stripped away by vandals or collectors. Felix hoped he could find what he was looking for.

He stepped across the blackened bricks near to where he guessed the entrance once was, brushing debris aside with his feet as he searched. Most, he knew, if not all of anything worth taking would have already been plundered by looters, but the thing he was searching for was something he hoped no one would have cared to take. It was just a cheap piece of hardware—cheap, but usually designed to take a pounding from would-be vandals. Felix hoped it had managed to withstand the building's destruction in some way that was salvageable.

After just over five minutes of searching, Felix found it. He pulled the book-sized piece of hardware from the rubble and examined it. It wasn't much to look at. A computer in the simplest form of the word, it was really nothing more than a common I.D. card scanner that had been linked to the lock on the building entrance. Simple, but solid, and from the look of the neighborhood, it was probably older than Felix himself. It would never open a door again, but it might still hold the list of the building's tenants in its memory.

That was what Felix wanted. He was guessing that the RavenTech connection here lay in one of the people inside. Once he learned who they were, he could start that search. It had crossed his mind that Diomedes did have his own link through Wallace, but he wasn't ready to highlight that as the connection until he'd had a chance to rule any others out. So far as he knew, the connection might even be with Flynn.

"Little late for lootin', man," came a voice from behind him. "Didn't think you were the type."

Felix turned, recognizing the voice. It belonged to Charlie Hobbes, a man whom he had consulted on more than one occasion for info about The Dirge. Charlie had his ear to the ground as much as Felix did, but Charlie prided himself on learning as much as he could in the small, dangerous part of the city he lived in. Felix didn't exactly trust him, but he trusted the man's information. He decided to take the opportunity.

Felix turned. "I have unique tastes," he said.

"What tastes?" Charlie asked. Though weatherworn clothing covered most of his thin body, his face was gaunt and unshaven, giving him a presence that was reminiscent of a skeleton. Even his eyes were slightly sunken. His entire bearing appeared meager, perhaps why so many allowed him to overhear the information that he made a living on. Felix knew there lurked craftiness behind the façade.

"Tastes?" Felix repeated. "I like piña coladas. And getting caught in the rain." After giving the reference ample time to go over the man's head, he said, "Raven Defense Technologies."

Charlie walked closer. "RavenTech?" He laughed. "Man, if you're scamming for anything RavenTech in that ash heap you *really* should've come sooner. This is The Dirge, not some damn sidewalk sale."

"Oh, so *this* is The Dirge? I thought we were in Disneyland!" Felix joked. "That's not entirely what I mean."

"So say what'cha mean, man! Yer always talkin' riddles."

"Of course I am! How else can I keep you from selling every word I say without paying for it first?" He winked.

"Don't know. Fuckin' honor system?" Charlie joked. He flashed stained teeth.

"How much do you know about the people who used to live here?"

"Might've heard a thing or two once in a while. You lookin' for someone who's worked for RavenTech?"

Felix gave his best noncommittal nod. "Worked, played, whatever. Anything that might be a connection."

"Why?"

"Make you a deal, Charlie. You tell me what you know, maybe do a bit of poking, and I'll tell you the why. Which *is* worth a little bit on its own."

"The man knows what he's talking about," Charlie said to himself. "I'm in. What's the biz?"

"I'm looking for a RavenTech connection here because there've been a few buildings out there that have had similar, ah, structural difficulties. All of them had some connection to RavenTech."

"You're searching for who did it, eh? Who's payin'?"

"Depends on who did it, don't you think?" Felix shrugged.

"Blackmail, eh?"

"I don't blackmail, Charlie. Or haven't I advertised my shining reputation?"

Charlie grinned. "Your loss, man."

"So do you know anything?"

"Might," he said, thinking. "Gotta do a little poking, though."

"Nothing off the top of your head?"

"Maybe. But I got a rep to think about, too. I don't want to give you junk without being sure."

Felix nodded, reasonably sure Charlie didn't know anything and was only trying to save face. "I need to know soon if it's going to be any use. You know how to reach me."

"You'll be hearin' from me." Charlie turned to go. "Don't dig around in there too much. You'll piss off the rats."

Felix watched him leave and wondered if Charlie not knowing anything was a good sign or not. He could usually be counted on to know the things worth knowing. Maybe Diomedes was the RavenTech connection, or maybe there was another connection just as hidden. Then again, it was too early to make a judgment. Perhaps if he could get the tenants' names out of the entry scanner, something else would surface.

With a glance at his watch, he carried his prize away to find someone able to get those names out.

XVI

WHEN HE HAD LEFT them the previous evening, Brian was uncertain if he would return to Felix and his group the next day. It would depend, he'd decided, on how much information he could glean from the CPMC data. No sense returning to the others if he'd found what he needed already. Before he had even gone through the files to cross-reference the install list with the cybernetic data on the vigilante he already knew, he had considered forcing the others to pay him for what he found out. Brian envisioned that Felix would have been happy enough to make a deal, but the freelancers, Diomedes in particular, were another matter.

After picturing just how and where the freelancer would hurt him, he threw out the idea.

Unfortunately, even with cross-referencing the data, he still couldn't narrow things down to a reasonable number of likely suspects—assuming that the vigilante's implants were even legitimately documented. He didn't have much choice in the matter other than to continue to play the tag-along.

Were he just working with Felix, Brian probably would have been less hesitant. Diomedes's presence in the whole composition had made him uneasy. He already resented the threats the freelancer had made to him. Brian had no intention of saying anything about the freelancer in his interview, even before Diomedes's assurance that to do so would be a deadly mistake. On the other hand, he didn't like the idea of being someone who was easily pushed around, either. Brian had practiced standing up to the man many times in the camera of his mind. As soon as he saw the opportunity, he would have to do so for real.

Felix, however, was another puzzle. The man's trust in Brian and willingness to help was perplexing and, as far as Brian could tell, genuine. It made him both proud and uneasy. Was he being patronized? He hated being patronized. If so, Brian resolved to prove Felix wrong. Either way, he realized, Brian would have to do more than merely tag along. Perhaps that was why he brought the footage with him for them all to see at the rendezvous.

*   *   *

Romulus watched Felix study the recorded news footage on the reporter's tablet screen and waited for his own turn.

"How long ago was this?" Felix asked.

"That first one is from a little over a month ago. When the first ganger slayings were found in the International District," Brian said. "The first with witnesses, anyway. Typically, none of them wanted to be filmed." Felix nodded silently as Brian continued. "The other two should have dates on them. There's not really much in there that isn't in my file, but it's a visual record and every little bit helps, doesn't it?"

"Anything could be helpful," Felix agreed. He finished scanning the reports and handed it to Diomedes. "See anything that clicks with last night?"

Romulus resisted the urge to look over his mentor's shoulder and waited for him to finish. Diomedes looked at the screen as the reports replayed, his eyes shifting occasionally to Brian. Romulus could see he was intimidating the reporter, and wondered if it was intentional. The report finished and his mentor grunted. "Nothing new," he said, passing it to Romulus.

Romulus scrutinized the video, marking information in his mind as the reports listed it. Diomedes was right, there wasn't much: the places, the times, and the witness reports telling of a figure in black. The reports really added more to the sense of mystery than to anything else.

"Do you recall anything else from last night?" Felix asked. "Anything, I don't know, noteworthy?" The man looked between Romulus and Diomedes.

Romulus opened his mouth to speak, glancing over to his mentor for approval. Diomedes gave a nod, so Romulus said, "There wasn't really much time to notice anything. He was already fighting the gangers when

I got there. After that I guess I was too busy to look, and when I finally made it over to him—well, I didn't even get that far. Next thing I know he's gone. Like Diomedes said, we got out of there pretty quick afterward."

"Did you?" Brian spoke, addressing Diomedes. "Have much time to notice anything, I mean?" Romulus actually winced from the reporter's own discomfort as his mentor answered, for a moment, with merely a dead stare.

"Long enough," Diomedes said finally, and mostly to Felix. "The face was the same as in the video."

"Did you hear anything, or see anything of him before he attacked?"

"No," Diomedes answered. "He jumped from the roof. No guns. Slashers and fists. When I closed on him hand-to-hand, he was already done with the others. Good fighter. Knew some sort of martial arts."

"What kind?" Felix asked.

"Don't know."

"Describe it."

Diomedes gritted his teeth. "Lots of blocks, dodges mostly. Kept me from getting to him."

"Sounds like Aikido, maybe a form of Karate," Felix said, thinking. "Hmm."

"Hmm, what?" Diomedes asked.

"How long was he fighting the gangers before you got to him?"

"Maybe a minute or so."

"Yeah," Brian cut in with a nod to Felix. "He takes out five gangers that quickly and then goes defensive when he fights you? Something's a bit weird about that, don't you think?"

"Diomedes is a little more dangerous than a few gangers," Romulus told him.

"Even so," said Felix. "What do you think, Dio . . . medes?"

"Defensive." Diomedes nodded. "For the most part. And he ran when Romulus came."

"Think he knew who you were?"

Diomedes shook his head. "If I was him and I knew who we were, I would've tried to kill us."

Felix shrugged. "Maybe he knew something you didn't."

"Talk straight, Hiatt."

Felix shrugged again. "I don't know. Just brainstorming."

"There are worse ways to stun someone than with a flash," Brian said.

"I've never seen one of those before. It was like his whole hand lit up," Romulus mused. He left out the obvious fact that there were probably a lot of things he hadn't seen before.

A moment of silence passed before Felix spoke. "Wait a minute, Flynn. You're sure it was his *hand* that flashed?"

"Pretty sure. I mean—" Romulus paused to check his thoughts. "Yeah, pretty sure."

"It was from his palm," his mentor confirmed. The two waited for Felix's reaction.

"It's just that there's no standard stun flash on the market right now that's in the palm. Never was, to my knowledge. Had to have been a custom job."

"Why put it in the hand, then?" Brian wondered.

"Not sure. From what I gather, there's problems with hand-mounting that sort of thing that makes it either too difficult or too expensive. That's why it's not really marketed. Either this guy's a tech himself, or he's close with someone who is."

"If it's that hard to put in, wouldn't there have to be a pretty good reason to do it?" Brian asked.

Felix shrugged. "I can't think of a single good reason—except just to see if they could," he chuckled. "One of my favorite reasons, actually. I wonder if we're looking for me?" The small man looked around in mock alarm. Romulus couldn't help but chuckle.

"Are we?" The question came from Diomedes.

Felix blinked. "I'd say you're joking, but to my knowledge Hell hasn't yet frozen over," he said. "So I'll just answer you straight and say no, we're not." Diomedes said nothing. "Besides," Felix continued to Romulus, "black's not really my color. I'm more of a spring."

Romulus smiled before his memory flashed on something. He pulled the pocket screen out again and replayed the reports.

"There's a lot of things that aren't making sense here," he heard Felix say.

"Tell us," Diomedes ordered.

"The RavenTech connection I told you about. Mostly it seems like our guy has it out for them, but why hit the second place, then? The only connection's that it's next door."

"Maybe he's got a problem with addresses," the reporter joked.

"Shut up," Diomedes said. Romulus continued to slow-motion scan the reports.

"Also," Felix went on, "some things seem to point to a corporate connection: the expensive flash job, the suspicious connections to RavenTech and such. I can see why a warehouse would be hit. No doubt there'd be some equipment loss. But why the apartment? I mean, we won't know until we've time to check those names, but if you're the only connection, Diomedes . . . I don't know. It just doesn't add up."

A moment of silence passed. Romulus moved to the second report.

"I don't suppose you'd tell us a little more about the nature of that connection?" Felix probed. Romulus looked up from the reports with interest.

"No."

Felix held up his hands in apology. "Just asking."

"Stop asking."

Romulus noticed the reporter was no longer saying much. He looked back down at the reports, still listening to the conversation but watching for what he hoped he had remembered correctly.

Felix just kept going. "The thing is, it would make more sense if he's corporate. The arsons would be his day job and this vagrant-rescuing, ganger-killing thing could just be a helpful hobby. You have to admit the two don't exactly mesh."

Romulus heard the reporter laugh. "Unless he thinks burning down buildings is helpful."

"True," said Felix, apparently taking the idea seriously. "But still. I mean, assuming he's a psycho—it's a good bet but there's no guarantee— he could be following any number of irrational behaviors. I just can't help but think that someone who would go through such trouble to install a non-lethal stun flash like that wouldn't be prone to torching an apartment where a great number of people could be hurt."

"A stunned enemy is easier to kill," Diomedes told him.

"Then why didn't he kill you?" Felix asked.

"Disappointed?"

"It just raises some worrisome questions is all."

"Talk won't get us anywhere," said Diomedes.

It was then that Romulus saw it. "Hey," he said quietly to himself in recognition. "Hey!" he said again and looked up from the screen. "I think I've got something!"

"What is it?" Felix asked.

Romulus handed the paused report to Diomedes. "When you said black—you don't look good in black—I thought . . . I remembered, I mean. Last night after he escaped I saw a black floater flying over. It was just after I woke up. There's the same one in the background." He pointed to the pocket screen. "Same color, same style. Or model."

"Let me see that," Felix said. Romulus watched as Diomedes peered at the screen a moment before handing it to Felix. "That's a Boeing Ursa Minor. Black, unmarked. Not too commonplace."

"Could it be a coincidence?" asked Brian.

"Yes," said Felix. "But it's worth checking out."

"How?" Diomedes asked.

"There're no plates visible," said Brian. "Wandering through the city trying to find that thing would be like looking for a needle in a haystack."

Felix grinned. "Someone I know once said that the likelihood of anyone ever actually dropping a needle in a haystack, much less trying to find one, is incredibly small. On the other hand, I think I know someone else who can make it a little easier."

XVII

IT HAD TAKEN all of forty-five seconds for Felix to get from the building entry to Marc's door. "Diomedes, Flynn," Felix said, pointing to the two men who entered the apartment behind him, "this is Lifesaver."

Diomedes and Flynn, Marc thought, matching the names with the faces he'd seen last night. His memory jogged, he remembered a few details about them now. Marc smiled and extended his hand. Flynn took it. Diomedes did not.

"Lifesaver?" asked the younger man. Marc wasn't sure if the tone was confirming or confused.

"Actually," Marc replied with a friendly scowl at Felix, "My real name's Marc. People just call me Lifesaver 'cause that's what Felix here keeps introducing me as."

"Well it fits, doesn't it?" Felix grinned.

Marc noticed the larger man was paying little attention to the discussion, looking instead around his living room. Flynn, however, still maintained an interest. Marc pulled out his omnipresent pack of peppermint Lifesavers. "Lifesaver?" he offered. Flynn chuckled but declined after a glance to Diomedes, who all but turned his nose up at the offer.

Felix took one, as always, and chuckled. "He always does that."

"No, I always carry them," Marc said. "Most of the time I offer them when you introduce me to someone so they don't think I'm some sort of medic."

"Though he does know the right maneuver in case you get one of those suckers stuck in your throat, speaking from experience," Felix added to the freelancers.

"This isn't why we're here," Diomedes told Felix.

"Ah, yes. Always keeping us on track, Diomedes is. I'm afraid I do have a bit of a favor to ask. I hope you're not too busy with . . . other things?"

"Tonight, no. Last night, yes. In fact I was up so late that I just woke up an hour ago, so you've got me fresh." Marc ushered them inside. "What is it you want, exactly?"

"What was last night?" Felix asked as they moved to have a seat.

"Oh, you know, work and such."

Fruitless work, as it happened. He'd kept his search going into early morning, growing more certain with every passing hour that he wouldn't find his target, yet still hanging onto the hope of chance. He had finally gone to bed as the sun rose. After he woke, he heard that the elusive man from ESA had been spotted boarding a plane out of the country. Whatever business he'd come to do, he'd most likely done already. Surely efforts were already underway to learn just what that business was. Marc wondered what the chance might be that Felix would have seen or heard anything useful.

They moved into the main room. "Pardon the mess." Marc took a seat at the computer by one of the windows and turned the chair to the rest of them. Flynn found a clear spot on one end of the sofa as Diomedes continued to stand and looked out the window at the street four stories below. Felix moved to the other end of the sofa and picked up some hardcopies that were lying on the cushion.

"Ah, mind if I put these somewhere?" Felix asked.

Marc cursed inwardly, recognizing the AoA papers even before he saw the Palladium. As there were other, more open places to sit, he guessed Felix had seen it too.

Marc sprang up. "Yeah, I'll put those somewhere." He tugged open a desk drawer and shoved them in, closing it after. He really needed to wake up. "Normally I'd just say toss 'em on the table, but that's a bit cluttered, too," he said, attempting to cover. He motioned to the electronic hardware and mess of cables that were scattered on a coffee table that he long ago had turned into a workbench.

"Is that Holes?" Felix asked.

"Yeah, or will be, I hope."

Felix turned to Flynn. "Lifesaver's trying to make an A.I."

"Artificial intelligence?"

"Yeah." Marc nodded. "And I'm not *trying* to make one, I *am* making one. It takes time to nurture the emergent programming so it turns out stable." He barely stopped himself from going into details that the others probably wouldn't appreciate. "I haven't had time. The name was Felix's idea, of course."

Diomedes slammed his palm against the wall beside the window. "Hiatt!"

"Ah, yes!" Felix exclaimed. "There he goes again! We need your help to find someone."

"Find someone?" Great. Another search. He might have been less irritated if the freelancer hadn't just made a sizeable dent in his wall.

"Or something, actually. To be brief—"

"You, be brief?"

"—there's a floater out there owned by a guy we're trying to track down."

"Got plates?"

"No, but it's a black Boeing Ursa Minor. Not too common. I'm hoping you could use something out of that bag of tricks. Provided it still works?"

Marc nodded. "Yeah, it still works."

Diomedes turned his attention on Marc. "What is it?" Marc wished the guy would sit down. He glanced up at the larger freelancer, thinking.

"Felix, can I talk to you for a second in the other room?" Marc asked.

Felix stood. "Sure."

Marc motioned to a door that led to a second bedroom that he used as another office and storage room. "Excuse us just a moment, sorry."

"We're not leaving," said Diomedes.

The door closed and Marc turned to his friend. After a moment of hesitation, he gathered his courage and said, "Felix, don't take this the wrong way, but I wish you wouldn't do this to me."

"Diomedes and Flynn, you mean? Sorry for that, but I couldn't come alone. I'm Dio's guide to finding this guy and I don't think he's willing to let me out of his sight for the moment."

"I just don't want every punk who's looking for someone to come knocking on my door. I don't mind helping you out, but too much attention causes problems. Right now the AoA doesn't have to pull strings to keep my little tap-in hidden, and we want to keep it that way."

Felix held up his hands. "You know I know that."

"So why'd you bring them?"

"Maybe it was a bit imprudent of me, and for that I'm sorry. But I know Diomedes. He won't tell anyone. He's not one to share his resources, and if this works, that's how he'll think of you."

"And if I can't find this guy?" Marc asked.

"Then he won't think you worth the breath it takes to mention your name."

Marc thought for a minute. He did trust Felix, but the man wasn't infallible. Maybe he could do the search without the freelancers knowing how. "And Flynn?"

"I think he's trustworthy. If I tell him to be discreet about this, he will."

Marc sighed. "You sound pretty sure about that."

"Call it a feeling."

Marc turned to the window and looked out over the dying city as the sun set. "You're not the only one who's got a feeling about him."

"What do you mean? Recruiting's got their eye on him?"

"Technically I'm not supposed to tell you those sorts of things anymore, but someone's got their eye on him, yeah." Recruiting wasn't Marc's area, but he did know that Flynn was targeted from his Aegis Security training psych profile as a possible candidate. Marc also knew that he was not to be approached while he still associated with Diomedes. Apparently they thought he still had some growing to do, or perhaps they considered Diomedes a risk. He didn't know the details, but it was something minor he was to look out for. And he really shouldn't tell Felix about it. Not yet, anyway.

A moment passed before he moved on. "As for the problem at hand, I suppose we could work around it."

*　*　*

Romulus sat staring at the jumble of circuit boards and fractal processors on the table in front of him as Diomedes moved towards the door behind which Felix and Lifesaver had closed themselves. "Well, he seems nice enough," Romulus said. His mentor made eye contact with him but gave no reply. "Though the Lifesaver thing is a bit kooky. And the thing on his eyes was a bit weird."

Romulus had seen a prosthesis twice before like the one Lifesaver wore: a single, stylish visor bubble around both eye sockets, like a pair of sunglasses without the frames. From what he knew, it was some sort of hybrid of optics implant and computer readout, and given the amount of hardware lying about here, Lifesaver probably had use for such a thing.

Diomedes's only comment was a quick "Shh!" Romulus felt stupid for not noticing that he was trying to listen in. Being taught by his uncle to respect people's privacy had likely kept Romulus himself from thinking of it, but Diomedes was doing it to watch their backs. He wondered briefly what his uncle might say about that, before he whispered to his mentor, "Hear anything?"

"Not clearly. Shh."

Romulus nodded and went back to thinking. He wanted to trust Lifesaver. Was that a weakness? He hoped they would be able to capitalize on his own discovery about the floater—he had to admit, he was proud of it—and Felix seemed to think Marc could help find it. He didn't want the information to wind up being a waste of time. Diomedes hated wasting time. Brian had been sent to check on some names for Felix, but Diomedes and Romulus were here. Romulus got the feeling that his mentor was putting more stock in their part of the search.

The closed door opened a moment later and Felix stepped out, followed by Lifesaver.

"Well?" Diomedes asked.

"I'll help," Lifesaver told him, "and as a favor to Felix there's no charge—except to ask that you let me keep my methods a secret. I'll be in the other room looking. If I find anything, Felix'll confirm it." Romulus smiled, glad to know they'd get to follow the lead.

"I want to know how," Diomedes said. Romulus remained quiet, though curious himself. "Hiatt knows, I know."

Lifesaver blinked and opened his mouth to reply but it was Felix who spoke first. "Those are his terms, Diomedes. Take it or leave it."

His mentor flashed an angry look at Felix, and Romulus found himself inwardly groaning. They had what was important and the offer seemed fair. As Diomedes and Felix stared in defiance of each other, Lifesaver stepped over to the computer desk in the corner and sat down. "That's the only way I feel comfortable."

Romulus felt the opportunity slipping. "Diomedes," he began in an effort to persuade. His mentor turned his glare onto Romulus. It burned away the rest of what he had meant to say.

Then without a word, Diomedes turned and moved across the room to where Lifesaver sat. "Find it. We stay until you do."

Lifesaver got up once more. "I'll give a shout when I find something," he said from the doorway. "Feel free to find some food in the kitchen. There's some leftover pizza in the fridge." With that he closed the door.

Silence seeped into the room. Diomedes moved to resume staring out the window. When he could stand the tension no longer, Romulus asked, "So what's Lifesaver do exactly?"

"Like I said, he's a programmer. Silker, Net-head, hacker, geek. You name it—if it's computers, he's on it."

"Yes, but what does he *do?*" Romulus pressed. "Who does he work for?"

Felix let out a laugh. "Flynn, you don't even know who *you're* working for! You're worried about somebody else's job, now?"

Romulus didn't quite know what to say to that. "We work for ourselves," Diomedes answered for him.

"You don't know, either, do you?" Romulus baited. "Know who Lifesaver works for, I mean."

"Oh, I know. And believe me, I would love to tell you, but that happens to be a thing I promised I wouldn't. I will tell you one thing, though, Flynn."

"What's that?"

Felix walked over to him and leaned in. "It's a damned lousy secret to have to keep."

"What do you mean?"

"I mean the secret itself isn't lousy, but keeping it a secret is damned frustrating for someone like me. On the other hand," Felix grinned impishly, "it's also a hell of a lot of fun being mysterious!"

Romulus scowled as possibilities filled his mind. A government group? Maybe a secret division of some Internet think-tank? Romulus had to admit that, being from a farm, he didn't even have a clue. "Do I get a hint?"

Felix shook his head and walked into the kitchen. "Nope. I already told you I made a promise. I made one to you, too. I can't be giving you the impression that I don't keep them now, can I?"

Romulus stood and looked into the kitchen to find Felix digging through Lifesaver's refrigerator. Felix pulled out a sealed plastic container and shook it. "You could always try just asking him if you really want to know. I think you'll eventually find out." Felix opened the container, sniffed it, and then quickly sealed it and tossed it aside. "One thing not to do."

"What?"

"Never sniff in the back of a man's fridge. I didn't know meat could *get* that color."

XVIII

"YOUR ATTENTION, if you please," she announced. The thirty-six men and women of the Saratoga mining team assembled in the outfitting bay turned towards Marette for an explanation. They had been sent to the Aristarchus site. They had found what they were unaware they should be looking for. They were deceived, uninformed, and a calculated risk. And now they were about to be offered a bribe. Marette prayed they would be wise enough to take it, for their sakes and for her own.

"I am neither a diplomat nor a public speaker," she began, "so I will apologize beforehand for my lack of eloquence. Important events have occurred at this mining site, some of which you are aware, some you are not."

A swell of grief boiled up inside and threatened to choke her. Marette paused to force back the all-too-recent horror and sorrow of events she had tried to put out of her mind before coming to the assembly. She must remain collected. Concerned murmurs floated amid those she addressed.

"I am not here to offer you an explanation," she continued. "What I can say is that the European Space Agency, which grants Saratoga the ability to mine this plot of the Moon, is engaging its legal option to shut down the mining to explore the area further. More ESA representatives will be arriving at fourteen hundred hours, at which time, after certain security measures are taken, you will be relocated to another site to resume the work for which you were trained.

"The events of the past few days are not widely known beyond this site. You may already know that a transport and communications lockdown has been in effect here for some time. This silence has been necessary for scientific purposes. On behalf of ESA, I apologize for any inconvenience it may have caused. To compensate you for this, and to further request your cooperation in our necessary silence, ESA has credited your personal accounts with a sum based on the original mineral yield estimate of the site. Your foreman, Mr. Andora, has details on specific amounts."

Marette paused to let this sink in, reasonably certain that the money would pacify the group at least a petite amount. The memory of the screams tugged at her and overshadowed the few tentative questions that floated out from the group. Marette took a deep breath and tried to shut away her emotions. She vowed to stay passionless outside. She ignored the questions. They would be answered, in time.

"In addition, in exchange for your further silence about the situation until such time as ESA is prepared to make public comment on the matter, you have been promised five times as much compensation once ESA reaches the point of full disclosure. Do not speak of this to anyone off-site. Not friends, not family, not anyone. Violation of this will result in forfeiture of future compensation and suspension of lunar certification for the entire group. In addition, the Saratoga Mining Company would be denied future permits to mine lunar sites, and would be well within their rights to bring legal action against those of you responsible. That is all. Direct any questions to Foreman Andora, who will bring them to my attention. Barring this, I would recommend that you now prepare yourselves to transfer to the new site. That is all."

She whirled and headed for the foreman's office. Behind her, Andora took over managing his crew. She would wait for him in the office to address any questions he would bring, though Marette doubted he would be happy, or even satisfied, with any answers she would be able to give. For his sake, she hoped that they would be enough.

The AoA had known that they would have to deal with the miners when they originally influenced ESA to send them to the site. The miners' silence was imperative to their objective in the eyes of both groups. She prayed the money was enough.

"Are you ready for me?" Andora asked when he arrived a short while later. He hesitated in the doorway, despite the fact that it was his own office that he was about to enter. Marette nodded and waved him in.

"How are the preparations for relocation?" she asked.

"Smooth so far. We know the drill."

"I need you to keep things that way."

The foreman nodded. "I will. We're a good crew and efficient."

Which is why you were chosen, Marette thought to herself.

"You're not catching us at our best, you know," he added. "I—we work better when we're following regular procedures and know more about what we're actually doing."

Marette was unsure if he was being defensive or fishing for an apology. She changed the subject slightly. "Does your crew have any questions?"

"Aside from the obvious of just what you think that is they found?"

Marette sat, waiting silently.

"Most seem content with the arrangement. The money, I mean. It's why most of them are here, after all. But some want to know when the communications lockdown will be lifted. Some have families who expect to hear from them more regularly. They won't violate the silence order, but they'd like to put some fears to rest."

"The Space Agency will send messages to your families assuring them that all is well, but nothing else will be allowed. This site will continue to be blacked out. The official explanation will be that there have been minor armed conflicts between mining companies. Pirating and so forth. If they must give a reason, that is it."

"There won't be a lockdown at the new site though, right?"

"No." It was a statement she knew to be only a half-truth. All transmissions would be monitored. The frequency of sudden comm-system 'failures' would probably rise. Officially, however, there would be no lockdown.

"I also have three of the crew scheduled for leave. Off-moon."

"I'm afraid I cannot allow that. All of your crew will relocate to the new site."

"They aren't going to take that well."

"I do not expect so."

"One has his daughter's wedding to get to."

Marette shook her head. "Not even if he were scheduled to be crowned the king of France." Her tone was calm but firm. "Everyone goes to the new site. That is to be the arrangement."

"And after the relocation?"

"I cannot say," she lied, knowing full well that they would not be allowed to leave. Not at first. "The ESA liaison officer at the new site will have that answer for you."

"ESA liaison officer," Andora repeated through subtly clenched teeth. "So we still won't be operating independently?"

Marette shook her head. "You will have full control of your crew to mine as normal. That will be standard and you will not be interfered with. All functions ranging off-site will require clearance from the liaison. ESA wishes to ensure the agreement is followed. The liaison officer will acquaint you with the standard procedures."

Andora nodded, with the appearance of being reassured. "As long as it's spelled out. I don't want any surprises."

"The function of the officer is to make things as smooth as possible," she said.

"I don't know how smooth things will go if the crew doesn't get their leave at the new site. They might not take well to that."

"Even so, they would find it difficult to leave without the blessing of the Space Agency," Marette reminded him.

"But not impossible."

"The Chinese National Space Administration is nowhere in this hemisphere. Elements of the Western Space Consortium would be almost as difficult to reach. It is a long journey across the lunar surface." Especially given the new plot they were to be assigned, Marette thought. Even then, the joint space venture of the American companies had limited lunar resources and would not be inexpensively persuaded to take a few extra passengers.

"I'm just letting you know that you can't keep my crew bottled up for too long."

Marette clasped her hands and tapped them against her chin for a moment. It was a nervous habit that she caught herself doing a second later. "Mr. Andora, I would suggest, for all your sakes, that you keep your crew as cooperative as possible."

The foreman looked at her a moment, seeming to summon a bit of courage. "Is that a threat?"

"To call it a threat would imply it is something I have control over. It is a warning."

The two sat in silence for a moment before Andora spoke again. "The discovery—" he said, not describing it further despite Marette's expectation that he had already guessed at what it might be, "we'll be told, well, more about it? Eventually?"

Marette nodded. "When the rest of the public is." It was technically not a lie. The public would not be told. Could not be told. It was vital that nothing be leaked.

"It's incredible to think about, really."

"I am afraid I cannot comment." Yet he was right. It was incredible. Marette only hoped that it would be what they were looking for, for the sake of the lives already lost, and the lives that were currently threatened. "If there is nothing more, you are dismissed."

Marette waited until the foreman had left before she took out the data disk she had kept in her pocket since returning from the site. It was the only record of events that officially had no record, even to ESA. The scanners carried by the team had their own recorders—recorders now lost beyond the memory of screams thick with pain and terror. Even the simple audio-visual records were gone, wiped somehow by the device that killed the team. Only the account of the data relayed by Alberto's transmitter remained.

Marette remembered.

The audio feeds had shut off a second after the video. The only clues she'd had of activity inside the structure were the flashes of light reflected in the small windows of the airlock. She kept transmitting, calling instructions to the team, telling them she'd lost her link, asking for some sign that anyone was hearing her. She continued to call to them until the light faded. She kept trying while she attempted to reestablish her connection to them, asking for their conditions until her requests turned to pleas.

And then she stopped.

And then she sat.

She just . . . sat. Watching. Blankly staring at the stillness outside the airlock. Watching, as nothing continued to happen, and listening to silence cloaked in the sound of what became her own breathing. She sat, not moving, not daring to think, letting the constant flow of null stimuli wash steadily into her senses and pass unprocessed through her mind. She sat waiting, timeless and dead.

It was the waiting that finally shook her—the realization that she was allowing herself to do so. It was not in her nature to wait.

Before she knew what she was doing, she was in a suit outside the airlock, peering into the structure through the window at the darkness beyond. Her team lay still on the floor of the black room inside. There was no sign of the object. No sign of the door it had come through.

A moment later, she keyed in the sequence to close the far side of the airlock. Her blood pounded through her ears while she opened the outer door, stepped into the lock a moment later, and closed the door afterward. She waited, impatiently, keeping watch over the prostrate bodies of her team for any sign of movement as the airlock refilled. When it opened, she pushed herself through to them. Alberto was second from the back; she reached him first. The vital readout of his suit was dark. In a flash, Marette removed his helmet. His eyes were open and blank. His pulse was gone.

He was dead.

In a daze, Marette moved on to another of the team: Henley, a weapons tech. Dead. Siri, the team commander. Dead. Freitz, his helmet still gone. Dead.

At the time, she had been rushing—half from fear that the thing that had done this would return for her, half to block out her own grief enough to function. Yet now, as she sat remembering, the full force of that grief hit her. It twisted her insides out and nearly wrenched a cry of anguish from her. She forced her emotions back under control now as best she could.

And it was control then that had probably saved her.

It was only through a burst of movement in her peripheral vision that she had noticed the soundless spillback of the black covering at the end of the chamber. She scrambled back into the airlock, shoved closed the door, and cursed her own foolishness with ragged breaths. Crouched behind the closed door, she hit the emergency decompress and then ran out of the airlock as quickly as she could in the bulky suit, not looking back.

In hindsight, Marette knew it had been foolish and risky to jeopardize the project by putting herself in such obvious danger. She also knew she would not have been able to live with herself without trying to see if anyone was left alive.

She had waited in the vehicle for any sign that the thing was following, any show of movement or pursuit, though she had not been sure what she would have done if any came. She had waited five minutes, fighting as she did so to keep a grip on the fear and loss of her team. She waited five more just to be sure. When nothing had come, she opened up the comm-channel to the mining site and gave the foreman the plain-word code phrase to send to Alpha Station that indicated a request for reinforcements. Marette had tried to sound as cool and confident as she could. She wasn't sure how well she had succeeded.

It had been another two hours until they had arrived, during which time Marette had spent in the rover at the tunnel entrance, alone with her thoughts. It wasn't a period she cared to recall again anytime soon.

By the time the reinforcements had arrived, armed, she had regained a measure of control. She gave them the simple instructions to guard the tunnel entrance. Anyone seeking entrance, though unlikely, were to be turned away and reported. Anything coming out was to be fired upon.

Back in the foreman's office, Marette looked at the disk she had omitted from her report to ESA. She slid it into the computer and keyed in the sequence to upload the scan data to her AoA contact back at Alpha Station. Uncertain of exactly what the next steps would be, she watched the disk transmit and hoped it would be worth the lives of the team. At the moment, the possibility that it would be gave little relief from the memory of their screams.

XIX

FELIX'S KNOCK sounded a moment before his head poked around the opening door. "Anything yet?"

Marc looked up from the image of the sky above the activity of the City Square Night Market and shook his head. "Not so far, but I can't go too quickly, you know. I have to break into each camera, I have to cover my tracks. It takes time."

Felix stepped into the room and closed the door. "Hope we're not putting you at risk." He held a glass of water from which he periodically sipped.

Marc shook his head at his friend. "Not so much. It's tedious, but it's more or less routine. And boring. The only real risk is my sanity after doing this all last night, too."

Felix moved behind him to watch the screen as Marc resumed the search. "So that's what kept you up."

"Yeah."

"Who were you looking for?"

"How do you know it was a 'who'? And, ah, you know better than to ask those kinds of questions anyway."

"No, I know better than to expect an answer." Felix chuckled. "But I always gotta ask. Especially when you practically beg me to. You didn't *have* to mention what you were doing last night."

Marc shut down the camera and began acquiring another. "Fine, so I can't keep a secret. What's your point?"

"Not the best trait to have in your line of work."

Marc shrugged. "Well, you're the only one I know who's not one of us that I can share this with. It's therapeutic, I guess. I'd go nuts otherwise."

Felix laughed.

"What?"

"Oh, I just find it amusing that the person you choose to vent these things to is a self-proclaimed information bounty hunter, even if that title doesn't exactly roll off the tongue."

"Still don't like 'private investigator,' huh?"

"I keep telling you, it just sounds wrong somehow. No oomph. Plus I think I'd need an office for that."

Marc chuckled. "Well, you may be a 'self-proclaimed information bounty hunter,' but you're a trustworthy self-proclaimed information bounty hunter," he said. "And you know, if you're trying to persuade me to say more, you have a strange way of doing it."

"Oh, I'm not trying to persuade you of anything. I'm sure you'll let it slip when you're ready. What's that?" he asked suddenly, pointing at a shadow that moved across the screen.

"Ah . . . MedEvac," Marc said when he saw the ambulance. "So who owns this floater anyway? What's Diomedes want with him?"

"Oh, I'm not sure Dio would like me sharing that."

Marc wasn't certain if he was being completely sincere or not. "Well, let me ask you this: does he have any connections to ESA?"

"ESA?" Felix gave an interested look.

It would probably be best to take that as a no and not risk giving away too much. "Never mind," Marc said. Then again, it was Felix he was talking to. "Well, does he?"

"Ah, not that I'm aware of. Are we talking European Space Agency or . . . ?"

"Yeah."

"Just making sure," said Felix. "Like I said, not that I'm aware of. So you mean there's something going on with ESA?"

Marc watched the camera a moment and wondered exactly what to say. "Have you heard anything?"

Felix gave it a few moments' consideration. "Not as such, no. Anything I should know?"

"How about this? As a favor to me in payment for the search, you keep your ears open and let me know anything you happen to come across involving them."

"I think I can do that," Felix agreed. "Some sort of security issue?"

Marc turned from the screen to face him. "That obvious, is it?"

"Not too hard to guess, given the fact that they've got you searching with the cameras for whoever it is. That, and where I figure ESA would fit into the whole agenda. Sounds like there's a leak."

"I don't know everything. Just keep your eye out is all I'm saying. By the way," started Marc, changing the subject as he turned back to the screen, "who was the redhead I saw you with last night?"

"My, you were busy last night. Where'd you see us?"

"I followed that floater you were in on a hunch." Marc panned a camera across the west end of the city. "I watched it until you got out at the justice tower. He got out first, then you."

"That was Brian," his friend replied. "He's a reporter we're working with. Part of the reason we know to find this floater."

"Nice guy?"

"Yeah, but a bit self-absorbed and paranoid. I think he's got a bit of a tendency to jump to conclusions, too. Ambitious, though." Felix shrugged. "I figure he might be a useful guy to know."

"Uh huh."

"Plus he's fun to argue with," Felix added happily.

"Ah, so that's it. Where's he now?"

"Off checking on another lead. Running some names through a press database to see if it turns up anything. Diomedes didn't really want him around, anyway."

"Yeah, well do me a favor: if I meet him, you want to introduce me as Marc? The Lifesaver thing is getting old."

"Hey, not my fault you always have some. Besides, it makes for good mental shorthand. You know how hard it is for me to remember things."

Though Marc was focused on the screen, Felix's grin was clear in his tone. "Oh, yeah, and I guess you—"

And there it was. "Hang on, hang on, hang on," Marc said. He zoomed in the camera to confirm. "Right there." He pointed at the screen. "Black unmarked Boeing Ursa Major." He popped a Lifesaver into his mouth. "Are you lucky or what?"

Felix leaned in over his shoulder. "Where?"

X X

ROMULUS HAD SPENT most of the three hours that passed at Lifesaver's place sleeping. Tired from his fitful rest the previous night, he hadn't felt much like talking after the first fifteen minutes. When Felix had left to check on Lifesaver for the first time, Romulus had quickly drifted off while Diomedes kept his vigil at the window.

It was Felix who woke him as Diomedes was grilling Lifesaver for details of where he'd found the floater. Romulus got himself together while Felix made a quick phone call, and then they were off, headed for a club called The Arena. Romulus had only heard enough about the club to know that it was dangerous, and during the flight he asked Felix for more details that the man was happy to provide.

"Gangers make up the largest percentage of people at The Arena on any given night," Felix said. "The rest are a mix of gang wannabes, gamblers, and the occasional freelancer or counterpart of my own, looking to score an easy and dubious job. It's not a place I like to frequent."

"Gamblers?" Romulus asked. "What, is it part casino or something?"

Felix shook his head. "Oh, there are plenty of things there: alcohol, music, drugs. But the main draws are the death sports," he replied grimly. "The Arena is the closest thing to holy ground for most gangers, though that's really more of a guideline than a rule. They use The Arena to settle disputes or just to quench a little bloodlust—legally, but definitely not non-violently. There are a number of different games and contests, some one-on-one, some for a," he paused to scowl, "team. All have their own strict rules, and nearly all involve some variant of death as the objective or means to an end. There's always betting, and any agreement between opposing gangs or individual gangers based on the outcome is usually honored. How a place like that came into being would be a fascinating sociological study if it weren't so bloody."

Romulus nodded, understanding a little more now about conversations he'd overheard in the past where the "law of The Arena" was mentioned. "And it's all legal?"

"For the most part. Couldn't operate so openly if it wasn't. All the combatants are willing, so the idea's that they know what they're getting into. Nowadays most people who even bother to think about it just argue that calling it wrong for two willing people to fight—even to the death—under controlled conditions is needless victimization. As I said last night, there aren't many who put up much of a fuss over gangers killing each other if it doesn't affect them."

"And what do *you* think?" Romulus asked, not quite sure of his own answer to that question.

"In a nutshell? I think it's barbarically Darwinian. While the combatants may be willing, the thrill of the spectators and the betting is deplorable. Draws more people than you might expect, and not just from the quote-unquote lower classes. As for whether it's right to let people considered the dregs of society go at each other with rusty hooks, well, that sort of brings up the question of how they came to be those dregs and just whose fault *that* is. Not the most cut-and-dried issue, is it?"

Romulus thought of his own luck. It hadn't been the best, but he couldn't argue that he hadn't had his share of good fortune, either. If he hadn't found Diomedes, he wasn't sure where he'd be now. The images of the beaten vagrant from the previous night entered his mind suddenly, striking him with the sadism of it all and making it hard to feel sorry for the gangers then, regardless of their luck.

They approached the large, renovated warehouse that housed The Arena. Spotlights and neon shone from the exterior walls and pulsed chaos around flat screens, which displayed scenes from inside that Felix explained were recordings of past matches. Atop the building, looking slightly out of place on the otherwise haphazard, gritty structure, was an enclosed floater lot. When he'd heard that it was their destination, Romulus had thought it odd that a ganger club would have a dedicated floater bay, and he commented on that that to Felix.

"Gangers aren't their entire clientele. More than a few rich types like to watch and gamble on the events, and they like to have a semi-secure place to park their toys," he said. "After all, who do you think owns the place? Some folks probably even have reserved parking."

"Looks like the lot is full," Romulus noticed aloud as they approached.

"He's still in there, or Lifesa—, er, Marc, would've called," Felix told them. "If we circle, we could wait until he leaves and tail him. It's a good bet he doesn't live here."

"Circling attracts attention," Diomedes said. "We'll land somewhere and go in."

"Ah," began Felix, hesitating a bit, "Marc can only keep watch on the area for five or ten minutes. If he leaves after that we might miss him."

"We'll land and go up," Diomedes insisted.

They managed to find a ground spot a block and a half away. They got out quickly, and while Diomedes showed Romulus how to better hide a holdout weapon, Felix said he'd see what he could do about getting them in quicker at the door. A crazed howling echoed from somewhere in the distance as Romulus, anxious to be after Felix, watched him hurry down the street. A moment later, he and Diomedes followed.

"What happens if we find him in there?" he asked Diomedes as the two walked quickly towards the noise and lights ahead.

"Depends on who's around when we do." Before Romulus could comment, his mentor spoke again. "Careful. Something's up."

Romulus looked ahead of them to find Felix being surrounded by four men that he assumed to be gangers. They appeared to be talking, but the way the gangers were posturing around the small man was anything but friendly. Diomedes increased his pace to a jog, and Romulus followed instantly.

Before they could cover the full distance, the men sprang on Felix. Romulus thought he saw the glint of a knife in the hand of the one that Felix dodged first. He managed to spin the attacker around into another, but the two behind Felix grabbed his arms and held him back.

He and Diomedes were nearly there, and Felix made eye contact with Romulus, alert but not struggling. Diomedes reached them a split second later and drove the butt of his gun down on the back of the head of one of the two standing in front of Felix, knocking the ganger to the ground and then aiming at one of Felix's captors. Romulus followed, subduing the other freestanding attacker with a one-armed grab from behind that ended with his gun aimed at the final ganger on Felix's right.

The rescue caught both off guard, and Felix spun down out of their grip a moment later, pistol suddenly in hand. "Now," he said calmly, "I can see you're none too bright so I'll repeat myself and I'll speak *slowly* this time. Yes, I *am* curious about the arsons, and what interest is it of yours?"

Romulus looked quickly between the gangers before him and tightened his grip on the one he held. He waited for any answer, realizing now that this was no random mugging. The two he could see glanced at each other nervously. They were twins, matching further in their shaved heads, tattoos, and multiple piercings. He didn't spare a look for the one Diomedes had knocked down, and all he could tell about the one he held was that he stank of alcohol and funk. He wanted to ask Felix what had happened, but in that split second he sensed Diomedes's own silence and decided to remain powerful and quiet. The man in his grip wasn't moving. Filled with adrenaline from the rescue, Romulus wasn't about to let him.

"Nothin', man!" His eyes were locked on the barrel of the gun Diomedes had on him. "It ain't our business—we just screwed up—"

"You guys looking for some fun?" the other spoke up. "Man, I've got this friend—she could give it to all of you—just—"

"Shut up!" Felix pushed his gun against the back of the second man's skull. "Yeah, you screwed up—you *really* fuckin' screwed up. You forgot to look out for my friends here, and that's a mistake that might give you a new hole to shit through." Romulus was surprised at Felix's language, but kept silent. "Now the next words out of your mouths had better be an explanation, or my large friend with the two free hands is going to get *angry*."

Diomedes's gun pressed to the first ganger's temple to punctuate Felix's point.

"Geez, man, we thought you were someone else!" he cried.

The sharp flutter of a siren cut through the conversation before anyone could respond. As red and blue light reflected off of the gangers' faces, Romulus saw his mentor pull his gun down quickly. Felix did the same. Romulus jumped and let go of his captive, turning around to look. A police car had turned the corner and was passing by the crowded entrance to The Arena.

A moment later there was a sudden shuffling and Romulus sensed movement behind him as his mentor swore. He turned to see all four gangers bolting into the alley. Romulus looked to Diomedes, panicked and frustrated. "What do we do?" he asked urgently.

"Shut up and act natural."

"I doubt they saw us," Felix said as the police car rolled by. "That was probably just something to keep everyone in the area in line. Cops won't normally go *in* The Arena, but they do patrol from time to time." With a sinking feeling, Romulus looked down the alley where the gangers were fleeing. He wanted to follow, but Diomedes wasn't moving.

"They're gone, Flynn," Felix told him. The squad car continued by without stopping.

"But we can't just stand here—"

"They'd lead us straight into an ambush," Diomedes grumbled. "They can go to hell. Our target is there." He pointed to the floater lot. "We're just wasting time now. C'mon."

They turned and continued towards the entrance. "Funny thing," Felix said as they neared it. "They only asked about the arsons. Didn't say a word about our Wraith."

"Same thing," Diomedes said.

"I don't know. I wish we'd had them a little longer. I hadn't expected we'd wind up with other people asking *us* questions here."

"Would you really have shot them if they hadn't talked?" Romulus asked.

"Of course not!" Felix replied. "But I didn't want them to think that."

"Never bluff," Diomedes said.

"Oh, now I wouldn't agree with *that* . . . " Felix said.

Diomedes looked at Romulus. "Stay alert." Despite wanting to ask more, Romulus nodded and focused.

A short while later, after making their way through the crowd of people talking, yelling and just generally milling about mindlessly in front of the entrance, they were inside. Felix had briefly talked to the bouncer, a staggeringly large man—larger even than Diomedes—with two immense red chrome arms and a matching skullcap that covered him from the brow on back. Romulus didn't make out what Felix said to the man; it was much too loud and Romulus was too focused on the people pressed against him by the crowd, but he guessed it was a combination of familiarity and the cash Felix pressed into his metal hands that allowed them past so quickly.

Felix led them to a steel stairway that stretched up along the outside of the building, and they climbed it to the heavy door at the second story. A moment later, Romulus followed Felix inside to see the club stretch out below them. Everything below was bathed in the violent light of flashing red, pulsing strobes and harsh yellows. Everything above was mired in darkness. They were on a catwalk that looked to run the width of the building. Smaller walkways spread out over the center where people sat, walked, or dangled. Harsh retro-grunge rock filled the place, pumped out by a band somewhere out of view below. A wild yell to their left, audible over the grating music due only to its ferocity, jerked Romulus's attention fast enough to give him a glimpse of a half-naked figure diving from the catwalk into a mosh pit below. His fall triggered a brief fistfight that ended when the topless man fell beneath the mass of jostling bodies.

Straight ahead of them, the catwalk continued toward a doorway leading to a large section of the second story. The section was closed off from the open air of the catwalks. It appeared to run the width of the building. It was toward this door that Felix was taking them.

"The way to the garage is through there!" he yelled over his shoulder.

Moving beyond the door, they found themselves in a small, clean hallway that had Romulus blinking with its unexpected brightness in comparison to the previous room. It led to a T-intersection, from the top of which faced an elevator. The door closed behind them, blocking out the music enough for Romulus to hear the noise of cheering and cursing that seemed to come from other doors down the corridors to the left and right. Combat arenas, he guessed. They walked to the elevator and stopped.

"Normally," said Felix, fishing in his pocket, "you can only use the elevator with a card you get when you land upstairs."

He took a few cards out and thumbed through them, comparing each to some markings on the card reader. "But," he continued, selecting one, "I hate being normal." The card slid in, and after a moment, they were inside watching the elevator doors close as a sudden wild cheering rose over a shriek from down the hallway.

Moments later the doors were opening on the floater garage. "Split up," Diomedes ordered. "Yell if you find it."

Romulus moved off to the right, checking the landing spaces and trying to plan for what he would do if he found both the floater *and* its owner. He checked the weight of his gun and made a note to scan for cameras like Diomedes had taught him. He saw none—in fact, he saw no other people or even an attendant. He guessed the garage was automated. All he heard were his own footsteps and the occasional sound that he was forced to attribute to the others. All he saw were floaters that were not the type he was looking for.

Though bigger than he would have expected, it wasn't a large garage, and a minute or two later he had met up with Felix and Diomedes at the elevator.

"He's gone," said Felix, stating the obvious. Romulus dropped his guard and found himself feeling a bit of thankfulness mixed with his frustration. The sensation was bothersome. Was he a coward, or just unsure of himself? He didn't like either possible answer.

"We took too long!" Diomedes grumbled.

"He couldn't have left too long ago," Romulus told them.

Diomedes turned to Felix. "Call your friend. Now. Find him again."

Felix scowled and looked as if he would say something in protest, but instead merely pulled out his phone and turned away.

Romulus glanced about the garage. There were more vehicles than he would have expected. "Why was he here, I wonder?"

"Gangers," said his mentor.

"He didn't attack any."

"We don't know that."

Just then Felix turned back to them. "He's not answering."

"Why not?" Diomedes demanded. "Where did he go?"

Felix shrugged.

"Tell me!" he shouted, stepping forward and nearly making Romulus jump.

Felix pulled back as well. "How the hell do I know? He *does* have obligations, you know. He's not just going to sit around all night to serve you. And even if I had gotten him and he had time to comb the city again, he couldn't find him instantly." Felix paused as the two men watched each other's gaze. "I asked him to call when he gets in. So just *relax*. In the meantime I advise we follow your protégé's suggestion and see what we can find out about why he was here."

Diomedes turned back towards the elevator. "Stay together."

Romulus went after him, followed by Felix. "Come on, Diomedes, cheer up," the small man said plainly. "This place is violent. You'll like it."

They rode the elevator back down, briefly discussing where to look and unofficially deciding to just move around the club a bit, keeping their eyes and ears open. Romulus was a little dismayed at their lack of direction, but it didn't appear that they had much choice, and Felix told him not to underestimate the benefit of pure observation.

They came out onto the catwalk, once again surrounded by the noise. This time, led by Diomedes, they squeezed their way down the stairs onto the main level to find that the view from the catwalk had actually been quite obstructed, and a good deal more of the place was now visible. Some of it was still obscured by small dividing walls or hanging sheets of wire mesh that some club-goers were climbing on, but Romulus could now see a small stage where the grating music pumping through the speakers had its source. Bars and mosh pits were also scattered randomly around the place, but there was one area that, from the distance, did not seem to hold anyone or anything at all. After a few moments he could tell that it was a deeper pit, but could only guess at what was in it. The chaos of the activity around him only mirrored his own feelings of what seemed to be the pattern of their search: they'd missed a chance, and they were lost again.

Diomedes was leading them to the nearest bar along one side of the club when he stopped and stared angrily across the place. For a moment he said nothing. Romulus tried to see who or what his mentor was glaring at, but Diomedes was taller than he, and the place was much too crowded for him to determine the object of his mentor's ire.

"Wait for me at the bar," Diomedes told them. A moment later he was off.

Felix and Romulus crossed the short distance to the bar, managing to avoid eye contact and arrive unmolested. They were almost immediately attended to, or at least glared at, by the bartender: a tall, gangly woman with a short cut of brilliant blue hair.

"What're the one-on-ones tonight?" Felix asked immediately.

The woman raised an eyebrow at them and gestured with a sneer to the screen behind her, where a list of color-coded names and gang affiliations were displayed that Romulus took to be a list of duels and results. Beside the names were references to what he figured were the names of arenas or combat types—names like "Free Fight," "The Pit," "Rip and Tear." As Romulus watched, two names next to the last listing changed from their previous blue: one to red, one green. Numbers sprang up beside them that he guessed to be somehow related to gambling payoffs. For a moment he was curious as to how to read the numbers, until the knowledge of the "sport" they were attached to reasserted itself.

Suddenly Felix nudged him, and he realized the bartender had asked him what he wanted. He shook his head in the noise and mumbled a "no thanks."

The woman scowled at him before she caught sight of something behind him. Glaring furiously, she pulled a shotgun from under the bar and fired into the ceiling. Even before the shot's retort had ended she yelled out, "No goddamn guns!" Romulus looked behind him in the direction she had shouted. A man and woman stood a short distance behind him. Each aimed a weapon at the other. The bartender lowered the shotgun at them both.

"No guns!" she repeated. "You want to fuckin' shoot each other you take it to the dueling range or you take it outside!" She motioned with the gun. "*Right* now or I do you both!"

They both glared back at her for only a second, then lowered their own guns and moved away until the crowd and noise swallowed them. The bartender cursed after them and then moved to answer a shout for a beer.

Felix laughed beside him in what sounded like relief. "Great service here, eh?" He glanced up at the screen behind the bar. "No unaffiliated fights tonight," he continued. "No one not in a gang, I mean. I wondered if maybe our guy came to fight."

Romulus took a moment to regain his bearings. The bartender returned and slid Felix a clear drink, which the man sipped at while Romulus tried to refocus on the job.

"Maybe he did—just not officially," said Romulus.

"I'm almost glad we didn't find him," Felix remarked. "I'm increasingly less confident about what you've been told by whoever hired you." Romulus wasn't sure what to say to that. Felix shrugged. "Part of it's just a gut feeling," he said. "Part of it's not. You heard what I said before about certain things we know about him not meshing with the arsons. And now after being jumped by those guys . . . "

"They jumped you because you were asking about him, right?" Romulus asked over the din. "Sounds like we're on the right track."

"No," said Felix, "they didn't. They only mentioned the arsons. Nothing about our Wraith or even an arsonist. Diomedes made that leap of logic. While it's possible that they may have been trying to protect him, that certainly wasn't the feeling I got."

Something occurred to Romulus. "And they jumped you, not Diomedes or me. You're the one he hasn't seen. That we know of."

"Given what we know, he could probably take me himself without much trouble. Why send someone else?" Felix said.

Romulus looked into the sea of people behind him and wondered where Diomedes had gone.

"They knew me on sight," he heard Felix say behind him. "The only times—"

"What the hell you think you're bloody doin'?!"

Romulus had seen the speaker approach from behind Felix, but the smaller man's back had been turned and he showed no sign of noticing until the question had been shouted. Felix turned on his stool and looked over the newcomer quickly. He might have been a ganger—it was difficult for Romulus to tell. He didn't recognize any markings, and the stranger didn't look emaciated like the average ganger. He wasn't huge, but he wasn't stringy, and the blue glow behind his eyes indicated that they were more than mere cheap street implants.

"I beg your pardon?" said Felix after a moment.

The blue-eyed man leaned in closer, eyes pulsing slightly with light and threats. "I said, what the hell you think you're bloody doin'?"

"Oh!" Felix said cheerily. "Having a drink with my friend here, thanks for asking!" Felix glanced at Romulus and smiled.

The blue-eyed man again moved closer, seeming to grow as he loomed. He wasn't bigger than Romulus, but next to Felix the man's advantage in size was apparent. "That's . . . my . . . seat!" he growled. "That's . . . Angus's . . . seat!"

Romulus turned, ready for a fight, ready to come to Felix's aid if need be, but his companion's composure was calm.

"No," Felix replied into Angus's glare. "This is my seat. It was empty, I sat down in it," he said simply. "Find your own. There's two over there."

Angus grabbed Felix by the shoulder and spun him out of the stool, though the smaller man's balance was good enough to keep him from sprawling on the floor completely. Romulus reacted immediately, standing in challenge, but as Angus turned to face him, Felix darted in between.

"You got a problem with that, little man?" Angus sneered. People were watching them now. There would definitely be a fight. Where was Diomedes?

Romulus pushed forward, but Felix backed up against him and held him back. "Yes, actually," Felix said. "I left my drink behind." He darted in and grabbed his glass. "Much better." With that, he turned around and motioned Romulus to the other two empty stools.

Romulus had been expecting a fight. The utter lack of any physical altercation at all had him stunned and confused, and he was sitting three seats down with Felix before he knew it. "Who was that?" Romulus asked.

"That, apparently, was Angus." Felix said with a smile as he glanced about.

"I know, but who *is* he?"

His companion shrugged and sipped his water. "Someone who has a great fondness for his usual seat, I'd say."

Romulus paused, wondering if he'd missed something. "I thought we could've taken him," he mumbled.

"Oh, there were two of us," Felix mused, still looking. "You're probably right."

This wasn't making sense. "Was there anyone backing him up?"

"I don't know, maybe. But they probably would have found some way to make their presence known by then."

"Then why—"

Felix quickly put up his hand and turned to Romulus. "Did I hurt anyone?"

"Er, no."

"Did I get hurt?"

"Well no, but—"

"Is the situation resolved?"

Romulus blinked. "I mean, I guess so, but . . . "

"So what's the problem?"

"Well he . . . took your stool." Romulus began to feel foolish.

"If you're going to get into a fight—if you're going to risk your neck, and especially if you're going to try to hurt someone else—you'd damn well have a better reason for resorting to violence than a replaceable barstool. The thing with using force is even if you win, it's going to hurt you, too. And I'm not talking about bruising your knuckles. That's something you really need to learn if you're going into your line of work."

"But he was pushing you around," Romulus argued.

"Yeah, he was. I'm not saying he wasn't being an ass, I'm just saying that it's just a barstool. Very much like the one I'm sitting on now. My self-image isn't so fragile that I'd let something like that get to me. 'Course, it wasn't always like that."

There was a sudden yell from above and out towards the center of the club. Romulus and Felix both looked to see a large man fall from a catwalk down into a mosh pit and disappear from sight.

"And it seems like our friend Dio's decided to help me out with a little visual aid of his own."

Romulus looked up at the spot from where the man fell and saw his mentor staring blankly down below. Some yelling rose up from beneath where Diomedes stood, but Romulus couldn't make it out.

"I think," said Felix, "that he's just been challenged to a match. If I heard right." He took a drink. "I wonder how many stools that was over."

"You don't even know what it was about," Romulus said with a defensiveness that surprised him.

"No, but I know Diomedes—or at least as much as you think you do."

Romulus said nothing, instead watching his mentor as he made his way across the catwalk to the stairs, and didn't notice Brian until he spoke.

"Well what do you know? You guys are here after all!" The reporter walked up with a freshly reddening welt across his forehead. "When you told me to meet you in this hell-hole I half suspected you were trying to get rid of me."

"Glad you made it," Felix said. His eyes were fixed on Diomedes. Romulus nodded a greeting.

"Oh, don't get me wrong," Brian continued in mock joviality, "I love this freaking place. Where else can you get knocked out in a fistfight and mugged three times before you hit the ground?" The reporter paused to gingerly touch his growing welt before glancing around uncomfortably. "So where's our vigilante?"

"We missed him, I'm afraid," said Felix.

"*Missed him?*" Brian cried before lowering his voice. "Missed him? Then what am I doing here?"

"What *is* he doing here?" Diomedes had reached them.

"I called and told him to meet us here before we left Lifesaver's," Felix explained with a shrug. "And I'm sorry, Brian, but he was here when I called. You find anything?"

The reporter scowled, moving uncomfortably out of the way of two men who pressed their way to the bar. "Not too much, and nothing RavenTech. There are a few minor things of interest, but if I'm going to stand around telling you tidbits I'd rather do it outside."

"Take him outside," Diomedes told Felix. "Romulus and me will keep looking in here."

Felix looked at Diomedes, then to Romulus. "Remember what I said, Flynn. We'll meet you two back at the floater. In the meantime, you know my number."

A moment later, Felix and the reporter were gone.

"Come on," Diomedes told him.

"Where are we going?"

"I have to take care of someone first."

XXI

THE BRILLIANT WHITE half Moon traveled through the night. It cast a pale glow on its twin reflected in the glass of the skyscrapers that seemed to meet it halfway in the sky. Below, smaller lights shone, and landing lights pulsed in a lonely rhythm atop the higher rooftops. A police floater rose steadily above the streets on its patrol. Streetlights glowed closer to the ground, and the steady, solitary glow of a camera's active LED turned along the scene. Below, a black limousine's perfect finish reflected them all as the car moved through the streets, slowed to a stop beside the man with the ponytail, and took him inside.

Ken Wallace waited within the car as the man, one of his most trusted tools, settled in against the leather. "Good evening, Mister Fagles," said Wallace once the door closed. "Nice night for a walk. Brandy?" He motioned to an empty glass and a bottle.

Fagles loosened his overcoat and nodded in acceptance before taking the bottle to pour a small amount into the glass. "Nice night for a walk. Though I do like your way better, I think." He sipped. "This is good."

"Oh, yes." Wallace smiled. "Simple pleasures."

Outside the window, the city lights gave way to murky blackness as the car traveled out along a bridge floating across the water.

"So," Wallace prompted.

"Everything is ready for the exchange," Fagles answered. "Tomorrow night, eleven p.m. outside their training facility. They've agreed to one guard in each floater. "

"Good," said Wallace. "I'll have two more men in here in case they try anything."

"I don't think they will. I believe they have accepted my implication that this partnership may become more lucrative as time goes on."

"I have no intention of that."

"Neither do I, Mr. Wallace." He grinned. "I don't see your point."

Wallace smirked back. "I'm just making certain we're clear."

"Crystal."

"Good. Everything is ready with the product. Your diligence will be rewarded. It appears that all we need do now is wait." Wallace lifted his glass. "And tie up loose ends, if there are any left?"

"The drugs with which we paid your 'associates' seem to be working well. I've managed to get reports of two of them dying from a, quote, overdose."

"Confirmed?" Wallace asked.

"As reliable as can be expected, considering."

Wallace shook his head. "It's inefficient, this idea of yours. Having to rely on unconfirmed secondhand reports in such matters makes me worry."

"As I've said before, what you see as inefficient, I see as simple, safe and elegant," Fagles replied. "We pay them in tainted drugs, they use them, and after a comfortable amount of time has passed, their heart stops. No one's going to care enough to do a detailed autopsy on some ganger passed out in a gutter. And with the delay, do you really think the others even have half the intelligence to connect the drugs to the deaths?"

Wallace shook his head. He didn't pick those punks for their brains. Hell, they didn't even get the right warehouse at one point. "No, but it still irritates me to leave open the possibility that we didn't take care of them all."

Fagles drained his glass. "What will they do, report you to the police? Even if it didn't mean incriminating themselves in the process, who would believe them?"

"I don't like loose ends. They come back to haunt you. Speaking of which, how is Diomedes?"

Fagles smiled coolly. "Nothing certain yet, but he is looking. I understand that after I spoke with him, he hired a man named Felix Hiatt, so I do think he's taking our offer seriously."

"Good." It *was* serious, if he succeeded. "Who's Felix Hiatt?"

"Someone with a knack for finding things out. Quite well, from what I understand."

"So they might have a chance," Wallace said thoughtfully. He was becoming glad that his attempt at killing the man the other night had failed. It would be interesting to see the outcome of this endeavor.

"Who will kill whom, I wonder?" Fagles asked, as if reading his thoughts. He grinned again. "I do so enjoy no-lose situations."

Wallace did, too, though in this case he was pulling more for the outcome that would relieve the larger irritation of the two. Diomedes hated him, but the psycho had done more that actually threatened Wallace's plans than Diomedes had. At least so far. He would not have his plans ruined by such an insignificant.

Wallace had received word of confirmation from his ESA contact earlier that day. It was definitely more than just an unusual mineral deposit. Lives might have been lost, but what mattered even more was that there was activity. Secrets. *Profitable* secrets, and with that came power. It was a promise that he was prepared to invest in.

The limousine continued along the highway, chasing the Moon to the horizon.

XXII

FELIX WAS MORE than a little concerned about leaving Flynn inside The Arena, though it struck him as ironic. From a physical standpoint, Flynn was better off than Felix was himself. Not that Felix wasn't comfortable in his ability to defend himself, but Flynn's larger size was more intimidating. Yet it wasn't Flynn's physical well-being that Felix was concerned with at the moment. On the other hand, there was only so much you could tell a person at once before you had to let their own experience teach them. Felix just hoped experience wouldn't be too harsh.

He followed Brian out of the place, amazed at how much the reporter drew attention to himself by trying to remain inconspicuous. He wove this way and that as they made their way to the exit, trying not to be noticed by the sea of people yet managing to get in the way of nearly everyone with his erratic course.

"Just bite the bullet and push through, Brian," Felix admonished from behind him.

"Bite the bullet, he says," Felix heard him mutter. "Exactly the thing I'm trying to avoid here . . . "

They did make it to the exit without any real trouble, but, Felix noted with some amusement, not before they passed by one particular man more than twice. Felix wondered a bit that Diomedes didn't insist on hearing what little information Brian had to share. Either he was angrier than normal with the man he was about to fight, or his opinion of Brian's help was now close to nothing. Or both, really.

"Well, that was fun, wasn't it?" Brian said as they left the mass of bodies in front of the building. "Come here often?"

"Not if I can help it. Their brunch menu is just atrocious."

Felix looked around, scanning the area with a bit of caution. This wasn't the best place to walk and talk, and while there was probably more violent energy inside The Arena than outside, it was more likely that they'd be chosen as a target while isolated out here in the open. He would have found the irony more interesting if he hadn't been attacked earlier. "Might as well head back to the floater," he said. He led the way. "So you weren't able to find much?"

"Virtually nothing we could use, from the building records. You told me to look for anyone with a RavenTech connection, right?" Brian shook his head as they walked. "Nothing. Not a damned thing. Not in the press files, anyway."

Felix nodded.

"Interesting thing though, there was a convicted arsonist living there." The reporter read from a palm computer. "One Casey Dodd, fifty-four. Served ten years."

"Fifty-four? Well if the arsonist *is* our Wraith, it sounds like Mr. Dodd might be a bit old."

"He also died in the fire," Brian added. "How's that for poetic justice?"

"An even better reason to rule him out," said Felix, a moment later ashamed of his own callousness.

"Yeah, I thought so, too."

Felix thought he heard footsteps behind them as they crossed the street under a crumbling sky bridge. He glanced around a moment to check but saw no one who seemed to be directly following. His near-mugging earlier was making him jumpy. Brian was looking ahead silently, and they walked a few feet more. Felix glanced up to watch a plane fly overhead. "So what is it you're trying to decide about telling me?"

"Hmm? I'm not trying to decide."

"Okay, so?"

Brian cleared his throat. They walked a few more paces. A spotlight arched across the clouds from somewhere to the east.

"I did some talking with a colleague who's looking into the arsons," he said finally. "I'm not her favorite person. I didn't even think she was going to tell me anything when I asked, but I guess she thought that she could get something from me in return. She was friendly enough. But, she doesn't like me."

"What did you find out?" Felix pressed. Were Brian's ramblings genuine, or was he was just stalling?

"It's possible that the arson was a cover for theft. I couldn't get too many details—like I said, she doesn't like me. Or maybe she doesn't know, herself—but apparently RavenTech's own investigation found that the surviving debris might not entirely account for everything that should've been there."

"How much?"

Brian sighed and shook his head. "I don't know, exactly. It'd have to be a decent amount for them to notice it gone in the rubble, no?"

"That's a lot for one man to move by himself," Felix thought aloud.

"And not a very subtle way to hide it, with an obvious arson."

A rush of thoughts hit Felix. He struggled to put them into a sense of order. "They'd be looking for whoever did the arson. Like you said, it's an obvious crime—so it stands to reason that the person or persons who stole the equipment didn't directly set the arson. They paid someone else."

"Well, maybe."

"It doesn't make sense, though. Even if they stole the stuff, they had to get inside. That's a high security warehouse. Anyone able to get in long enough to move the stuff out should be able to cover their tracks better than just burning the whole—" Felix gasped as another thought hit him. "Unless . . . "

Brian stopped. "What?"

"Unless the stuff was never there in the first place. Stolen, or rerouted by someone on the inside, maybe? Destroy the records of the reroute, then destroy where they're supposed to have gone so they're less likely to notice it missing."

"What, you're saying that RavenTech stole their own product?"

"Maybe," Felix said. "Making a lot of assumptions, here, but . . . it fits."

"So why the other fires? Drawing attention to the arsonist instead of the theft?"

"Maybe. Or maybe there were thefts at the other places that just weren't noticed? Or maybe they had a different purpose."

They continued to walk. "I'd say it's a good bet a Dirge apartment wasn't theft."

"And if it wasn't theft, then . . . " The realization hit him suddenly. As quickly as he had it, Felix reminded himself that it was held together by assumption. Still, could it be Wallace? "Diomedes was the target," he announced aloud with a trace of wonder at why he'd dismissed it so easily before.

"Care to explain that?"

A noise from the alley—just the skid of an old can against concrete— made Felix turn suddenly. It was the same alley down which the men who jumped him had fled. He was definitely twitchy. Trying to relax, he was about to answer the reporter when something caught his eye. Felix stopped and peered, enhancing the light with his implants, and saw a leg extending from behind a corner down the alley. It looked to be at an odd angle, but around it was . . .

"Felix?" Brian asked. He followed Felix's gaze into the gloom.

"Your sight's probably a little better than mine," Felix whispered. "Can you tell: is that blood?" He felt more than heard the reporter's reactive wince beside him.

Brian looked. "I'm—I can't tell. But I'd be willing to bet."

"No bet." Still peering cautiously down the alley, he moved into the unknown.

"Uh, Felix? Felix?"

Felix waved for Brian to be silent. He pushed himself forward, and it was harder than it should have been. Brian hurried up beside him.

"What do you think you're doing?" the reporter whispered harshly.

Felix continued creeping forward. The noise coming from The Arena up the street overshadowed any in the alley. He focused his hearing and still heard nothing. "I already know this is a dumb idea, Brian. I don't need you to remind me."

"I think it is blood," Brian said. He pulled out his taser.

Felix couldn't help but grin. "Take the safety off this time?"

"Shut up."

The reporter paused at the corner, covering him as Felix stepped around it.

* * *

"You're going to fight?" Romulus asked after Felix left. He was following his mentor across the sea of people out towards the center of The Arena.

"He challenged me."

"Why'd you throw him off the catwalk?"

They reached the open area that Romulus had noticed before. It was a giant pit dug out of the floor about twenty feet by forty feet, and twelve feet deep. He stood at the edge with Diomedes while he waited for his mentor to answer.

"Not him," he said finally. "The one he fell on."

Romulus thought about some of the "games" he had seen on the board above the bar. "And so just because he challenges you, you're going to fight him to the death?"

The glare Diomedes gave him all but slapped Romulus across the face. Romulus shrank back and said nothing.

Below them, the pit waited. Patrons gathered closer to the edge, alerted by some unseen signal that there would soon be a fight.

"Probably not to the death," Diomedes muttered.

"But it could happen."

"Might."

"But—" Romulus again tried to form a protest but couldn't find the words.

Diomedes pulled out two handguns while his eyes burned through Romulus in a dead stare. He handed the weapons to him. "Hold these." On the other side of the pit, a man jumped in. Romulus took the weapons and nodded to his mentor. For a moment Diomedes said nothing. The anger briefly dropped from his eyes and he said sternly, "You want to learn? Watch." With that, he jumped down, landing heavily on his feet in the dirt.

Romulus wasn't quite certain what to expect. Would they just fight? Or would there be some sort of announcement? Both Diomedes and his opponent seemed to be waiting for something.

The opponent was smaller than he would have expected. The man was about Felix's size, wiry and thin. He paced and darted around his end of the pit, rubbing his hands and arms rapidly and bouncing in a frenzy of disorganized energy that made Romulus wonder what drugs he was on. The man glared at Diomedes the entire time, but he looked to be no match for Diomedes's sheer bulk. Perhaps his quickness would give him an edge, but Romulus found himself relieved despite that unknown. His mentor would probably take him easily.

A knot formed in his stomach.

Yet still, nothing happened. Romulus glanced around for someone or something that was supposed to trigger the fight. Reader boards appeared unchanged. Screens still continued to show various videos and TV channels.

What the hell was Diomedes doing accepting this challenge, anyway? They had a job to do. It didn't make sense, but then how does a freelancer gain respect if he runs from a challenge? The question bothered him. He wondered what Felix would say.

Spotlights from above flashed to life to shine down through the smoky air into the pit. Romulus instinctively looked down only to find both Diomedes and his opponent looking upwards. He followed their gaze to where the four beams crossed. He could see nothing in the glare, but something was happening.

"Ladies! Gentlemen! Wretched worms I see beneath me!" The voice, shrill and wicked, sounded suddenly as the music in the immediate area stopped. "We! Have! A! Challenge!"

A roar went up from the crowd. Romulus could now see a man being lowered down into the nexus of the beams, hanging upside down with his knees bent over a sort of trapeze. Nearly naked, with skin dyed deep red, the announcer held a yard-long pipe in each hand. The red man swung slowly as he talked, motioning with the pipes as he addressed the crowd with the demeanor of either a circus ringmaster or a gleeful devil. His voice screeched over the club's sound system, caught by an unseen mic.

"Direct your attention to The Pit, where our latest combatants will entertain you with their own bloodlust!" Another cheer went up from the crowd with a vehemence that sent a shudder up Romulus's spine. "Our latest match is a nameless challenge—" (here a number of boos echoed) "—between this immense bald hulk," he gestured to Diomedes, "and the fool who challenged him, this spindly rat-man! Shall we call him Rat Face," the announcer cackled, "or just a dumbass with a death wish?"

More yells went up from the crowd, crying out both names and profane suggestions for others, or just clamoring for a start to the fight.

"But first, the rules! Simple enough for even you putrid scabs to grasp! No weapons but those in the pit!" Here he hurled the pipes down to the center of the dirt below. "*No* audience participation!" He shook his head and waggled a fingertip. "And the first one to stop moving . . . is the *loser!*" The crowd cheered and screamed in approval. The ringmaster gave another cackle as he started to rise back into the darkness. "Have at it, boys!" he cried as he disappeared.

With that, the fight began.

Both men bolted toward the weapons. Diomedes's opponent was quick, but Diomedes himself covered the distance in four great strides, overshooting the pipes and barreling into the small man before he could reach them. Rat Face was knocked onto his back and had to move quickly as Diomedes continued to ignore the pipes and lunged in with a kick that knocked the other's feet out from under him. He tumbled to the left as he fell to avoid the strike of Diomedes's fist, and then regained his feet and backed away. Diomedes stood his ground. The crowd urged him on.

Romulus guessed that Diomedes's immediate goal was to keep his opponent from the pipes and maintain the advantage that his own size and strength gave him in a hand-to-hand fight.

Rat Face made a feint in either direction, seeming to test Diomedes's reflexes. In each case, equal movement from Diomedes blocked his attempt at progress. Another feint. Then another that ended in an indignant yell. Diomedes said nothing, and once more the small man moved. This time Diomedes flinched in the opposite direction. Rat Face bolted for the opening, but Diomedes was too fast. It must have been a trap; his mentor changed direction instantly to hurl his body around and land a solid blow square across his opponent's shoulder blades. Both continued forward, off balance, but Rat Face slammed into the dirt a moment later while Diomedes stumbled around him.

The wind knocked out of him, the smaller man struggled to rise as Diomedes regained his balance, turned around, and rushed in anew. Rat Face had just started for the pipes again when a kick from Diomedes slammed him in the jaw. He tumbled back down with a yell of pain that spat blood. The crowd whooped and hollered as Romulus winced. This time, however, the small man got to his feet quicker and came at Diomedes in a furious rush with fists flying.

Diomedes, seemingly caught off guard, fell back. Rat Face managed no real damage through the larger man's defense but managed to batter him back far enough from the pipes to gain an opening. He rushed for the opportunity, practically diving for the weapons, arms outstretched, but too soon: Diomedes grabbed him before he could lay a finger on the pipes and forced him to the ground in a tackle. The two wrestled in a wild grapple of arms and legs. Though Diomedes was clearly overpowering the man, he could not gain a firm hold; Rat Face flailed and twisted like a farm hen struggling to forestall its slaughter, giving Diomedes little opportunity to do more than struggle back. They grappled and tumbled through the dirt. Around the pit, the crowd above cheered them on with traded bets and shouted curses.

Soon Romulus could tell that his mentor's opponent would be able to make a grab for a pipe in a moment if things continued. Could Diomedes see it? He was too close to the struggle, possibly blinded by proximity, the pipes at his back. Romulus tried to yell out a warning, but his shout was lost in the noise. A split second later, the small man seized a pipe and beat it across Diomedes's face with a pounding that Romulus nearly felt himself. His mentor released his hold and rolled off the smaller man. He lay there, reeling, as Rat Face snatched up the other pipe and got to his feet.

His mentor was down and vulnerable, maybe even in danger of being killed if he didn't get up! Romulus found himself yelling, screaming for Diomedes to stand. Rat Face moved in and swung a pipe hard and downward. It smashed into the dirt a fraction of a second after Diomedes twisted out of the way. The smaller man exploded to the offensive, swinging one club after the other as Diomedes, now on his hands and knees, tried to regroup. One swing hit Diomedes in the thigh, a blow that Romulus expected to knock him back down, but his mentor continued to move and rolled out of the way.

His momentary advantage lessening, Rat Face began to jump around Diomedes, still swinging wildly while Diomedes dodged. His mentor struck out, trying to catch his opponent or the pipes, but Rat Face was too quick. He rained blows amid gleeful cackles onto Diomedes's hands and arms. Frustration punctuated every counter-attack that his mentor tried. The laughing jackass's every swing felt like it went straight in Romulus's own face to taunt him, threaten him, and he couldn't do a damned thing to stop it.

"Hit him!" Romulus whispered. "Come on!"

The fight continued, and with every pipe swing, every failed catch by Diomedes, every throb of his pulse, Romulus felt the growing urge to leap onto Rat Face's back and knock that smug look off of his face. Every grab his mentor attempted made Romulus wince in anticipation. Every time he caught only air was like a burning brand in Romulus's side. Rat Face was taunting him, taunting his mentor. Diomedes should've been able to stop him, but the man was floating out of reach. Every swing and cackle was a twist of the knife that threatened Romulus's mentor, his protector, his own safety! The threats, the taunts, they had to stop! Diomedes was so close!

The pipe clanged again across his mentor's reaching hand. The voice screaming for Diomedes to get him was Romulus's own.

Suddenly Diomedes backed off. Rage burned in his eyes. The other held his ground, still taunting them. Again Romulus yelled for his mentor to get the man.

Diomedes suddenly scooped his arm down into the dirt and hurled a handful at his opponent's face. It hit the bastard square in the eyes. He stumbled back, surprised and blinded. One of the pipes fell from his startled grip. Romulus roared with the crowd.

And then Diomedes was rushing forward with a running punch that smashed the man hard in the face. The full force of the blow pounded Rat Face into the ground and released a whoop from Romulus's lungs.

Rat Face was doubly stunned. Diomedes took full advantage with a series of kicks that shoved him across the ground. Wracked by blows to his entire body, the man struggled to get up. Diomedes grabbed him by the shirt and hurled him forward with one hand. He skidded across the dirt like a rag doll. Again Diomedes was on him. He picked up the small man once more and this time threw him into the dirt wall of the pit. The man hit it head first and fell back as blood rushed from his nose and mouth, covering his face.

It was then that Romulus recalled Ranth's blood on his own face, the warm flood that had splashed him as Diomedes's bullet took the Nosferatu's life.

He stopped cheering.

Diomedes picked the barely moving man up again by the neck. This time Romulus wasn't in danger. He was watching from above, comfortable, as his mentor struggled for sport against a foolish man half his size. As the memory of his own cheers came back to sting him, Romulus saw Diomedes pause. The now broken-looking man in his grip was not moving but still seemed to be alive. Time hung still in the air. Romulus breathed a sigh of relief that it was over. He looked up to see if the ringmaster was coming back to announce the winner.

Suddenly Diomedes attacked again. He pounded his victim against the wall with both hands and wracked his already broken body with more punishment, the motivation for which Romulus couldn't understand. The crowd around him pressed in with wild screams. Romulus's own pleas for his mentor to stop were drowned out by the calls for blood that surrounded him.

The man's battered body leaned limp and beaten against the wall, held up only by the force of the blows impacting his helpless form. Diomedes tugged him forward by the collar, lifted up his body, and hurled the man over his shoulder. His beaten opponent sailed sickly through the smoky air, the force of the throw twisting the body in odd contortions under the red light shining into the pit. The man's eyes were open in vacant observation of his plight. His gaze caught Romulus's for a moment before he hit the ground like a piece of meat, and did not move.

The crowd roared.

Diomedes advanced, pipes in hand.

Romulus couldn't speak.

And then his mentor stopped short. He stared upward, out of the pit, at a point behind Romulus. Romulus turned to see what he was staring at but found nothing but the chaotic flash of lights and the blackness beyond. When he turned back, the devilish ringmaster above was concluding the match with a flourish of words that Romulus couldn't listen to. Romulus only watched, silent, as Diomedes climbed out of the pit.

"We're leaving," his mentor said as he reached for his weapons. Romulus handed them back in reflex.

"What?" he finally managed.

"We're leaving." Diomedes pointed up behind Romulus. "He's there."

Romulus followed his arm to one of the TV monitors that showed a female reporter among flashing sirens on a street in the night. Behind her sat a familiar black floater.

Romulus glanced back into the pit. The small man's body was being pulled out. Romulus couldn't tell if he was breathing or not.

"Hurry up," Diomedes said, moving away already.

Romulus turned, let out a shaky breath, and followed his mentor.

XXIII

THERE WERE, in fact, two bodies. Felix only gave them a moment's glance before checking up the alley and then behind him to make sure they weren't walking into an ambush. Aside from the bodies, the alley remained dark and deserted. Belatedly, he looked upwards. Still nothing.

Motioning then for Brian to step out, Felix crouched to examine the men and winced. One was covered in blood that looked to be his own, his chest and face cut as he lay unnaturally against the wall. Felix checked his pulse and found nothing. The other body, a little farther around the corner, looked undamaged and much more relaxed. For a moment Felix thought he could be sleeping, but, like his companion, his pulse was silent. Felix recognized them both.

"Nasty piece of work," Brian said from behind. "What happened to the other guy?"

"Don't know," Felix replied. "Doesn't look like he was attacked. Looks like he just . . . died."

"Looks like we've got another Wraith attack."

"These are the men who jumped me," Felix said. "Two of them, anyway."

"Jumped you? When?"

"A while ago, when we arrived. They implied I should stop asking questions about the arsons. Diomedes and Flynn showed up a few moments later, but the cops came and they ran off before we could find out too much."

"Doesn't look like they got very far."

"Maybe. There were four of them, though. Why did these two stop? I didn't hear any attack then."

"Maybe the one had his heart attack or whatever and the other stopped to help him," Brian suggested.

"And the other two kept going? Makes sense; then Wraith attacked after we'd gone. I'd sure like to ask these two some questions."

"Given their current state, I'm sure they'd prefer to be able to answer."

Felix knelt down beside the one who hadn't been slashed and wished he knew the signs of death by heart attack so he could check Brian's theory. He began to search the body.

"They obviously had some connection with the arsons. And given what happened to him," Felix motioned to the bloody one, "I'm even less convinced that Wraith sent them." He wished they had some other name to call the vigilante. He found some cash and decided to ignore it, continuing his search.

"Maybe he sent them to take care of you and this is their payment for failure?" Brian supposed.

"I admit I hadn't thought of it that way," said Felix. "Still, if he was close enough to do this to them, why not just do me himself?"

"Mmhmm."

"Still, I'm not going to rule it out." Felix found a phone in the ganger's pocket, a more expensive model than he would have expected. He pulled it out and scanned through the recent call history. Only numbers, no names, but Felix still recognized one.

"I'm an idiot," he said.

Brian looked down from a nervous glance about the alley. "What is it?"

"Charlie Hobbes," said Felix. He told the reporter about his encounter with Charlie in the rubble of Diomedes's ruined building and how the man had claimed to not know anything about the arsons. Or, rather, that he "might" and had to do some checking.

"You think he tipped them off?" Brian asked. "Or maybe he had a hand in hiring them?"

"The former, if it's anything. If he was directly involved he'd have fed me some false information to throw me off his trail. I'd bet he sold the fact that I was looking for them. Probably why he wanted to wait to tell me anything: he wanted to see how much they'd pay first."

"So you think these guys are the arsonists?"

"I'm starting to think that's a definite possibility. If that's the case, then how does our vigilante play into things?"

"A patsy?" Brian offered.

"Expensive patsy." Felix dialed Charlie's number from the ganger's phone. It rang.

"Yeah?" It was Charlie's voice.

"Hello Charlie," said Felix, certain the caller ID displayed on Charlie's phone.

A pause. *"Who's this?"*

"This is Felix, Charlie. You said I'd be hearing from you. I hope you don't mind me calling first. Care to tell me whose phone I'm calling you on?"

<click>

Felix hung up the phone and smiled wryly. "I don't think he was very glad to hear me."

"Can't imagine why."

Felix put the phone away and finished searching. All he found remaining were a few more dollars, which he put back.

"What, you think he needs the money?" Brian asked.

"No," Felix said as he stood. "But we don't exactly need it either. Might as well leave it for someone who does."

Brian was about to say something more when he stopped short. After a moment, he said very softly, not moving his lips, "There's someone watching us."

Felix froze, then rethought and pretended to fish through his pockets. "Where?" he whispered.

"Behind you. Lying on the fire escape."

"So where do you think the other two ran?" Brian asked a moment later in a louder voice.

"I don't know," Felix said in his regular manner. He turned around, trying to appear casual. "They could've just as easily went one way or the other." His gaze swept the alley, sliding across the fire escape about thirty feet away. A figure lay there in the darkness, just barely visible, and Felix turned his eyes skyward a moment after spotting him. "Though I suppose they could've gone up . . . " He looked down, once again passing his gaze over the face to get a better look before turning his back on the watcher to address Brian.

"He must've followed us from The Arena," Felix whispered. "We brushed past him twice on the way out."

"So . . . what do we do?"

Felix paused to think. The man hadn't seemed too threatening before. If he'd wanted to kill them, he'd had plenty of time already. That was some comfort. "Follow me," he mouthed. He then turned and moved down the alley towards their watcher. "Maybe the others aren't far away," he said aloud. "C'mon, let's see."

Brian moved in closer to walk behind Felix in the alley. They approached the fire escape and pretended to concentrate their search at ground level. Felix fought the urge to look upward. The man made neither move nor sound as they neared him. Felix reached into his jacket.

When they were under the platform, Felix pulled his gun and aimed up at the man on the wire mesh. The figure above was startled and flinched visibly, but moved no more and said nothing. Between the grating and the shadows, Felix could make out nothing beyond the eyes looking down at him.

"Hi," Felix said sternly. "My friend has sharp eyes and I don't like being watched. Who are you, and why are you following us?"

The man above slowly shifted up onto his knees.

"Ah!" Felix declared in warning. "Slowly. Come down here." The silent figure hesitated. "Now."

Time stopped.

Felix waited.

Brian waited.

The man ran. He stood and leaped down from the platform in a fluid motion that caught Felix so off guard that he was watching the man take off running down the alley before he realized it had happened.

"Stop!" Felix yelled only to have the man ignore him. "Damn!" he whispered, putting away the gun. "He called my bluff. Come on!"

Then he was off, with Brian following.

They raced through the alleyway. The figure ahead of them, half-cloaked in the darkness beyond, soon turned a corner that led back out to the main street. Felix charged after him, now a little less worried that they were being led into a trap. The clatter of trash cans and the rattle of a fire escape ladder echoed around the corner, but Felix rounded it just in time to see their eavesdropper run out of the alley and around onto the sidewalk. He ran past the fire escape and leaped the overturned cans, breathing hard and hearing Brian right behind him.

Felix turned out of the alley and stopped. This street was more crowded than the last. He looked helplessly in the direction the man had gone, but blinded by headlights and chaos, he saw nothing.

"There!" Brian pointed and took off again. Felix followed, still unable to spot the man himself. They ran one block down, across an intersection, and around a corner. Felix was starting to get winded.

Brian stopped and cast about. "Do you see him?"

"I didn't see him the last time." Felix caught his breath and looked vainly for any sign of the man. Cars passed by and a few people wandered down the sidewalks, but their spy was gone. "I think he lost us."

"I bet he doubled back on us. That or he's somewhere very close, watching us right now." Brian peered around again.

"He's a sneaky one," Felix agreed. It had been nicely done. Creeping to that vantage point on the fire escape without them hearing couldn't have been easy. He looked around at the area, mentally mapping their location. "Hmm."

"Hmm?" Brian asked. "Hmm, what?"

"Hmm, hmm," Felix answered. "Follow me."

He half walked, half jogged down one more block to a side street. A light rain whispered down on them and coated the streets in the glare of reflected lights. Felix took Brian past a cement staircase that led down to a basement door, glancing down at the door as they passed. It was closed. He ran across the street then and ducked into a doorway to crouch in the shadows. Brian settled in beside him.

"What are we doing?" Brian asked with audible impatience.

"Shh. Watch across the street."

Brian scowled but said nothing. They crouched and waited. For a few minutes, Felix only watched as cars and pedestrians passed. No one noticed them there in the doorway, but no one was their quarry, either. Another few minutes ticked away. The reporter shifted nervously. Felix was about to give up when he spied their man walking to the stairwell and going down. Felix grinned. He did love being right.

"How'd you know he'd go down there?" Brian whispered.

"Know who The Scry are?"

"I think so. They're kind of information gatherers, aren't they?"

"Yeah. Competitors to me, in a way, though I talk to them from time to time. C'mon, looks like now's one of those times." Felix stood and started to cross the street.

"Maybe I'm missing something here, but if they're spying on us, wouldn't it be a little stupid to go knocking on their door?"

"Nope!" Felix said. "I mean, even if they are collectively spying on us, which isn't really a guarantee with how their own little hierarchy works, they won't do much beyond tell us to go away. They're pacifists." Felix trotted down the stairwell with Brian at his heels, rapped against the iron door, and then added, "Well, pretty much."

"Pretty *much*?" was all the reporter got out before the metal shutter in the door slid open. A pair of eyes scrutinized them.

"Yes?" a woman's voice demanded.

"Ah, hello," Felix said. "I'm wondering if you can help me find something out."

"And what is it that you seek, Felix Hiatt?"

Felix smiled back, surprised neither that the gatekeeper knew his name, nor that she chose to use it. The Scry tended to have a love for flaunting knowledge that rivaled his own. "Well, for starters, I'd like to know just why one of you was tailing us."

"We follow people. Other people follow people, too. If someone was following you, congratulations for noticing, but why assume it was one of us?"

"We trailed him here. And I need to know: was it business or pleasure?" It was perfectly feasible that, being known to The Scry as a kindred spirit, one of them may have just decided to follow him and see if they could learn anything. If one was being hired to watch him however, knowing who had done the hiring could offer some valuable answers.

The gatekeeper's eyes glanced from Felix to Brian and back. The shutter slammed shut without warning.

"So, is this how they usually do things here?" Brian asked after a moment.

"Ah, if she comes back in a few moments, yes. If not, then no."

A few moments passed. "That'd be a 'no,' then?"

Felix scowled. "I get the distinct impression we're being ignored." He knocked at the door again.

The shutter slid open. "Go away."

"Look, I—"

The shutter closed before Felix could say more.

"Not terribly friendly, are they?"

Felix turned to Brian. "You're enjoying this, huh?"

The reporter smirked.

"Third time's the charm." Felix knocked again. The shutter didn't open.

"Apparently not."

"You know, if anything this just makes me even more suspicious."

"Why? They could just as easily lie to you if they were being paid."

"The Scry don't lie," Felix told him. "Pardon the rhyme. A reputation for honesty is what keeps them paid."

"'Trust no one' is a good rule to live by."

Felix shrugged. "Your loss."

"So what now?"

"Not sure," Felix answered truthfully, "but there's not much we'll accomplish standing here."

"We could wait here until one of them comes out—or sneak in another way."

Felix shook his head. "Pretty sure they could outwait us. Even if we did sneak in, I don't think we're likely to discover anything that way." He made a move to the staircase. "We'd better get back to the floater. At least for the moment."

Felix trotted up the stairs with Brian following. No sooner had he arrived at the top than a purposeful clearing of someone's throat behind him made Felix turn. Leaning on the railing around the top of the stairwell was a woman Felix hadn't even noticed. Short, dressed primarily in dark blue denim and without any visible piercings or tattoos, she looked rather ordinary for the area. Even her hair, though no less attractive for it, was merely a natural brown and pulled back in a ponytail. Her hands clasped, her eyes calm, she watched them.

In a poor attempt to hide his intrigue with how this woman had presented herself so stealthily, Felix glanced at Brian. The reporter seemed equally surprised. "And how long have you been there?" Felix asked her.

The woman smiled slightly. "What," she replied, "would be the point of being so quiet if I were to tell you that? Rather ruins the effect, wouldn't you say?" Her voice, deeper than he'd have expected from her size, was different from the one at the door and held a UK accent. Welsh most likely, Felix thought. The woman remained where she was, smiling confidently with one eyebrow arched.

"Point," said Felix, "but it rather ruins the point of getting our attention if you don't tell us anything at all."

"Who are you?" Brian shot.

"Caitlin," the woman answered. She straightened and then walked towards them into the light, which showed enough of her features for Felix to put her in her early thirties. Felix caught his guard dropping and readied himself for any sudden movements.

"Felix's name I know by reputation," she continued, speaking to Brian. "Who in the bloody hell are you?" She stopped, still smiling, and tapped her fingers on the rail.

The reporter hesitated a moment. "Brian."

"Mmhmm," she said. Felix got the feeling they were being looked over.

"Would I be right in assuming you're one of The Scry?" Felix asked.

"A good assumption," said the woman called Caitlin. She turned and indicated with a wave of her hand for them to follow.

"What do you think?" Brian asked.

"Don't know." The woman was walking away. Felix noticed that her hair was actually braided and likely longer than it looked. "But you know what they say about opportunity."

"And curiosity."

"Okay, so we'll be careful," Felix said, following after her.

She led them up the street a short distance to an empty bus shelter and sat down. Felix checked to make sure the bench was clean and sat a moment later. Brian apparently preferred to stand.

Caitlin spoke before Felix could say a word. "You're partly right. The Scry haven't been hired to follow *you*, but those two freelancers you were with. You just happened to pick up a tail when someone saw you with them outside The Arena. You're working for them?"

Felix nodded. "I guess that's pretty apparent, yes."

"To do what?" she asked.

"I was under the impression that you led us here to tell us something, not the other way around."

"Your impression is accurate. You're looking for the vigilante, the . . . 'Wraith.'" It was a statement. "Why?"

"If I tell you, will you be telling me something in return?" Felix asked.

"If your answer is what I expect it will be."

From how much they'd been watched, Felix guessed that The Scry already had a pretty good idea. "Those two freelancers were hired by someone who thinks he's behind the warehouse arsons. So we're looking to find him."

"He's not," she said. "Behind the arsons, rather."

"And how do you know that?" Brian asked. Felix nodded his approval of the question. Something made him want to trust this woman, but he tried not to let his guard down too much. She did have very nice eyes, though.

"Because he's had us keep our ears out for information as well."

"He's who hired you to follow us," Felix stated.

"To follow your friends, yes."

"Why?" Felix pressed.

Caitlin shook her head. "I don't know. He's not the kind of bloke that takes to telling us much at all. Matter of fact, I get the feeling he knows a lot more about the bloody arsons than we do."

"Sounds like he has The Scry do a lot of things for him?" Brian asked.

Caitlin looked at both of them sternly. "I need your promise that what I'm going to tell you doesn't go beyond us. I hear you're trustworthy, Mr. Hiatt, and I'm willing to risk that. Can you vouch for your friend here?"

Felix glanced at Brian, wondering. "I think I can," he said. Brian nodded. "And call me Felix."

The woman paused, thinking. "He gets a lot of information from us, to the point where he's become an honorary leader to some. He's done favors for some of us—helped some of us out of a bollocks or two. I think he regards The Scry as his flock. What I've gathered is that a lot of what he gets is news on other groups, mostly gangers, and he uses it against them. Which is why I don't want this to get out. It could send the wrong kind of attention our way. I have the luxury of being in the city by choice, though I've got some friends who aren't as lucky."

"No one's going to hear it from me, I give you my word," Felix said. "Or from Brian." He turned to the reporter, still speaking to Caitlin. "I'm sure he knows that I could make things very difficult for him if he tarnishes my vouching." Felix suddenly rethought how that sounded and patted Brian on the shoulder genuinely. "But I'm not worried."

"Thank you," Caitlin said. It came with what Felix read as a faint smile of relief despite the hint of uncertainty in her eyes. "So what do you think about the arsons?"

"Seriously starting to doubt that it was him."

"He's hinted that he might've been set up. He hasn't said by whom."

"Maybe by whoever's behind it." Felix opted to keep his suspicions about RavenTech to himself for the moment. He guessed Caitlin had approached them with more information than she'd told so far.

Caitlin nodded. "Or maybe just an enemy who'd like to pin it on him."

"Maybe both," Brian added.

"Someone who'd hire two freelancers to go after him," Caitlin finished.

Felix looked down, uncomfortable. "Apparently he had the chance to take out Diomedes last night when he attacked him. He doesn't seem like the kind not to take that opportunity if he felt threatened. Any thoughts on that?"

"As I said, the bloke doesn't tell us much. I suspect he knows something about your friend. He needs him, or wants him alive."

Brian spoke up again. "Why should we even believe you?"

The woman arched an eyebrow and shot Brian a glare that Felix thought could have stopped a bullet. "You're a bloody obnoxious sod, aren't you? Don't believe me, see what good it does you!"

Felix attempted a disarming chuckle before Brian could say more. "I, ah, do get the feeling that you have something more to tell us, though," Felix said.

Caitlin looked down from her glare. She nodded silently, seeming to compose herself. "Well, first of all, he goes by Gideon. At least it's what he has us call him. And secondly," she paused again, looking to the ground for just a moment, "we—I—know where he lives."

Neither Felix nor Brian said a word. Felix leaned in closer.

"You're still bound by your promise," she confirmed. Felix nodded. Brian did the same. "It's an older flat on the corner of Fortieth and Twelfth in the University District. I don't know which unit, but that's where others have met him. He's told us to look for him there if need be."

"Not exactly the safest place in the city," Felix said. "I wonder where he keeps his floater." Caitlin didn't respond. "At the risk of offending," Felix continued, "why are you telling us this?"

"Because The Scry are the only ones that know, and if you find out, I think he's paranoid enough to suspect that one of us told you. I want him to stop trusting us."

"To *stop* trusting you?" Brian repeated.

"To stop using us. He's getting too controlling. Putting us at too much risk for his own purposes. As I said before, putting the wrong kind of attention our way. I want it to stop. I don't want to harm him, just his trust in us."

"By telling us where to find him."

Caitlin nodded. "He wants a meeting with your Diomedes anyway. All I'm doing is letting you find him first."

"You realize that Diomedes may be trying to kill him," Felix said. It seemed only fair to warn her.

"Oh, hell!" Brian blurted. "Not before I get my interview, he's not! I thought he was just trying to find him! You didn't tell me he was going to kill him!"

"I don't know that!" Felix declared. "But it's a possibility."

"Oh, great, so Diomedes goes out there and offs him and then where am I?"

"Crikey," Caitlin said in the middle. "You said you didn't think he was the arsonist!"

"*We* don't! But Diomedes doesn't know yet," Felix told her. Brian's outburst had caused Felix's own voice to rise. He tried to bring it down. "He even thinks Gideon torched his apartment."

"Bloody hell," Caitlin cursed under her breath.

"But we don't have to tell him," Brian said hurriedly. "We can just go there ourselves, I can get my interview, and—"

"Diomedes is still going to be looking for him," Felix argued.

"Yeah, but he's not going to find him without us! Look, let's just go there now and find him ourselves!"

Caitlin was shaking her head. She cursed again.

"Gideon is going to find him," Felix continued calmly. "Diomedes is going to shoot first and ask questions later unless we get to him first."

"Do you know where he is?" Caitlin asked, somber.

Felix nodded quickly. Brian was backing away.

"Fine," said the reporter. "You tell Diomedes, I'm going to get my interview."

Felix somehow felt bound to keep Brian with him. "So you're going to just go by yourself, knock on his door and ask to talk? You think that's safe?"

"I'll be okay," Brian replied as he turned away. Felix fought the urge to chase him down, neither able to think of a real reason why he should nor what good it would do if he did. "Don't worry!" the reporter yelled back as he jogged away. "I'll keep our promise!"

"Bloody hell," Caitlin muttered again beside Felix.

"If it's any consolation, I think he will that, at least," Felix told her.

"Bugger it, he'd better. Where's your Diomedes now?"

"Close by. We're due to meet back up shortly, actually. I'll find him before it's too late." He found himself wanting to reassure Caitlin despite his impression that she could obviously take care of herself. "I'm sorry you misunderstood me about who thought what."

Caitlin only shook her head. "I'm going with you to talk to Diomedes. Where is he?"

"I really don't think that's a good idea," Felix said, worried. "He's already in a bad mood. We just missed your vigilante before and—"

"He's not *my* vigilante."

"And he's not *my* Diomedes. My point is that he's less than jovial. I hate to say this, but Dio might hurt you just for being connected to him."

She stared back at him. "Then we'll tell him carefully. I need to make sure he's straightened out."

Felix considered arguing for a moment, but despite his worry, he had to respect her determination. Plus, based on the stubborn defiance streaming off of her, he didn't think he'd win. Had the situation or time permitted though, he'd have enjoyed the debate. "Brian and I were supposed to meet them at a floater a few blocks away. I'll show you."

Felix stood and Caitlin followed as he began to think of what he'd tell Diomedes and how to keep Caitlin from getting hurt.

"Danae," she suddenly said.

"What?"

"I know your last name," she stated as they hurried up the street. She motioned to Felix. "Hiatt," she said, and then pointed to herself. "Danae."

Felix smiled despite his worry. "Caitlin Danae," he repeated, searching his memory. "*Clws i gwrdd â chi,*" he tried in greeting.

"*Clws i gwrdd â chi, hefyd,*" Caitlin responded with a smile, not missing a beat. "You speak Welsh?"

Felix smiled to himself. "I remember a little."

XXIV

ROMULUS WOKE from his haze as the floater lifted off. While technically awake for the entire time between the fight's end and lift-off, he could recall no single thought of his own during that period. Now, as the nearby buildings gave way to the gritty brilliance of the city skyline beyond, that dead calm broke with the awareness of his own shame.

He'd been cheering, and the memory of it burned him. Why had he been cheering? One minute he was as worried for Diomedes as if his own life were being threatened, the next he was thrilling at the sight of the brutal hand-to-hand as Diomedes destroyed his opponent. Romulus couldn't believe he possessed the savagery to take pleasure in such a thing. It hadn't really been him—he'd been drunk on the energy of the crowd and relieved that his mentor would be okay. The thought was a buoy he clung to in a storm of doubt. He would not be the kind of man to find sport in that brutality. He refused the possibility.

But when the bloodlust and relief had subsided, the fight had kept going. And going. Too far. Why didn't he try to stop it then? The small man in the pit had been beaten long before the fight ended. Romulus should have done something. He should have yelled out and got them to stop it. Or had he? Guilt turned in his gut. He couldn't recall. It was all a haze of violence and regret. If he had yelled, he should have yelled louder. Had he yelled at all?

He looked over at Diomedes. His former roommate piloted the floater with grim determination. Diomedes had driven his fists furiously into his opponent's limp and beaten body, ignoring Romulus's own cries for a reprieve.

Romulus should have yelled louder. He should have jumped into the pit and pulled his mentor from the man. His opponent had forced Diomedes to his fury. He had to use it to defend himself and then he got swept up in it, unable to regain himself until he saw the news footage. Diomedes was a freelancer, after all; Rat Face had provoked him. Romulus should have seen that and pulled Diomedes out of it. Guilt rushed over him again as he realized he probably would never know if the man was alive or not. It was his fault for not reacting.

Romulus looked over at Diomedes again, brooding over thoughts he would not allow to form. The cityscape sped in confusion beneath them, and everything was moving too fast. He needed time to think.

Siren lights flashed up the approaching buildings and reflected on the insides of the cockpit. "We're here," Diomedes announced.

Romulus pushed his thoughts to a shadowed corner of his mind and forced his concentration to the moment, looking out the window at the activity below as they descended. A police car was parked at an odd angle on the sidewalk, where it separated a small gathering of people, including the news crew, from an area of darkness next to the buildings. Romulus could make out no details in the shallows, but the black floater was still there, crouched on the far side of the street just a small distance up the block.

"He's still here," Diomedes said. "Look for him."

Diomedes's phone rang. He didn't answer it.

They drifted upwards again and Romulus began to scan the rooftops. The city lights were ruining his night vision. Though he tried to avoid letting his gaze fall on them, they seemed only to get brighter as time went on and pulled his focus towards the light. His mind was turning to sludge, thick with walls and barriers that would only let him look.

Diomedes took them in a path that swept the rooftops, cruising slowly at a steady altitude while they both looked down. Despite the ambient light from the city, the shadows were many, and Romulus had to concentrate on the edges of the buildings where things were less dim, hoping he might catch a glimpse of their arsonist peering down at the scene below. They had to find him. Without that, without the money to help him rebuild . . .

He couldn't finish the thought. Doubts of the nobility of their purpose whispered to him with Felix's voice. The floater seemed to close in around him. He adjusted his seatbelt, trying to get some relief.

They continued to sweep the area. Diomedes moved them into a wider pattern.

"I see something!" Romulus said.

"Where?"

Romulus was looking down, nearly beneath them. "On top of the last building. Someone's up there. You just passed it."

Diomedes swung them around. There was no sign of anyone when they'd turned, but still they closed in, descending, until the floater hung over the top of the building.

"There." No sooner had Diomedes said the word than a dark figure fled across the roof away from them. "It's him." A shaft of light split the roof down the middle, and it was clear that Diomedes was right when their man dashed through it. The floater lurched into motion, launching across the roof after him.

The vigilante had reached the far edge of the building in an instant and jumped down. The floater overshot the edge in its momentum, and they banked around in time to see him swing himself over the top platform of a fire escape down to the one below. Diomedes held their position in wait as the vigilante nimbly swung and jumped down, platform by platform. It was a six-story journey, but the man was nearly to the ground already. Still Diomedes waited. The vigilante hit the ground and was off.

Diomedes grabbed a monitor atop the console and spun it to face Romulus. "Watch the ground view," he ordered. "Don't lose him!"

The screen held a wide view of the area below. Diomedes was already flying in the direction he ran, keeping a constant distance above the ground. Romulus tracked their target and called out directions, concentrating on the chase.

On they tracked the vigilante. On he ran, twisting and turning but always, Romulus noticed, away from where his own floater was parked. He showed no sign of stopping or even hiding; he had a destination in mind. Romulus glanced ahead and guessed where it was: the vigilante was headed straight for the West Center Transit Station. Except for the large open arch of the entryway, the place was entirely below ground.

"He's going underground, we're gonna lose him!"

The floater plunged with a lurch that left his stomach in his ears.

"Jesus!" Romulus cried. The ground rushed up to meet them and for a moment he lost all sight of their man as his eyes closed by reflex. He was all but thrown to the floor a second later as Diomedes stopped them just before they hit the ground. Ahead, the vigilante ran straight for the open archway in the ground floor of an approaching skyscraper.

"Oh, God," Romulus began. He pressed himself into the back of his seat. "You're not—!"

Shock held the rest of his protest in his throat. His mouth hung open, paralyzed, as his hands grabbed onto whatever they could and his foot stomped on an imagined brake pedal. The entrance loomed before them. Diomedes skimmed the floater even closer to the ground and plunged them inside without a word.

Romulus cried out, reeling and out of control as Diomedes steered them to the right, avoided a wall, and flew them down a bank of escalators after the arsonist as the mercifully small number of pedestrians before them dove for cover. The ceiling, thankfully high, allowed the floater clearance down to the next level. Romulus once more tried to cry out in protest, but a sudden clang and tearing shocked him to silence again as they smashed a hanging light at the bottom of the escalators and sailed under a low archway before scraping the floor and leveling out.

The vigilante continued to run, only a few yards ahead of them, and turned right into a wide corridor a little over half the length of a football field. Diomedes nearly didn't react in time; they careened across the width of the hall to narrowly miss smashing into a bank of ATMs.

"What the hell are you doing?!"

Diomedes ignored his shout. He swung them around to face the vigilante, who was still running down the bay towards a railing that marked the drop-off to the space below, where the subway trains ran. Narrower balconies ran the length of the upper area where the floater's engines whined and people scattered. Escalators led down to the tracks, but their quarry headed straight for the railing.

The floater lurched to movement once more, and they launched forward to close the distance to the railing. The vigilante looked behind at them through the tinted windshield. Romulus doubted he could see through it. They were coming up fast. The engines screamed in acceleration.

"I'm not losing him," Diomedes swore.

Romulus tried to protest.

The man jumped the railing.

They didn't stop.

Romulus yelled as the floater smashed through the railing and tipped forward to give them a full view of a receding subway train on the tracks below. Before he knew what was happening, Romulus was thrown back in his seat from the acceleration. Everything was a blur of chaos and motion. He was vaguely aware that the floater had somehow leveled out. When he managed to shake the shock from his senses, he realized that the lighted surfaces rushing by on either side of them were the walls of the narrow subway tunnel. They'd left the station behind and were gaining on the train ahead of them. Romulus's eyes widened when he saw the vigilante clinging to the rear.

The floater took up nearly the entire width of the tunnel. Diomedes pitched them back and forth, trying to maneuver through the constricted space. They were faster than the train, but it had the benefit of rails. Every time they got close to the train, the wall swiped the floater, knocking it back with a scrape so violent that Romulus kept expecting to ram straight into the side of the tunnel. He wanted to yell at Diomedes to stop, but they'd committed themselves. He could only hold on and try to keep his heart from pounding out of his chest. The vigilante merely clung to the train, a black silhouette against solid dingy gray. Like Romulus, there seemed to be little he could do until he was out of the tunnel.

Even Diomedes was silent. A determined grimace of anger held his face, growing harsher with every scrape of the tunnel walls. The engines whined as they sped on. Corners closed in on them as they turned, and still the floater plunged through the tunnel, trapped and pursuing.

And then they were out. The cement hole opened up into another station—Padelford Place near the university—brick and open to the air. A sigh of relief aborted back into Romulus's lungs in panic. The train was stopping blindly while they screamed forward; their momentum would ram them into it from behind!

The vigilante looked back at them. Romulus cringed and braced, yet the horrible impact failed to occur. He found himself thrown sideways and for a moment felt nothing beyond the crush of his seatbelt on his chest as they slowed.

They'd missed the train.

Diomedes had swerved to avoid it, but barely. People stared at them from across the tracks as they coasted to a halt beside a brick wall that ran along one side of the open-air station. Prying his hands off the armrests, Romulus looked for any sign of the vigilante. There was none.

Sirens began in the distance as Diomedes cursed.

*   *   *

The floater was gone. It was either that, or Diomedes had somehow managed to disguise it as a broken-down '35 Uhatsu two-door. Felix looked around in frustration. "I don't suppose you see any invisible floaters lurking about?"

"What?" Caitlin responded.

"It's gone," Felix said. "They're gone." For a moment he considered the possibility that Diomedes had just gotten nervous again and taken off, but last time he did that, he'd left Flynn to wait, too.

"Well," the Welshwoman demanded, "where did they go?"

"I don't know." Felix pulled out his phone with a grimace. "But Dio's not one to leave me behind unless he thinks he doesn't need me anymore." He dialed as Caitlin waited and scanned the sky. "Don't worry, they couldn't have gotten far. I'm almost certain that they stayed at The Arena for a while after Brian and I left." Of course, they were in a floater while he and Caitlin were on foot. Felix decided not to mention that.

"You're calling him?"

Felix nodded as it rang. And rang. Felix hung up. "He's not answering."

Caitlin scowled and cast about. "What about the other bloke?"

"If Flynn has a phone, I don't know the number."

"Then what," she asked, turning back to him, "do you propose we do?"

Felix glanced up at the empty sky and began to think aloud. "Like I said, Dio wouldn't have left unless he didn't think he needed me anymore. So he either found Gideon, or he thinks he knows where he is. If it turns out he's wrong, I'm sure I'll be getting a call."

"But that's not the option we need to worry on."

"Right. If he's not wrong—"

"If he's not wrong, then he might wind up at the flat I just told you about," Caitlin finished for him.

"It's our best bet," Felix agreed. "C'mon, we can get a cab on Fifteenth."

Caitlin grabbed his arm when he turned to go. She released the touch quickly as he stopped, and Felix found himself wishing it had lingered.

"Wait," she said. "I can't go with you. I don't want to run the risk of having it look like I led you there. It's one thing if he suspects The Scry, quite another if he is certain. I'm already playing with fire as it is."

"I'll find him," Felix told her.

"What's your number?" she asked quickly. Felix must have paused just a bit too long as she continued, "You're not the only one with resources, Felix. If I can find out where they are, I'll call you."

Felix agreed. "I'll do the same if I find him first. But don't The Scry have my number somewhere?"

"More polite this way," she said with a small smile. "And I prefer the direct approach."

They exchanged numbers. Felix found himself wishing she could have come with him, and for one shocking moment he actually couldn't think of a thing to say. Caitlin looked back at him with an urgent gaze that reminded him he needed to hurry.

"Good luck," she spoke in Welsh.

"*Hawddamor*," he returned.

He rushed into the night, alone, with Caitlin's face not the least of the things on his mind.

XXV

THEIR FLIGHT OUT of Padelford Place was nearly as harried as their flight into it, though almost certainly less dangerous. Once again, Romulus sat in silence as Diomedes launched them away from the closing sirens. It seemed that they had escaped before any vehicles made visual contact with them, a fact for which Romulus was very grateful.

They fled quickly from the station. Their only objective just then seemed to be just getting away from the place. Even so, Romulus could read the frustration in Diomedes's face and was sure he was keeping an eye out for their man. Now that the adrenaline had withdrawn from his own system, Romulus kept his mouth shut. Diomedes was visibly steaming.

They took a winding path through the streets, skimming behind buildings and heading for the university campus. A small wooded area among the buildings hid an outdoor theater with its tall pines, and it was there that they landed, hidden in the shadows on the grass.

As the sirens faded in the distance, they stepped out. Diomedes began to take some supplies from the floater as Romulus looked at the trees. It struck him how much of a difference they made; they had the power to block out the rest of the city and shield them from the chaos. Most of the trees on the farm had been barely beyond twenty feet tall, much shorter and sparser than these tall evergreens, but somehow he felt at home and at peace here among them.

Diomedes stepped from the floater with a gray equipment bag slung over his shoulder. With only a determined look, he ordered Romulus to follow.

They traveled a short distance through the trees, following a silent, dark path until breaking out into the open. Diomedes kept a swift pace ahead in the direction they had come. Were they just going to wander the area on foot and hope they got lucky? In the floater it made more sense; without it, such a thing seemed futile.

Diomedes continued to lead him along the silent, empty buildings.

Then again, did they have much choice? Sometimes persistence paid off. They had followed the vigilante this far. To stop now would be to throw away the good fortune they'd had in finding him. Yet they'd already lost him again.

For the first time, his head was suddenly clear enough to realize that they should have seen Felix at the floater. He had been planning to meet them, hadn't he? He tried to remember what the man had said when he and the reporter had left, but Romulus couldn't recall specifically. The reporter was going to tell Felix about what he'd found. Was it something that caused them to miss meeting at the floater? Maybe something that spoke to Felix's doubts about Wraith really being the arsonist? Where had he gone?

Romulus began to worry, both that Felix knew something vital and also for the man's general safety.

They left the campus, turned onto Twelfth Street, and then crossed it. Diomedes's pace began to slow. Romulus closed the distance to walk beside him and tried to figure out how best to breach the other's mood. For a moment he couldn't bring himself to say anything. They stepped onto the sidewalk and continued on. Romulus opened his mouth but merely cleared his throat. Diomedes turned his head to scrutinize him.

"Uh," started Romulus, looking forward, "shouldn't we call Felix?"

"Why?" Diomedes turned his gaze away to scan the area.

"Well, he was going to meet us, wasn't he? At the floater?"

"He can take care of himself. We don't need him now. We haven't lost the mark yet."

Romulus looked around as they walked, keeping his eyes from Diomedes. "Maybe he found something else out."

"Don't be stupid. We stop to call Hiatt, we lose the mark."

Romulus felt his initiative weakening. But what if Felix had gotten jumped again? "Let me use the phone to call him while you look," Romulus tried quickly so as not to be cut off. "He said this guy might not be the arsonist, maybe he found some other evidence—"

Diomedes turned and glared, his voice a harsh whisper. "We don't get paid to get evidence! We get paid to—"

A nearby burst of gunfire cut Diomedes off.

* * *

The echo of the nearby gunfire reached Felix's ears just after he stepped from the cab that had taken him to Fortieth and Twelfth. For a moment he paused, listening. There was no more gunfire, but the sounds of wicked laughter followed in the distance.

There was also no sign of Diomedes's floater. He stopped and listened again.

* * *

Minutes later, Romulus galloped up the poorly lit apartment stairwell. An obviously broken lock on a door had let him inside seconds earlier, and now he rushed up towards the roof like Diomedes had told him. They'd found the vigilante in another fight, and did not want to be stunned again. Diomedes was at that same moment rushing to the top of another building. Romulus didn't know exactly what he planned, only that it was Romulus's job to cover him.

Romulus had reacted to Diomedes's instructions in the sudden chaos after the gunshots without thinking. Things were moving too fast again, and it looked like everything was going to end a bit sooner than he was ready for.

The roof door was unlocked from the inside. A moment later he was out and vaulting the barrier that divided the small rooftop deck from the rest of the roof, landing on the other side with one foot smashing down six inches into the fragile surface. For a moment he paused, fearful of dropping through to the level below. When it was apparent he would not, he gingerly withdrew his foot from the hole and crept the rest of the way to the edge.

Two L-shaped buildings framed a parking lot between them. Four stories below was the chaos of a fight. Two gangers already lay on the ground near where the vigilante stood fighting another three. A short distance from them, their backs to parked cars, stood two more gangers holding a man and woman hostage. All of the gangers had grotesquely painted faces, and the two with hostages shouted taunts and cackled in a way that made Romulus shudder in remembrance of the howlers in The Dirge.

Diomedes was nowhere to be seen. The far rooftop was empty.

Romulus pulled his gun, unsure what to do. The fight below continued. The gangers laughed as their hostages struggled, their mouths muffled. His first instinct was to try to help them, but if he fired from here with just the auto-pistol . . .

A crack echoed upward as another ganger went down. One of the remaining two fighting the vigilante lunged at him. Romulus could see he was off-balance even before the ganger knocked him back against a car. The other pulled a gun and started firing. In the commotion it was impossible to tell who was hit. Romulus felt himself watching, impotent, before movement straight ahead caught his eye. Diomedes crouched atop the opposite building, working quickly to set something up behind the retaining wall.

What should he do? Felix's words came back to him, arguing what they didn't know. Wraith was fighting again below. The ganger with the gun was out of bullets and backing up towards the hostages as the vigilante advanced. Diomedes hurried to assemble what Romulus saw to be a rifle. As the vigilante knocked the ganger aside. Diomedes began to take aim. Romulus was doing nothing. Just like at The Arena.

With a flash of light from his palm, the vigilante stunned the last two gangers along with their hostages and then ran forward to catch the woman as she started to fall. Diomedes corrected his aim. He was about to fire. Miles away, Romulus cried out in protest.

A blur of movement came from behind Diomedes as the gun fired.

*   *   *

Felix didn't have time to make more than a hasty assumption before he dove against Diomedes's shoulder to defeat his aim. The bullet sounded like it hit a car, but there wasn't time to look. In a few brief seconds the freelancer shifted and pulled his auto-pistol, shoving Felix off his back and onto the rooftop before he aimed the gun at him.

"Wait, dammit it's me!" Felix shouted.

Diomedes's eyes blazed. He shifted his gun and fired.

The bullet shot through the rooftop beside Felix and reflex alone darted his body further away. At that range, Diomedes had missed on purpose. Felix pushed himself to his feet, forcing himself to calmness and gambling that the shot was just a release of anger.

"He's not the arsonist!" Felix told him.

Diomedes paused, and for a moment the look the freelancer gave him was balanced between unreadable or uncaring. "He's the job," he stated finally, picking up the rifle and crouching down to brace himself against the low wall guarding the building's edge. "Get in the way again and I'll kill you."

Felix believed him. He took a chance. "Wallace hired you!"

Diomedes stopped.

"What?"

Felix wasn't completely sure of it, but it made sense. It was also probably the one thing that might stop Diomedes. "He's playing you for a fool, using you to take out another enemy. Do you think he's going to pay you when you're done? Or is he going to finish you off when you come to collect from his lackey?" He hoped to God his instincts were right.

Diomedes did not move. Felix fought the urge to find out what was happening below. His attention had to be focused on the freelancer. Where was Flynn?

Diomedes screamed. He stood up, howling out a primal yell of fury as he rose. Still yelling with an intensity that paralyzed Felix, the freelancer spun around, swinging his rifle like a club and letting it go just before it would have hit Felix. It smashed against the door to the stairway behind him.

Felix stood before the freelancer, watching him shake with rage and frustration. He honestly didn't know what to do. For an instant he thought he saw genuine pain in the freelancer's eyes. It was gone in the same instant.

The vigilante was there a moment later. Felix figured he'd crawled up over the side of the building somehow, but Diomedes's body had blocked him from Felix's view such that he seemed to just appear in the space behind him. Diomedes hadn't noticed. The vigilante made no further move.

"Diomedes," the vigilante spoke. "Wallace wants us dead." His voice was calm and distant in a way that Felix found eerily soothing. "And I need your help."

At first Diomedes didn't move, standing silently in a near-match of the masked figure behind him. And suddenly he was turned around, a hidden weapon drawn and pointed directly at the dark figure's head.

"He wants us to kill each other," Gideon spoke.

"He's telling the truth, Diomedes," Felix warned. It was like watching a lit match tumble towards a pile of gunpowder. "Let's hear what he has to say. You've caught him." Another long second crawled by. "You can always shoot him later."

It was one of the stranger things he had said in his life. Felix tried to flash Gideon a helpful smile but his gaze was leveled straight at Diomedes.

Diomedes stepped forward and put his gun to the man's head. "This is a bad place to talk."

"Yes," Gideon spoke. "It is."

*   *   *

Brian watched Felix and the freelancers follow the vigilante into the side door of the apartment. They had gotten to him first. Just his luck, thought Brian. He had been waiting just across the street in the dark of a bus shelter for the last twenty minutes. He had stayed put when he heard the gunfire, foolishly choosing to await the outcome rather than run into a firefight. It was the safe choice, and he should have known it was no time for playing it safe. Now he might be completely screwed. If he messed this up, his editor would have all the pull he needed to can him, no matter what strings his dad could pull.

Then again, the vigilante was still alive. Felix could have been wrong about the freelancers' intentions. That would be a break, at least . . . unless Felix told the vigilante not to talk to Brian out of spite for ditching him. That's probably what he was doing right now. "Don't talk to the reporter," and Felix would have the information for himself. Brian was unsure what exactly that would accomplish, but he was willing to bet that Felix would try to get back at him.

Brian watched as the door closed, and he tried to feel better by telling himself that he made the right choice under the circumstances. Unless it had all been a trick. Brian shook the thought out of his head.

If he wasn't careful, he'd get paranoid.

XXVI

WHEN FELIX HAD BEEN in college, an art student lived across the hall from him who had a special fascination with the color black. The vigilante might very well have paid her to be his decorator: Everything was black. A fire could have swept through the place and it would have looked no different. At least, Felix amended, the part they had seen so far, which consisted of a long room with a black curtain divider running the length of one wall. Only a single fluorescent lamp on the ceiling bathed the place in harsh light.

What it lacked in color, it made up for in dinginess. The room was made to appear larger by its lack of any furniture, save for a single black table and chair, a black bit of shelving beside them, and a black antique chest. The shelves contained numerous bits of cybernetic parts. The table supported a single laptop computer. The chest sat closed. If the room had any doors besides the exit, they were behind the curtain. No light came from beyond it. Felix searched Gideon's hard, silent eyes and wondered at the things the curtain hid.

The four of them stood uncomfortably in the room as Flynn closed the door. Diomedes kept the gun leveled at Gideon's head. "So," the freelancer said. "Talk."

"Put the gun down," Gideon spoke.

"Fuck you."

"I could take it from you." The masked man's voice was still calm and flowing smoothly.

"Try it."

"I thought we were here to talk," Felix tried.

"Shut up, Hiatt," Diomedes hissed. "You don't need to be here."

"Why?" Felix asked with more anger than he thought wise. "Because I'm the one who's been trying to tell you that you've been looking for the wrong guy?"

"We were hired to find *him*."

"By Ken Wallace," Gideon said.

"You said that."

"You didn't start the arsons, did you?" Flynn suddenly asked.

The vigilante turned slowly, his eyes still on Diomedes, and walked to the computer. "There's something you should listen to." The screen blinked to life, and a moment later a conversation played. Felix didn't recognize the voices, but he could make a guess.

"*I don't like loose ends,*" began a man's voice. "*They come back to haunt you. Speaking of which, how is Diomedes?*"

"*Nothing certain yet,*" said the second voice, another man, "*but he is looking. I understand that after I spoke with him, he hired a man named Felix Hiatt, so I do think he's taking our offer seriously.*"

"*Good. Who's Felix Hiatt?*"

"*Someone with a knack for finding things out. Quite well, from what I understand.*" Felix couldn't help but smile. It was nice to be known, after all.

"*So they might have a chance.*"

"*Who will kill whom, I wonder? I do so enjoy no-lose situations.*"

The vigilante stopped the playback. "Do you recognize the voices?"

Diomedes nodded, his face twisted into a scowl. "Wallace."

"And the guy from the 'Pyre," added Flynn.

"There's more on the recording if you have any doubt."

Diomedes shook his head but refused to lower his gun. "Where did you get this?"

"A bug," Gideon spoke. "Inside his limousine."

Felix blinked. "How did you manage that?"

Gideon just smiled. It was a bit unnerving, and Felix reminded himself that this man was a killer. "There's more you should see."

He keyed in a quick sequence and an image appeared on screen that spun into a video. The image was shot through a barred window that looked into a warehouse. Low-light enhancement filtered the frame; it was night. The cameras zoomed in to a group of three men.

Their heads were shaved and their ears shined with the glint of metal—no, there were four men; the three kibitzed around a fourth, who was setting a bomb of some kind. The picture did not linger long, and soon vaulted upward onto the roof. Felix guessed it was either a head mounted or direct optic camera. The image ran across the roof, swung down into a larger window and dashed across to the bomb. Felix recalled the freelancer's description of the video they'd seen and wondered if it had been shot at the same time.

"Who are they?" Diomedes asked.

"I think those are the guys who jumped me outside The Arena," Felix answered. "Or two of them were, anyway."

"And the filth who burned your apartment," the vigilante whispered.

"You know a lot for someone who didn't do it," Diomedes shot. His gun was still drawn.

Felix had to stop himself from saying that the vigilante had used The Scry to look into things. He thought about Caitlin and wished there'd been time to call her.

"They did it," Gideon repeated. His eyes remained calm behind his mask.

"Prove it," Diomedes challenged.

"I can give you as much proof as Wallace gave you on me."

"I remember them," said Flynn suddenly. He looked to be trying to recall something. "When we were coming home that night—those howlers we dodged—I mean, that might have been them." Flynn glanced to Diomedes for confirmation.

After a moment, the larger freelancer nodded. "Might have been." He put the gun down.

"Wallace hired them as well."

"I knew it," Felix grinned.

"How did you know?" Diomedes shot. The freelancer moved to face the entire group.

Felix winked. "It pays to have me around."

The freelancer turned his glare on Gideon again. "I want to know what's going on. Everything."

"Wallace is stealing from his own company. Stealing guns." A fire crept into the vigilante's eyes. "Weapons. Bullets! For the killers that stalk the streets and prey on the innocent. Guns that give power to the terror, terror that I fight every moment . . ."

Felix took a tiny step back as the vigilante's tone grew into a tirade against gangers and the like. The man almost literally pulsed with wrath. " . . . murdering, kidnapping, violence that preys on the innocent. Cold, heartless, *filthy* subhuman dogs! They think they can do as they please? They think they will not know *consequences*! Not know *justice*!"

Felix couldn't determine the source of the hatred, but it had a raw grip on Gideon. His eyes flamed. His breath grew ragged. Artificial hands clutched at artificial biceps and wrung his own body as if to tear himself apart, and still he went on.

"*Get to the point!*" Diomedes yelled.

The vigilante turned his anger on Diomedes for a split second, but before Felix could brace himself, Gideon had calmed like a switch had been flipped. A silence descended.

"So he stole the guns to put them on the street?" Flynn asked after a few moments.

"He's selling them," spoke the vigilante, lucid again. "I don't know who's buying. Wallace needs the money for something. I don't know what. Something he plans to buy into. Something evil, I know it."

Felix raised an eyebrow. What might Wallace have done to this man to warrant him becoming such an enemy? Or was it anything at all beyond a manifestation of the man's own psychosis?

"He stole the weapons somehow and hired the street trash to cover it up with the fires," he continued. "Of the three fires, the first one was a test. They botched the second. The third was the real thing."

"He burned my place, too," Diomedes growled.

Gideon nodded. "To kill you."

Felix smiled. "Hey, I guess as long as you've got a few pyromaniacs on your payroll, you may as well use them," he joked. He supposed he couldn't blame anyone for not smiling.

"And where are the arsonists now?" Flynn asked.

"Dead. Mostly Wallace's own doing. One was mine."

"And then he hired Diomedes to take care of you, hoping that one would take out the other," Felix finished. Diomedes bristled as the vigilante nodded. "Everything he says meshes with what I know, by the way," Felix added as an afterthought. "I just recently found out that some inventory was missing from the third site. And the lack of any alarms set off does point to an inside job."

Diomedes cursed. The four men stood together in the black room.
"So what now?" Flynn asked.

Gideon looked at the young man as if he'd been waiting for the question.

*   *   *

Some time later, Felix stepped into the chill of the night air. Somehow it felt like a morning darkness: dead, or at least asleep. It was the hour before dawn when everything was intrinsically hushed. He checked his watch. Okay, so it was only one thirty and his internal clock was off. Or maybe the time spent with the vigilante seemed longer than it truly had been.

Or maybe it was the guilt. He hadn't yet called Caitlin to let her know that he'd found Diomedes in time. Just in time.

Felix sighed. He was tired. He took out his phone and pulled up Caitlin's number on it. His enhanced memory had recorded it as soon as she'd said it, yet he'd felt the need to put it in there anyway. He dialed the number and reminded himself that there hadn't been any opportunity to call before now. He still felt sorry for having to leave her in the dark.

It went to voicemail without ringing. Either she was on the line or her phone was off. *"Hullo, you've reached 326-3827. I can't answer just now. Leave a message at the beep."* Felix chuckled. Over half a century since answering machines and voicemail were widespread, and still people left instructions, himself included.

"Caitlin, it's Felix. Sorry I've not gotten hold of you 'til now, but I've been with him for most of the time since. Dio found him about the same time I did. Right now things are stable, but I'd like to talk to you. Give me a call when you can."

He hung up and glanced about the street. It remained quiet for the moment. Music drifted faintly from various sources. Somewhere far off two lovers were enjoying each other. Cars rumbled intermittently from the nearby highway. "Quiet" was a term whose meaning depended on where in the city you applied it.

Diomedes and Flynn were nowhere to be seen. They had left before he had while Felix stayed behind and spoke to the vigilante a bit more. He had an agreement to uphold—and an opportunity to teach someone the value of trust and patience. And, okay, maybe to feel a little smug, too. Felix stood awhile, breathing in the night air and watching the area. His day had been stressful, and fatigue was beginning to settle about him like a welcome cloak. It would feel good to sleep.

Felix stood a while longer to watch for any stir of movement. Unless he was wrong, he'd probably catch sight of the reporter soon. He started walking. Someone lay on the bench inside a bus shelter down the street. Felix couldn't tell who it was or if the person was sleeping or hiding, but it didn't matter. Felix wasn't in the mood and didn't see any reason for sneaking.

He strolled around the shelter with casual caution and stopped when he could see the entire prostrate figure. He did turn out to be hiding.

"Hi, Brian," Felix said.

The reporter looked quite uncomfortable as he slowly pulled himself into a sitting position, and Felix wondered how long he'd been staked out there. "Ah, hi." Brian glanced about while hardly taking his eyes off Felix. "Where're the others?"

"Others?"

"Diomedes, Flynn, Gideon. That woman. Anyone else you might have been hiding around here."

Felix shook his head at Brian's suspicions. Maybe he should just leave right then? Not quite yet. "Only me. Dio and Flynn left a bit ago."

"Ah."

"Waiting for a bus?"

Brian rolled his eyes. "Yeah. I'm waiting for a bus."

"How long have you been sitting here?"

"Since before you all went inside. I got here first, you found him before I could."

"You'd have been with me if you'd waited."

"I'm the one that found the news footage—and the one who found out about the theft! You wouldn't be this far without me."

Felix rubbed his temples. He was too tired for this himself. "You're not exactly making me want to help you, you know. And I could point out that neither of us would've gotten this far without help."

"Sure."

"Apartment 7-F. I told him you'd like to have a few words with him, so he's expecting you." The shock on the reporter's face was priceless.

Felix would have taken more pleasure in surprising the untrusting man if he weren't thinking about sleep so much.

The reporter's surprise turned into suspicion. "What's the catch?" By the look in his eyes, Brian had stopped a breath short of asking if it was a trick.

Felix just shook his head. "I made an agreement with you, Brian. I keep my agreements." He turned to go. The reporter could wrestle with his suspicions by himself if he wanted. But after a few steps Felix stopped and turned, adding with an afterthought, "Trust *some*one."

He turned again and left, wondering if he'd blown the man's mind.

XXVII

DON'T SHOOT THE MESSENGER. It was a motto that Marette tried to take to heart when she could. At the moment, her heart pounded with frustration as her eyes glared at the monitor. At the moment, she was failing.

"Christ! They are sending them now? What the hell are they thinking?" English may not have been her first language, but she did know at least a little about how to swear.

"Chief, I can assure you that I only know what I've told you." The man looked calmly back at her from the monitor, waiting for her to respond. Higgins was his name. He was a gruff-looking man, yet his bearded face struggled for gentleness as he listened. He didn't outrank her. He even had lower security clearance in ESA than she. But he had just told her that ESA was sending another team and relayed orders for her to take them back into the structure when they arrived.

"So they want me to shovel bodies into that thing, like coal into a fire! No. I shall not do that! Hold them at Alpha Station. I will talk to Command."

"I can't."

"The hell you can't!" Marette hardened her gaze. "This is not a favor I am asking of you, Higgins. I am giving you an order!"

Higgins just sighed. "Ma'am, even if I didn't have orders from Command that countermanded that order, I couldn't hold them. They've already left the station."

She bit her tongue before she tried to order him to call them back. He had been ordered to get them to her. *Merde.*

She closed her eyes and drew a long breath. "Do you have anything else to report?" No use wasting any more time on Higgins.

"No, ma'am."

"Clarion out." She clicked off the channel.

She wasn't ready for another team. This one would be even better armed than the last, but Marette didn't know if that would help them. At least now they could safely assume that thing, whatever it was, to be hostile. Or dangerous, at the very least. Logically, she realized, no one knew its intentions or purpose. Emotionally, she felt it had attacked. She struggled to remain objective, but would objectivity get more people killed? Or was it her fault for not suspecting it would have some sort of defense at all? Was it even a defense? She just did not know.

They needed more information. They needed to study what had happened, but how to tell ESA that when the only data to be studied could not be shown to them? She had sent a copy to the AoA, but while they were scanning it, the Space Agency had no such copy to go on, and so moved with an urgency that the AoA agents within had been apparently unable to halt.

She could stall the team, of course—maybe buy a bit more time on her own—but it made things more difficult with the new team at the site instead of Alpha Station, and the AoA had to maintain a presence there. The AoA was the reason that anyone had found the place at all. She could not do anything to jeopardize her position, but she could still try to stall for time.

Marette began recording a message for transmission to Earth. Perhaps an appeal would give their agents the chance they needed to stall ESA's zeal for further action.

The AoA needed more information, and, Marette recalled, they needed to find the mole. Though of course finding him was not her responsibility, it was another thing she could not risk telling ESA herself. How could she alert them to a security leak she could not possibly know about through resources she should not have been able to access? Yet someone had been planning to sell secrets about the site, and the AoA could not allow that. She needed to stall, not only to save the lives of the new team, but also to keep them from discovering anything for the mole to leak. Such a thing was blatantly unacceptable.

It was not her area, Marette reminded herself again. She knew little beyond the fact that the mole had been traced to—and lost in—

the American city of Northgate. Other Agents would find him, but she needed to give her comrades time.

So much was in jeopardy. So much uncertain.

Normally, Marette loathed a bureaucracy. Maybe for once it could work to her advantage. It was time to stop up the works.

XXVIII

FELIX HAD EATEN too much. What was it about blueberry pancakes that made them expand in one's stomach minutes after eating them? Not that he'd paid any attention to that and stopped eating, of course. He always hated leaving food that he'd ordered on the plate, and the fact that they were particularly good wasn't helping. Besides, he had slept until nearly noon and awoke famished. So far he'd managed to down nearly two giant pancakes, a glass of orange juice, a side of eggs and, of course, a glass of water. He was mopping up syrup with the final bite when he looked up to see her.

Caitlin's rich accent greeted him as he met her eyes. "Enjoying your breakfast?" she asked, one eyebrow arched.

Felix smiled and lowered his fork. "Probably a little too much, from what my stomach is saying." He offered her a seat. "Can I get you something?"

She sat down across from him. "How is the tea here?"

"Oh, I'd be the wrong person to ask," Felix apologized. "I can tell you they have tea, but as I've never really developed a taste for it, I doubt I'd be much more help than that."

"Not a tea drinker? And you seemed like such an intelligent bloke." The Welshwoman gave him a teasing smile. A waiter approached before Felix had time to attempt a defense, and Caitlin ordered a cup of English Breakfast.

Felix wasn't even going to bother to ask how she had found him. Something told him that Caitlin probably wouldn't tell him anyway. "How'd you manage to find me?" he asked after a moment. He had to see if he was right, after all.

"Well now, I can't tell you everything, can I?"

Felix grinned. "Going for the air of mystery, are you?"

"Would you do any different?" she asked in a friendly manner. Felix admitted silently that he wouldn't and realized that was probably the reason he hadn't expected her to. "I did receive your message," she continued, "but by then the situation seemed stable enough to wait until now."

"I'm sorry I wasn't able to call you sooner. I was too busy trying to keep everyone else talking."

Caitlin nodded. "Was convincing your freelancer friend as difficult as you thought it might be?"

Felix fought the urge to correct the "friend" part. Now was not the time to explain the dynamics of the relationship. "Depends on if you consider being thrown around and shot at 'difficult.'"

"Crikey."

Felix chuckled. "Well, technically Dio did the hard part, I just let him throw me," he joked. "He burned all the calories." Caitlin raised her eyebrows as if she wasn't sure if she should laugh or not. Felix continued. "I had just ruined his rifle shot at Gideon. Dio was . . . irritated."

"So he was planning to kill him."

Felix nodded. "But when I got in his way, it gave me his attention for long enough to start feeding him the facts. Gideon got there soon after and we managed to get him to listen." Felix told her about Wallace hiring Diomedes and his involvement with the arsons.

"How did he take it?"

"Not well," Felix said. "But it redirected his anger—just a little at first—enough for him to listen to more proof. Did you know Gideon had a bug in Wallace's limo?"

Caitlin thanked the waiter as he brought her tea, and then shook her head at Felix. "Until a few moments ago I didn't even know about Wallace to begin with." She sipped the tea.

"How is it?" Felix asked.

"How is what?"

"The tea."

"What I expected," Caitlin said.

"Is that bad or good?"

She flashed an admonishing smile. "Do you want to listen to me talk about the tea, Felix, or are you going to tell me what happened next?"

Felix felt a slight warmth rise to his cheeks. He wasn't actually blushing, was he? "Ah," he began. The amusement on the Welshwoman's face seemed to widen a little. "Most of the rest of the time at Gideon's apartment was spent plotting."

"Plotting what?"

Felix hesitated. "Ah, this isn't something that's going to find its way into common knowledge, is it?" Again, he felt he could trust her, but it didn't hurt to make himself clear.

Caitlin shook her head. "Not if you don't want it to."

"I'd rather it didn't."

She nodded and took another sip. "Alright."

Felix told her about the meeting, elaborating on how Wallace had set them up to kill each other while he stole from his own company for unknown purposes, and about the plan that the vigilante and freelancer had developed to deal with it.

"And you're involved in that somehow?"

Felix nodded. "I want to keep an eye on Flynn." He told her of the young man and his worship of the older freelancer. "I don't want Wallace getting away with anything, either."

"Now that I think of it, Gideon did mention Wallace once to another Scry. I only half heard it at the time. I'd forgotten it until now."

"So do you know why Gideon's got it out for Wallace so bad?"

Caitlin shook her head. "He didn't tell you?"

"Not directly, no. I don't really know if it's something specific that Wallace did to him or just the fact that he sees Wallace as adding to the chaos of the city. He's not a stable man, Caitlin. He's got enough hardware on him to give CPMC a heart attack, and he goes off on tirades about the 'filth that rapes the life of the city.' He's trying to do some good, but . . . "

"You're not the only one who's spent a little time with him, Felix."

"Right. I'm preaching to the choir, huh? What I mean is that Wallace works for a company that puts out guns. He's torched a few places. He may have just fallen across Gideon's sights."

Caitlin nodded. "I think you may have a point." She sighed. "I'm afraid of him, but because of how he's helped The Scry, I care about him, too. Is that silly?"

Felix shook his head. "I don't think it's silly. Heart and mind seldom speak the same language."

"I have compassion for him, but—" She hesitated. "I don't want him endangering us."

Felix sat for a moment, just listening. Caitlin merely sipped her tea. He let a bit of silence pass, and then spoke. "Which reminds me of something else. I caught up with Dio *after* he found Gideon. Apparently they actually chased him across town through a subway tunnel."

"I'd heard something about that," she said. "The police didn't know who it was. That was them?" Felix nodded. "Bloody barmy lot you run with."

Felix grinned. "Makes life interesting. Though I'm just as glad I wasn't there. Ah, but anyway, what I'm getting at is that Gideon thinks that's how they made it to his place, by following him."

Caitlin frowned. She already saw his point. "So he has no reason to suspect The Scry might have told them."

"Not a one," Felix said regretfully. "I'm sorry."

She smiled, gently. It was a lovely sight. "Not your fault."

"I just wished your idea had worked. You care about them a lot, don't you?"

"The other Scry? Yes." She chuckled quietly. "Well, some of them."

"If you come up with another idea I can help with . . . "

"I should let you know?" she finished for him after a sip.

"Ah, well, yes." Felix smiled back. "So you said you had the luxury of being in the city by choice. Does that mean you don't live here all the time?"

"Not all the time, no. I rent a house a fair distance outside the city."

"What brings you here, then?"

"The Scry."

"Oh? That's it? No job here or anything?"

She raised an amused eyebrow. "Well, I can't tell you everything immediately now, can I? But even if I were just in the city for The Scry, that seems to surprise you?"

Felix shrugged with a chuckle. "Maybe, but pleasantly so. It's not often I meet someone who shares my love of discovery, you know."

She grinned. "You don't hang around with many Scry, do you?" It was a rhetorical question. "I do rather enjoy the hunt. Leaves me well chuffed."

"Chuffed," Felix repeated. "Been a while since I've heard that word."

"Ah. *Very pleased with myself*, then," Caitlin explained.

"Oh, I know what it means, just remarking on the fact that I hadn't heard it in a while."

"Aha." Caitlin smiled. "Do you do that often?"

"Only when I'm comfortable," he remarked. "I get the feeling you may hear quite a few remarks." Felix paused for a moment to see if Caitlin would object to the implication. Her eyes met his but she said nothing. He continued on before the pause became awkward. "So then I suppose it begs the question of why you don't live here all the time?" It seemed foolish as soon as he'd uttered it.

"You mean why leave this wonderful utopia we have here?" She winked and flashed a grin that quickly faded. "I need a break from it. I think if I lived in the city all the time . . . " She seemed content to let the melancholy in her tone finish the thought. "It's good to get away. Besides," she finished with a grin, "that's where the horses are."

As she said "horses," a gleam sparked in her eyes. He asked the obvious question with a grin kindled by her own. "You ride?"

She shook her head, still grinning. The gleam became a glow. "I fly."

XXIX

THE SKY WAS DIVIDED. Above the treetops that swayed in the wind, there stretched a stark expanse of separation. To the south, dark clouds muted the sky like a blanket, heavy with gray rain captured in billowing sheets. The mass formed a forbidding border along the open northern sky where blue and haze rallied to meet it. Shining somewhere behind the clouds, the sun's light spilled over the edges of their darkness with an eerie glow that painted gold the green of the evergreens and budding alder.

Romulus stood in Weatherby Park, Northgate's largest, and took in the sight. He could feel the sunlight's warm hum as it trickled sparsely over the clouds. The trees surrounding him reached up to it in their longing as the grass spanned the area between them. He closed his eyes and breathed in the life. The air was sweeter here, cleansed by the green as it swept the grunge away. The park absorbed the sounds of the city beyond. He could actually hear a bird singing and the call of a crow above.

He . . . existed. For a moment, that was all. No thoughts, no confusion, no pain. He existed. He simply was.

He'd done this before, but not since the farm. Sometimes he'd found himself in the fields, just watching the life blowing and swaying like simplicity in the wind. Thoughts and cares vanished in those moments, surrounded by the bounty that could spring from what impossible force lay within a single seed. Not from will or desire, but from the pure and simple nature of what it was. It was a kind of magic, and it brought him as much peace now as it had then.

It was peace he needed. He had woken from a troubled sleep in the floater that morning and been unable to rest anymore. When they had returned after the meeting with the vigilante, it was sheer physical fatigue that had allowed his slumber, but once the sun had risen and the basic needs of his body were minimally satisfied, a clutter of thoughts swarmed his mind. His future, his mentor, his entire view of the world. Uncertainty and unwanted choices had chased each other around in his mind. Diomedes had been his anchor, his only solid ground since his uncle had gone. Was that crumbling now? Had it ever really been solid? Or was this just a storm that would pass and leave everything as it had been? Storms rarely left things unchanged.

He'd followed the knots of reason and emotion that his choices had woven in his mind, until he could take it no more.

After they'd finished at Gideon's place, Diomedes had taken the floater across the city to a place near the park, and upon seeing it, Romulus had recalled the relaxing feeling of the trees in the wooded theater they had landed in the night before. He'd gone for a walk, and, for a time, his troubles remained behind.

Yet now, something was wrong. The sense of it arose within him like an alarm going off, even before he heard the crack of the branches or the screams and sirens that came moments after. Yelling followed: a mix of screams, shouts and a bellow of fury. Romulus stood in a long clearing lined by bushes on one side and trees on the other, poised on a winding path that forked ahead of him. He turned towards the yelling. Fifty yards away, the bushes literally exploded.

Romulus dropped to the ground immediately. Someone screamed out of the smoking hole in the brush and hurled himself into the clearing. It was a man, in a rage, literally throwing his body about in a fury of frenetic movement. He wore no clothes, and even from a distance the hardware on him was clearly visible. A thin metal exoskeleton clung to the back of his body. His entire scalp was metal, and both legs and one arm had been replaced and were now bristling with pop-up weapons and other hardware. He screamed again and raised his arm to fire a grenade across the clearing, where it ripped apart an evergreen in its wake.

Romulus remained pinned to the ground. Three projectiles launched toward the man from where he'd come. One sped past him as he turned; the remaining two made contact with his hip and shoulder, where they flared in a tiny storm of electricity. The man's right leg gave out and he fell like a collapsing building to slam down on his side with one arm flailing wildly and the other completely limp.

Four people rushed into view. Each wore the uniformed red and black body armor of CPMC. They sprinted as a team towards their screaming target who, though he now lay crippled, had not ceased his flailing. As he thrashed around and turned a weapon on the approaching officers, they split formation as if rehearsed. Two broke off in an arc around the man's left; the third arced to the right. The fourth raised a bat-sized tube and fired a mass of wire that expanded into a net and knocked the struggling man backwards where he screamed and began firing. Bullets sprayed the area, and as Romulus watched, two of the officers returned the fire as they darted in front of the man. Romulus swore a bullet hit the man in the net, but he showed no sign of pain and kept firing at the two as best he could. The remaining two officers completed their end-around to sweep in and blindside him, thrusting stun rods into the netted man's back. There was another electric flare as he screamed again, struggled briefly, and then collapsed to the ground, motionless.

Romulus got to his feet as the officers unwrapped the net. The two holding the rods stood a vigilant watch over their captive's unmoving form.

"You know, from what I hear, those stun rods aren't as pleasant as they look."

Romulus jumped and spun around. It was Felix. The short man waggled his eyebrows briefly in greeting. "I talked to a guy once who said it's got all the pleasure of being hit by a train, but without the unpleasant after-effects. Once the twitching stops, anyway."

Romulus looked back to where the officers worked around the body. "And he got two."

"Unless I'm wrong, he just got one."

"Sure looked like two to me," said Romulus. Two of the officers had pulled out tools and were rapidly performing some sort of work on the man's body—or the metal attached to it. He couldn't see well enough to tell which.

"No, just one would be enough to stop a rhino. Trouble is, there's never a rhino around when you need one. One of those was a stunner. The other's an EMP rod."

Romulus nodded. It made sense. An electromagnetic pulse would short out most of the cybernetics on the man's body.

"Standard procedure," Felix said, "even if he's already on the ground. The EMP knocks out any remaining hardware in or on him, and the stunner knocks the rest of him out, even if he's working off boosted adrenals or just simple PCP or Jack. 'Course, sometimes the system can't stand the shock, but when a guy's gone hardcore CP like that and is gardening with grenades . . . "

"They hit him with a *lot* of EMP, then," said Romulus as he continued to watch. "At least I think that's what they fired at him. That's what got him on the ground."

Felix nodded. "I didn't see it. Probably EMP grenades, though. They have to be pretty low power to be shot like that, so they take him out a little with those until they can use the rod to do the rest."

One of the officers now held the man's detached leg in his arms. "God," Romulus whispered, "they just take him apart now?"

"They get rid of all the hardware that they can strip quickly in the field. Then they take him back and see if they can rehab him."

"Does that work?"

"Sometimes," Felix said grimly. "Sometimes they don't even get this far. I saw a guy go full bore in the middle of a mall once. Just snapped. He killed over a dozen people before CMPC just put a railgun slug through his head from two hundred yards." Felix grimaced and massaged his temples with one hand. "Having a photographic memory isn't always a good thing," he whispered.

Romulus swallowed hard. What might he have seen if CMPC hadn't arrived in the park? A blink of what Felix just said gave him an excuse to push the thought away. "You have a photographic memory?"

"Guess I let that slip, huh? Yeah, I do. Mostly photographic. Bit of a side effect of a memory experiment I participated in a time ago, when I was a little more reckless."

"If that was a side effect, what was the experiment?"

Felix paused. "Keep a secret?"

"Okay."

"Memory transfer. They were playing around with taking someone else's memories and encoding them onto a device that would interface with a host's existing brain tissue." He turned his head and peeled back a small flap of artificial skin. A small connector sat behind his right ear. "It's built into the side of my skull."

Romulus boggled. "So you've got someone else's memories?" God, if they could extract memories like that, and store them? It was both fascinating and frightening.

"The transfer wasn't perfect, but yes, most of them." He replaced the skin flap and smiled. "Pretty damn cool, huh?"

"Is it from someone who's, well, still around?"

Felix shrugged. "He could be. He'd be about seventy-five now."

"You haven't tried to find him?" That would be a remarkable conversation to have.

Felix shook his head. "Nope. I mean, I'm curious, but I know this guy quite intimately. From what I can tell, he's a very private person. I don't think it's a meeting that he'd want."

"If he's so worried about privacy, why donate his memories?"

Felix paused. "I don't know. The memories stop before any idea of being an experimental donor shows up. I suppose it could be that he was killed and had been an organ donor. But if that's the case, I don't think I would've had to sign a non-disclosure agreement about his life. No writing a book about the guy or selling his story."

"What's his name?"

Felix grinned. "Oh, what's in a name?"

"Not going to tell me?" Romulus found himself smiling back.

"Nope. As a result of all this, though, I'm scared to death of EMP. I don't know what I might lose."

At the mention of EMP, Romulus looked out at where the man's body was being taken away. "They did a good job," he remarked as he watched them.

"Some say you have to be crazy yourself to work the psycho squad."

Romulus shook his head. "That's the sort of thing I want to do."

"Dangerous job."

"I want to protect people like that. They stopped the guy, stopped him from hurting anyone, just swept in as a team. Neutralized him. They probably saved a lot of people."

"That was one of the cleaner 'neutralizations' that I've seen. It's not always so easy. Sometimes there's a lot more violence. Brutal. More often than not in this sort of situation, CMPC officers have to kill, and a full bore CP doesn't ever go quietly. That's a terrible thing to have to do."

"But they're protecting the rest of us when they do it," Romulus argued.

"Oh, I'm not saying it's not for a good cause. But killing for a good cause is still killing. I've seen what it can do to someone inside. It's damaging." Felix rapped his fist over his chest. "In here."

"Someone had to do it."

"Yeah, I know. That's part of the problem." He sighed. "I'll put it another way—and hold on, 'cause I'm about to go all philosophical on your ass." After a moment, he went on. "Malicious violence, hate—it's part of the nature of evil. It's destructive. Absolute best way to oppose that's with creation. Or, love, really, depending on how you look at it."

"Good and evil?" Romulus asked. "That's a little too black and white, I'd guess. If that guy came after us, a hug's not going to stop him."

Felix chuckled. "Valid point, but that's not what I mean. 'The world is gray' is something I've heard a lot. But what's gray but a combination of black and white, if you follow me?"

"Um?"

"Put it this way: it's like, say, cancer. Fifty years ago they treated cancer with radiation. Killed the cancer cells just fine, but also destroyed healthy tissue. Reasonably effective, but at a cost, destroying your own good cells to be rid of the bad. Now we have nanocellular treatments. Kills the cancer, leaves the good cells alone. It took longer to come up with, it costs more, but it works so much better."

"Okay . . . "

Felix went on. "Violence—evil, for the sake of argument—is insidious. One of its greatest weapons is speed and ease, and if we're not strong enough, it forces us to fight it on its own terms. Fire with fire, violence with violence, what have you. Even if we're successful, a part of us is eaten away.

"They took that man down without killing him, and now he'll be taken to rehab. With patience, time and care, his mind might be healed and he won't be the same raging thing that we saw here. But if he'd been too violent and forced them to kill him, he'd have been lost completely, along with anything positive he might have ever done, and those agents would have had a death on their heads. Necessary— I'm not saying it's never necessary—but still a terrible thing. I count myself lucky at never having been put in the position where I've been forced to kill."

Romulus frowned, mulling it over. "They probably get used to it, though, at least?" he finally said.

"Some do, I'm sure. But those are the ones to feel sorry for. And to fear. Not caring about having to kill is one step closer to enjoying it. Why do you think cops get psych evaluations whenever they kill someone in the line of duty? You have to be careful."

"I wonder if Gideon's used to it," Romulus said quietly. They were both silent for a moment.

"Don't know," Felix said. "He's got to be CP. Not full bore, but . . . he's not well. If I had to guess, I'd say the killing either pushed him over the edge or pushed him deeper. Maybe deeper, given all his hardware, but it's hard to know."

Romulus thought of how the vigilante had saved the old man, protected the couple outside the apartments, and taken out five gangers by himself. He remembered the tortured look on the man's face as they had talked to him. Despite all the anger and rage in Gideon's eyes, he was trying to do good. He was trying to do what he thought was right. And yet . . .

"Flynn?" Felix asked quietly. "Was Dio the same when you knew him on the farm? Before he got his own implants and turned freelancer?"

Romulus felt where the question was leading. He heaved a sigh. "It's hard to remember things clearly, anymore."

"How many people has he killed, I wonder?"

Shut up! Romulus nearly said it aloud. The CPMC officers were taking their man away. "Let's go somewhere else."

He strode a distance up the path and Felix followed. Again Romulus walked in silence, seeking solace in the green. Felix simply walked beside him and remained quiet. Given how talkative the man was a moment ago, he guessed it was intentional. At first glad for it, he soon began to feel rude for not speaking himself. Troubling thoughts of his mentor still pressed at him, so he asked. "You never told me how you heard about Diomedes and Wallace."

"I didn't, did I? Sorry for that. We got sidetracked, and I forgot," Felix chuckled. "Just because I remember things well doesn't mean I can't forget to recall them." Felix turned to him and grinned. "And when we think a thing, the thing we think is not the thing we think we think, but only the thing that makes us think the thing we think we think."

He rattled it off so quickly that the words flew by before Romulus could follow them.

"Um, what?"

"Exactly! But to answer your question, I found out from a cutter."

Romulus nodded. Cutters were street doctors who specialized in quick procedures and very few questions, usually seen for illegal implants or getting patched up when a licensed doctor would either charge too much or ask too many questions.

"Did Diomedes go to see him?"

Felix nodded. "Yeah. Apparently he took a small time bomb off of your roommate's spine. From what he told me, Wallace had it put there to give Dio some incentive to do a job for him. Possibly double-crossing a previous contract Dio had, I'm not sure. I *think* Wallace had also paid him a small amount and promised to remove the bomb once Dio's loyalty was secured and the job was done. According to the cutter, it wasn't a promise he kept. Dio would've had his spine blown out if the cutter hadn't gotten it out in time."

"Shit," Romulus whispered. He couldn't blame Diomedes for his anger. "He didn't tell me a thing."

"He called me looking for the best I could send him to, otherwise I wouldn't know so much."

"What did Diomedes do for Wallace?"

"That I don't know."

Romulus thought about the other things Wallace had done and realized a part of him didn't want to know. Frustration welled up inside him. "What are you doing here, Felix?" he asked.

"Dodging goose droppings, at the moment," he answered and sidestepped a spot in the grass. "Gotta watch where you step around here."

"That's not what I meant."

"Still good advice," Felix returned with a grin.

"Hiatt . . . " Romulus had said it like Diomedes. The tone surprised him.

"Well, okay. So I got up late, went out for breakfast, spent some time with a very attractive woman I met last night, asked her out, got a very definite 'maybe,' and then decided to look for a friend of mine that I thought might be having trouble." They trudged through the grass for another few steps. "And I got a walk in the park out of the bargain."

"You don't need to look after me."

"No man's an island."

Romulus began to walk faster. "I came here to find some peace," he warned.

The smaller man increased his pace to match. "You sure you didn't come here to hide?"

"You can't take a hint, can you?" he asked through gritted teeth.

"Hiding from this doesn't make it go away, Flynn. I heard about the fight—about what Dio did to that guy. He's not who you thought, and it shows in your eyes. I could see it last night, and I see it now."

"He's what I want to be!" he whispered. Or used to be, he added silently. He couldn't look Felix in the eye.

"No," said Felix. "He's not. He's not and you know it. Like it or not, you know it."

"And just what the hell am I supposed to do?!"

"Get out of it. Get away from him."

"And do what?" he demanded. "Without him I'm just some homeless . . . jobless *loser* with nowhere to go!"

Felix grabbed his arm. "You're not a loser, Flynn. Unlike a lot of freelancers I've met, you've got a heart. You've got a purpose. I'm sure of that."

Romulus jerked his arm out of Felix's grip. "I *thought* I had a purpose! And now it's just a pile of shit!" Romulus lowered his voice out of pain and shame. "Just get out of here."

"Flynn, look—"

Romulus punched him across the face. "I said go away!" He turned and rushed across the park, heading back to the floater and leaving Felix behind on the ground. Shock and anger flared inside of him as he ruefully rubbed his knuckles after the punch. Maybe he wasn't so different from his mentor after all.

Hell, it was all he had.

X X X

MARETTE'S ATTEMPTS at stalling the second team bought her nearly another day. She sent requests confirming orders, sent counter-appeals through channels, and even orchestrated a comm-system failure that would appear to be equipment malfunction if anyone checked on it. Every hour was more time the AoA had to sift through the data. The more the AoA knew, the more they could do, and the greater their chances became of finding what they were looking for, and of lowering the cost in lives.

No more would die, Marette had vowed. Not if it was avoidable. She stated this clearly to the Space Agency as much as she dared — as much as she could in hopes that they would share her view. She walked the line between insisting that they listen to her and being so insubordinate that they would merely replace her with someone who would follow their orders. ESA was eager, but they did share her caution. They simply had less cause than she did to consider patience a virtue. Marette had pushed as hard as she dared. It bought her some time.

She had absolutely zero assurance that it made any difference.

ESA Command had grown increasingly irritated with her as the day went on. Literally five minutes before her ESA superiors transmitted a deceptively polite ultimatum that she send the team in, her compatriots in the AoA had signaled her. The gathered data had proven mostly inconclusive. They were still studying the scans, but they felt she could stall no longer. The tactical options that ESA had devised could not be proven viable, nor were they deemed futile or disastrous. As for the ESA mole, there was no new information, and a step forward might help bring his plan to light. There were no certain solutions, yet no cause to abort.

Some might consider news that a plan still could work to be a positive thing. Marette thought it a worthless uncertainty and a frustrating lack of progress, but they were no worse off. They had done all they could with the extra day. They had tried. She cursed. Trying was no comfort when it got them nowhere.

The new team was ten strong, with two eight-man rovers to carry them and their gear from the former mining camp to the dig site. They rolled and rumbled along the grey lunar surface as the team leader, an Italian woman Marette's age called Altieri, reviewed the operation plan with the rest of the team. In reality, it was less an operation than an assault.

ESA's plan was to use EMP and Geiger cannons to neutralize the device that had killed the first team—unofficially tagged a security drone. It was thought that the EMP's effect on what appeared to be an automated device—coupled with the Geiger cannons' more powerful dose of the same radiation that had affected the midnight coating—would shut the drone down. Other members of the team carried the recoilless ARG-rifles that the first team never got the chance to use. They were to attempt to stop the drone without destroying it, if possible. Marette knew it would be her call as to when destructive force would be brought into play. She did not intend to hesitate this time.

They rolled to the entrance of the tunnel and the team disembarked.

Protocol and Marette's position as field chief required her to oversee from the rover, but as she watched the second team set up their equipment, guilt at not being able to join them more closely tugged at her. Pushing such useless regret out of her mind, she tested cameras and checked suit mics and sensors while the team readied their weapons and fanned out to defensively flank the command rover.

This time she was the only double agent. With ESA's rush to get a second squad out, the AoA had no time to find a replacement for Alberto. Both organizations fortunately had similar goals in the current situation, yet Marette would have felt better having another of the Agents there with her. She closed her eyes, drew a slow breath, and tried not to hear screams echo in her memory. She had a job to do. Having to do it by herself had never bothered her before. She forced her head to clear. It would not bother her now!

"*F.C. Clarion, all systems prepped and ready,*" Altieri reported.

"*D'accord,* Lieutenant," Marette acknowledged. "Maintain formation. We are going in." She eased the rover forward at a pace that the soldiers could match in their suits. They negotiated the simple incline and crept through the mouth of the tunnel until it engulfed them. Lights and scanners swept the area. A steady beep indicated nothing moving in the space ahead as the rover continued on course along the slate grey of the buried structure.

The Space Agency had yet to confirm that it was a spacecraft. The AoA was betting on it. Scientific analysis of the crater and sheer, optimistic hypothesizing had led them to hope that what they would find would be a crashed spacecraft containing the technology they desperately needed to bring them leaps and bounds closer to their ultimate goal.

"*Levy, O'Brien,*" Altieri ordered, "*check the tunnel supports. Confirm they haven't been damaged.*"

Marette nodded her satisfaction as the two troopers acknowledged the request. It was a concern that she had discussed with Altieri before they had gone in. She took her eyes off of the team readouts to check the supports with her own eyes. As yet, they appeared normal.

"*Checks out so far.*"

They continued deeper. The opening would be visible in a few moments. Their lights blazed a path before them. It was impossibly still.

The tunnel supports remained untouched all the way to the end. The airlock sat as it had before, perpendicular to the tunnel with one end open to the vacuum and the other flush against the structure.

"Hold," Marette ordered, and stopped the rover. There was no sign of movement on sensors. Nothing could be seen through the narrow side windows. She waited longer than needed, just to be certain. "No sign of activity, Lieutenant. Send two of your people to make a visual inspection inside the lock."

Altieri acknowledged the order and Marette watched as the two forward troopers moved ahead. The team adjusted formation to cover them as they stepped around to the side and peered into the open airlock hatch with weapons ready.

"*Looks clear,*" one reported. "*The hatch on the other side is closed.*" He moved forward into the airlock. The second followed, and then they both disappeared from view. Marette glanced at their video feeds.

Everything appeared normal. The lock was empty. The hatch at the far end remained shut.

"*All clear inside,*" they reported. "*Zero activity.*"

"*Understood,*" Altieri replied. "*Check behind the lock.*"

Marette watched on the screen as the two troopers turned their backs to the closed hatch. A moment later, they emerged from the airlock and moved out to continue their inspection outside. "Blue squad, move up." Half the team went forward to join them. Marette waited and watched. All readouts were clear. A moment later, the team reported the same.

Marette took a breath but resisted the urge to let herself relax. "Lieutenant Altieri, I want two people watching the inner hatch at all times. Is that understood?"

"*Contois, Dietrich, you heard her. You're on hatch duty.*"

"Have we checked the airlock seal yet?" Marette asked.

"*Checking it right now, ma'am,*" another reported. She waited. "*Looks like seal integrity has been compromised. We'll need to reseal it.*"

"Wait until the rest of your prep is taken care of, Crewman, then worry about the seal."

"*Yes, ma'am.*"

"*Uh, Lieutenant?*" It was Dietrich. He'd moved close to the hatch, inspecting it by the view from his camera. "*Come take a look at this.*"

"Report, Dietrich. What do you have?"

"*Well, it looks like the door behind the hatch is closed.*"

The lieutenant walked into the lock while Marette tried to see what she could on the video feed. "*He's right, Chief,*" Altieri reported. "*We didn't bring cutting tools with us. Isn't that how the last team got it open?*"

Marette scowled. It made sense that if the lock seal was breached, the door behind it might seal up. Whatever the structure was, it obviously had power. The last time, the door had opened on its own when the lock had been pressurized; actual cutting had gotten them nothing but a cracked helmet. Would the door re-open under the same conditions as before? If it did not, at least it would buy her the time she had been unable to get earlier. Perhaps more time than even she wanted, if they had no way to get inside.

"Ignore that for now, Lieutenant," she ordered. "Finish your preparations for entry."

Guards stood watch as the rest of the team unloaded further equipment from the rover. Remote-controlled mini-turrets were set up inside the lock, each about the size of a large dog and modified with an additional, if limited, supply of EMP pods. Only two of the four they had brought could fit in the lock itself, but once it was safe to continue behind the hatchway, all four would be placed in the structure as sentry guns. It was hoped that the miniature weapons platforms would prevent further loss of life.

Marette had tagged one with a sensor feed. While the AoA hadn't been able to place an agent, she could at least secure an additional source of data beyond ESA's control.

The mini-turrets were set up. The seal against the structure was reestablished. Once the team evacuated the lock and all that was left inside were the sentries, Marette did one final check on all systems. A moment later, she gave the order. "Seal the outer doors, Lieutenant. Then stand by for my command to pressurize the lock."

Altieri stood at the exterior controls of the airlock. "*Order acknowledged. Lock doors closing.*" Marette couldn't help but imagine the sound of a giant dungeon door creaking shut. "*Outer door secure.*"

Marette scanned the turret readouts. All systems nominal. "Pressurize the lock."

"*Pressurizing . . .*"

The hiss of filling oxygen played over the turret's audio feed. "*Pressure at thirty percent . . . fifty percent . . . seventy . . . eighty-five . . . ninety-five . . . ninety-seven . . . ninety-eight . . . ninety-nine. Pressurization complete and holding steady.*"

Her fingers settled over the controls of the turrets. They were designed to work autonomously—if necessary, to fire at anything that moved—but she wanted to keep them in check until she had to fire. Marette did not know what she would find inside. A part of her even hoped that perhaps some of the first team might have survived. Unlikely as that was, she did not wish to kill them upon their moment of salvation.

"Open the inner hatch."

Marette heard the hatch bolts disengage over the transmitters and watched as the lock door slid steadily open. Bit by bit, the grey of the structure took its place behind it. It remained, solid and unmoving. Marette counted her heartbeats as she waited. She could see no sign of a mark from the first team's attempt to drill. What sort of metal could absorb and reflect energy so well?

It moved.

It opened as soundlessly as before, a simple and elegant motion made ominous by the sweat of her palms on the controls and the sight of the bodies that still lay on the blackness beyond. The door stopped.

The void stood still.

Marette switched on the floodlights. They flashed to full and bathed the motionless bodies in harsh illumination. The midnight coating that covered all else absorbed the rest of the light. She reminded herself to breathe.

"Structure doors have opened," Marette broadcasted. "No sign of hostiles. Stand by." How long had it been until the drone had emerged the first time? Just under four minutes, by the data.

Marette waited. She watched the chronometer as seconds ticked away. She tried not to look at the fallen forms of the first team. Her gaze kept sliding from the darkness onto the still bodies. She willed for the drone to come, if only to give her a distraction.

Two minutes. Still there was no movement.

Three minutes. She tried to visually gauge the distance to the back wall and found it impossible.

Four minutes. She glanced up from the screen and out the rover's window at the lock, inside which the team waited. She would make them wait longer.

The chronometer read five minutes before she ordered them in. "Carefully," she warned.

The team entered in twos. The first four moved to stand abreast in the structure entry and guard the lock as two more prepared the sentry guns for movement. Ordinarily Marette would have been able to steer the sentries by remote, but the hasty armament refit had sacrificed movement for firepower. The turrets' purpose here was defense, not exploration. The troopers released the sentries' surface anchors and started to roll them forward manually.

She watched on the video feeds as Altieri led them into the structure. Troopers fanned out while the turrets were ponderously lifted over the airlock's edge and into the maw.

Levy saw it before she did. "*It's opening!*"

As the lieutenant began giving orders, Marette fixated on the rapid rectangular spillback at the end of the chamber. Troopers trained weapons on the appearing door. Marette hastily checked the turrets. Only one had been lifted inside; the trooper carrying it was reengaging the anchors. The other—

"*Shit!*"

The curse came loud over the channel as the trooper with the second turret dropped it at the lip of the lock, blocking the entry. Two more of the team rushed in from behind to help clear it. The rest of the team was cut off from the chamber.

Within the structure, the grey door opened.

Marette cursed and reinitialized the first turret, locking onto the far doorway just as the drone hovered through it like a ghost.

She did not wait. "Open fire!"

Tiny bolts of EMP leaped through the darkness from the four troopers' weapons as Marette fired an EMP pod at the thing. The pod flared in contact with the drone as the troopers' bolts slammed into it one by one. It faltered, dropped a few inches, and then continued forward. "Geiger cannons! Rifles! Fire!"

"*Get that damned turret out of the way!*" Altieri yelled to the team in the doorway. The sound of gunfire followed her voice. Crimson ghosts fired from the Geiger radiation cannons ripped out at the drone and were absorbed or flew past it into the black-coated wall behind it. Darkness shattered from the walls in craters where they hit. Rifle slugs flew forward and tore into the drone as Marette fired the same from the mini-turret. The drone stopped and faltered in the air. Dented and damaged, it endured, and began to glow red. Marette cursed again, remembering what would come next.

"*Turret two online!*" a trooper shouted.

In a flash she set it to automatic. The three troopers beside it added their weapons to the deluge as EMP pods slammed into the drone. Lightning burst around it in a ball of burning energy. It engulfed the floating mass in a maelstrom until gravity suddenly seized the drone and dropped it, powerless, to the floor. The lightning winked out. The drone lay still.

At once, they all ceased fire.

No one moved. They waited, watching the motionless metal hulk lying amid the blackness.

The silence was stunning.

Chilling . . .

Motionless . . .

Dead . . .

"*FUCK!*" someone shouted in a release of tension.

"*Stow it, Soto!*" the lieutenant snapped.

Marette breathed again and studied the shattered thing suspiciously on the video feed. "Lieutenant, how does the drone look from where you are?"

"*I'd expect to see my great-grandfather up and around before that thing, Chief. From here it looks pretty well gone. Are you reading anything on it, Dietrich?*"

"*No, ma'am. No energy output that I can read. We bloody well fragged the bastard.*"

"All right. Finish setting up the mini-turrets. Then I want two troopers to bring the bodies out while the rest stand guard. Absolutely no one is to approach the drone until we see if any more are on their way."

The team acknowledged her orders and went to work. She waited until the turrets were able to run autonomously and then keyed in the sequence to remote pilot the second rover down from the surface.

If more drones lurked in the structure, they did not make themselves known. The far door had closed shortly after the first had come through, and while the team stood guard over the removal of the bodies, the door showed no sign of opening again. Regardless, she could sense the contained tension in everyone, even fifteen minutes afterward when the last of the first team had been borne away.

"All right," Marette began. "You have done well. For the moment, we will hold this chamber for study. At no time are you to regard the area as secured. Be on your guard. Lieutenant, I want to know what that black material is."

Marette sat back and watched the team do their jobs. Altieri divided them between guard and study. Troopers became techs with more equipment retrieved from the second rover, and the scanning began. As Marette watched, her thoughts drifted back to the Space Agency mole problem. If they could hold this area, their first solid step inside, real discoveries could be made. They needed to control that security leak before they could continue. She had faith in the AoA. They would solve the problem, but how long would it take?

Marette frowned, reminding herself that her own task was before her. As she herself had said, the area was not secured. She refocused, watching the blackness of the chamber as the team worked diligently and meticulously, recording everything bit by bit. The far door remained closed.

And then it happened.

"*Oh my god . . .* " It came from Levy where he was studying the black material. "*Sir, ah, Lieutenant—have a look at this.*"

Marette turned her attention to his camera as Altieri approached. The wall was still black but for four glowing symbols arranged in a square. Each was about three centimeters wide and glowed just as clearly as the readouts on her own monitors. And suddenly they were gone.

"*What did you do, Levy?*" the lieutenant asked.

The crewman held up a sample bottle. "We were all set to take a sample of the stuff. I put my hand against the wall for just a moment to steady myself and those things just started glowing."

"Touch it again," Marette ordered over the comm. She watched as the glove of his suit made contact with the black wall. It was a gesture that up to this point, she realized, had not occurred. A moment after he touched it, the symbols appeared again around his hand. He let go, and, again, they disappeared shortly thereafter.

Altieri touched the wall before her, first with one hand, then the other. Marette watched in amazement as the symbols appeared around each contact point. The first team had said the material was largely organic, but what *was* it? She weighed a risk quickly and made a decision.

"Touch one of the symbols," she said.

Altieri touched the wall again as Levy stepped back. After a moment, she brushed a finger across the upper left symbol. Almost immediately, a glowing area expanded out from the center of the arrangement to form an oval along the surface of the wall. Over half a meter wide and half as tall, it shined a luminescent blue over the faces of the team. At least twenty more symbols arranged themselves inside.

"*Chief,*" said Altieri. "*If I didn't know better, I'd say we were looking at a computer screen.*"

"What," Marette replied in barely contained awe, "makes you think you know better?"

XXXI

IT WAS TEN THIRTY, and the Moon was nowhere to be seen. Romulus found himself searching for it despite the near-total cloud cover that wrapped the sky and reflected the dirty, amber light from below. As he and Diomedes flew over the city, Romulus tried to guess where the Moon might be, but the truth was that he had not paid much attention to its location the previous night.

Romulus was unsure why he suddenly wanted to see it, other than the possibility that it could have helped him relax to look at it for a time. He still needed peace of mind, but the green of the park was gone. He sighed and tried to put the park and Felix out of his thoughts for the moment. He was just anxious about their plan for the night, he told himself.

He and Diomedes were en route to the meeting point. Gideon and Felix would meet them there. Already he could see the vigilante's black floater waiting for them. Not looking forward to facing Felix after the previous afternoon, Romulus hoped he wouldn't arrive until the last moment. He turned away from the window to focus on checking the straps of the body armor Diomedes had loaned him. A few moments later, they landed.

Romulus carried their equipment out of the back as his only mentor went to talk to Gideon.

"What's he doing here?" he heard Diomedes ask. Romulus closed the door and looked up to see to whom Diomedes was referring.

"I'm with Gideon," Brian answered. The reporter stepped around from the vigilante's side, dressed in black with an armor vest strapped over his jacket. He held a small news camera, currently switched off and at his side.

"He's with me," the vigilante confirmed.

Diomedes's eyes narrowed. "Why?"

"He records what I do. He will show my justice to the public, and assure that Wallace is exposed."

Diomedes advanced on the reporter, stopped just an inch away to glare down at the man, and then wrenched the camera from Brian's grip. "I see you point this at me, you're dead. I see me on the news, I'll hunt you down and pull out your lungs."

Brian shuddered visibly but eventually met Diomedes's gaze. He did not, however, reach for the camera. "I'm only shooting Gideon. That was already the plan."

Diomedes frowned and continued his glare a few moments longer before he pushed the camera back into Brian's hands and turned away.

"He's with you," he rumbled to the vigilante.

"Diomedes is big on safety. Always handle a camera as if it's loaded. Looks like we're all here!" Felix appeared from the shadows with a grin. He stepped up to the reporter and remarked, "Hey! Disaster Man! I like the vest." Felix tapped the armor until Brian scowled.

"Disaster Man?"

"Sorry, inside joke." Felix turned to face them all. "So, it looks like we're all locked, loaded and armored up here. We missing anyone? Hello, Flynn." He gave Romulus a simple smile and nod. His left eye was bruised and purple.

Romulus found himself nodding back. "Hi. Is your eye okay?" Damn it, why did he ask that?

Felix touched a hand to the bruise. "Stings a bit, but it's nothing that can't be healed. At this point."

Gideon spoke. "We're running out of time."

"We are," said Diomedes. He turned to Felix. "You remember the plan?"

The question was met by a laugh. "You're asking *me* if I remember the plan?" When Diomedes's expression didn't change, Felix continued in an imitation of him, "Yes, I remember the plan."

"Get going."

Felix gave a salute and an overdone, "Yes, *sir*, captain, *sir!*" and trotted to Diomedes's floater to climb into the pilot's seat. "You guys be careful," he told them. With a last look to Romulus, he closed the door. The engines rushed back to life.

"Let's go," spoke Gideon. Moments later Romulus was ducking into the vigilante's black floater and watching Felix ascend.

Diomedes sat in the pilot's chair with the vigilante in the seat beside him. The Ursa Minor was much smaller than Romulus was used to. It was flatter and shorter than his mentor's floater, and though he and Brian fit comfortably enough in the rear seats, there was room for little else beyond a very small storage space. As his mentor oriented himself to the controls, Romulus checked the safety on his weapon, a small assault rifle he held in his lap.

The strange-looking weapon that Gideon brought out caught his attention. Shaped like a sniper rifle, it held a peculiar, cylindrical pod at the end of the barrel. "What is that?" he asked.

Gideon did not turn but simply told him, "Takes care of the first transport. Custom made."

The reporter looked over at Romulus. "Nervous?"

Romulus paused a moment, and then gave a deliberate look at Brian's camera. "Why should I be nervous? I'm not the one without a gun."

The reporter simply cocked his head and grunted. Romulus turned to the window, satisfied. He wasn't in the mood to talk to him. For a moment though, he wished he were the one with the camera. It was an odd thing to be wishing. He had a responsibility to cover Diomedes while he flew.

He silently wondered if that would be possible without firing a shot himself.

They flew across the city, making for the location where Gideon had claimed the stolen weapons were stored. Somewhere not far off, Felix was waiting for their signal. Romulus checked his weapon once more, cleared his mind, and waited.

They circled the area once and landed on the side of a hill overlooking a span of private warehouses. As they waited in the darkness, seeing no sign of Wallace's transports, Diomedes twice used veiled threats to question the accuracy of Gideon's information. Twice the vigilante assured them that they need only wait.

The minutes passed by. Brian drummed his fingers with an irritating half rhythm.

Drum-drum . . .

Romulus watched outside and listened to his own breathing.

Drum-drum . . .

His mentor sat, radiating impatience.

Drum-drum . . .

Gideon adjusted his rifle.

Drum-drum . . .

"Oh, for crying out—*Stop* it already!" Romulus burst.

The reporter shot him a scowl but stopped. "Touchy."

"Both of you shut up," Diomedes whispered.

Gideon opened his door and leaned out as it folded upward. He cocked his head as if listening. All Romulus could hear was the sound of far-off cars and other distant noises. "I think I hear them," the vigilante whispered. Brian lifted his camera and began to film the dark man.

"Where?" Diomedes asked.

"Close. Out there. I hear their engines starting."

Diomedes brought the floater to life as Gideon lifted the odd rifle.

"Too soon. Can't hear them now."

"They're coming," Diomedes said.

"Stay down until I say."

"Hurry up."

Gideon said nothing but sighted down the rifle into the distance. Moments later, the blocky shape of a transport floater lumbered upward into the sky fifty yards away. From the silhouette it looked to be just larger than Diomedes's own—smaller than Romulus had expected. He leaned forward, his eyes searching rapidly for the second.

The transport turned away from them.

Gideon's rifle fired with an igniting hiss that sent the cylindrical pod at its end launching off like a rocket, vanishing into the darkness. The vigilante sat perfectly still as Romulus waited for . . . something.

"It's marked," Gideon declared, closing the floater door. "Lift off."

Diomedes hardly waited for the vigilante to get completely inside. They ascended rapidly as the second transport, their main target, appeared from the buildings ahead of them. Romulus shifted in his seat and prepared to take Gideon's place, as was the plan. His pulse raced in his ears. They launched forward after the transport.

"He's on course. Follow until he crosses the river, and get above him."

"I remember the fucking plan," Diomedes growled. "Shut up and get ready."

The transport flew at an inconspicuous pace ahead of them. Somewhere beyond it was the first, and in the distance beyond that lay the river that crossed the city.

Romulus released his safety belt as they crossed the river, and he pushed himself forward to hunch just behind the front seats. His mentor took the floater higher. He held on between the seats as they rose, their speed increasing to catch the transport. It was gone from view now, somewhere below them. He felt the reporter brush across behind him, sliding to Gideon's side for a better view.

A rushing roar of wind filled the cabin as the vigilante released the door hatch on his side. It opened out and upward to show the transport flying fifty feet beneath them. They continued to pass above it.

With a jump, Gideon was out.

Romulus scrambled up into the front seat so quickly that he nearly tumbled out himself. The whir of Gideon's spooling support line stopped abruptly as Romulus strapped himself quickly into the seat. The vigilante flew below, his arms open and steady as the floater towed him through open air just behind the transport.

Watching in awe, Romulus had to shout above the wind to be heard. "He's not on yet!"

His mentor said nothing, but he could feel the floater's acceleration as they pulled Gideon closer. Thus far they hadn't been noticed as anything but a passing vehicle rising to a higher vector. Romulus held onto the release for the support line, waiting for the vigilante to reach the transport and feeling vulnerable for how much the position exposed him. It would be difficult for those inside the transport to see Gideon flying in their blind spot, but if they held this course much longer . . .

Gideon reached the back of the transport and grabbed on. "He's on!" Romulus shouted. He waited just a moment to be sure, and then released the line. "Cable off!"

Everything happened at once. Romulus caught a glimpse of the line detaching from the vigilante's harness and whipping free behind them. A second later he yelled in surprise when Diomedes banked them into a turn while the transport veered evasively away below. Romulus clutched his weapon in one hand and grabbed the frame of the open door with the other as the safety belt strained against his chest. It was all he could do to pull back from the hatch.

They sailed away through the sky.

"Holy crap! Did you *see* that?" Brian hollered. Romulus took a second to breathe. The entire maneuver had taken less than ten seconds, and he hadn't yet had time to be impressed. "Damn it, I can't get a good angle!" the reporter cried from the back. His camera was up and shooting through the window.

"Shut up or get out!" Diomedes ordered. They flew away from the transport until he turned them on a parallel course.

"They're still on course—I think!" Romulus shouted when he could see the transports. "I don't even think they've seen—Uh oh."

The transport, previously flying simply, suddenly began to pitch and weave. In the darkness, Romulus could only see its lights and a faint outline. The plan called for Gideon to now be clinging to the back and attempting to sabotage the engine, but it was impossible to tell if he was still there.

"He'll be fine," Diomedes told him. His voice boomed without yelling. "Transports can't maneuver well. Watch if the first comes back."

Romulus looked ahead. "I thought you said they wouldn't stop to turn around!" Both Gideon and Diomedes had previously agreed that two transports with stolen cargo would be too worried about attracting unwanted attention to risk a firefight.

"I did. Watch for it."

Romulus cursed again and tightened his grip on the rifle. Wind filled the cabin. Lights buzzed across the sky in front of them. None of the lights seemed to be heading for them.

Sparks flew from the transport. "I think he's got it!" Brian yelled.

Diomedes braked at once and swerved around behind the transport until they were following it. It continued to weave and dodge, but Gideon—now visible—clung to it as he had to the subway train, standing on the bumper with one hand anchored on the side.

"He's clamped on!" Brian told them as he shot. "His fingers are *in* the metal! Damn, that's some good hardware!" Blue light flowed from Gideon's other hand and reflected off the hatch where the sparks flew. Romulus couldn't tell if it was from a tool in the vigilante's hand or the engine itself. The transport banked and shook in front of them. It tossed Gideon about like a rag doll, but what force the crippled and clumsy transport could muster was not enough to break his grip.

A blast of sparks burst again around Gideon's hand from the tampered hatch. Immediately the transport began to drop in front of them. Romulus's stomach winced as he watched it plunge off course and out of view.

XXXII

"DAMN!" BRIAN EXCLAIMED. "Those things do *not* glide!"

Romulus leaned out to watch as much as he dared. "They've still got landing thrusters, don't they?"

"They'd better," said Brian. "Our psycho's still on there!" He was still filming. "Yep, there they go. It's slowing down. Gonna be a rough landing, though."

Lightning flashed nearby, and thunder rolled in behind the light. The clouds were nurturing a storm. Diomedes banked the floater downward after their quarry. Romulus held on, rifle in hand, and tried to keep an eye on their target. It did appear to be slowing, descending on the edge of the open land where a shopping center was being built. The ground below was sparsely lit, rough with dirt, and bounded by iron frameworks and stacks of materials.

Diomedes had his phone out. "Hiatt, we're at the site. Dead on. Get here now." Felix's response was too quiet to be heard.

The ground below twisted and turned as Diomedes took them in to land. Another peal of thunder rolled through them, and moments later the transport slammed into the dirt. The thrusters had slowed it, but not completely. The impact threw up a cloud of dust that followed the floater to a mound of gravel into which it slid with a crunch. Romulus tried to spot Gideon or the pilot through the dirt and dark.

"I can't see anything! Can anyone see him?"

"I can't tell!" the reporter called back.

"Cover the transport!" Diomedes ordered.

The dust rose higher. They continued to circle as the storm approached. Diomedes didn't seem willing to land yet.

Their course took them around again where the dust was clearing. Romulus squinted and saw the door open. From behind it came a man with a gun. Instantly Romulus trained his rifle on him—and waited. The man looked around for them through the dust. A guard? Part of Wallace's operation, or just some unlucky guy like Romulus who needed the money enough to take a simple job for one night?

"Shoot!" his mentor ordered.

The guard, clearly dazed and shaken from the landing, seemed to catch sight of Romulus, yet only watched as if trying to decide who they were. The guard clutched his weapon but hadn't yet raised it. If he did, he would have a clear shot at Romulus.

"Damn it, fire!"

Romulus nearly squeezed the trigger just from the sound of his mentor's voice. Still the guard had not raised the gun. Romulus cursed, muscles tensed.

The guard raised the gun.

Romulus froze in surprise.

A blinding light flashed from below and Romulus fired. His shots went wide from lack of control. No gunshots came from below. The light faded fast. A second later the guard slumped to the dirt.

"About damned time," Diomedes said to Romulus.

"It wasn't him." Brian pointed. "Look."

Below, Gideon appeared from the shadows. He bent over the fallen man for a moment, and then waved them down. Romulus let out the breath he'd been holding. A short time later they were on the ground.

They stood as a group around the unconscious guard. Gideon had already tied and gagged him with some rope he had apparently scavenged. Another man slumped in the pilot's chair.

"Pilot's dead?" Diomedes asked.

"Just out. From the crash."

"I thought you kill everybody," his mentor said.

"I kill for justice. You kill for money. Neither would be served here. Leave them be."

Diomedes regarded the bodies. For a moment, Romulus thought he might kill them. A sudden knot tightened in his chest. Those men were helpless. Romulus moved forward without thinking, ready to protest or even push the gun away if it looked like Diomedes would fire. He tried to think of something to say.

Before he could, Diomedes just shrugged. "Can't I.D. us." He turned to Romulus. "Tie up the pilot."

Romulus nodded, relieved. It was silly to think Diomedes really would have killed the captured men, he told himself, but he wasn't completely sure if he believed it. He took the rope as his mentor reached into the transport and opened the loading hatch.

"Hurry. Hiatt should be here by now."

As if on cue, the sound of a floater's engines came from above. Lightning flashed once again and thunder followed immediately. Romulus looked up just long enough to make sure it was Felix and then went back to tying the pilot. By the time he was done, Felix was out.

The small man surveyed the area. "Transport's disabled, pilot and guard unconscious and bound, and all perfectly in the planned-on area with no sign that we've been spotted." Felix chortled. "You know, this is going way too well."

A sudden rain rushed down from the sky. Wet drops shattered the dust on the ground below. Felix grinned. "Ah, that's much better."

The transport's cargo door opened on hydraulic cylinders. Diomedes stepped up. "Open the hatch," he ordered, motioning to his floater.

Felix walked back and did so as Gideon and Diomedes began to unload the crates from the transport. The crates were gray, sealed to the rain, and locked with bolts screwed into the sides. As the rain began to soak his hair, Romulus went to help.

"Where's the other transport?" Felix asked.

"Deaf and mute," came Gideon's reply. "And on its way to Wallace's exchange."

Diomedes stopped. "I thought you said it was taken care of."

"It *is* taken care of." Gideon turned to Brian. True to his word, the reporter had stopped shooting since they'd landed. "It is time for you to go."

Brian nodded. "Right." He gathered up his camera. "Gentleman, it's been a pleasure." With a self-satisfied grin, he turned and hurried away.

"Now where's he off to?" Romulus asked.

"You said you were going to destroy it," Diomedes growled. He had not taken his eyes off the vigilante.

"I said it would destroy Wallace. That pod I fired at the first transport? That pod built to my specifications, to my needs, to my plan?

That pod jams the transport's communications and records the meeting. The reporter brings the footage to Wallace's superiors and the media. He is exposed for arson and the betrayal of his company. Publicly disgraced and arrested. If RavenTech lets him live."

Romulus blinked. "They'd kill him?"

His mentor actually grinned.

"Given the evidence against RavenTech, he could probably turn against them to save his ass if he's indicted. I wouldn't be surprised if they tried to keep him quiet," Felix said. "Not to mention making an example of the guy for stealing from his own company," he finished grimly.

"They'll gut him," Diomedes declared, still grinning. "Finish loading the crates."

They continued in silence, working in the pouring rain. The thunder and the deluge masked their sounds as they filled Diomedes's floater to capacity and then loaded what little remained into the vigilante's.

"It is a tragedy that the tools of death that remain on the other transport must continue to exist," Gideon intoned, "but such sacrifice shall serve to be a bane to Wallace. And now we shall destroy what has been captured here."

"Destroy your share," Diomedes said. "The rest is mine."

Gideon turned to him, wide-eyed. "*All* must be destroyed, else they find their way into the hands of those who would bring chaos and death to our streets!"

"Fuck you. Wallace torched my place, my gear, stole my money. It's payback."

Fire erupted in the vigilante's eyes. He lunged at Diomedes and stopped only moments away. "If you would sell them, you would be no less guilty than he whom we've destroyed tonight!" He stood glaring at Diomedes, body tense, poised to strike. Romulus stepped back without thinking as his mentor stood defiant. Felix was behind him somewhere. His mentor returned Gideon's gaze in a stare that betrayed no emotion.

It had been going so well! Romulus struggled for words to diffuse the situation amid an eternity that ended in barely a few seconds.

Diomedes moved first.

"Fine," he spoke. "We destroy them."

The vigilante loosened. "I'll lead you to where we can melt them down."

He turned to go.

Diomedes pulled his auto-pistol and shot Gideon through the back of the head.

Instant and terrible, there was no surviving it. Romulus staggered; outrage bulleted through his own body with equal violence. The shot echoed and was absorbed into the rain before Gideon's body tumbled face first into the mud. He twitched once and then lay still.

Diomedes—his *mentor*—had slain the man in cold blood! Horror threatened to vomit up from Romulus's stomach as he fought the shock freezing his mind and body; he could only stand there, gaping.

"Maybe we can still get the reward," Diomedes rumbled.

"Jesus Christ!" The yell came from Felix. "What—what—what the . . . Shit! What the hell did you *do?*"

"He wanted to burn our money." Diomedes put his gun away. "You heard him. He was a damned psychotic." He knelt down and turned Gideon over. Mud clung to the body. Blood ran down his face. Diomedes pulled off the mask that hid his features, revealed now to be stained in red and shattered where the bullet had forced its way through.

Romulus was still frozen. He'd let it happen. He'd stood by and watched it happen before him, just like he'd watched in The Arena.

No! This was *not* his fault. It was his mentor's. *His mentor's.* God. "What . . . " he managed. His own voice was distant and unresponsive.

"Wanted to see who he was," Diomedes said. He stood up. "Let's go."

Felix didn't move, staring hard and cold. "Oh! 'Let's go,' is that it?! Gun him down, have a look, and be on your fucking merry way?!"

With a strange calm, Diomedes met the smaller man's eyes. "He was a goddamn lunatic. He had it coming, sooner or later."

"And when someone blows you through the back of your head and leaves you dead in the muck without so much as a thought," Felix shot back, "that's the exact damned same thing they'll say about you. He was a goddamn psycho! He had it coming! And they'll be fucking right!"

It was a dream. It had to be. Rain surrounded them in ethereal haze. Romulus was there, watching it all, but numb. Powerless. Distant.

His mentor's eyes burned dangerously. "Get in the floater," he hissed.

"I don't know who you're going to get to help you sell those guns," Felix shot, "but you can be damned sure it's not me!"

Diomedes's auto-pistol was out and trained on the small man in a blink. "Bullshit. You're going to get in the floater and you're going to help us sell. You're going to get Romulus and me the money we earned, or I'm gonna leave you in the mud with the psycho."

Romulus flinched. Diomedes hardly ever used his handle. At any other moment he would have been proud to be counted as a partner. Now everything within him recoiled on instinct. It was all falling apart.

Felix pulled his own gun. Diomedes didn't flinch.

"Back off," the smaller man demanded.

Rain poured down, washing over Romulus's face. His two companions stood before him, guns out, each mirrored in the other. Diomedes towered above with Felix in his shadow, just as he had stood over his smaller, battered opponent at The Arena: poised to strike.

Diomedes fired.

Anguish caught in Romulus's throat and Felix dropped his gun with a shout. Diomedes's aim had merely disarmed Felix, but now he stood vulnerable.

In that instant, Michael remembered.

He remembered the man who enthralled him as a boy with stories of glory—and he saw the same man standing by as gangers beat a vagrant. He remembered the man who recognized him and took him in when he had nowhere else to go—and he saw that man nearly push him into the flames of a burning building to salvage some equipment. He remembered the mentor that tried to teach him how to reach the dreams he had himself inspired—and saw that mentor beat a weaker man within an inch of his life. He remembered a knight imbued with the strength to protect, a strength that Michael wanted so badly—and he saw that "knight" use that strength to hurt and destroy. He remembered skill and courage, and he saw rage and violence. He remembered the man who called him a partner . . . and finally saw that partner shoot Gideon from behind.

Michael rose between Diomedes and Felix. He stood, shielding his friend from the freelancer's gun, and forced the word out. "Stop."

His former mentor's glare cut into him. "Don't be insane. Move!" Something lurked in Diomedes's eyes that Michael hadn't seen before, but he wasn't backing down.

Michael was aware of Felix behind him and of the freelancer's weapon aimed straight at his chest. For a moment, Michael faltered, trapped between a wasted past and an unguided future. And then he remembered how Felix had listened—and remembered himself striking the one person who had truly been there for him.

"No," Michael said. He brought his own weapon to bear on Diomedes.

They stood facing each other, eyes locked. Michael's entire being was tensed. It took all his strength not to look away. He held the auto-pistol with both hands. Any shot that might make him drop it would have to take off his own hand as well.

"What the hell are you doing?" Diomedes growled. He turned his aim on Michael's head.

Something moved in the rain behind Diomedes. A woman Michael didn't recognize lunged from the darkness and pressed a gun up into the back of Diomedes's neck. "Bloody move a hair and I pull this trigger," she swore in an accented voice.

Diomedes cursed but didn't move.

The woman glanced behind him at Felix for a moment, then back to Diomedes. Her eyes were hard. "Hullo, Felix."

"Felix . . . ?" Michael asked.

"Yeah, she's with me," Felix answered. "You've incredible timing."

The woman glanced at Gideon's body and said nothing.

"Fuck you all," Diomedes growled.

"Put the gun *down!*" she yelled.

Michael's pulse pounded in his ears. He fixed his old mentor with the strongest look he could muster. "Put it down, Diomedes." Each word was a struggle. "Get in your floater . . . and *leave.*"

Diomedes lowered his weapon an inch.

"*Go!*" Michael shouted, nearly bursting.

Diomedes dropped the gun completely. For a moment, his former mentor just stood there, watching him. Days ago this man had been his shelter and his greatest hope. Now all that had crumbled to dust. Anger swirled in Diomedes's eyes and Michael felt it searching through his soul. Accusation and betrayal regarded him, and, for only a moment, the freelancer's gaze held a flash of pain and loss. It was the thing he'd never seen before in Diomedes until moments ago.

And then it was gone.

Without a word, Diomedes turned and moved to the floater. He pitched out the bag containing Michael's remaining insignificant possessions, closed the door, and started the engines. The floater lifted into the rain.

Michael watched Diomedes go until he faded into the downpour, and then stared into the rain. Alone.

XXXIII

IN THE END, they decided to leave Gideon's body where it was. Though it seemed to Felix that they were all reluctant to do so, they agreed that doing more would only serve to involve them in matters they now wished to avoid. No one wanted to leave the body in the mud without a burial, but Caitlin had argued that to bury the man themselves would leave him missing to the rest of the world. If Gideon had family or friends, however distant, they should be given some chance to know what had happened. But bringing him in themselves threatened to catch them up in a net of questions. They'd found an emergency medical beacon in Gideon's floater, and so had activated it and left the tiny transmitter with the body. The ambulance would find him. His loss would be known.

As Felix lifted the three of them off in the dead man's floater, it seemed a hollow thought.

They didn't speak much after deciding what to do. Felix had introduced Flynn and Caitlin, but both were understandably somber and didn't speak beyond exchanged hellos and practical conversation. They flew, withdrawn, and Felix found himself wanting to break the silence with a joke. Somehow he managed to be silent and leave them both to their thoughts as he focused on his own.

He was more worried for Flynn than for Caitlin. While he found himself growing quite fond of the Welshwoman, with her flashing eyes and free spirit, he knew Flynn was probably suffering the greater pain at the moment. The young man had finally lost the blinders he'd worn for so long. It was the best thing for him, and Felix sensed Flynn had the strength inside him to move on, but . . .

Felix stopped himself before he began to assume too much of what either of his companions was feeling. He would speak to them both when the time was right.

As for himself, Gideon's death both distressed and relieved him. Diomedes had ended the man's life without warning and over a reason as hollow as greed. People had died for less, Felix knew, and just as senselessly. Gideon had been snuffed out with less than a thought, and without even a chance to prepare himself. Felix mourned the man as he would any taken life.

Yet Gideon had not been well. The pain in his soul and the madness in his eyes was now gone. Whatever pain had caused his deadly crusade—whether an event in his past or the mystery of a hardware-induced psychosis—was now at ease. No more would his unstable mind carry the weight of his vengeance. Caitlin and her friends were safer for it. The man had fought violence with violence, and his sanity was arguably the cost.

Felix had already mourned Gideon when he had met him. Now, at least, he was at peace. Felix sighed. It didn't make his death less tragic.

They chose to respect one of Gideon's last wishes. After departing the construction site, they flew out over one of the wider sections of the river where they pushed the crates out and let the water take them down to where no one would find them. Though only weapon-filled crates had dropped into the dark waters, Felix realized that, in a way, it was as close as they would come to a burial for Gideon. For a while, they watched the water without speaking. Felix found himself unsure of what to say. He supposed they all felt that way. They hovered awhile longer before moving on.

Caitlin shared with him the location of her apartment in the city. It was a small but secure building about ten blocks from the place they'd first met, and it was there that they flew next. Soon they had touched down on the street outside.

"I'll see you to your door." Felix made it a question, and was glad to see Caitlin nod.

She turned to the rear seat where Flynn sat. "You did a good thing tonight, Flynn," she whispered. "It took courage."

Flynn looked up at her, poised on the edge of choosing his words. "Thank you," he said at last. It felt sincere.

"It was nice to meet you," Caitlin finished. "Good night."

"Good night."

The two smiled briefly at each other before Caitlin left the floater to walk with Felix to the door of her building.

"How are you doing?" he asked her.

"I'm all right," she answered, hesitating. "No, I'm not all right. I don't know what I am." They came to the door and stopped. Felix waited patiently, just listening. "I'm relieved," she admitted. "God, that sounds terrible of me. Crikey. I don't mean it that way, I don't mean I wanted him dead. I didn't. I just . . . "

Felix gave her a moment, and then said, "You're not glad he's dead, but you're glad he'll leave The Scry alone."

Caitlin nodded. "Yes. Though it's the same thing, isn't it?"

"I don't think so."

"The ends don't justify the means, Felix."

"No, they don't. But you didn't cause this."

She looked at him, eyes strong. "No, I didn't. I didn't say I had. But he's dead, and instead of mourning, my first reaction is relief. I don't like the thought of that." She looked away at the floater as if to hide her pain from him. "He was disturbed, and he was dangerous. But he protected us. He deserved to be mourned. And my first bloody thoughts are of why I'm glad he's gone. No different than if I'd shot the poor bloke myself."

Felix scowled; it hurt to watch her beat herself up. "That's not true and you know it."

"Of course I know it!" she whispered. "But I don't feel it."

Felix regarded her for a moment and tried to resist the urge to put a compassionate arm around her, for fear she'd retreat from him. "So then tell me," he said finally, "how are you not mourning him? By wishing he didn't have to die, or by caring enough about honoring his memory that you're standing here beating yourself up for not doing so?"

Caitlin stood silently for a few moments. "I suppose you're right."

"But?"

"But right or not, it will likely take a bit of time to sink in."

"I suppose I can understand that." Felix nodded and flashed a quick smile. "After all, we only just met. You haven't learned I'm always right, yet." He winked.

To his relief, she smiled back. "You're just as obnoxious as the reporter chap, aren't you?"

He chuckled. "Oh, probably, but I like to think it's a more endearing brand of obnoxiousness."

Her eyes softened and she brushed her knuckles gently down his cheek. It was a warm, soft touch. She had lovely hands. "I'll not be about for a little while," Caitlin told him. "I need to get out of the city and ride. Clear my mind."

He nodded. "Think you'll come back?"

"I can think of at least one reason to." Caitlin smiled again and continued before he could respond, "And what is your next move?" She nodded to the floater.

"Abandon the floater somewhere, then see what I can do for Flynn. He's going to need somewhere to go. I think I can help him with that. He'll have a place to stay for a while, at least."

"You care about him a lot."

Felix smiled at her. "He's a good kid. And I don't know, there's a . . . potential inside him. I can't really describe it. Just a feeling I have."

"You seem a good judge of character."

"And what makes you think that?"

She grinned. "Well, you like me, don't you?" She kissed him then before he could speak, quickly but firmly on the lips. "Take care of yourself," she ordered.

"You, too, Caitlin." He watched her go into her building, hoping she'd be okay. It wasn't until the door had closed that he realized he was blushing.

XXXIV

MICHAEL STAYED with Felix over the next few days; it was a blessing for which he was very grateful. For a time, he had returned to the mood that had haunted him immediately after Diomedes's and his apartment had been destroyed: hopeless, lost, and purposeless. Staying with Felix gave him a place to go where he could rest and have one less worry on his mind.

After a while, the feeling of being lost left him too, and Michael began to grow aware of a strength inside himself. It was a strange feeling. So often before, he'd sought that strength from an outside source. Diomedes had been his strength since he had found him, with an essence that Michael had struggled to capture for his own and qualities he had wished to draw into himself. It struck him as ironic that he only gained that strength after breaking free of the man.

Felix suggested that it had always been within him, merely overshadowed by his worship of Diomedes. After all, Michael had projected honor, courage, and righteousness onto Diomedes that the man did not possess. Perhaps he might have possessed them once, but no more. Perhaps they were merely a side effect of the image that Michael had created in his mind when he first knew him on the farm. Had those qualities ever been real? Michael didn't know. In the days after he'd broke from Diomedes, Michael wondered if those qualities actually had come from within himself—qualities that had lain dormant, seeking to become alive in the simulacrum of the dour freelancer.

It was the feeling of purposelessness, however, that in those three days he could not escape. Having discovered his false conception of a single freelancer, he now doubted his entire preconception of the profession itself. Was there room for noble pursuits in such a mercenary concept? He didn't know. If there was a place for him somewhere, where was it? Felix was sympathetic to his doubts, but offered no concrete assurances beyond suggesting that, sometimes, purpose could find the man better than the reverse.

So Michael waited, and rested.

Brian Savagewood's interview with Gideon—and the subsequent connection to the RavenTech arsons—populated the web and news broadcasts. The pod that Gideon had placed on the first transport had done its job, and the reporter had done his. Scandal raged around Wallace's scheme. Footage of the illicit deal seemed plastered everywhere, and the evidence that Gideon had passed to Brian had found its way to public knowledge. Wallace was wanted for murder, arson, theft, and industrial espionage. The public, though normally jaded and apathetic to one more murder in a violent city, responded to the production with the zeal of the crowd at The Arena. They seized Wallace as a scapegoat for corporate transgression while RavenTech distanced itself from the man, citing Wallace's theft from his own company.

Ken Wallace was found dead within two days. Michael wondered if Felix had been right. Had RavenTech killed him as both an example and to prevent him from drawing them deeper into the scandal? Theories and rumors erupted, but none had yet been substantiated. Michael doubted if any would ever be, and often wondered what had caused Wallace to embark on the scheme in the first place.

According to Felix, the streets abounded with rumors about Gideon and where he might turn up next. There was no mention of his death. The recovery of a nameless body from a construction site received no coverage.

As for their part, Michael, Felix, and Diomedes had been left out of Brian's account of things. Maybe Diomedes's threat still hung over the reporter's head, or maybe he just didn't want to share the spotlight. Whatever his reasons, neither Michael nor Felix were of a mind to complain.

Michael had come to realize that he had resented the reporter a little when he first met him. Brian had a purpose, or at least a career. They were about the same age, but the reporter was on his own and doing well. Though Michael wasn't sure that he resented the man anymore, he still envied him that purpose—even if Brian was, as Felix admitted, an ungrateful putz.

Michael tried not to think of Diomedes. Felix had already offered to look into what had become of the man, but Michael had declined. He wasn't ready to deal with that yet. He wanted to separate from his old mentor as much as he could, feeling guilty just for knowing him. For so long he'd thought of himself in terms of being Diomedes's partner. Michael wanted to stand alone. He tried to put the man out of his mind.

It was during the afternoon of the third day that Felix turned to him and said, "Well, they should be just about ready for you now."

Michael blinked. "What?"

"Them," Felix replied with a grin. "Them! Them!"

Michael smiled. He was getting used to the man's joking manner. "Oh, yes. 'Them.' How silly of me to forget."

"Yes, well, I'm sure you're forgiven," Felix replied. "Come on, get your coat. Let's go."

"Are you going to tell me who 'them' refers to?" he asked as he rose.

"Oh, probably, probably. You sure you don't want to guess? I'll even give you a hint: it's got nothing whatsoever to do with giant ants."

"Giant ants."

"Nothing at all."

"Uh huh."

"Well, it doesn't!"

They headed out the door and made their way down to the street. Wherever they were going, Felix insisted they walk. "So do I have to guess, or are you going to eventually tell me?" Michael asked. Felix had a glint in his eyes that was making Michael increasingly curious.

"Not even going to try to guess? I did give you a hint."

"You said it has nothing to do with giant bugs."

"Ants!" Felix corrected. "Giant ants. 'Them!' It's an old, old movie from the 1950s. Giant nuclear-mutated ants crawl out of the desert and generally cause havoc. They eventually go to Los Angeles."

"And this has nothing to do with that." Michael shook his head. The man was perpetually weird, but it was a good quality.

"Yes, I already said that. Weren't you listening?" Felix shot him another grin as they walked up the street.

Michael shook his head again, smiling. "I'm not much in the mood to guess, Felix."

292   MICHAEL G. MUNZ

"Oh, sure, I've got this great secret I'm actually able to tell you, and you're going to take away all the fun of dangling it in front of your face."

"I'd guess you're having quite a bit of fun already."

"Yeah, well, can't deny that, I suppose. Fine." He paused as a group of teenagers passed them on the street. "Ever heard of Aeneas?"

Michael thought about it. The name seemed familiar, though he couldn't place it. "Not quite, no."

"Heard of the city of Troy?"

Michael nodded.

"Aeneas was, as the story goes, a cousin of the king of Troy. Just before the city fell, his mother Aphrodite—goddess of love, in fact—came to him and warned him. She told him to leave Troy before it was destroyed completely, to lead a group of his countrymen to another land and start a new kingdom. He did, and, to make an epic poem short, supposedly founded what would eventually become the Roman Empire."

"Okay?" Michael said, wondering at the point of the story.

"Yeah, I know, great story—actually it is. Pick up Virgil's Aeneid sometime." He chuckled. "But I'm babbling. On to the point! There are people who consider our modern society something of a present-day Troy. Only this time, it's not the Greeks coming to destroy us, but the nature of what humanity has become that will eventually tear us apart. Violence growing as compassion shrinks. Environmental destruction. Power centered more and more in the hands of those who wield it for their own gains. They're worried our self-destructive tendencies are very near to winning out, that we may have already passed the point of no return."

Michael said nothing as he listened, inwardly agreeing that these people might have a point. He'd seen a great deal of humanity's dark side in the past few months alone.

"Some of these people have formed a sort of secret society that's been around for—well, I'll spare you the details, but it suffices to say that it's been a while. Time enough for them to have established fields of quiet influence in a great number of other organizations."

Michael looked at Felix with more than a little skepticism, though the man had never lied to him before. "So they're controlling everything?"

Felix chuckled. "Oh, no. Heck, no. Nothing that drastic. They have a great deal of eyes, but not as many hands, so to speak. They do have some influence, but they wield only as much as they can without being discovered. Where they can though, they act for good. You asked once who Lifesaver—er, Marc—worked for. (Call him Marc now, by the way, or I'll owe him dinner.) This's the secret I couldn't tell you at the time. He's part of the Agents of Aeneas."

"Agents of Aeneas?" Michael hadn't heard of them anywhere. "So if they think this is all another Troy—they're going to try to leave before it crumbles?"

Felix nodded. "That's one of their main goals, yeah."

"And just where do they think they'll go? I haven't heard of any newly discovered continents lately, have you?" he joked before a thought jolted him. "God, they don't mean to kill off anyone who's not with them, do they?"

Felix laughed. "Oh, no, no, no. Nothing like that. They don't want to do away with society. For one thing, they're not killers. The whole group works on the assumption that society will do away with itself. They don't want to get rid of society, they just want to leave it."

"So where are they going to go?"

"Where, indeed?" Felix gave him what might have been a knowing smile. "Like I said, that's *one* of their goals. The other, which I'm guessing will perk your interest more, is to try to prolong the life of society by doing as much good as they can."

"Like what?"

"Oh, things. Building shelters, organizing humanitarian aid groups, aiding the police, exposing corruption. Sometimes they'll keep watch on important figures who've made enemies through positive acts, protecting those that need it. Maybe even a little redirection of funds now and then. Not always legal, but . . . positive."

"Like what?" Felix was being rather vague. Michael suspected it was deliberate.

"Can't tell you specifics. Not yet, anyway."

"But you do know."

"I might know some things," he said with a wink that all but screamed yes.

A question that Michael realized he should have asked by now sprung to mind. "I'm assuming we're going to talk to someone from this group, but I'm guessing you're one of these 'Agents of Aeneas,' too?"

"Well, based on all I've told you about a secret society, that'd be a pretty valid assumption, wouldn't it?"

"That's what I thought." How many secrets did the man have?

"Although," Felix added, "it'd be an incorrect one."

Michael shot him an amusedly annoyed glance. "You really like doing that, don't you?"

"Oh, now I'm *sure* you know the answer to that one." Felix grinned.

"So how do you know so much about them?"

Felix smiled and glanced skyward. "Oh, that's a story I think you'll have to wait to hear," he mused. "Best not to complicate things too much for you today. I will say that I am currently, oh, a friend of the organization."

Michael nodded and remained silent awhile as they walked down the sidewalk. Ahead was Marc's building, and Michael guessed it was not a coincidence. He also guessed that the reason for this journey was not simply to say hello. An excitement born of curiosity and hope sparked within him, and he picked up his pace as more and more questions filled his mind. Before he could form them into words, Felix spoke.

"They've had their eye on you, Flynn. They trust you enough to let me tell you about them." They reached the entrance to the building. "And you're under no obligation to join. It's not the mafia. I wouldn't bring you here if it were. But they will ask you to keep their secret."

Felix raised his finger to the door buzzer. Beside the button was a small outline of a shield-bearing figure that Michael hadn't noticed before. "This is the Palladium, an artifact that was said to guarantee the safety of any city that held it, and one of the things Aeneas was said to have carried out of Troy. It's their symbol." He paused. "Do you trust me?"

Michael nodded.

Felix pushed the button. A moment later, Marc answered and released the door locks. Michael considered what Felix had told him so far: " . . . *protecting those that need it* . . . " Perhaps, as Felix predicted it would, purpose had found him. He stepped through the door first, leaving Felix to follow.

EPILOGUE

HISTORY WAS NO STRANGER to exodus. Life had left the oceans to crawl its way up to existence upon the land. Humankind had spread across the globe via ice bridges and precarious ocean voyages. Countries had formed of former refugees settling in a new land after fleeing persecution or searching for their own freedom. The Earth, once a vast expanse of seemingly endless frontiers, had now grown small from exploration, settled over seemingly every inch of its surface, and had seen doubling after doubling of human population. An exodus, in the true sense of the word, was no longer feasible within a global frame. They had journeyed to the planetary shore, and they knew not how to swim.

It had been nearly a century since mankind had first launched a simple beeping transmitter into orbit. A century of aircraft development bridged the gap between the rudimentary glider and the surface-to-orbit fighter craft. Yet in a century of space flight, they had barely learned to travel in a cost-effective way beyond the Moon.

No one in the Agents of Aeneas doubted that faster and further travel was possible. Progress had never been forged from the fires of doubt, and to believe their goal was impossible would serve no purpose. They had researched and studied. They had searched. And when a survey scan of the Aristarchus crater had turned up a solid mass of extra-lunar material, one emitting faint levels of energy, they dared to hope that their search had been fruitful. A simple asteroid or meteor would have been obliterated in the ancient impact that had formed the massive crater. That the mass remained solid and undistributed hinted of something designed to withstand such an impact—designed to weather the violence of cosmic radiation and the theoretical stresses of interstellar travel. It had hinted at the AoA's holy grail, a means to their exodus: an ancient, derelict starship buried beneath the Moon's surface.

And so they had released a hint of the data to ESA, a nudge to lead the space agency to direct its resources towards an investigation. The Agents of Aeneas had observed and influenced that investigation. Marette Clarion herself had been placed as the overseer, waiting for the moment when the protocol-obsessed mining foreman would uncover the alleged vessel and report to ESA.

The presence of an active defense system inside the ship had been a tragic and unexpected element. That anything at all functioned after the centuries the ship had lain dormant had been a surprise that became both a blessing and a curse. That *any* lives had been lost was disastrous, but the discovery of both the drone and the black substance—which appeared to be some sort of computer system—held so much promise: it was operational, drastically increasing their chances of both salvaging the technology and understanding the science that had got it there.

In the few weeks that passed after Marette's first team had lost their lives, five more of the security drones had appeared. Three had challenged the second team's turrets. Crewmen Soto and Dietrich had given their lives to ensure the drones' destruction. When the entry was declared secure two quiet days later, they discovered two more drones lying in the corridors beyond. Neither functioned. They had been removed for study to the small field base that ESA had rapidly set up just outside of the ship.

Everything was kept contained at the immediate site—a technological quarantine that the AoA had pushed for. The mole inside the space agency was still operating, but the Agents of Aeneas had discovered that he had not had a chance to make his deal. His initial buyer, the American named Wallace, was dead. He had not as yet attempted to find another. For now, they watched him and let him remain with ESA where they could trace his movements. He would not be exposed. Not yet. Handled properly, he could be turned to their advantage. For now, the roadblock he had posed had been removed. They were free to continue.

And so they did, cautiously, beginning to explore the interior of the ship. The black substance coated nearly every surface they found inside. The eerie displays that the second team had discovered would appear wherever a wall surface was touched, and techs had managed to decipher the simple sequence that would open a door in some places. They had mapped a very limited section of corridors, including a small, empty room thought to be the source of the drones, when suddenly the sequence stopped working, and, for the moment, they could go no further.

Marette watched a full Earth hang above the lunar landscape. Slowly, their exodus was taking shape. More scientists were inbound to help unravel the nature of the black substance. Was it truly a computer of some sort? Did it contain the data they were searching for, or was it more than that? The first sensor techs had reported that the ubiquitous material was at least partially organic. They later determined that it displayed properties of photosynthetic respiration, absorbing carbon dioxide and releasing oxygen like a plant. It was both solid and liquid, both mysterious and baffling. Was it the key to the puzzle, or the puzzle itself?

Somewhere inside its unexplored reaches, the ship concealed the technology they needed behind—or within—the blackness. Wherever it hid, Marette vowed, the AoA would find it.

It waited for them.

MICHAEL FLYNN'S JOURNEY
CONTINUES IN
A MEMORY IN THE BLACK

As the Agents of Aeneas struggle to unlock the secrets
of the alien craft, word of its discovery has leaked, and
various groups conspire to seize its technology for
themselves. While Michael Flynn protects a fellow
Agent from those who believe he knows too much, the
two are tasked with renewing contact with Diomedes,
who is wanted for the assassination of a man suspected
of trying to sell the technology.

Meanwhile, Gideon has been seen alive . . .

Keep reading for a glimpse of what's in store.

THE UNFOLDING TROLLEY DOORS released Caitlin into the late-afternoon warmth. Air cooled by the river that flowed a block south provided small relief from the stifling atmosphere that had surrounded her moments earlier. Ahead waited the grey stucco of her flat, and she took to the bits of shade beneath the sapling maples that the city had been kind enough to plant along the sidewalk. Against the colour of a clear blue sky, they could be verdant and gorgeous as leaves danced with golden light, yet today they seemed mere refugees amid grey concrete and white haze. They resonated perfectly with—or perhaps because of—her mood.

A cloud of worries and personal demons hounded her thoughts with troublesome whispers. What Felix referred to as a second wave of grief over Gideon's fate again forced her to examine the guilt she felt over her own part of it. Then and now, she'd told herself that she'd done what she'd thought was right. It was the solid ground she had found to stand on; though she inarguably felt safer with Gideon gone from her life and the lives of her fellow Scry, the means were not her choice, and she certainly hadn't pulled the trigger.

And yet the possibility that she had not left a dead body there that night—that he had continued on and could have been aided somehow instead of simply discarded in the mud—had sewn a seed of remorse in her heart. Had she been so anxious to be rid of someone—someone to whom she and others owed their lives, even—that she'd treated his life as no better than trash? Though his association with The Scry put all of them at ever-deepening risk, she never believed that she wished him death.

Could she have been wrong about herself?

Shame was a significant part of what she was fighting, Caitlin knew. And yet hadn't they made certain he was dead? Even summoned an ambulance to find him? After seeing Gideon again, she could no longer be sure how much of what she remembered was real and how much she had created to protect herself. That Felix remembered the same events that night should be reassurance enough, but Gideon's return created a doubt that continued to fester.

They would find out. They had to. It was an assertion that had given her some comfort. Though a part of her hated to admit it, Felix's commitment to aid her had bolstered that comfort. Then Diomedes's appearance had brought another element of that night back to the forefront of her troubled thoughts, and that comfort was no longer enough.

She wanted to clear her head with something soothing, for a time at least, if she couldn't banish the source of the problem. She needed a cup of tea.

She laughed ruefully to herself. What she *needed* was a ride, or at least a soak in the tub. There was no horse around for the former and likely no time for the latter. But the tea would be a help.

Caitlin reached her building, trotted up the few steps to the door, and keyed in her pass code. The light smiled green at her, but the door still took a second yank to open off of the catch. Her landlord was taking his time with fixing that little quirk.

Taking its time as well was the lift, and as she stood waiting, her craving for a cuppa growing, she considered taking the stairs up the eight flights. But her flat's lift had a way of ascending that made the speed rather palpable, and though she wouldn't admit it to anyone, she rather enjoyed the sensation. It wasn't a horse, but it would have to do until she could next get out of the city. Who knew how long it would be before that happened?

Perhaps she could tear herself away if she needed to. It would have been easier that morning than it was now that Diomedes had re-entered the mix. For the first time, Caitlin wondered if the murderous freelancer had recognized her on the street. The only other time he'd seen her was when he'd shot Gideon, and she didn't think he'd gotten a very good look during those few minutes in the dark. Yet there were cybernetics that might do the remembering for him.

She had put a gun to his head to defend Felix. If he did remember, it would be an understatement to say he would not be well chuffed to see her again. But he'd never bothered her since that evening.

The bell for her floor chimed. She stepped off of the lift and realized that in her brooding she'd completely forgotten to enjoy the ride.

Bollocks.

Her door was immediately across from the elevator. Moments later she was through it and making a beeline for the kettle when the sight of a figure on her balcony made her nearly jump out of her skin.

Standing outside the glass, watching her, was Gideon.

Caitlin froze. Again she had the feeling of being confronted by a ghost. Though dressed in the same sweatpants, t-shirt, and jumper he'd worn earlier, now those clothes were torn and dirty. They made him look considerably more haggard than he was a few hours ago, even without the fatigue apparent in his eyes. This time the ghost stood only meters away. All that she need do to speak with him would be to cross the distance and slide back the door. Then he reached up and rapped on the glass, and she was suddenly less concerned with whether or not she'd find the answers she was looking for than whether she'd like what they turned out to be.

"Gideon." It was a greeting that she whispered, though very nearly a question as well. Hearing her through the glass, or perhaps just reading lips, he nodded and rapped again.

He waited patiently, but as she moved closer she could see an uncertainty in his eyes. Though small, it stood out in contrast with his previous and sometimes crazed confidence in a way that, for a moment, made his expression seem pleading.

She reached the door and paused with her fingers on the handle of the sliding glass. If he'd been at her front door she'd have preferred to step into the hall to speak to him. But he wasn't in the hall, and there seemed little point in joining him on the tiny balcony. She stood, torn.

Oh, sod it! The door was unlocked and open a moment later. She stepped aside to let him in.

The large man took the wordless invitation and came inside. "You are Caitlin Danae," he spoke. The voice was the same as it had been before. "I need your help."

A myriad of questions bottlenecked in her throat. Her thoughts jumbled, words became elusive, and she stared without speaking until she became conscious of gaping at him.

"Gideon," she managed, "what happened to you?"

"Are The Scry working for anyone?" His voice was calm in a way that had her taking a step back.

"What?"

"I need to know if I can trust you or not. Are you working for anyone?"

"Anyone who?" she demanded, taken aback by the question. "No—no, I'm not."

"You were at my apartment. How did you find it?" he continued. "Were you following me?"

"You told us to find you there. Months ago, when The Scry were working for you. I was looking for you."

He waited, watching her, sizing her up. She was aware she hadn't actually answered his entire question, but then she hadn't asked how he had found her flat, either.

"I don't remember telling you that," he said finally.

"I'm not a liar," she said. "Gideon, what—"

"Who's the man who attacked us?" he pressed. "What does he want? Did you help him find me?"

"What? No! He—You don't remember Diomedes?"

"You say this as if I knew him. Who is he?"

She gaped. Had he repressed the shooting? Did he have amnesia? "Gideon, what is going on? What happened to you?"

He frowned as if trying to decide what to say. "There was an accident. I've been away for a while."

"An *accident*?" She saw him again, face down in the mud. Bloody. Violated. Murdered.

"Why are you looking at me like that?"

"An accident!" she repeated, appalled at the word. "I saw you dead!"

He stood staring, unsure. Confused. "I was never dead . . . "

"Then, what happened?"

He blinked, off-balance, as if the question surprised him. "It . . . it doesn't matter."

"Doesn't *matter*? You were shot, you were—you were gone! We checked, we made *sure* there was nothing we could do for you! You can't just tell me you got better!" She was vaguely aware she was glaring at him.

"You say . . . " he began, steeped in confusion. "You say I was shot?" Gideon turned away like a toddler separated from a parent.

"You truly didn't know?"

"I don't remember." He blinked again, becoming more composed. "You seem to know a great deal. Tell me. Why? Have The Scry been following me?"

She leaned against her dining room table, still feeling vulnerable from his presence in her flat, but somewhat more at ease as his tone softened. "The Scry were working for you. You more or less recruited us. You don't recall that, either?"

"You assisted me, once. You and a few others of your group. Once, that is all. You proved yourselves valuable, but I remember no further contact."

"There was further contact." The first time he'd come to The Scry to get extra eyes and ears on a particular night, it was Caitlin and a few others with whom he worked. "But The Scry haven't been following you. I have."

"Why?"

"As I said, I thought you were dead. *Buried.* Then I saw you alive, just last week." She hesitated, uncomfortable explaining her full motivation to him. "I needed to find out what really happened."

"It doesn't matter."

"Bollocks, why do you keep saying that?"

"Saying what?"

"That it doesn't matter."

He frowned, confused again. "I don't know. I'm unsure I even mean it." Again his gaze recomposed itself and hardened, as if his mind were a ship rocking back and forth. "I barely know who you are, and you claim you know so much of me. You swear to me you're not working for anyone."

"Yes! Crikey, how much do I have to say it?"

He gave no answer, merely staring back at her as if deciding whether or not to take her at her word. Whatever inner conflict she felt regarding this man, she did know that she was working only for herself. She met his gaze, daring him to say things were otherwise.

"Alright," he said finally. He turned first and looked out the window towards the street, then at the sky. "I can't see the Moon from here." He went on before Caitlin could ask what he meant. "I need to know what you know. About this Diomedes. About me. I can't—I require your help."

"What sort of help?"

He shook his head. "Later."

"Later," she muttered with a sigh. She was being carried into Gideon's world again, riding on her obligations, her remorse, and her curiosity. It was the place she'd been trying to escape before he'd been shot, and it now loomed again on her horizon. She was losing control of it. Would she be able to do more than simply hang on? "I have some questions of my own," she answered.

"Then ask."

"Who is Ondrea Noble?"

Gideon rose and paced the room once, watching her like a cat before relinquishing his answer. "My sister."

"Your sister." She considered his answer. "You two are close? I think every time I've seen you in the past week, I've seen her. But you'd not mentioned her before."

"I had a brother once. My twin." His eyes glazed as he drifted a moment. "But he's gone now. She is all I have. She helps me. She's helped me recover, got Marquand to pay for it."

"Pay for what? What did they do?"

"There was some head trauma. They said my body was broken also. Some of my cyberware was damaged. They replaced that as well." He sat again, elbows on his knees as he leaned forward in a portrait of weariness. "Ondrea could tell you the specifics. She was always more technical than I."

"And Marquand just covered the entire cost?" His sister must have some clout.

"Mostly." Gideon opened his hand slowly, as if studying it. "I'm told I'll need to do some work for them after. But she said it was the only way to get them to save me."

"Did she say what sort of work?"

He shrugged in a way that made Caitlin think he didn't know. "Nothing until I'm healed completely, but I owe them." He dropped his head away, and then looked up at her again. "Except I don't think they trust me."

"Why not?"

"I'm not to leave the building. They say I'm still healing and need to be observed. I'm supposed to sleep sixteen hours a day, hooked up to monitors. Why is my sister out to get me? They'd keep me locked in that room completely if they could!" He shouted the last part suddenly before catching himself. "I am sorry."

"It's alright." She waited for him to calm a bit before asking about what had caught her ear the most. "Ondrea is out to get you?"

He shook his head as before. "I didn't say that—didn't mean that. She's always helped me. She's the one who got them to let me out, to help me remember things." He shook his head vehemently. "She's trying to take care of me!"

Though it felt like he was telling himself that as much as he was Caitlin, he said it with such force that she wondered if it would be wise to question the assertion. She settled for a middle ground. "But you don't want to go back."

"Something . . . " he started, and then cut himself off. "No."

"Will you be alright if you don't? Will it affect your recovery?"

"I want you to answer my questions now. Tell me what it is you say I'm recovering from. Who did it? Why?"

"Your sister really only said it was an accident and left it at that?" It wasn't so much that Ondrea hadn't offered more information that struck her as off, but that he hadn't asked the woman for any further details.

"Yes. Whenever I spoke to her, learning more about it felt unimportant compared to other things we had to discuss. I would know what you claim to have seen."

She told him then, keeping the story brief. She described to Gideon his own search for Diomedes, their pairing to bring Ken Wallace to justice, and the argument that ended with Diomedes pulling the trigger. She told him of how they'd run off Diomedes, of the difficult decision to leave Gideon's body—beyond help, they believed—to be found by the authorities, and finally, how they had destroyed the captured weapons in accordance with his original intentions.

When she was finished, she waited, watching Gideon where he sat. At first he continued to simply listen as he had before, giving no reaction to indicate that he'd just heard the tale of his own violation. She was trying to decide what more to tell him when suddenly he spoke.

"You said this Felix was the one you were with today. Can you trust him?"

"Very much. Felix was the first to believe you weren't the arsonist Wallace had painted you as, and he's the one who got Diomedes to work with you. I've never known him to break his word. He has a reputation for keeping it, as a matter of fact. And," she added finally, "we've been seeing each other for the past five or six months. I could hardly do that without trusting him."

"But you let Diomedes go."

Though his implication took her by surprise, there was so little emotion in the statement that she was not entirely sure how he'd meant it. "I'm not a killer," she said after a breath. "Diomedes is wanted. There's a bounty."

"For what he did to me?"

She shook her head. "I made sure word got out around town about what he did, but there's footage of him assassinating a man in the Corporate District last week."

"The man is a killer."

"Yes," she whispered, "he is." *But you let Diomedes go.* It had never occurred to her to second guess her part of that decision. To let him go. To let him be free to kill again. Now . . .

No. She would not hold herself responsible for every action the bloody freelancer had chosen to take since that night.

"He is a killer, and today he tried to kill me." The tone in Gideon's voice jarred her from her own thoughts. The wrath she would have expected from him was absent, and what was there was something she had not anticipated: fear. Though she had never conversed with Gideon directly at any great length, she never knew him to show a trace of apprehension. Yet there it was. He was afraid.

Her immediate instinct was to try to comfort him. That the thought made her immediately uncomfortable was not helped by the fact that, moments later, Gideon himself shook his head and scowled in a portrait of self-loathing.

"What do you intend to do?" she asked instead.

"I don't know. I need to stay out of sight. From him, from my sister, from everyone. It's important I remember more. I have to remember. Have to. I need to stay here."

Caitlin's stomach tightened. She knew as soon as he said it that she couldn't let him. But then what? Simply turn him away? Turn her back on him again? She liked neither choice.

"What if they find you again? Either of them."

"They won't. After they found me at my apartment, I began to suspect Marquand had placed a tracer on me. If they did, I started jamming it after leaving my apartment."

"Jamming it?"

"Marquand didn't just heal me. They added features to my cyberware."

"You are jamming Marquand's tracer with their own equipment?"

"Yes." He scowled. "I am aware of the irony."

"It isn't irony so much as I'd expect they would ensure that such a thing wouldn't work."

"I was on your balcony for an hour without any sign of them."

Caitlin stood, went to her desk, and fished in the bottom drawer. She found the device by feel, tucked back beneath a stack of envelopes. "I can check for any unusual signals coming from your implants."

"You are an engineer?"

She shook her head. "Not so much. But this is useful for finding bugs, and I don't need a PhD to use it. If you'll permit me?"

Gideon stood with a nod. She passed the scanner in an arc across the front of his body and then along each arm and leg. There was no indication of a signal.

"Anything?"

"Nothing yet." Perhaps it wouldn't be foolproof, especially if Marquand was using anything fancy. She moved around to his back, continued the scan, and still found nothing. Caitlin was closing the scanner and realizing how little comfort it gave her when she noticed the bullet hole.

"Oh my god. Gideon, you're shot."

He looked over his shoulder at her. "It's small. Just a ricochet knick."

"You've got a hole through your jumper here. It's big enough to have a care with so it won't get infected. There's hardly any blood, though."

He strained to see it, though the wound's location on his back must have made it impossible to get a good view. "It doesn't feel like much," he told her, but removed the jumper nonetheless.

The shirt he wore beneath it had a similar hole, and again, far much less of a stain around it for the amount of blood loss she'd anticipated. Caitlin knew of blood augmentations that would result in faster wound clotting, but even so, the colour of the stain didn't look right.

As he lifted his shirt, her gasp was one of both revelation and shock. "Gideon," she whispered, "what did they do to you?"

Read more in
A Memory in the Black:
Book Two of the New Aeneid Cycle,
now available!

ABOUT THE AUTHOR

An award-winning writer of speculative fiction, Michael G. Munz was born in Pennsylvania but moved to Washington State at the age of three. Unable to escape the state's gravity, he has spent most of his life there and studied writing at the University of Washington.

Michael developed his creative bug in college, writing and filming four exceedingly amateur films before setting his sights on becoming a novelist. Driving this goal is the desire to tell entertaining stories that give to others the same pleasure as other writers have given to him. He enjoys writing tales that combine the modern world with the futuristic or fantastic.

Michael has traveled to three continents and has an interest in Celtic and Classical mythology. He also possesses what most "normal" people would likely deem far too much familiarity with a wide range of geek culture, though Michael prefers the term geek-bard: a jack of all geek-trades, but master of none—except possibly Farscape and Twin Peaks.

Michael dwells in Seattle where he continues his quest to write the most entertaining novel known to humankind and find a really fantastic clam linguini.

Connect with Michael G. Munz online:

Website: www.MichaelGMunz.com

Twitter: @TheWriteMunz

Facebook: www.facebook.com/MichaelGMunz

OTHER NOVELS IN THE NEW AENEID CYCLE

A Memory in the Black

A Dragon at the Gate

OTHER BOOKS BY MICHAEL G. MUNZ

*Mythed Connections: A Short Story Collection
of Classical Myth in the Modern World*

Zeus Is Dead: A Monstrously Inconvenient Adventure

www.ingramcontent.com/pod-product-compliance
Lightning Source LLC
Chambersburg PA
CBHW020339180626
46812CB00001B/271